LISA HELEN GRAY
MYLES
A CARTERS BROTHER NOVEL BOOK THREE

Copy rights reserved
2015
Lisa Helen Gray
All rights reserved
No part of this publication may be reproduced or transmitted in any form or by any means, electronic or mechanical, including photocopy, recording, or any information storage and retrieval system without the prior written consent from the publisher, except in the instance of quotes for reviews. No part of this book may be scanned, uploaded, or distrusted via the internet without the publishers permission and is a violation of the international copyright law, which subjects the violator to severe fines and imprisonment.

This book is licensed for your enjoyment. EBook copies may not be resold or given away to other people. If you would like to share with a friend, please buy an extra copy, and thank you for respecting the author's work.

This is a work of fiction. Any names, characters, places and events are all product of the author's imagination. Any resemblance to actual persons, living or dead, business or establishments is purely coincidental.

AUTHOR'S NOTE

I'd like to remind people that Myles is a work of fiction. Every place, business, street name, school and characters are all made up from my imagination.

The same goes with the school ages and exams. I understand that it doesn't meet UK requirements, and that it's way off base, but I wanted my characters young, but not *that* young. So please, when reading Myles, remember it's fiction, and not real life.

Thank you for understanding.

DEDICATION

Donna Mansell
July 1983 – July 2010
When someone you love becomes a memory
The memory becomes a treasure.

R.I.P

MYLES

PROLOGUE

Life for me was meant to be easy, it was meant to clear and straight forward, also, incredibly dull and boring. Nothing bad was ever going to happen to me because, well, things like that don't happen to people like me. But then I went to Grayson High and my whole world changed.

You see, my mother sent me away when I turned five to an all-girl school in Dartmouth. I came home when I was thirteen, but only because there was no other choice. Miss. Niles, the woman who raised me in Dartmouth, only worked during school terms. Any other day of the year she went back home to see her family, leaving me to head back to my own.

Miss. Niles raised me until I was thirteen before she sadly passed away from cancer. She was the only mother I knew growing up, and the only person I felt loved by. After that I refused to let anyone else raise me, my father agreed, excited at the prospect of raising a child.

It's how I ended up in the town of Coldenshire, attending Grayson High school.

The place that caused me so much anguish, so much misery, and caused endless nightmares. Grayson High changed me.

Grayson High is where I was bullied, torn apart, humiliated, and completely victimised. I'm not just talking about your average high school bullying; I'm talking about being cornered and beaten, shed of dignity, and left feeling every bit afraid. Some days I dreaded going to school, but then I had my reasons for escaping to it.

Like people say, evil isn't just those unknown around you, but can be those who are the closest to you.

It just so happened that one day I took the worst of those evils and ended up in school, already beaten and lifeless. I'd given up.

That's when Craig Davis raped me. He dragged me into a forest by the park near the back of my old house, stripped me bare, beat me, and raped me.

That was the day that changed my whole life forever. Not only did it tear me down from the inside, but it tore apart everything I ever believed in and saw on the outside. I no longer saw happy families, the two point four kids and picket fence; I only saw the hatred. I felt the hurt, the pain, the anguish that people can cause you. The trust I had in mankind got torn away from me in a blink of an eye, causing me to be scared of my own shadow, my own father.

My story isn't pretty, it took me two and a half years to stand up to what Davis did to me. My own mother, at the time of the rape, tore me down, didn't even believe me, so I let it go and cowardly isolated myself from the rest of the world until my father got a promotion and we moved. I'd hoped I could just forget all about it, that being in a new town would help me forget what he did to me, but the nightmares only got worse with each passing moment.

Then one day a friend of mine, Charlie, emailed me about Craig, telling me what he did to another girl called Harlow. At the same time my father announced our move back to Coldenshire and that's when I came clean about the whole thing. About Davis, how he raped me, how mom told me to drop the charges, and how he had done it to another girl.

I went to court, he got sent to prison and I... well I, I still can't seem to move on. I thought it would help. Kill my demons. But I'm still stuck inside my own head, breaking a part bit by bit.

I'm Kayla Martin, and this is my story.

ONE

KAYLA

THEY SAID RETAKING MY last year of school would be good for me. That I'd be able to catch up easily enough if I put my mind to it.

How wrong could two people be?

My first day back at Grayson High and I'm still sitting in the passenger seat of my dad's BMW trying to find the courage to even put my hand on the door handle; I'm that nervous and scared. The last time I walked these halls everyone was shouting abuse at me. Calling me the girl that cried wolf, a whore, a liar; the list is endless.

"Darling, you're going to have to actually leave the car if you want to complete school." My father's voice cuts into my thoughts making me jump slightly. I smile at him softly, not wanting to show him how scared I really am about today. If he knew then he'd send me to an all-girl school again, and that's something I really don't want. Not when I'm fighting so hard to be normal again.

Taking in a deep breath, I slowly but surely put my hand on the door handle, my fingers trembling as I take one last look at my father.

"Have a good meeting, Dad," I tell him before jumping out of the car. The spring air cools my heated skin as I slam the door shut behind me. The smooth rumble of the car pulling away spikes my anxiety. I tap my pocket where I have my mobile phone ready and handy in case of an emergency. Dad even spoke to the school Principal to make sure it wasn't confiscated during class, and assured her I wouldn't use it unless I really had to. How she agreed is still a mystery to me, but then, people do find it hard to say no to my dad. It's his job to negotiate after all. I'm also guessing a generous donation was thrown in too.

The smell of cut grass fills the air as I walk across the field to the school entrance. One good thing about coming back to Grayson High, I know all the exit routes and where to go for some peace and quiet. The worst thing is coming back with everyone knowing my business, and facing the people that are left who bullied me endlessly throughout the entire year I was here.

"You made it?" A deep, husky, quiet voice startles me from the side and I jump, clenching my fists.

My head turns slowly to the boy... Okay, more like a giant man, standing next to me.

"Myles," I breathe out, feeling a blush rise to my cheeks. Myles Carter is a boy I talked to when everything went down. He was the one person I never felt was judging me. He supported me more than he knew and I've thought about him countless times since. I was even excited to see him when I found out I'd be returning to Grayson High, but then when I went to go see Denny, an old friend and a friend of Harlow, the girl who Davis nearly raped, he didn't seem so pleased to see me. In fact, I'd go as far as to say he looked tortured, a look I know all too well.

"Hey," he smiles, a slight dimple showing in his left cheek. All of the Carter brothers are movie star hot, but something about Myles has always drawn me to him. It's not just about his looks either. He's incredibly clever, knows his left and right, which is probably more than you can say for his twin brother, Max, who is the polar opposite of Myles. It's not only that he's clever, but he's kind, generous, funny, charming, and he cares about people. Not just people he knows, although he is loyal to the bone with them, but he genuinely cares about the people around him. He comforted me at a time I was ready to give up, the time I had sat and contemplated how many of my mom's anti-depressant tablets and my dad's pain killers I could find, and swallow, before anyone found me. Not that I think they would care, but at the time, I only wanted the pain to go away, but then Myles came over and sat down next to me. We only spoke for about twenty, maybe thirty minutes, but in that time I knew giving up wasn't an option. I don't know; it was something about his presence that made me feel at peace for the first time since the attack and I felt clean being around him. And being clean is something I have not felt since *him*, Davis.

"Hey," I breathe out, then realise I'm awkwardly staring at him and also repeating his words, so I shake my head and look down to the floor.

"Mrs. Collins sent me. I'm to accompany you to your classes," he tells me, trying to talk in a posh voice that sounds nothing like Mrs. Collins.

"Ahh, well, I hope she's paying you well to babysit me," I tell him dryly, my hopes of him coming to see me voluntarily dying in an instant. I start to walk away, but stop when he stops me.

"Okay, I lie. I wanted to accompany you to your classes."

"How do you even know we have the same classes?" I ask stopping short, then turning around sharply as we reach the science building. When I turn his body is close and for once my skin doesn't break out in a cold shiver, or my heart race with fear, but instead, it starts to race for an entirely other reason, causing butterflies to swirl in my stomach.

"I got a copy of your timetable from the teacher?"

"Are you asking me or telling me?" I ask, fighting back a smirk. I can't help it. Whenever I'm around him I either get lost for words, or end up having a permanent smile on my face.

"Both?" he answers and when I raise my eyebrow at him not believing him, he throws his hands up in the air in surrender, the action causing me to take a step back way too quickly and I end up falling backwards. I close my eyes anticipating the landing on the hard floor, but it doesn't come. Instead, two large hands cross against my back, stopping me from the fall I'm sure would have sealed my fate for the rest of the school year as the laughing stock.

When I open my eyes Myles is staring down at me with a concerned look on his face. It's then I realise what I did and I feel humiliated. Why can't I just be a normal teenage girl? One that doesn't jump easily at the littlest of noises, and who is free to be whoever she wants to be and not what she's been moulded to be?

We can only wish, right?

"You steady?" he teases, making light of the situation.

"Yeah," I whisper back, not able to look him in the eye again.

"Come on, we have English after registration," he smirks when I finally look up at him.

We walk through the empty halls of the science building, heading towards the English building where our registration and first class will be. By the time we make it there the halls are crowded with other students and I become more and more nervous.

I recognise a few people's faces and I don't miss curious glances from the other students trying to figure out who I am. It won't be long for the rumour mill to get around, and for the people who didn't know who I was or my story, to know every detail by the end of the day. It's what they do. It won't even be through gossip either; it will be through texting, Facebook, and Twitter. I'll be surprised if I'm not trending by the end of the day.

My face pales when I see a group of Davis' friends that he hung out with. They were in the year below at the time and did anything and everything he asked. I should know. I endured their name calling, pushes, and kicks that he ordered them to do whenever I was around.

One word, 'lapdogs'.

My palms become sweaty and for the millionth time today I wonder what the hell I'm doing back here. I should have been happy with the exam results I got, but with everything going on last year I found it hard to concentrate, which is the reason I failed more than half of my classes. I need at least a B in childcare, instead of the measly D that that I got.

"You okay? You're looking rather pale?" Myles asks, concerned. My mouth opens to tell him I'm fine, but only a gush of air escapes, no sound. Then a booming voice and hard touch creeps up from behind me and I end up turning around with a loud scream, and falling back into Myles' chest.

My breathing is heavy and I'm wrapped up in Myles' arms and the notion isn't lost on me. For over two years I've shied away from any sort of touch, although a female touch doesn't scare me as much as a male's.

"You fucking dickhead," Myles snaps, his body tensing.

"Shit, I didn't think. I just got overexcited when I saw you and Kayla. I didn't think," I hear a familiar voice to Myles' speak.

"You saw me this morning you jackass," Myles snaps again, not sounding pleased. His fingers run up and down my back in a soothing gesture. My whole body is still shaking, my heart racing from him scaring the shit out of me.

"I know, but we're connected and shit. When you're not around I miss you, bro," Max tells him dramatically.

"How so?" Myles asks dryly.

"Well, you know, you cry, I cry. You smile, I smile and all that bollocks. So when you're not around for me to know what I should be doing, I get jittery and nervous and shit. Then I got excited when I saw you, well sensed you with my twin power..."

"Jesus cut to the chase, Max," Myles snaps.

"See? Now I've got to go to registration cranky. Oh look, Jessica Seymour," I hear him sigh before his presence moves away from us.

"He's a bit much," Myles says apologetically.

"It's okay, I was just startled," I tell him, moving away from his warm embrace. When I take a step back giving some much needed room between us, I start to feel the cold surrounding me. It's then it dawns on me that I let him touch me without freaking out, without having a panic attack and lashing out at him. My head snaps up to his and I look up at him with wide eyes. He's looking at me curiously and I wonder if he knows I'm freaking out inside right now about him touching me. It might seem stupid to some, and kind of weak, but for me it's about power. I need to be in control of who and who doesn't touch me, it makes me feel stronger, not that I can control who does and doesn't. That's the sad part, but something about Myles touching me relaxed me.

"You sure? He can be a bit aggressive when it comes to being around people. He acts like a kid on Christmas morning, every day," he grins and I look up at him and smile, then take a look behind his shoulder to where Max has a girl I vaguely remember up against the locker door, his tongue playing tonsil tennis with hers.

"And he looks like he got his present early today," I blurt out, then turn bright red. I face plant my palm over my face when I realise I said that out loud. I peek through my fingers only to see Myles grinning before turning to see what I'm talking about, and then bursting into a fit of laughter.

"As long as he makes it to first class I don't care," he tells me still laughing, and then ushers me away and into our registration class where a new teacher is starting today. I'm glad I won't be the only newbie.

My dad made sure to get a detailed timetable for me so I could prepare myself for each lesson, and who would be in what class. It's the only way for me to handle my anxiety. The unknown and being cornered scares me, and plus, I needed to make sure I wasn't going to be in any of the other boys classes who played a hand in bullying me.

Walking into the classroom the tables are set out differently than I remember. Instead of being seated in pairs, the tables now seat three and I turn to Myles looking wide eyed and nervous.

"Come on, we'll sit at the back in the corner."

"Yo, wait up," I hear Max shout, but I don't turn around to look, I just keep walking behind Myles, following him to our table and ignoring the curious stares.

"Katie, Katie, Katie, do you need a picture, babe, because I'm gonna have to disappoint, I just gave the last one away to Mr. Hawks," he says and I turn around in time to watch him give her a cheeky grin. I look back quickly thinking what an arrogant jerk, but then the girl in question speaks.

"What? Huh? What are you going on about, Max?"

"You were staring, stop it. Didn't your mother ever teach you not to stare?" he says, his voice laced with warning and he doesn't wait for her to answer before walking up behind me.

"Shot gun the window," he shouts near to my ear and nearly bursting my ear drum. I wince and move my head away and look to the floor glaring.

Yes I'm that much of a chicken I can't look up and glare at him. I'm always, *always* scared of the consequences. Though, I do seem to be getting more confidence.

He quickly barges past me, nearly knocking the bag off my shoulder as he does. Myles notices and punches Max in the shoulder giving him a warning glare. This protective side of Myles is what warms me to him. He doesn't even do it intentionally; it's just in his nature. But something about him looking out for me and not really questioning it does something to me that I can't describe. If only he knew how much I needed him today, how much his presence is already making this hard day more bearable.

"Here you go," Myles smiles, giving me the middle seat.

Jesus! A Kayla, Carter, sandwich.

My eyes look to Myles, then to Max, and I can only imagine that I look like a scared lost puppy right now staring at them. I nod my head and my fingers automatically reach out for a loose piece of my flaming red hair, and I start to twirl it around my finger. I'm actually screaming at myself now for pulling it up in a messy bun, because all I want to do is use it to shield me against the two boys sitting beside me.

Myles' leg brushes against mine and instead of the normal anxiety and fear that usually creeps in, all I feel is a blush rise in my cheeks and butterflies flutter in my stomach.

What is he doing to me?

"Sorry," he whispers, looking at me nervously. I nod my head quickly before looking back down at the table where I've dumped my bag.

"You two are just too talkative," Max whines like we're getting on his nerves. "The conversation is so stimulating, I might just need to cool off outside."

His sarcasm isn't lost on me and my lips pull up at the corners. My head turns a little to get a good view of him. He's the total opposite to Myles. Max has this easy-going charm and banter going on. His easy, carefree attitude and his sociable personality could quite easily make him friends in an empty room. There is just something about him that draws you in. His hair is also darker than Myles', and his eyes are a shade lighter than what Myles' chocolate brown ones are. Don't get me wrong, they have similar facial features, and I guess if you were meeting them for the first time you could get confused as to who is who. It's their personalities that separate them apart from being twins. Max is out-going, sharp, bubbly, and so flirty. He's also more athletic, his build bigger and defined. Although Myles is no slouch, his body build is more natural than his brothers. He's also intellectual and more interested in where he will end up once school has finished than Max is. They both have great personalities, but Myles just seems to come with a filter, whereas Max, I dunno... I guess that's why people worry about him so much.

"Do you have a game this weekend?" Myles asks Max, and that's how I spend registration, listening to the two of them talk back and forth. They soon go on to a game being shown on the television at the weekend, and my heart clenches just thinking about the weekend I just endured.

Luckily, I'm only in the room next to my registration class once the bell rings, and I wait for Myles to get up before following. Max follows us out of the room before looking left and right down the corridor.

"Who are you looking for?" Myles asks.

"Oh, Maddie. She's turned into some kind of stalker and the police won't put a restraining order on her."

"You actually asked the police to do that?" I ask horrified. I know all about Max's reputation, so the likely case a girl is stalking him is pretty high, but still, don't sleep with them if you don't want anything else to do with them.

"Um, yeah. She tried asking for my number, and after we fuc- made love, she wanted to take my shirt home," he puffs out looking disgusted at the thought.

My face flames and I nod my head like I understand, but I don't, it's a huge lie. I turn towards the next classroom and notice Myles looking down at me grinning.

"Clearly I got the brains," Myles chuckles, shaking his head at his twin brother.

"Yeah, up there maybe," Max says poking Myles' head with his finger. "But clearly I got the brains down there," he tells us holding his junk.

"Could you please refrain from touching your junk in the hallway, Mr. Carter," a teacher snaps.

"Oh, Miss. French, you love my junk," he winks.

My eyes widen at him, and then over to the teacher, waiting to see what her reaction to him is, but she just shakes her head with a sigh before walking off.

"She totally wants my cock," he grins, and Myles and I both snap our heads to him.

"Seriously, bro, do you have a filter anywhere inside of you? I'm pretty sure she's in her forties."

"More experienced," he winks, then laughs at my expression. "I'm off to maths before Mr. Hugh has my ass."

Myles opens his mouth to say something back, but he just shakes his head at Max's retreating form.

"Come on," he grins, gesturing to the English room door.

The halls have quietened down now, so when we walk into the classroom most of the class is already seated and listening to the teacher. Mrs. Perry worked here when I attended previously. She's really nice and I'm glad I don't have the other English teacher, Mr. Roberts; he was a complete arsehole to us.

"Kayla, Myles, how lovely for you to join us. Come in and take a seat," she smiles, ticking our names off on the register.

Following Myles' lead I walk behind him to the back of the class, where he takes a seat at a table one from the back, and in the middle row. Everyone watches, some of the girls give me curious glances and some just give plain death stares as I throw my bag down on the floor, and settle in to listen to the teacher.

As I'm late in the school term after being a witness for the Davis court case, everyone else already knows what they're doing. The only advantage I have is the fact I've already taken the classes and learnt the criteria once before.

Myles brushes his leg up against mine again and a shiver runs through my body. I try to move my leg away a little without letting on to what I'm doing, not wanting to be obvious, but then his arm brushes up against me.

I'm still baffled as to why the normal panic and fear I feel when another person, especially a male, touches me isn't there when Myles touches me. It's like my body knows to trust him, although my head isn't on the same line as much just yet.

Don't get me wrong, I do trust him, I just don't trust myself or my judgement anymore. I think it's one of the reasons my panic attacks are so severe.

"You okay?" Myles whispers, leaning in closer.

I nod my head, swallowing, not wanting to show how much his presence is doing to me. Not that I think he would take advantage like most lads his age would.

He gives me a knowing smirk and I blush furiously, dropping my gaze back down to the table, not meeting his. I try to ignore him for the rest of the lesson, but there is just something about having him this close to me that distracts me, in a good way. I've never been like this around a boy before. Not even before... Well, you know who I'm talking about. I've just never felt this connection for someone before, and if I'm honest, it's scaring and exciting all at the same time.

TWO

KAYLA

THE REST OF THE DAY goes by pretty much the same. Myles walks me to my classes, even if we aren't in the same classroom, which I'm grateful for. Without him I wouldn't have made it to registration. Even in the lunch hall he knew when I needed my mind occupied with other thoughts, or when I just needed to go and have some alone time. It's been really good having him there. I know my dad won't approve, so when he picks me up at the end of the day I lie to him.

"It went fine. I spoke to a few people I knew, but that's about it."

"That's great news, darling," he smiles and I hate that I'm lying to him, but if he knew the truth he'd either send me to an all-girl school or home school me, neither are what I want. If only my anxiety didn't get in the way of me enjoying the last year of school. "Did you get any homework?" he asks mindlessly, as he manoeuvres the car through the busy streets.

"I only got a little light reading," I tell him, staring out the window and watching the streets pass by in a blur.

"Sweetie, your mother called this morning on the way to work. She said she wants to have you for the Easter holidays, is that okay?"

"But that's two weeks," I panic.

"I know, but I'll be working a lot and you'll be at home alone all day and night; that's not good for you," he tells me.

"Dad, I'm eighteen, I'll be fine. I'll just go weekends like I usually do," I tell him, hoping he won't pressure me into going.

"Okay, that's fine. I'll call her back later to tell her."

My mind races knowing what will happen if he calls her. "Yeah, maybe you should just tell her you need me to do some odd jobs around the house, and to get up to date with my school work, so it doesn't hurt her feelings."

"Good idea," he grins, looking at me briefly before directing his attention back to the road. As soon as I know he's not looking I breathe out a sigh of relief. I hate going to my mother's house. I've had to put up with her for years and years, and when dad divorced her after he found out that she lied about my rape, I thought that would be the last I would ever see of her. Apparently not, because as soon as their divorce was final he told me she had custody for weekends. I'm eighteen for fuck's sake, but I know if I don't go it will only make everything ten times worse, and believe me, that is something you don't want.

"Want me to make Spag Bol for dinner?" I ask, changing the subject as we pull up on to our street.

"That sounds delicious. I'm going to be in my office so shout me when it's ready," he smiles as he parks the car and shuts the engine off.

Another thing I love about living with my dad, he's not breathing down my neck every two seconds. He leaves me to my own devices. It's never even bothered me. I could have a party with a bunch of random strangers and he wouldn't notice or hear a thing when he's in his office. It gives me the peace I need to be alone. As soon as I'm free to, I'm moving out and getting my own flat. Nothing against my dad or anything, I just want my own independence.

After helping me clean away the dirty dishes my dad goes back to his office. I won't see him now until the morning when he drops me off at school.

I'm startled when the front doorbell rings. I look towards it with a shaking body, my feet itching to run upstairs and hide.

"Can you get that, darling?" my dad calls, and I know I can't just ignore it now that he's heard it. He obviously didn't make it into his office before it rang the first time.

I walk over to the door, thanking the person who invented peep holes, and look through it seeing Harlow and Denny standing there with a pushchair. I open the door slowly, surprised to see them both standing there.

"Hey guys, what are you doing here?"

"We brought some chocolate cake to celebrate your first day of school," Denny smiles and Harlow nods her head grinning.

My eyes begin to water and I shuffle nervously. "Thank you," I whisper.

"Don't thank us just yet, Denny still hasn't lost her appetite after having Hope, so I'd hurry if you want some cake," she smiles and I smile back. Harlow is lovely. She's one of the nicest people, apart from Denny, and my best friend, Charlie, that I really know. All the girls I've ever known can be downright bitches and so mean to one another. I was thankful when I met Charlie and Denny, neither was like the other girls I had come to know and hate.

Harlow's brown hair whips around getting in her face and I stand there wide eyed realising how rude I'm being.

"Oh, God, come in, come in," I tell them, opening the door wider. Harlow walks in first and helps Denny pick the pushchair up the step and through the door. I look into the little car seat attached to the pushchair and smile down at baby Hope who is lying down, wide awake, and sucking her thumb. She's so freaking adorable and looks the spitting image of her father. The only trait I think she gets from Denny is her fair hair. It's turned lighter since I last saw her too, so I can only imagine how much lighter it's going to get.

"Come into the kitchen, my dad's in his office down the hall," I tell them.

"Where are the plates?" Denny asks, ever eager for chocolate. I point to the cupboard as I grab some forks from the drawer and grab a knife out of the board. I walk over and hand her the knife, letting her do the honours. She cuts off a massive piece and I nearly have a heart attack.

"I can't eat that much," I gasp, horrified.

"Oh, that piece is for me," she laughs, then cuts off another piece half the size which makes me relax and let out a chuckle.

"You're lucky we got the cake out of the house. Max walked in from school to see Hope and nearly took the whole thing home with him," Harlow laughs as she takes the fork and starts munching on her cake.

I give her a smile and look to Denny who is really demolishing her piece of the cake. "Thank you, both of you."

"Don't thank us yet, we have another motive for coming round," Denny interrupts. The grin on her face is wide and mischievous. Both girls are looking at one another before turning their sneaky eyes back to me. "We want you to come round mine at the weekend for a girls' night in."

I smile in giddy excitement. This is what I've missed the past two years, and what I want back. I've missed out on so much with my depression that when I was told I was moving back to Coldenshire I told myself I'll be stronger, do things I wouldn't normally do. I soon lose my smile when I remember where I have to be this weekend.

"I'm sorry, I can't. My mom has me on weekends," I tell them sadly.

"Tell her you've been invited to mine; I'm sure she won't mind," Denny says hesitantly, but I know from the look in her eyes she doubts it. Denny only met my mother a few times, and every time my mother was rude and condescending towards her. The only time she's polite is when she wants something.

"I'll ask and let you know," I lie, already knowing the repercussions if I did ask her.

It's not long before we finish the cake and I invite the girls to watch a movie in my room, not knowing what else to ask. I'm nervous as hell. I've never had girl friends over before, so I'm stuck on what I should be doing. They agree and we both grab some drinks to carry upstairs, carrying Hope's car seat up with us, along with her changing bag. I swear, it's like she packed for a holiday and not for a visit.

"What would you like to watch?" I ask, moving towards the DVD shelf.

"I don't mind. God this room is amazing," Harlow says absentmindedly as she gazes around my room. It's the one thing I pride myself in because I spend the majority of my time in here. The living area feels informal and nothing about it feels 'living', so I've always made sure to have the essentials in my room to make it look homely.

The room is purple, and above my bed I have a huge blocked star which has little twinkle lights shining down. I made my dad get it fitted when we moved. My bed looks more like a sofa than it does a bed, its huge; it also has blackbirds printed on the wall behind it flying towards the large window.

I have a white bookcase in the one corner that has lights behind the shelves. It's brilliant for when I have one of my nightmares and just need something to erase the shadows in the dark room. I have a matching DVD shelf, but instead of light up shelves I have twinkle lights at the bottom of each shelf that shine down onto the shelf below them.

My desk is next to my bookshelf, which is a simple white wooden desk with a simple white chair with a purple cushion attached.

My wardrobe is on the other side of the far wall. It dents in a little, enough to fit in poles to use to hang up my clothes, and then in the centre are two built-in white wardrobes; one is open with storage boxes and the other is closed by wooden doors. Then to finish it off, the other side, instead of hanging more poles, I asked for some hooks which are in a shape of stars to hang up coats, scarves and bags and stuff. I really do love it. It feels homely and lived in, especially with all my bits and bobs still lying around from organising everything when we moved in.

"Thank you," I smile, glad they don't think it's too girly. When my dad brought my mom round to see the new house, in case she ever needs to stay when he's away on business, she told me afterwards my room looked like a two year old's. She's wrong though. It maybe a girly colour, but the room is sophisticated and elegant, and I couldn't have wished for a better bedroom.

Denny takes a seat on my bed, kicking her shoes off just as her phone rings.

"Hello?" she smiles, but then a frown appears between her eyes, right before she rolls her eyes towards us. "She's fine. We've been gone half an hour, an hour at most, for goodness' sake. No. We're watching a film. What? No. We're with Kayla. Go away. No. She's fine where she is," she snaps, before putting the phone down shaking her head.

"Mason?" I question, smiling. Denny's always had a crush on him. When we used to hang out she would always talk about him and her plans to marry him someday. I guess she got her wish.

"No, worse... Max."

"Max?" I ask confused.

"Yeah, since Hope was born he won't leave her alone. He's constantly around," she laughs and Harlow and I laugh with her. I can't picture him being a child person; he seems too... childish himself.

"That's kind of cute," I murmur after a second or two.

"No, trust me, it's not," Denny giggles and Harlow nods her head in agreement. Harlow walks over to the DVD shelf and looks at my collection of DVDs.

"Oh my God, *Labyrinth*. I love this movie. Can we watch this?" she asks, and I nod my head smiling. I love this film.

Hope stirs in her car seat and I freeze mid-step, worried I'll wake her up, but

Denny doesn't seem to mind as she talks normally to me.

"So then, how was your first day of school?" she asks me while Harlow busies herself putting the DVD in the DVD player like she's done it a million times before. I relax a little more knowing they feel comfortable and it's just me making the situation awkward. It's then I realise I've been in my own mind and that I forgot to answer Denny.

"Oh, um, it was okay. It went good," I smile, taking a seat on the end of the bed, nearest where Hope is lying in her car seat. Her eyes are wide open and she's sucking her tiny fist into her mouth. She's so freaking adorable I have the urge to get her out of her car seat and munch the hell out of her.

"Do you want to hold her?" she asks, surprising me.

"Oh. I... I don't know. I've never held a baby before."

"It's easy, don't worry," she smiles and leans down to un-strap Hope from her car seat and her arms start wriggling about. Like I said, so freaking adorable.

She gets her out and holds her out to me, and she gently places her in my arms. I hesitantly take her, my arms shaking a little, scared I'll drop her.

"She's so tiny," I whisper, then jump when I hear the front doorbell ring. "Oh shoot, I should get that," I tell them, my body shaking. No one ever rings our doorbell. I never get guests, and if my dad is expecting someone he usually gives me a heads up.

"You stay there, I'll go get it, if that's okay?" Denny asks, and I nod my head, my throat tightening. I bet they think I'm a freak, freaking out over the door being knocked.

Denny leaves, the door shutting quietly behind her, and Harlow comes to sit down next to me. "You don't have to be shy around us, Kayla, or embarrassed. We understand you know. We may not know exactly what you're going through, but you're not alone anymore. I promise. I'm glad you've moved back, Denny missed you a lot."

"Denny spoke about me?" I ask, shocked that she even remembered me. It wasn't like I was a memorable person, not unless you count the rumours everyone spread around the school about me.

"She missed you," she answers smiling.

I'm completely overwhelmed. I thought for sure after treating her the way I did before I left she would hate me forever, even forget about me after a couple of weeks. This though, this is just something else. I don't think I've ever felt I mattered to anyone before. Before I can open my mouth to reply to Harlow, the door to my bedroom flies open, with Denny storming in. I'm so surprised by her hasty entrance that it takes me a few seconds to see who has followed in behind her. I look to Denny first for answers, but then my eyes flash back to Max when he storms over to me.

"Please don't," I shout, jumping back a little, but then I stop, remembering I have Hope in my arms.

He pauses, looking at me like I've lost my mind, but then his eyes soften and he looks at me and then down at Hope.

"I just came to see if my niece was okay," he smiles gently and my breathing starts to calm somewhat. My hands are completely shaking as I hold Hope out to him. He excitedly moves towards me, taking the bundle of joy out of my arms, unaware of the turmoil going through my mind right now, or the fact my heart is racing to the point I'm about to pass out. As soon as Hope is safely out of my arms I shoot up off my bed and head for the door.

"I'll be right back," I mumble, feeling Myles' heated stare on my back as I rush out of the room. I didn't even see him walk into the room. Tears fall silently down my face as I make my way down the hall to the bathroom. I feel completely mortified by my reaction to Max. I had the same one when I first came close to Malik, when I went to Denny's to speak to her and Harlow.

I make it to the door when an arm reaches out, snagging me around my elbow, stopping me. A startled squeal escapes me then I find myself face to face with Myles, and my heart starts beating faster for a whole other reason.

"Hey, shush, it's me, don't panic," he says gently, and I find my body relaxing instantly. It confuses me. I find it hard sometimes to relax around my own dad, but every time I've come in contact with Myles I've felt calm and relaxed.

"I didn't mean anything by it. It's just that, I can't help it," I mumble, feeling so embarrassed about it all. I must have looked like a right freak. It wouldn't surprise me if they've all disappeared and hightailed it home before I get back.

"Don't worry. We all get it, okay? You don't need to be sorry, or worry about your actions around us. Just be yourself, even if it means you lash out at one of us. None of us are judging you, Kayla."

"What if I'm always like this?" I find myself asking. Shocked isn't the word I'd use right now. I've never even asked my therapist that question.

"Once you trust us, trust in the people around you, I don't think you'll need to ask that question again. We'll all help you through it, even if it means getting in your space," he winces, looking back at my bedroom door with a guilty expression.

"What do you mean?" I ask tilting my head, trying to figure him out.

"Max," he sighs, his cheeks flushing a shade of pink. "He went back round to Denny's after dinner and found she had gone out. As soon as she let slip where she was on the phone, he was rushing over here. I caught on to the end part of where he was going, so I thought I'd come as backup in case he got too much."

"Oh, you mean like charging in a bedroom?" I smile, blushing.

"Yeah, that," he laughs. "Are you okay now? We can go if you'd like."

"NO! I mean, no, it's fine. He had just taken me by surprise is all. Hope you guys don't mind watching *Labyrinth?*"

"Ha, I love that film, but Max will probably have nightmares," he chuckles and I feel lighter for just talking to him, so I easily follow him back to the bedroom.

Walking in, everyone is sitting on my bed and I have to bite on my bottom lip when I realise what we've walked into.

"She shouldn't be watching this, Denny. Does Mason know you coerce your child into watching this?"

"It's a freaking kids film, Max, and for one, she is far too young to understand," Denny snaps back.

"It's not good for her. They kidnap a baby for Christ sakes and you want her to watch this?" he dismisses looking irritated, his eyes looking to the television before flickering away quickly.

"Because she's going to wake up in the middle of the night and panic about a hot, bad, Goblin King coming to kidnap her, Max. Seriously, grow up," she snaps, but I can see the amusement in her eyes.

Looking at Max's expression as he takes in the film with a wince and back to baby Hope, I can only find it freaking adorable. Who thought Coldenshire's one and only big time football player would be all mushy when it comes to babies. Usually guys like him run a mile in the other direction when the word 'baby' is even mentioned.

"Oh, hey, sorry, we're hogging all the bed," Harlow says, going to stand up, but I wave her off.

"It's fine. I'll go get the beanie," I smile and walk over to my closet. I grab the beanie I shoved in the corner by the coat racks, nearly falling on my ass doing it. Dragging it over next to the bed so I can still see the film, I hesitate when I realise

Myles is still without a seat. The beanie is big enough for the both of us, but that would mean sitting close to him and I don't know if I'm ready for that.

"It's okay, sit down," he tells me, and I do, not wanting to have everyone's prying eyes on us. My palms are sweaty and my heart rate picks up when I think he's about to take a seat next to me. When he doesn't and he takes a seat on the floor with his back leaning against the beanie I begin to relax.

His head turns and he gives me that half dimpled smile that has always made me a little loopy and tongue tied. Thank God we're all watching a film.

The film turns into two and when my dad walks in a few hours later he's completely stunned when he sees a room full of people. His eyes widen more when he sees Max holding Hope, bottle feeding her.

"Oh, hi. I didn't know Kayla was having any friends over," he tells them slowly before giving me a questioning look.

"Hi, Dad, this is Denny. You remember Denny, right?"

"Oh, hi, Denny. How's your mother and father?" he asks smiling.

"Hopefully my mother has landed herself in jail and my father is wonderful, thank you. How are you?" she asks seriously, and my dad opens and closes his mouth like a goldfish.

"Good," he says before giving me another quizzing look.

Jeeze!

"The baby is Hope; she's Denny's daughter. Mason, her fiancé, isn't here, he's at work. These are his twin brothers Myles and Max. They go to school with me and this is Harlow, she's um..."

"I'm a recent friend of Kayla's. We met through Denny," she smiles, getting up to shake his hand, which he shakes back.

"Oh, I know, are you Miss Dean's granddaughter?" he asks, and I'm surprised he knows that.

"Yes, Sir, I am," she smiles big before going to sit back down.

'Sir?' Max mouths to Myles and I try hard not to giggle.

"Sweetie, it's getting late. I just wanted to come see how you were doing. I can see you're fine, but..."

"We should be going anyway, Mr. Martin. I need to get Hope to bed," Denny cheerfully interrupts, and my shoulders slug a little. Harlow must catch on because she looks towards me and smiles.

"Maybe we can do this again sometime?"

"I'd love that," I smile shyly, before looking at Myles and blushing. I've gotten so used to him being here, I'm sad to see him go. Even when his arm would brush against my leg, or we'd move closer together I'd get these shooting tingles spreading through my body and not the usual bolts of fear that I'd normally get. The feeling is exhilarating. I feel like I keep repeating the fact, but to me his touch is something I've craved for a while, and not just by him, but by anyone and not feel the sudden need to run and hide.

"Come on then, guys. Let's leave Kayla to get some sleep," Harlow claps as Denny puts Hope's coat and things back on. Max hovers close by and once she's settled in the car seat, Max picks her up, smiling.

"Bagsy pushing the pram home."

Everyone turns to roll their eyes at him, and my father just smiles shaking his head, but when he looks back to where Myles and I are sitting, rather closely I might add, his smile falls and a concern look washes across his face. It's weird seeing this side of my dad. He's never been overly protective, but I kind of like it. Sometimes I wish he'd see more of what was going on under his nose, though, but I can't really blame him for ignoring certain things.

Anyway, Myles coughs uncomfortably, and I shift in the beanie before getting up. Myles follows and looks to everyone standing in the doorway with smug looking smirks.

"Need a minute or two, bro?" Max coughs looking down towards Myles' legs. Myles coughs, his head snapping up giving Max a glare back in return.

"Yeah, just need to talk to Kayla alone. Wait for me outside."

"Son, I don't…" my dad starts, but I interrupt.

"Dad, it's fine. Go on off to bed, I'll lock up downstairs," I tell him, even though I lock up every night. It's something I've accustomed to do since the rape. I've just never felt safe and although being alone with Myles scares me, it's not because I think he'll attack me.

My dad reluctantly leaves with the others following him down the stairs. It seems he's not going to go to bed until Myles is safely on the other side of the door.

Fine with me.

"So…" I begin, when he doesn't speak for a few seconds.

"Yeah, so, I was wondering if, um, you wanted to be my partner in childcare tomorrow? Last week the teacher warned us that we'd be picking partners for our essay and presentation, so we needed to pick wisely. It marks most our grades…"

His pause lets me know he's finished, but I'm taken aback for a few short seconds before I find my bearings.

"Oh, um, sure. I'd love to. I'll warn you, though, I'm not good with vocal presentations."

"That's fine, I'll do most the talking," he winks and turns towards the door before hesitating. "Want to walk to school together in the morning?" he asks, and a blush tinges his cheeks.

My face reddens and I know he's only trying to make me feel more comfortable, but the prospect of him wanting to walk with me to school has me feeling giddy and special.

"I'd love to, but my dad, he um, he drives me. Maybe another time?" I ask, not wanting him to think I'm brushing him off.

"Sure," he says and he looks a little disappointed, but I'm tired so my eyes could be deceiving me. I give him a toothy smile and walk him downstairs. My dad is standing near the door looking flustered as he talks to my friends.

Friends.

It feels so weird calling them that. Well, mostly having someone *to* call that. They all turn their heads our way when they hear us approach and another blush rushes up my neck and Max grins when he notices. My eyes harden a little before I remember what happens when I show defiance. Max notices, and a strange look flickers across his expression.

"See you tomorrow," Max calls as Denny and Harlow ask me to call them. "We'll all have to meet up again soon," they finish, and it's not long before I'm watching their retreating forms down my driveway. Well, mostly *one* retreating form. He really does have a nice figure. His jeans fit him snugly in all the right places.

"Are you sure those boys are just friends?" my father asks when the door shuts behind them.

"What?" I ask. My mind is still upstairs with Myles asking me to walk with him to school.

"I just don't think hanging out with those boys will do you any good, sweetie. You need to make girl friends too."

"Dad, as much as I love your concern, it's fine. Plus, I'm pretty sure Harlow and Denny are girls Dad. I think baby Hope proves that," I giggle, hoping to lighten the tension.

"I guess, I just don't want to see you getting hurt."

"I know, Dad, but I'll be fine. I promise. They're good people," I tell him, hoping to ease his worry. It's not like I'm lying either. They may have been raised by their grandfather and their life before may be a mystery to people, but when I look into Myles' eyes, all I see is goodness in them.

"Hope so. Just let me know next time you have guests over," he grunts, before walking back upstairs.

I smile shyly back at the front door, remembering Myles' light touches when we were sitting close together. After a few minutes of blank staring I shake my head and move over to the door to lock it, then follow my nightly ritual and lock everything up for the night.

Once satisfied I've got everything done, I walk upstairs, my mind still daydreaming over Myles as I get ready for bed. Going over the day's encounters with him I come to a point where I know I have to keep my heart protected. Myles has the power to hurt me if I let him in, especially if all he wants is friendship.

Could I have a relationship? Am I really attracted to him? God, I can't. I feel dirty even thinking about it. No one should have to be with used goods. I'm dirty, unclean, tainted, and for someone like Myles, he doesn't deserve that.

With that, I vow to keep my heart at a much needed distance. Let's just hope my heart gets the memo in time for me to go to school tomorrow morning.

THREE

MYLES

WALKING INTO SCHOOL the next day my eyes scan the crowd for bright red hair. When I don't see her my shoulders slump with disappointment. I had really been hoping I would catch her out on the field again, but I haven't seen her or her father's car since I arrived twenty minutes ago.

I feel like a fucking pussy sitting around waiting for her, but ever since she returned I've not been able to get her out of my mind.

Registration is about to start, so I'm hoping she had to get dropped off early, and is already waiting inside the classroom. It's the one place I haven't looked since I got here.

Not that we planned to meet up this morning. I just want to be around her, to protect her, but mostly, I just want to be her friend. I've missed her. She's the only girl that has ever gotten me so worked up. We've never even dated, or had more than a few conversations between us, but there has always been something about her that has drawn me to her.

When I first heard the rumours about what Davis had done I had beat the shit into him in the toilets. It ended up with me getting my ass kicked by him and his mates after school, but the kicking he got from me was well worth the few bruises they managed to get in. No one knows about what I did and never will. I didn't do it for praise, but for some kind of justice.

Now, having her back, within touching distance, is killing me. It's giving me blue balls too. The way she smells when she's around me, the way her hair shines when the light touches it in a certain way, it's all addictive, like a drug to me. I can't get enough. And although she's still hiding behind her shell at the moment, her personality is one I've always admired. She always stood up for what she believed in.

When she first came to Grayson High and everyone took the piss out of her for wearing red glasses, she carried on wearing them anyway. It was the same with anything they took the piss out of. She was scared a lot during that time, but for the most part, she would give as good as she got. I know that side of her might be gone forever, or I could have imagined that whole part of her in my head all along, but the need to help her find herself again is too overpowering. I'll do anything to help her through this, I can see she's still haunted by what happened, and fights against it every day.

Walking in I find her already sitting down, Max sitting down next to her with a girl sitting in front of him on the desk. The teacher hasn't arrived yet, which isn't uncommon with the new teacher, but seeing Kayla sitting there looking uncomfortable and sad, does something to me inside. I rub at my chest trying to erase the sudden pain that's shifted there and take a step towards her. On a closer inspection, I notice she has bags under her eyes and that they're are swollen from crying from the looks of it. I want to reach out and ask what's wrong, but the way her eyes flicker uncomfortably towards Max and the girl sitting on our desk tells me that won't be such a good idea.

Fuck, Max and his fucking fuck buddies.

Shit, that's a lot of fucks.

She must sense me approaching because she raises her head and finds me, her eyes burning into mine and captivating them just like she always does. Her eyes are a dark, emerald green and, for a red head with green eyes, she's awfully tanned. Everything about her screams 'unique' and that is something I'll never take for granted.

"Hey," I smile, taking my seat at the end, boxing her in the middle of me and Max.

"Hey," she whispers, tucking a strand of hair behind her ear, her eyes nervously looking towards me, then to the girl sitting on our table.

"Myles," the girl sitting on the desk squeals, and I wince at the sound. I have to hold on to the edge of the table for dear life, to stop the urge to cover my ears as she gives me a queasy look, or it could be a grin, I can't be sure with the way she's looking at me with her crazy eyes.

I nod my head not wanting to engage in any conversation with her, and turn back to Kayla and smile. She returns it with a small one of her own, but then flinches when the girl slides her ass across the table directly in front of me. I give Kayla an apologetic look before looking up to the girl in question with a raised brow.

"Can I help?" I ask, trying not to sound rude, but I can't help it when it comes to girls like her. I don't exactly remember who she is, but I've see her type before and all they want is one thing. I'm hoping this is some prank my brother has put her up to because everyone knows the easiest Carter to get with is Max, and not me. So I don't know why she's wasting her time.

"Oh, you most certainly can. I heard you're a legend at chemistry, and was wondering if you'd tutor me after school," she asks, and her fingers run down the buttons on her shirt. Rolling my eyes I turn to look at my brother who looks as dumbfounded by the whole ordeal, which only makes me believe he didn't put her up to this. He knows I like Kayla, so he wouldn't do something like this, especially not in front of her. So it begs the question, who has put this girl up to this. Everyone in the school knows I'm unapproachable. I don't do the whole 'bag um and sack um' bullshit.

"Sorry, but you heard wrong. I'm not that good. You should ask George, he gets straight A's," I dismiss her.

"George?" she asks confused and in disbelief. Like the thought of me blowing her off is shocking. Jesus, I hate being rude, but she is seriously one of those girls who never get the picture, even when it's painted on a piece of paper and given right to them.

"Yeah, George. He sits over there," I tell her, pointing to the pimple-nose kid at the front. As if hearing his name he turns around, pushing his glasses further up his nose whilst looking our way. When he sees we're watching him, he gives us a smile and a wave before turning back to his notes.

"No thanks," she mutters. "I want you to teach me," she whines.

"Sorry, but no can do." I smile, but I'm certain it looks like a cringe. "Plus, my girlfriend wouldn't like it," I blurt out, pushing my arm around Kayla's chair.

"Oh, I didn't know you two were dating," she tells me, before giving a look to Kayla. The girl must really be clueless because she blushes and jumps off the desk. She gives one last wink to Max before sauntering off back to her seat.

"Wow, bro, talk about subtleties," he laughs.

"Girlfriend?" Kayla chokes out. I forgot for a second about her fears.

Shit.

"Yeah, about that. I'm sorry. It slipped out. I can't stand girls like her. They get my back up and they don't leave you alone. I'm sorry."

"No, it's fine," she blushes before finishing off some notes she was taking.

I'm about to say something else when the teacher finally walks in five minutes late. If that was one of us we would be in detention or getting a warning. It seems teachers get a free pass to do whatever they want.

God, I'm sounding more like Max every day. Although we're twins, we've never had the same similarities in personalities. We both want different things from life. I want to be a social worker, whereas he is happy running the V.I.P with Maverick. I want to go to college, get married, have kids, but he doesn't. He just wants to go on lads holidays, get rat assed, and live for the day, which is all good, but he can still do all that and take life seriously. I'm worried one day he'll meet a girl and get knocked on his ass, but she won't be interested in a male whore who only thinks with his dick. I mean, what girl would, right? Whereas I want to make a career, get married and have kids. I want to buy a house, drive a nice sports car, and live the dream. I don't want to end up like my family did. Although we are in a good place financially, we weren't always. There were times I can remember being so hungry my belly felt like it would explode. How I remember this from such a young age is anyone's guess. I just know I never want to be in that situation ever again, one where I'm literally starving, worrying if I'll ever eat another meal after the last. I guess my childhood is what's driven me.

"Max, turn your phone off and put it away before I confiscate it," the teacher snaps, glaring at Max beside us. From the corner of my eye I notice Kayla put her head down and her cheeks flame red. Fuck, she's so beautiful. Even blushing, timid, and quiet, she's the most attractive girl I've ever laid eyes on.

"Sorry, Miss. Two more minutes, I'm just checking to see how my baby girl, Hope, is," he gushes, not looking up from his phone as his fingers fly across the keys. I turn to my brother with a glare. Mason already warned him to stop texting Denny in the day in case she's taking a nap. Hope hasn't been sleeping through the night and with Mason working all day, and most nights, Denny is the one staying up most of the night doing night feeds.

Kayla looks at me with an amused smile and I can't help but feel the wind has been knocked out of me. Every time the damn girl smiles it does something to me. If only I could put it into words.

"No, Max, I will not wait two minutes. Either you turn your phone off and put it away, or I'll take the phone away from you, and you won't have it back till the end of the day. You should be able to refrain from texting your girlfriends in the day by now," she snaps and the whole class erupts with laughter.

Max frowns, looking disgusted as he lifts his head to address the teacher. "One, ewww, she's my niece, Miss, and two, she likes it when I check in with her. When she doesn't hear from me she doesn't settle for her mom," he brags, and my eyes flicker back to the teacher's and I watch her give Max a 'how naive do you think I am' look and I have to grin. The teacher hasn't been here long, but already she has Max pegged out.

"What?" he shouts, offended, making Kayla jump and out of gut reaction I grab her chair and slide it closer to mine. I notice her breathing pick up and I smile down at her to help her relax. Her eyes are wide and glassed over, and for a second I mistake it for tears, but then her tongue snakes out and licks her bottom lip and my groin tightens. God, how am I supposed to be friends with the girl if all she has to do is lick her lips and I'm hard? Max's voice cuts in and I snap my attention back to him, my hard on disappearing.

"It's a true story, Miss; I made it up myself," he whines, shoving his phone into his blazer. The other classmate's chuckle at him amused.

"Max, you have detention after school Friday." The teacher dismisses him on a snap, and he throws his hands up in the air frustrated.

"Honesty is the best policy, Miss. You can't give me detention for being honest," he whines, sounding like a girl. I'm thankful when the bell rings because I can't take any more of their arguing back and forth. I have to listen to enough arguing involving him at home.

"Max, you can have detention for lunch today too," she snaps, sending him a glare.

"Jesus, if I give you a straw will you suck the joy out of someone else's day instead?"

A few snickers erupt in the room, but I tune them out shaking my head. My brother never learns when to keep his trap shut.

"We have childcare now, don't we?" Kayla's small voice asks, and I turn gesturing her forward, to guard her from people bumping into her.

"No, we have history first, then childcare. I'm not sure what you have for the rest of the day. I have P.E. after lunch and then biology," I tell her, feeling gutted I couldn't work in all of her lessons with mine. I tried to when the principal asked me to arrange her timetable. I just didn't want to come off strongly and look like a total stalker.

"Oh," she frowns, looking unhappy.

"I have chemistry third, and P.E. for last period, but I don't think I'll be going to P.E. I'm hoping my dad remembered to get me excused," she blushes. Then with a shaky hand she moves another loose strand of hair behind her ear. The move is innocent if you're not close to Kayla, but because I know her, I know she's nervous about P.E. Maybe she heard about what happened to Harlow? If that's the case then she can be assured nothing like that will ever happen to her. Not again anyway.

"Why are you excused?" I ask interested, as we make our way through the buildings to our next lesson.

"Oh, nothing," she mumbles, looking worried and nervous.

"Tell me," I tease lightly, hoping she trusts me. Something about needing her to trust me burns deep down inside me.

"I have some scars." She whispers so quietly I can barely hear her over the noise of chattering students. I pull her to the side, down an empty corridor and position her against the wall. Her breathing picks up and even through her shirt and blazer I can see her chest rising and falling heavily. My hand lifts slowly, so not to scare her, to move another loose strand of hair and tuck it behind her ear.

"Scars?" I croak out, emotion clogging my throat.

She looks up at me startled and for the first time I see fear in her eyes. I take a little step back, not enough for her to escape, but enough for her to try and relax around me to talk.

"Can we go, we're going to be late?" she tries to side step me, but I put a hand firmly on her hip, the movement causes her to jump.

"Tell me," I tell her gently, my eyes staring down into hers and pleading.

"From when... From when Davis," she starts. But then her eyes begin to water and her body starts to shake. I feel like a complete fucking jackass for pushing her. I should have fucking known it had something to do with that jackass. I pull her into my arms and try to comfort her. Her body is as stiff as a surfboard at first, but once I run my fingers gently up and down her back she begins to sink against me, her body softening.

"I'm so fucking sorry, if I'd known-"

"You couldn't have known. It's okay," she whispers, but I feel her shudder beneath me and it kills me that she has to live with this day in, day out.

"I shouldn't have pushed, I'm sorry," I tell her honestly, wishing there was something I could do to fix this.

"I'm being stupid," she tells me as she pulls away, her fingers wiping the wetness away from under her eyes. I feel the coldness seep in between us when she takes a step away and this time I let her.

"No you're not. Come on, let's get to class before *I'm* the one getting detention," I grin, but I know it doesn't reach my eyes. My mind is too focused on how I can help Kayla and make it up to her.

Arriving in childcare, Kayla and I take the seats at the front nearest the door. We both have lunch after this, so we want to be the first ones out.

I like our childcare teacher; she's pretty cool for an old chick, and she's pretty lenient with things other teachers give out detentions for.

"Hey, class. I've come baring gifts," she cheers, holding out envelopes with our assignments in them. Each will have a different subject and topic to discuss, and we will write a twenty thousand word essay, along with a five minute presentation.

Students groan, but it's not heatedly. You can tell they enjoy this lesson just as much as any of the others. I'm not the only male in the class, a few other kids picked it as a G.C.S.E. thinking it would be an easy grade, but the joke was on them, now they're stuck with it until we finish up with school.

The teacher walks around handing everyone their assignments and when she gets to our table she gives us a big grin.

"Hey, you must be Kayla?" she says looking towards Kayla.

"Yes," Kayla answers, looking embarrassed.

"I'm Miss. Watson, I teach childcare and health and social care. Myles told me you were transferring so he paired himself with you, but if you'd like to change, I can try move some people around," she smiles, pulling a chair out to sit in front of us.

"No, I'm okay working with Myles," she answers quietly, her chair moving closer towards mine. She's nervous, that much I can tell, but the question is why? Why is she nervous around Miss. Watson when she's a woman?

It's probably because she's never met Miss. Watson, jackass.

I scold myself for not thinking of it sooner. "You've not met Miss. Watson yet have you?" I ask, looking to Kayla. I notice the teacher looking between us with a curious expression and I know it has more to do with Kayla's reaction to her than it is with anything to do with me.

"No. It was Mrs. Deer."

"I only got to meet her a few times. She was a lovely lady," Miss. Watson grins, and then opens the envelope with our papers in them. "Here is your assignment. Most of the class already know how they're going to work on their projects, but I wanted to come by and check in with you both before I leave you to do it. Do you have any idea how you'll work on it?"

Kayla looks at me and from the corner of my eye I can tell she is panicked, but I give Miss a nod and smile.

"Yeah, if it's okay with Kayla she can come round mine to study. I haven't thought much about it, but we did discuss the presentation and was wondering if I can do all the speaking?"

It's worth a mention while we have the teacher's main focus. I know Kayla isn't going to like being in the spotlight, so may as well get this over with just in case the teacher is grading us on our speeches. It will give Kayla more time to prepare herself.

"Not big on speaking in front of the class?"

Kayla shakes her head, no, not saying anything else and Miss. Watson looks at her more curious than before.

"That's fine. As long as you contribute somehow, like stand with him, hold up cards, or even press a button on a computer if you're using Power Point, then it's fine. Your topic is a difficult one. You'll need to do a lot of research, and if you can get some interviews and back up your research that would be even better."

"What's our topic?" Kayla asks seeming more interested, but I can feel her leg bouncing up and down beneath the table.

"Well, you'll be writing a presentation and an essay on the effects and after effects of an abusive home. You'll be finding out how it affects kids long term, like in relationships, jobs, having their own kids, and school and such. You can use your own experiences, or others, as long as it's kept confidential," she says smiling at us.

"What makes you think I have experience?" Kayla squeaks, wide eyed.

"Oh, I worded that wrong, I'm sorry. I know a little about Myles' background," Miss. Watson answers, wide eyed herself, struggling to explain.

"Oh." Kayla breathes, her body slumping back into the chair.

"So, whatever you both feel comfortable with. Let me know your schedules when you work them out. I'll need some idea on how much time you'll spend on it. It won't need to be completed until three weeks before school year ends, so it's going to be no rush. Just make sure you put in the hours."

"We will," I grin, then grab the worksheets off her and put them in front of me and Kayla so we can both see them. "So, when shall we get started," I grin, liking the fact I get to spend more time with her over the next couple of months.

FOUR

KAYLA

THE FIRST WEEK OF SCHOOL passes really quickly. I've hung out with Myles a lot; it's an excuse I've used for why I haven't made any friends yet, but really, I like being with him. Sometimes I wonder if I'm getting in the way with him, but when I try to give him space he always seems to seek me out. If I get on his nerves he doesn't show it.

It's a new week and after the weekend I'm glad to be at school. I need the work to keep my mind off things. My back is stiff when I sit down in my chair and I have to bite my lip to stop myself from whimpering.

The bell has only just rang for registration. I got my dad to drop me off earlier than normal so I had time to get into class and take a seat without people wondering what was up with me, but also because I didn't want anyone knocking into me to get to Max, mostly the girls that pour all over him.

The pains in my side are burning and all I want to do is soak in a long, hot bath, or take a nice, long, hot shower, but dad wouldn't let me have any more time off school. If only he knew why I really wanted the time off.

My eyes flicker towards the classroom door, and I hate that my eyes search for him whenever he's not around. When I try to focus on my English work, a noise at the door startles me. I lift my head in time to see Max walk in with a girl wrapped around his arm. It's nothing I've not seen before, since I started back. In fact, I'm pretty much used to it now that whenever I see him with a girl, I just roll my eyes. I'm about to focus my attention back to my English work when the hairs on the back on my neck stand on edge, which can only mean one thing.

Myles.

My stomach drops when my eyes catch one of the girls from another registration class lift up to kiss him. Not able to stomach it, or the feeling it provokes inside my chest, I quickly look back down at the table. My chest hurts and I can feel my face redden and my eyes water. It's not like I have the right to be jealous. I mean, I am jealous, right? This is what I'm feeling? God, how can I be so clueless? No wonder he doesn't want to be with a girl like me, not when he has girls like her hanging off him.

His large hands pull out the chair next to me and my heart beats ten to the dozen. I try to ignore him, but it's hard to when I'm in his presence. I end up squirming in the chair, trying to act like I haven't noticed him sit down yet.

"Think she's ignoring you, bro?" Max chuckles and I nearly jump out of my seat. My head jumps to his direction, wondering when the hell he got there and how I didn't see him take a seat.

He gives me his signature smirk and knowing eyes, which just make me blush further. God, did he see me looking at that girl kissing Myles? Did he see my reaction? Oh no! What if he tells Myles and then Myles doesn't want to hang out with me anymore?

"Calm down, Little K, your secret's safe with me," he whispers, just as Myles interrupts him causing me to jump again.

I'm getting them both bells. Yes, bells.

"Who's ignoring who?" Myles asks confused, and unaware of the turmoil going on inside my head right now.

"I was being sarcastic, what was that about with *Layla?*" Max asks, emphasising her name. Layla! Even her name is pretty.

"No idea. Did you see her nearly kiss me? I swear, some of the chicks in this school have no boundaries," he grumbles, and my heart skips a beat knowing he didn't kiss her back. Is that sad of me? Shit, who cares?

"Just the way I like um," Max cheers and a few classmates turn around to see what all the excitement is about and I bury my head into my book, nearly screaming out in pain doing so.

"Hey, Kayla, what you reading?" Myles asks, his voice closer to me than before.

I turn my head with it still resting on my book and look up at him. "Nothing, just tired," I tell him, but the movement is stiff and I start to panic how I'm going to hide my reaction when I go to sit back up. I don't have to think for long because the teacher walks in and asks us to take a seat and settle down. I lift up, my body in agony, and I curse myself for letting my dad bully me into coming in this morning. Funny thing is, I'll be like this most Mondays, depending on what happens the previous weekend. Who am I kidding, most of the week I'll be recovering, and it doesn't matter what day of the week it is.

"You okay?" Myles asks, his eyes scrunched up with worry.

"Yeah, I must have slept on my side funny," I shrug, wincing at the movement. He looks at me for a few more seconds, like he's gauging my reaction. I keep my face passive not wanting to give anything away. He still doesn't look convinced a few minutes later and I end up blushing and looking away. I'm surprised I got to hold his gaze as long as I did. I'm not one for confrontations.

"What are you doing at the weekend?" Max asks. Looking at him to see who he's talking to I'm surprised to find out it's me.

"Um, I go to my mom's," I whisper, so the teacher doesn't hear me.

"Want to come round Denny's?"

"I'm at my moms," I tell him, wondering if he heard me the first time.

"Yeah, but you can ditch the rent and come have some fun with us," he grins.

I wish. "Yeah, I can't. Since they broke up I only get to visit mom on weekends. She'll be pissed and probably take my dad to court if I miss a weekend," I half lie. I really do go on weekends, but I don't think my mom could afford to go to court again. I hope!

"That's shit. So you don't get a weekend off?" Max interrupts sounding interested.

"Yeah, I get the last weekend of every month to do what I please with, it's why she gets upset if I don't make it on her weekends."

"So that's in what, two weeks?"

"Yeah," I smile looking over to him. My heart skips a beat like it always does when I look at him. The teacher calls out our names and I jump, my gaze moving away from his.

"We'll make plans for then," Myles whispers in my ear, and a shiver runs down my spine. What is with me today? No, what is with me when I'm around him? I'm not supposed to feel like this, it's wrong.

"So, are you okay to start our project after school?" Myles asks during lunch. We're sitting at a table with a group of his friends. I'm tucked into my normal corner away from everyone else. I struggled sitting here when he first invited me to eat with him, but then when I realised no one could approach me, or sit anywhere near me, I started to relax. I think the fact no one can sneak up behind me from this position helps to ease my apprehension too.

"Yeah I am. What time were you thinking?" I try to remember if my dad will be home or not. He wasn't back from work until way past midnight last night and I'm pretty sure he said it would most likely be the same tonight.

"About half four? I need to go back home to change and take a shower."

"Where do you want to meet up?" I question nervously, not really wanting to go out in public somewhere, especially at that time.

"Is your place okay? Or do you want to come to mine?"

The cafeteria is bustling with noise, but I'm so nervous the only sound I can concentrate on is the thumping in my ears. "Cool," I smile, wringing my hands in my lap nervously.

The bell rings when lunch is over and I get up grabbing my bag from under my chair. Myles stops me just before I go to step past him. "I'll see you later then?" He smiles and it's so warm and genuine my heart stops for a few seconds, basking in his beauty.

I shake my head and give him a smile in return, hoping it looks genuine. "Yeah, sounds good. Oh, I'm cooking pasta bake for my dad so there will be tons left over if you fancy some."

"I'll look forward to it. I haven't had a cooked meal all week," he smiles. He opens his mouth to say something else, but then his friend who I've seen him hang out with, Liam, pats him on the back, getting his attention.

"Hey, Myles, a few of us are heading over to the skate rink after school, do you want to come?"

I can feel myself stiffen and as much as I try to relax, I can't. I'm waiting for Myles' reaction, but he doesn't give anything away in his expression. I don't even know why I'm reacting this way, it feels foreign and I start to squirm feeling uncomfortable.

"I've got plans mate, maybe another time," he smiles down at me and my body instantly relaxes. He's blown off a night out with the lads to come and study with me at mine. I want to interrupt, to tell him we can rearrange it for another night, but something inside me stops me from opening my mouth. It's selfish of me to keep my mouth shut, but I like Myles, I like spending time with him. I like the way I feel when I'm around him, the safeness he cocoons me in. It's refreshing from the normal fear that clouds my mind. Even with my dad I don't feel the same safeness I do with Myles, which is weird because I've known him my whole life, whereas Myles I've only known for a short amount of time, yet I feel the safest when I'm around him.

"See ya later," Liam shouts as he rushes off to class.

I wave timidly at Myles who just gives me a cheeky smirk in return. My cheeks flush red, but once I've turned and out of sight, I grin from ear to ear.

At the end of school, I hurry home, rushing through the door and up the stairs, straight into the shower. Once showered and dry, I quickly look through my choice of clothes and groan. Most of my clothes are baggy, boyish, or just boring. I want to look nice, not that I want to do anything, or for him to try something, but I want to make a good impression for the first time in my life.

"Why are you even bothered?" I mutter to myself, knowing I'll never be able to have a relationship with him. I'm damaged. I'm broken and I'm completely messed up. Just the thought of letting someone be intimate with me after what *he* did makes me want to vomit. I couldn't do that to someone.

So instead of going for a girly nice look, I just grab my normal casual wear. I grab a Guns and Roses t-shirt with a pair of faded washed out jeans and put them on. I continue to move at a fast pace, wanting to get dinner on the way before he comes over. I'm in the middle of blow drying my hair when my phone message alert goes off. I quickly grab my phone, my heart pounding at the thought of Myles texting to cancel tonight. But when I see my dad's name on the screen my body relaxes.

Dad: I don't know when I'll be back tonight so don't wait up. I'll grab something to eat at work. Dad x

I grunt into the phone still planning on leaving him some leftovers. He will only moan come morning that he hasn't got anything ready for lunch. I'll box it up for him to take to work. I fire off a quick text, telling him I'll leave it boxed up in the fridge and quickly carry on drying my hair.

Once it's done I decide to run some product through it, a bit of hairspray before leaving it wavy down my back. It's redder than it normally is due to the sun being out. You'd think with my red hair I'd have extremely pale skin, but I don't. I'm actually quite tanned, and don't burn easily like my mother does in the sun. I opt for some lip gloss and a thin layer of mascara before making my way downstairs.

It doesn't take me long to prep dinner and get it cooked. I'm just putting it in the oven to keep warm when the doorbell rings, startling me. Wiping my sweaty palms down my arms I walk towards the door, standing there for a few seconds to gain my composure.

Shit! What if it's not him?

Cursing myself, I quickly move to the peephole to find it is indeed Myles. He's standing there with each hand in his front pockets, his bag dangling off one shoulder and rocking back and forth on his heels. He looks like a magazine model. He's lean, muscular, and is taller than most boys I've seen my own age. It's not as intimidating, though, as it should be for me. In fact, little Tim in my cooking class, who is shorter than me, intimidates me more than Myles. There's just something about him that doesn't make me crouch back into myself, or jump when I'm around him, even though whenever his presence is around me it's like he's dominating my thoughts.

The doorbell rings again and I realise I've been peeping through the peephole ogling Myles. What the hell is wrong with me lately? I need to give myself a good talking to because I'm only setting myself up for heartbreak and I've had enough of that to last me a lifetime.

Rushing over to the door I open it and quickly jump back when I nearly swing the door in my face.

"Shit," I jump, my face flaming red from embarrassment.

Way to go Kayla.

"Hey," Myles chuckles. "Excited to see me?" He teases and my shoulders relax.

"Yeah, I nearly knocked myself out from not being able to contain myself," I tell him. Then my eyes widen when I realise I just flirted with him. Or is he just teasing? I don't know. God, I'm such a loser when it comes to things like this. I don't know what to do. And now I'm standing in the doorway staring at him like an idiot and I realise he's trying to talk to me.

"What? Sorry?"

"I said something smells good," He chuckles, not commenting on my flabbergasted state.

"Oh, yeah, crap, come in. Dinner is done if you want something to eat now?"

"That'd be good, if that's okay with you?"

"Yeah, I didn't really eat much earlier," I tell him, not wanting to admit it's because of my bruised side. I lost my appetite Friday night, but I'm actually hungry now I've had a warm shower, although the dull ache from rushing around when I got back is there pounding away. It's like a constant reminder of what a failure I am.

"Take a seat; I'll just dish this up," I tell him, gesturing to the chair at the table. He walks over to the chair and plonks himself down gracefully and I can't help but stop and stare at how good he looks doing it.

"Where's your dad?" he questions and for the first time, being in Myles' presence, I freeze. Should I tell him the truth; that my dad won't be back tonight, or should I lie and tell him he's in his office upstairs? Knowing I won't be able to lie, I look over to Myles with a sheepish smile, hoping he understands how much trust I'm putting in him by telling him this.

"He's at work and won't be back until later," I tell him, opting at the last minute not to mention the time. It's not like he asked me what time he's coming back or anything. I've not lied. *Jesus, Kayla, get a grip of yourself.*

I busy myself getting the plates out, before dishing out our food and bringing them over to the table. Forgetting to offer him a drink I ask him what he would like.

"Just a coke or something if you've got it," he smiles, then scoops up a fork full of food before shovelling it into his mouth, moaning when he does. "God, this is so good," he mumbles around his food, and I smile wide before getting up to make us some drinks. My nerves are slowly evaporating, which I'm thankful for. I didn't want the entire night to be stiff and awkward on my part. I'd never live it down if I was.

We eat the rest of the dinner in silence and after we've finished Myles helps me clean up before he gets his books out. I look at him confused for a second and it takes me a few minutes to decide what to say.

"Um, Myles? We, uh, can we go to my room?" I shake my head embarrassed.

"I just...My work is up there and I feel more, um, comfortable. Forget it, I'll go get my books," I stammer, my voice low and unsure.

"No, wait, it's fine. If you want to study in your room then we can. Lead the way." He smiles and I relax. Then I begin to panic. I never thought about it being just the two of us alone in my room. I turn on the stairs, my eyes wide and probably full of fear. Myles nearly bumps into me and when he looks up his eyes soften.

"We can study down here if you'd like. I'm not going to hurt you," he says softly and I scrunch my face up. Am I that transparent? Does he really believe I think he'd hurt me? But that was what I was thinking even though deep down inside my heart I know he wouldn't hurt me. God, my head hurts with all this backward and forward shit going on. It's confusing the hell out of me.

"No, no, it's fine. I um, I was just going to ask if you want another drink and some snacks?" I lie, hoping he believes me.

He smiles back and I relax. "I could use another drink if you've got one. I'm not fussed about snacks. Maybe something for later?"

I nod my head, grateful to have a few minutes alone to gather my thoughts. "I'll just go get them, you head on up," I smile before rushing past him down the stairs.

It's late when I roll onto my back and groan. We've been going over our project for hours and my back is beginning to hurt. Myles chuckles and I lazily turn my head to watch him. He's leant up against my bed, his legs stretched out in front of him and crossed at the ankles.

"So we've done the outline of what we can do, now all we have to do is research and stuff. It's a pretty sore subject to bring up to other kids at school, so I might just use an anonymous source."

"What do you mean?" I ask, sitting up and leaning back against the bed the same way Myles has.

"You know my brothers and I come from a broken home, right?" He asks softly and I can hear that the subject is hard for him to talk about. I nod my head opting to keep quiet as he talks, wanting to know everything about him. "Well, I don't remember our mom, but our dad, our dad was a sick son of a bitch. He beat us, mostly Maverick and Malik, though. They think we never knew or heard him, but we did. Max and I, we had trouble sleeping because of the noise, so we would hear things," he shudders and I reach out on instinct for his hand, covering it with my own. Tingles shoot up my spine from the touch and a nervousness that I've never felt before seeps into my body. Our eyes lock and my palms begin to sweat.

"Go on," I croak, my voice not sounding like my own.

"I think it affected us all in different ways. Max and I got less of the brunt because of how young we were, or because Maverick protected us. I'm not sure. Either way you look at it, Max and I got off lightly compared to the others."

"How did it affect you?" I whisper, the conversation hitting close to home. I'm interested in his answer though which surprises even me.

"We all came away with something different from our time with him. I want to help other kids that go through what we did. None of us spoke up to an adult because we didn't think they'd care or take us seriously, but most of all, we didn't speak up because we didn't want to be separated. I don't remember a lot, but I remember our dad telling us our granddad didn't care, that he sees us as worthless brats just like he did. I think it was the main reason none of us spoke, we didn't have any other family that would take in five boys.

"I guess if I could just help one kid in my life it'll make everything worthwhile. I don't know."

His demeanour changes to sad and helpless, and I wish I could take some of his pain away. I know all too well what he's going through. I just wish I had a quarter of his courage.

"You'll be a great social worker, Myles. Tell me the rest, about your brothers," I encourage, then realise I'm sticking my nose into his business. "Only if you feel like it. I'm sorry, I'm being nosey."

He gives me a soft smile before moving his writing pad onto the floor next to him. "Max, well, he doesn't do commitment or even love. It's why he sleeps around, I think. He doesn't want to get attached to anyone because he thinks in the end that they will leave or hurt him. He doesn't talk about our mom, so I'm guessing he has what people may call 'mommy issues'. Malik is angry all of the time. Well, he was until he met Harlow. He changed when he met her."

"She's a great girl," I agree.

"She is," he smiles. "He was just angry all of the time before her, always getting into fights and being broody all the time. He was angry at everyone for a long time. Then Mason, well, Mason slept around a lot. I don't think he knows it, but I think he used sex as a coping mechanism. He'd also leave them hanging high and dry before they could do the same to him," he shrugs.

"What about Maverick? He's the eldest of you lot isn't he?" I ask, not knowing much about the guy.

"Yeah, he's been like a dad to us, always getting us to school on time, fed, clothed and shit. I think when we moved into Granddad's he lost a part of himself not being our full time carer. He still bosses us about, has our asses, well, Max's, if we don't go to school and shit. But how, the abuse our mom and dad put him through, I have no idea. I've never been able to work him out. He's still a mystery. It could be it never affected him much, but I'd hear what he went through at night and I know there just isn't any way it didn't affect him."

"Maybe his need to look after you guys is how it affected him. It could be that he feels like he failed you all somehow and that's why he's so protective of you. I don't know," I shrug, my heart hurting. They all had each other growing up, someone to talk to when things got bad. I, on the other hand, have no one to confide in, no one to talk to or ask for advice. It's hard and I hate it. It's like I'll be forever stuck in some sort of nightmare, one I'll never get out of.

"What about you?" he asks lazily. I can feel the heat of his stare of the side of my face.

"What about me?" I squeak out nervously.

"Do you have a good relationship with your parents? Abuse isn't just physical, it's mental as well. Abuse can come in all sorts of ways."

"Um...why are you asking me this?"

"It's our project," he reminds me looking at me confused.

"My dad and I get along fine," I redden.

"What about your mom?" he asks, and I know he already knows the answer to his own question by the look in his eyes. I start to feel cornered, like he can read my mind, and I have to wipe my palms down my jeans in a nervous habit.

"We clash I guess," I whisper. "I'm tired, do you want to watch a film or do you need to go?" I blurt out, hoping he doesn't question my quick subject change.

"I wouldn't mind watching a film. My back and ass are killing me though, so can we move to the bed?" he questions and my heart rate picks up again. I swallow the lump in my throat and nod my head in a quick jerking movement.

We both pack our books away together. When Myles takes a seat on my bed I pause to watch him there. You'd think having him on my bed with just the two of us in the house, alone, would cause me to have a major panic attack, but looking at him getting comfortable, fluffing up all my pillows causes something else to constrict inside my chest.

Blushing, I turn away quickly to look at my collection of DVDs. There's a few I haven't seen yet, so I grab the pile and turn back to Myles.

"So, I have, *The Voices, The Boy Next Door, Two Night Stand,* or *X-Men: Futures Past*." I read them off slowly, flicking through one DVD to the next.

"*X-Men: Futures Past*, if that's okay? I've not seen it yet."

"Me neither," I smile, excited to finally be watching it.

FIVE

KAYLA

"WHERE THE FUCK DO YOU think you're going?" he shouts, and I can hear his feet running towards me as I try to pump my feet faster. Why can't I run faster? My feet feel heavy and I can't get them to move as quickly as I'd like. My heart picks up. The adrenaline is spiking through my veins, overriding the fear looming there.

The edge of the forest is getting closer, I can see it, but then it moves further away in a blink of an eye and I scream out in frustration, my scream too quiet for my own ears. I try screaming louder, but it's muted and I start to panic.

He's picking up speed behind me.

His hand reaches the back of my blazer and I scream out, flying forward to the dirty ground. Mud and dried leaves blow up in my face and into my mouth. I cough rolling over, kicking out and trying to fight him off, but my fists and feet kick out at thin air.

It hurts.

His hands are everywhere, touching, slapping, grabbing and I can't wiggle myself out. The sound of a belt undoing has another scream tearing from my mouth, until his hand clamps over it, muffling the sound. I try to break free, to scream harder for help, but nothing *works.*

Another sharp pain, another muffled scream, my voice is hoarse, then I hear people, their voices, and my eyes open to find my mother stood above us, she's watching him with sickening delight, laughing that laugh that sends chills down my spine.

"Help me, Mom!" I cry, but she just looks through me, not seeing me or caring.

I'm thrown onto my stomach, the sickening sound of them laughing echoing into the trees. I try to crawl away, the pain unbearable, but I fight it, I fight him. A sickening whistle sounds through the air, and all time stops until that whack of leather hitting my back, the belt buckle cutting into my skin and I scream in excruciating pain, but I still try to wiggle free. In the midst of trying to wiggle away I aid him in removing my knickers, the cold air hitting me below and I scream.

My face is shoved into the dirt.

Please no! Please don't do this. Please don't let this happen.

"You deserve this you little bitch. Enjoy it while you've got it," my mother's voice rings out sweetly from somewhere nearby.

"You'll enjoy it, I promise," he laughs, no compassion or remorse in his voice.

"Please don't, please no!"

Then he pushes in.

"No! No! No! No! Get off me, get off me," I scream, shoving a large body off me.

"Hey, it's me, Kayla. It's me, Myles. It's okay, you're safe," he tells me through my terror.

"Please don't touch me," I heave out through my tears before rushing off the bed and out into the hallway towards the bathroom. As soon as I enter I turn on the shower before I can't take it anymore and turn, emptying the entire contents of my stomach into the toilet. Once I'm finished I strip out of my sweat coated clothes.

I notice the time on my watch when I take it off and gasp. It's half two in the morning. Oh my God, did we...did we fall asleep together? I nearly rush back over to the toilet to be sick again, but the need to get *his* touch off me is overwhelming.

The temperature of the water is scalding hot when I step in. It doesn't cool in the slightest as I begin to scrub my body raw, making sure to pay extra attention between my legs. It's moments like this that I do feel clean, but I know the second I step out of the shower I will again feel *his* dirty hands on me.

I don't know how long I've stayed in the shower for, but when I begin to feel lightheaded from the heat I shut the shower off, grabbing the towel out of the rack before stepping out.

I'm hoping Myles has left by the time I go back into my room. It's not like he has a reason to stick around. I basically just freaked out on him and screamed at him not to touch me. I don't even want to think what I cried out in my sleep. Mortified, I grab my dressing gown off the back of the bathroom door and tie it securely around me before walking back down the hall to my bedroom.

I'm surprised to find my bed sheets have been changed and the old ones are in a pile by the door, but what surprises me the most is Myles sat on the edge of the bed, his shirt forgone and his head in his hands. He looks like a dark angel sat there, the muscles in his shoulders tensing and the muscles in his arms bulging from where he's leaning them on his knees.

"Hey," I whisper, and he must not have heard me walk in because as soon as he hears my voice his head snaps up. His eyes look tortured when he looks at me, and I look down embarrassed.

"That was about *him* wasn't it?" he questions, but it sounds more like a statement.

"Yes," I whisper, still not able to look at him. "We must have fallen asleep."

"Yeah, I... um, here, put this on," he tells me, walking over with his lost shirt. I take in a huge gasp of air when I see the outline of his abdominal muscles. They're cut to perfection and he has that V thing going on that I read about in my books. He has a faint line of hair trailing down to his um, nether region, it looks sexy as hell. I swallow the lump forming in my dry throat and the sudden need for water feels almost painful.

Moving closer he lifts his arms with his t-shirt scrunched up, and moves closer towards me, pulling the t-shirt over my head.

"Um, you should do the rest," he coughs before turning around. I slip my arms out of my dressing gown and push my arms through the t-shirt before pulling it down over the towel.

"Stay turned," I whisper, my voice hoarse from the dryness and from the crying I've done. With shaky fingers I walk over to my chest of drawers and find a pair of knickers and shorts, slipping them on under the towel. Once I've done that I drop the towel, picking it up and chucking it over the chair. His shirt smells like him and I find it oddly comforting. I inhale the smell, loving his intoxicating scent before dropping it back down. It falls loosely just above my knees. "You can turn around now."

I move over to the bed to sit down, too embarrassed, and confused on what I should say. It's late, I'm tired, and I just want to curl up in a ball and forget about my nightmare.

"You should probably go," I choke out, then jump, startled when I feel him sit on the bed next to me.

"I'm not going anywhere," he starts, and when I go to protest he holds his hand up stopping me. "I'm not leaving you here alone when you've just had a nightmare. Your dad isn't even back yet, so I'm not leaving. Come on, get into bed. I'll lie on top of the covers," he tells me, opening up the duvet.

I crawl inside the duvet, lying down so I'm facing him and watch as he tucks me in and lies down in the same position, but on top of the covers facing me.

"Do you want to talk about it?" he whispers, his fingers brushing a strand of wayward hair from off my face.

"Not really. I have a nightmare every night. Sometimes it's about what happened, sometimes it's different, my mom or someone will be there taunting me," I shrug, feeling another tear slide down my cheek. My hand tries to reach out from under the duvet, but Myles' hand reaches out, his thumb wiping the tear away, and I sigh.

"What does your mom say?" he asks. My heart stops, but I pause, a feeling I've not had since the rape happened. I want to talk; I want to tell Myles all of it. How my mother taunts me in my nightmare, laughs at me and encourages Davis to hurt me. It's how I find myself opening my mouth and telling him. I tell him everything, about how she stands there watching, laughing, taunting, how sometimes there's other voices, but I don't know who they belong to. It's mostly the same every night, but on the rare occasion it will be what actually happened that day, from the very minute I took the shortcut home so that I could be back on time.

"I'm sorry that happened to you," he whispers softly, but his jaw is hard and his eyes look distant and lost.

"Life happens," I mumble, not believing a word of what I say. Life is cruel and unfair. Sometimes I feel selfish because there are people all around the world with a harder life than mine. "There are people far worse off."

"That may be true, Kayla, but it doesn't excuse what happened to you. Just because someone out there has it worse doesn't make your pain any less significant. It happened to you, not them. It's your pain that you suffer with. You're a brave, strong, woman, and I don't think you should blow off your pain just because someone else has it bad."

My mind runs over what he said and I can understand what he's trying to tell me. It still doesn't excuse the fact that life keeps fucking me over. I must have been a worldwide known serial killer in my previous life, because I know I've done nothing in this life to deserve what I'm going through.

My eyes flick to Myles' deep, dark brown ones. We stare for what feels like hours, neither of us talking, and before I know it, I'm drifting off to sleep.

My body is warm and the bed is comfortably hard beneath me. I groan when the stiffness in my neck cricks. The bed shifts beneath me, and I freeze when I hear a male groan. My body is curled around Myles like a blanket. My leg is thrown over both of his. My girly parts shoved against his hips, and I can feel his... I can feel his morning wood against my legs.

Nervously I lift my head off his shoulder and lean up to look at his sleeping form. Asleep he looks relaxed, peaceful, and much younger than he does when he's awake. With a mind of its own my hand reaches up and I lightly run my finger along his eyebrow, his features scrunching making him look adorable. I find myself smiling as I trace my finger down his beautiful straight nose to his full plump lips. His bottom lip is fuller than his top one, it's sexy, and I run my finger along them, loving how soft they feel under my touch. His lips pucker, kissing my finger tips, and a delicious shiver I've never felt before runs through my body.

"Was I drooling?" he asks, his hard body rumbling against me and I fall back squeaking.

"I'm sorry, I'm, oh God, I'm so sorry," I blurt, my face heating like an oven.

He chuckles and I notice my leg is still over his and when I try to move it slowly, hoping he doesn't notice, my knee grazes against his morning wood.

Oh crap, now what do I do.

It's taken out of my hands when Myles reaches down and grabs my knee, lifting it off him as he follows, rolling onto his side to face me.

"Morning," he breathes huskily, his voice still full of sleep. His eyes are half mass, still full with sleep.

"Morning," I blush.

"Did you sleep okay?"

"Better than I have in a long time," I tell him honestly. There's no point in lying. We both know he would have heard me if I had had another nightmare.

"Sweetie, it's half seven, you're going to be late," my dad calls. I jump back from Myles, banging my head against the bed frame.

"Yeah, Dad. I'm up," I shout back. I'm so glad he isn't one of those fathers who walk in to wake their kids up.

"I'm going to bed, kid," he shouts, and I look to the door to my room, confused. Before I can think much else of it, I'm straddling Myles. His hard erection pressed up against my core and I nearly fly sideways off the bed with a squeal.

"Hold up, Dad," I shout, sounding out of breath. I don't look back at Myles. I'm too scared of what he'll see in my expression. I can't believe I just got out of bed like that, pressing myself unintentionally against his penis. Jesus, it was hard. And long. And, my God, something else.

I rush to open the bedroom door, before slamming it shut behind me and walk down the narrow hallway to my dad's bedroom. His bedroom is at the back of the house, his room the farthest away from any of the others.

"Have you only just gotten in?" I question, worriedly. He's been working a hell of a lot lately, and it seems to be since we moved back to town. I feel like he's not telling me something, but then, he's never really discussed his business with me before, so I don't expect him to start now.

"Yeah, Darling. We've had a lot going on opening up the new branch. I'm hoping my hours will die down once it's all settled."

"Are you sure everything's okay?" I can tell when he's hiding something or lying, his eyes always flicker to the left before landing back on me.

"Yeah, get to school and I'll speak to you later. I probably won't be back until ten tonight, but I do promise to call this time if I'm going to be out all night. I should have called your mother or something," he tells me.

"No. No, that's totally fine. I'm a big girl Dad; I'm eighteen, nearly nineteen. I'm old enough to look after myself. You know this."

"I know, Sweetie, but until you turn twenty one, you know the rules," he smiles and I groan. Because of everything that's happened I have to wait until I'm twenty-one to legally become an adult as such. While most kids my age are off to college, out drinking in nightclubs, I'm stuck living with the rents like a sixteen year old child. All because of the state my mental health was in when everything happened. Legally, I can leave when I want to, but it means I won't be able to finish school, or support myself financially. I'm classed as unstable until they do another consultation at the end of the month.

It's one of the reasons I see my mother on weekends. You see, the real reason isn't because we're mother and daughter and I'm legally bound, it's because she's blackmailing me. She's pretty much done it since I gave in my statement a few months back. She said if I didn't keep up appearances she would make sure a court sees me as unfit to live on my own ever. I believe she will do this, especially since she wants legal rights to my trust fund, and the fact my father pays for her house and bills. And the only reason he does this is so I have somewhere safe to stay when I'm with her.

I was supposed to inherit my trust fund as such when I turned eighteen, but because of my mental health at the time they decided against it, so now I have to wait until I'm twenty-one. Which I'm not really bothered about, I never earned the money in the first place, but it's the fact I could use that money to get away from her. So one wrong move on my end and she will make my life a living hell more than she already does.

"I know, Dad," I say rolling my eyes. "When I have my examination at the end of the month you'll see I'm better. I'm not bothered about what I get or don't get, I just want my independence back."

"You are independent, and I can see a massive change in you since we've moved back here. To be honest, I was worried at first about coming back, but I think facing your fears has helped in some way. I know I can trust you, but after, after last time, Honey-"

"I know, Dad," I tell him, giving him a small smile. I don't need to hear about the mistakes I've made in the past, but if only he knew what it felt to be that worthless, to be that dirty, maybe then he could somehow understand the reasons why I did what I did.

"Go get ready for school," he smiles gently, his eyes worn and tired.

I nod my head, waving goodnight, or good morning, whichever way you look at it, and head back into my bedroom. My mind is running through all those bad memories that I forgot Myles is still in my room. So when I find him standing there, shirtless, and looking hot as hell, I jump, a scream nearly escaping my mouth.

"Jesus, I really need to buy those bells," I mutter and he grins looking at me questioningly. I just give him a shrug and he smirks in return.

"I'm going to get going so I can get a shower in before school. Do you need us to come get you? Mason is taking us today because he's heading that way for work."

I'm about to decline, but then the conversation with my dad runs through my mind again and I find myself nodding my head 'yes' and smiling. I need this. I need to move forward, to prove to my parents that I can do this; I can go off to college without them having to worry. Not that I think that's the part my mother cares about, no. I just feel like I'd have more freedom once I prove myself.

"I'll be back here just before half eight, make sure you're ready," he grins, taking a step forward. At first I think he's going to kiss me, but he stops himself, looking at the floor with wide eyes before quickly grabbing his backpack and hightailing it out of my bedroom. I look to the door and shrug, knowing I can't let him get inside my heart, or think things that aren't really there. It will only leave me more broken and for some reason I don't think I'll ever get over being hurt by Myles.

THE REST OF THE SCHOOL week is really slow, and come Friday I just want to go to bed and sleep the whole weekend away.

Myles and I haven't seen each other out of school again this week, he's been busy studying and other things, but something inside me can't help but feel like he's avoiding me. After the night we spent together, Myles hasn't been back. He texted me that morning to meet him at the end of my street and that was that. We still hang out all the time at school, but something feels different between us now. I could just be imagining it, and with my track record I could be right, and I'm just blowing this up out of proportion.

"Good you're here. It's about time," my mother snaps, and I want to roll my eyes at her and tell her to fuck off, but I keep my mouth shut and my eyes focused on her mouth. Heaven forbid I don't pay attention when she's talking.

"The bus was running late," I tell her, but I already know there's no point in telling her anything, she will only see it as an excuse.

She clucks her tongue, looking at me with so much disgust. I squirm where I'm standing, waiting for her to blow. "Go put your stuff in your room and get started.

I have a '*friend*' coming over for dinner and I want the place looking sparkling."

I nod my head feeling defeated. We all know what she means when she says 'friend'. It's just another word to describe the obscenely rich men she's trying to get her claws into. Because she knows my father will cut her off soon, she needs another cash point. My mother didn't get anything from the divorce because of the circumstances, so she's now on the hunt for another male she can manipulate, just like she did to my dad.

"Speak when you're spoken to," she snaps, and quickly for her, she swings her hand out, slapping me in the face, the force whipping my head sideways. My hand covers my stinging cheek, tears welling in my eyes as I look at her. I hate her. I've never hated anyone as much as I hate her. "Do you understand or do you need to be taught a lesson?" she snaps, her voice grating on my nerves.

"No. I understand. I'll get it done," I politely confirm, my voice high and clear so she doesn't find another excuse to lash out at me.

"So why are you just standing there?" she roars, her face murderous, vein lines pumping in her forehead.

I don't reply, instead I rush off upstairs. My room is the small storage closet that should be used to store the hoover and stuff.

No. No, it's not what you think. It's actually pretty cool here. It fits a bed and a chest of drawers and there's enough room in between the two to walk down to get out. I'm just lucky she didn't have a cellar, that is somewhere I know she would've put me to sleep, and enjoyed it. I quickly chuck my bag on the bed, and change out of my school clothes. Once I'm changed I quickly rush down to the kitchen and get to work. The place isn't a dump, but she's not used to doing things herself. She's lazy and I'm pretty sure she's never worked a day in her life. It's another reason I hate her. She expects everything handed to her on a silver plate. I wish I could walk into the front room where she's watching some snooty show about housewives, and tell her where she can shove her goddamn broom and mop, but I know the consequences of speaking out of term when it comes to that woman.

A few hours later and I'm just finishing cleaning up the dishes, waiting for my mother's companion to arrive so I can go to my room. When there's a loud knock on the door I jump, and then rush out to go answer it. My mother stands glaring at me, looking at me like I took too long to answer it. The fact she is standing right next to the door is obviously lost on her. As soon as she can't see my expression, I roll my eyes. She moves to stand over near the fireplace, looking elegant and beautiful, it's just a shame her vile personality doesn't match her looks. Although, she can look an evil witch on most days, it's just a matter of who is in her presence.

I answer the door to an overweight man wearing a suit. His receding hairline makes his forehead look double the normal size. He's wearing silver rimmed glasses that look like magnified glasses; his eyes are popping out that much. His eyes leer at me and I have the urge to go and have a shower, but since my mother has to save as much money my dad gives her for her designer clothes, she doesn't let me shower here. Water doesn't come cheap, apparently, so she doesn't even let me make a cup of coffee in the mornings, even though it's already boiled from her making her one.

His eyes rake up and down my body, and I nearly end up vomiting in my mouth when he runs his tongue along his bottom lip, his eyes staring at my chest. I know I'm big chested, but to have someone old enough to be my granddad eyeing them up is just beyond gross.

I send him a glare, hoping my mother doesn't see, and step aside. I don't speak; I don't want to. The guy creeps me out and I know I'll have to pay for it later, but I'd rather suffer my mom's wrath than have him thinking he can leer at me all night.

"Good evening, you must be Kayla, Jessica's daughter?"

"Yes, Sir," I smile tightly, before moving away and walking back into the kitchen. I hear my mom laughing and flirting with him, it makes me want to vomit all over again. God, how can she even pretend to be interested in him? The guy screams sleazebag.

"Kayla, drinks," my mother snaps, and I roll my eyes walking back into the room to see what they want.

"What would you both like to drink?" I ask quietly and sweetly.

"Well, champagne of course," she says irritated, and I look away nodding my head. Once in the kitchen I pour both of them a glass of champagne before putting the bottle back into the fridge to cool. I'm sure I'll only get called in a few times to make them another drink, because there is no way I'm taking a bucket of ice out there to put the champagne in again. Who does she think she is? Royalty? God, she gets my back up.

With shaking hands I move into the dining room and place both drinks down in front of my mother and her guest.

"Oh, Harold, you are so funny," she giggles flirtatiously, and I have to bite back a groan.

"Thank you," Harold says leering at me with a sneer, which I'm sure he thinks is a smile. I nod my head not caring if he's thankful or not, and move back to the kitchen to plate up their food. Once it's done I move back out into the dining room and place both of their dinners in front of them. When a hand reaches out, touching the back of my thigh near my ass, I jump back startled and frightened. The plate of food I was placing in front of Harold nearly lands in his lap, but thankfully his other hand reaches out and catches it. His other hand, the one that was copping a feel, moves back towards me and I jump back again, feeling my throat start to close and my body break out in a hot flush.

God, please don't have a panic attack now, not here.

"You stupid little - urgh, get to your room now," my mother shouts, and I unfreeze long enough to get my feet moving away from Mr. Perv. I'm about to head to the kitchen to get my dinner when her voice cuts through me. "If you even think of helping yourself to food after what you just pulled, young lady, then you've got another thing coming," she snarls.

Sighing, I don't even bother explaining why I jumped, because in the end she wouldn't care why it happened or who caused it.

"I'm so sorry, Harold. She's such a clumsy young girl. We tried to raise her the best we could, but there's only so much you can do, right?" I hear her tell him, and I shake my head, feeling tears fill my eyes. Why can't I just have a normal mother, one that is proud to call me her daughter, and one that will stand in front of a loaded gun for me? I'd be lucky to get my mother to stand in front of me in a queue.

"Kids nowadays need discipline, a firm hand, and a voice of reason. I'm a firm believer in kids should be seen and not heard," I hear him chuckle as I make my way to the top of the stairs. My skin prickles from his choice of words and I wonder if he has kids of his own.

"I couldn't have said it better myself, Harold. She will be getting punished don't you worry, but I'm not going to let the girl stand in the way of what is turning out to be a delightful night," she coos and I literally just vomited in my mouth. Talking about disciplining her own daughter is what gets her hot and bothered, she's freaking sick, but then I've always known that.

I decide to get into bed and don't bother with my pyjamas. I feel safer with as much clothing as I can when I'm in this house, and with a complete stranger who just happens to be as cruel as she is in the house, I decide to keep my mobile phone under my pillow. I don't usually leave it where my mother will find it. She will only break it like she did the last five mobiles I had, so it's best to keep it out of sight. If I'm honest, I believe she breaks them because she thinks I'm recording her or some shit, and believe me, I've tried. It was just when it got to the blackmailing part that I chickened out and ended up having a panic attack. I'm not strong enough to hold my own, at least, I wasn't back then, but maybe I'm stronger now. Like Dad said, he can see how much I've changed since moving here.

A sharp pull on my hair has me falling out of bed with a loud thud. I cry out in pain when I knock my previous injuries.

"Get up," she screams, sounding like a banshee. Before I get chance to get my bearings, she's grabbing my hair again and lifting me up. In the small room, I use the bed as leverage to get up faster. When we're face to face, her eyes are bloodshot and I can smell the alcohol on her breath. From the corner of my eye I look at the clock out in the hall, shocked when it reads three thirty in the morning. How long has she been drinking? Is Harold still here? Oh my God, what if he is?

"Please, Mom, stop," I cry out, her hand in my hair tightening.

"Did you deliberately try to make a fool out of me tonight? Do you think it's a joke?" she shouts, her hand rearing back before coming down hard across my cheek. My hand reaches up to cover the sharp sting and more tears fall from my eyes. I don't argue back with her, there's no point, and even though she's asked me a question I know there's no point in answering. It's not the answers she wants to hear. "I should have given you up at birth. You're a useless, selfish brat."

This time, instead of a slap, she lands a solid thump to my already sore ribs. A loud cry leaves my mouth, the pain excruciating. I cower back, my ass hitting the bed and I move backwards to try and get as far as I can as I watch and listen to her shout expletives at me.

She leans over the bed, her nails digging into my thigh and I'm thankful I left my normal clothes on because if I hadn't, I'd have more than a bruise on my thigh right now. I'd have cuts from her nails that are sharply digging in. I'd actually be surprised if she isn't already drawing blood.

"You're going to regret what you did tonight. Why can't you be a good daughter, one that listens? Instead I get a whiny, snivelling, ugly, useless, thickhead for a daughter. No one will ever love you, no one, because you're not fucking worth it," she spits out.

Her words cut deep, hurting more than her physical blows and I bow my head in shame, which only makes her snicker. I don't look up. I already know what expression her face will be masked in, one of pure enjoyment and evil as she continues to throw insults at me. How I ended up with a mother like her is anyone's guess.

It's reaching five in the morning when she finally leaves my room. My face is throbbing, but thankfully she hasn't drawn any blood, and I'm pretty certain the only bruise forming that will be visible to other people will be the one of my forehead where she whacked it against the chest of drawers. With the room so small, it's hard to avoid hitting something.

I groan, rolling over and reaching down to grab my small bag of change of clothes and begin to quietly grab my stuff before heading into the bathroom down the hall. Luckily mom's room is down the other side otherwise she'd have my ass for even contemplating using her shower. But if I want to soothe any of these bruises, new and old, I need a hot shower.

Hoping it doesn't wake her up; I quickly turn on the shower, but not before opening the window wide to let the steam out of the small room. I make quick work peeling the clothes off my sore aching body, the fresh bruises making it hard for me to keep the tears at bay. I choke on a sob when the hot, steaming water first hits my skin and I clench my hands into fists.

I don't bother looking down at my body; I just do what I have to do before slowly getting back out of the shower. I know I'll never be able to get back to sleep now. There's no point when I have to be at the church shelter in just over an hour. It's the only thing my mother lets me do when I'm with her, and that's only because she made me volunteer, not that I minded. I actually really like it there and it gets me out of the house and away from her.

I quickly dab on some concealer to cover up the dark bags under my eyes when I'm finally dressed. Not wanting to spend another second in her house, I rush downstairs, nearly stumbling on my ass when I see a half naked Harold on the sofa snoring his head off.

Ewwwe!! No wonder she was in a bad mood.

I avert my eyes away from the large man and open the front door silently, enough so it doesn't creak and I can slide my slim frame through. I shut it behind me and make my way over to the church, the one place I can find peace, away from my hell of a nightmare life. I'm actually startled when I picture Myles, and it occurs to me then, he is another form of peace in my life, although, lately, he feels a lot more than that.

"You're early." The voice is soft and instead of my usual jumpy self, I turn around with a smile.

"Hey, Joan. I thought I'd get an early start on the food boxes that are being delivered."

Joan is Harlow's nan. She's a sweet lady, and I would say old lady, but apart from her looks, there is nothing old about Miss. Joan.

"You don't need to do that, I had it covered, but thank you, Sweetie. They've already been delivered and I got the nice, fit men to put them in the back room. Nothing to do with watching their muscles and bending over to pick up the boxes," she cackles, and I can't help but laugh with her. Can you see what I mean about not being old? The woman can flirt with the best of them, and I've even seen grown men blush around her. She's a hoot.

"I don't mind. I'll go get started," I smile, before moving towards the back.

"Wow! What happened, Kayla? Are you okay? Oh my God, why didn't you say anything?" Joan's hysterical voice has me snapping back around and I wince at the quick movement, my neck is stiff and sore, and I'm wondering what wound she could have seen when I have them all covered.

"W-what?"

"Your neck, Honey, has bruises on it," she tells me eyeing me up. Her eyes flick to my wrist and I curse for not covering myself better.

"Oh, it's nothing. I fell down the attic stairs getting some boxes for my mom," I smile, hoping my lie will be enough to get her off my back.

"Why didn't you say something, sweetie? You should go on back home and rest up."

Panicking that she's going to send me home, to *her*, I rush on, hoping she will let me stay. "No! No, it's fine. I'm fine. Honestly, it's not as bad as it looks I promise. Can I stay?" I plead, feeling my eyes begin to water. I know what will happen if I go back there now. Mother will wake up around eleven and will take her hangover out on me. The day will only get worse from there. I have one more night to suffer through, and then I'm safe for a whole five days.

"Of course, if that's what you want, honey. If it gets too much, though, you come find me, okay?"

"Okay," I answer quietly, before quickly rushing off to the back room, furiously wiping away the tears that have spilled over.

An hour later a girl around my age walks in looking like she's hardly had any sleep. I know that feeling too well, but there's also a sadness in her eyes that I can also relate to. I've seen her once before when I've helped out with the food bank, but I've never actually approached her or spoken to her. She's got long brown hair that falls in limp, messy waves to her waist. I'm not usually one to judge, but it could do with having a few inches cut off. It's her expressive eyes that stand out the most; they're large, round, and a stunning sharp blue colour. They look so innocent, but so full of pain and sadness.

"Hi, I'm Lake. Joan sent me in to help you. What do you want me to do?" she asks, and her voice is sweet and kind.

"Oh, I'm Kayla. I guess you can help date everything with me. Is that okay or would you like something else to do?"

"No! No, that's fine. Do you need me to get some more labels?" she asks softly, and I turn to look at her to find her gaze studying me.

"Yeah, if you don't mind."

"Not at all," she says and walks off to the storage cupboard where Joan keeps all the supplies.

She walks back in at the same time that everyone helps out; around the food bank arrives. I haven't had chance to meet everyone just yet. I've mostly kept to myself. But I know there are a few people around my age, and younger, that help volunteer. So I'm not fazed when a few girls a year younger than me and a few in the same year at school walk in.

"Did you hear they had some deodorant go missing?" one girl tells her friend. Her friend giggles behind her hand, giving Lake a funny look. I look to Lake to find her mindlessly minding her own business, but I can't help but notice the twitch in her jaw when her friend replies.

"Yeah, but I heard that the person who took it, needed it," her friend laughs back evilly.

The girls are trying to get at something, and I'm not sure whether it's to do with me or Lake, who's helping me. The look of Lake's hard gaze and the way she's gripping the table suggests that this isn't the first time she's had a run in with these two.

"Can I help you?" I ask the first girl that spoke, hoping the firmness in my voice is convincing. She's not the normal type of girl I would usually talk to or even see here. I can tell by looking at her she isn't here by her own free will. Her expression is bored, and I reckon the only kick she gets out of being here is picking on the other volunteers and people who need our help.

"No, but you should keep an eye on this one," the girl snarls, rolling her eyes at me.

"And why is that?" I flicker my gaze over to Lake, and I can see tears pool in her eyes.

"She steals things."

I don't know which one of the girls speaks up, but it gets my back up either way. I hate bullies like her. They always think they can intimidate whoever they want, say what they want, and to hell with the consequences.

"Well, she can't steal something that's free. Joan has already made that clear," I tell them sweetly, and both girls glare at me. I stare back, my expression not changing, although my body is shaking with nerves and fear on the inside.

"Whatever, she's a tramp. She doesn't belong here," the other girl, the second one to speak when they walked in, says.

"Listen up, bitches, I'm only going to say this one more fucking time, and that is to back the fuck off. I've listened to you go on and on about what you think of me, but there is something you've still failed to pick up on, and that's that I don't care. I don't care what you think of me, what you say, or what you think I've done. It's people like you who waste minutes, hours, weeks, *hell*, years picking on people and wormin' your way into people's lives just to gossip and be bitches that have no life. In the future, next time you think I've stolen something then report me. It's only going to come back to bite you in the ass."

I stand shocked. It's the most Lake has spoken since I've met her, or even been here. She doesn't speak to a lot of people; she mostly keeps to herself or goes to Joan. Now I can see why. These girls are ruthless. When they leave with a huff, I can't help but smile. Lake has got some bark. I envy her. She is someone I wish to be. I've never stood up for myself, but I have no problem doing it for other people.

"Thank you," she whispers after a few seconds. I turn my head away from the door and give her a big smile.

"I'm sorry. I wish I could have said more, I'm just not...Just not good with conflict," I tell her, ashamedly.

"I can get that," she says softly, then when she sees my confusion she carries on. "I heard one of the volunteer's mention who you were and a bit of your story. That's when I realised I'd read your story. I'm sorry... for bringing it up," she says, her face turning red.

"No it's okay, well, it's not something I talk about, but it's fine," I whisper.

"I'm sorry," she tells me, and her hand reaches out for mine and she gives it a light squeeze. The suggestion startles me at first, but then I realise she is just trying to be nice to me.

"Right, it's nearly lunch time, do you want to go grab something to eat with me?" I ask with hopeful eyes. It beats sitting in the cafe, or the chippy around the corner on my own for an hour and a half.

"No, I um, I'm saving money at the moment. I'll eat later. I really should get these finished," she rants, her eyes wide.

"That's okay, we can do this later, and it's my shout. I honestly could use the company, and if you like we can share a meal deal. They have a large bag of chips either with sausages, fish, or doner meat for two people. It's no problem." She looks like she's about to decline again when I interrupt. "Please, I hate going on my own, I honestly don't mind. It's not that much."

"Are you sure? I really don't have any money," she tells me, chewing on her nails as one arm covers her stomach. She looks unsure, insecure, and more than anything, shy and scared. I wish there was more I could do or say that would ease her mind. I honestly have enough money to buy everyone in the building food, but I'd never rub it in her face like that. I can tell there's a story behind those broken, sad eyes, so no matter what, I'll make her feel at ease as much as possible.

"Honestly, it's totally fine. I wouldn't offer if I didn't mean it. Plus, I don't fancy sitting for an hour and a half looking outside a chippy window," I giggle, and she giggles with me.

"Okay then, I'll just go grab my coat," she smiles and I smile back, heading over to where I dumped my coat and purse when I first came in.

SIX

MYLES

Another weekend has passed being bored out of my mind, so walking down the corridor to registration I begin to feel my shoulders relax. I don't know whether it's because I'm getting to see Kayla again or what. I just know I'm excited as fuck to see her.

All weekend I've had to listen to Max go on about some chick he met up with or some other crap. We were meant to be having a movie night at Denny's, but Hope got sick so we stayed away. And as the old Gunners' house is now burnt down, the parties have been getting less and less. And if they think I'm hanging out in a park when it's pitch black outside then they've got another thing coming. Most kids my age go, but I'm not like most kids, and there is no way you'll get me hanging out in one either. Kids have to play in the place, and they all seem to forget that when they're smoking, drinking and doing drugs. It makes me sick. I don't even want to comment on the immature idiots that vandalise the playgrounds with shit kids don't need to read.

So anyway, my Saturday consisted of watching bad movies, catching up with homework, and listening to Max whine about being bored, until he finally gave up and went to the park to get drunk and laid.

My Sunday wasn't much better. Max woke me up at the crack ass of dawn to go watch him play footy. I don't usually go, but he said he was fed up of looking at me sulking all the time, so I went along wanting to prove him wrong. I stood in the pouring rain for two hours watching him play. It was hell.

Walking into the classroom my eyes seek out Kayla first. She's beautiful sitting in her usual seat, leaning back, and gazing out the window. But today her eyes hold more sadness and pain in them than they usually do. She was like this last Monday too, and it burns my heart to see.

As I draw closer I notice her body tense a little before relaxing, and I grin to myself. She's leaning her head in the palm of her hand while still gazing out the window and I notice a purple bruise covering her wrist.

What the fuck?

"Hey," I call, sitting down in my seat. "What did you do?"

"What did I do? What?" she asks me, looking adoringly confused, which makes me grin at her. Her mouth opens and her tongue sneaks out, lightly running along her bottom lip. I have to clench my teeth and will my dick not to get hard.

Like it listens.

"Your wrist, it's bruised," I tell her, pointing to the offending bruise.

"Oh, I fell down the attic stairs getting a box down for my mom on Friday. It's fine. It just caught between the box and the door," she rambles, and for some reason I feel like she's lying to me. I'm pretty good at reading people, but when I'm around Kayla, every brain cell I own turns to slush.

"Must have been some fall," I grumble when I notice her wince again for the third time since sitting down.

"Yeah it was," she says quietly.

"What did you get up to at the weekend?" I ask making conversation, hoping the tension in her body relaxes, when it doesn't, I sigh, coming to a dead end.

"I helped at the food bank Miss. Joan helps run."

"You did?" I ask shocked, although I really shouldn't be. She's the most selfless, kindest person I know.

"Yeah, it's actually pretty relaxing," she smiles and it's genuine for the first time since I walked in, but then her choice of words describing her time there confuses me.

"Yo! Yo! Yo!" Max's loud voice comes booming through the classroom. He high fives, knuckle punches, and winks his way through other students like he's King of the school.

"God, he's something else," I mumble, and then hear a faint giggle to my side. My head snaps to the sound, my eyes raking over Kayla. Her hand is covering her mouth, but I still hear the faint giggle, and it only becomes louder when I send her a glare. "You think it's funny?"

She nods her head still giggling when Max comes barging past our seats to take his by the window.

"How's my future wife this morning?" he asks, swinging his arm around the back of her chair. Immediately her giggling comes to a sudden stop and it's my turn to burst into a fit of laughter at her wide eyed expression.

"Don't think she likes the thought of being your wife, bro."

"Everyone wants to be my wife. Hey, Alisha, you'd be my wife, right?" he shouts across the classroom and the girl in question, Alisha, looks back over to Max with crazy eyes, nodding her head furiously and grinning like a fool.

"See, Alisha wants me," he grins.

"I'm pretty sure Alisha would have said yes to her pet dog," I laugh. Alisha is one of those girls if you pay her an inch of attention then she will stalk you for the rest of your life. It so happens, I'm probably not far off with the dog comment.

"You're just jealous. Kayla, you'd be my wife, right?" he asks her and she's looking between us with wide eyes. "Right?"

"Um, not to hurt your feelings or anything, but no," she says quietly, fiddling with the sleeve on her blazer nervously.

"Why not?" Max whisper-yells, outraged, actually looking genuinely hurt, which confuses me more. Does he have a thing for Kayla? Just the thought has every muscle in my body tensing up and I want to actually punch my own brother in the face, although it wouldn't be the first time.

"Y-you're pretty high maintenance," she whispers back, and I burst into another fit of laughter, loving the shocked expression on Max's face.

"I am not," he tells her outraged.

"You really are," I tell him chuckling which earns me a glare.

"What about Myles? Is he high maintenance too? We are twins after all."

"Uh. I...He-"

"Don't answer him," I interrupt, not wanting to cause her anymore embarrassment. Her speech is stuttered, and her cheeks are flushed red. She looks so freaking cute. I want to kick myself for interrupting her when I was interested in her answer too, but for different reasons than my brother.

"No! She has to. My ego is on the line here, bro," he whines looking at Kayla with puppy dog eyes, but then as soon as her back is turned he gives me a smug grin, knowing what he's doing. The bastard.

"No she doesn't. Ignore him," I tell her, glaring holes into my brother. He's doing this on purpose. He knows how I feel about her, even though we've never actually spoken to each other about her.

"No it's fine," she says quietly. "No, Myles isn't high maintenance, he's anything but," she smiles and my heart warms at the sight. God, she's so goddamn beautiful it kills me not being able to touch her, to feel if her skin is as soft as it looks, or if her lips taste like cherry.

We're all silent for a few minutes and I can feel Kayla become stiff next to me, the silence making things awkward.

"In all honesty, I think he's high maintenance. I'm easy," he grins, leaning back in his chair, so it's resting on the two back legs and looking cocky.

"Too easy," she whispers, but I hear her and my head flies back and I roar out a burst of laughter.

"Myles, Max, please keep it down back there," the teacher shouts. Max groans muttering at how unfair she's being with us.

"I swear she wants a piece of me," Max mutters. "She always singles us out. Have you noticed?"

Jesus, he has no filter. "Bro, we're the only ones making so much noise."

"And?" I swear sometimes I worry about him, and how we can even be twins. We're polar opposites. We have nothing in common like normal twins and we act completely different.

"So," I start, grabbing Kayla's attention. "Do you want to work on the project tonight? We can meet at mine or yours again, up to you."

"Oh, I-I can't. Charlie and I arranged to meet up. She wants to come over to talk about something. I'm sorry."

"No. It's fine. I guess we can arrange for another night when you're free?"

"Definitely! Is tomorrow good for you?"

"Yeah," I smile as the bell for first period rings. "I'll speak to you later then."

By fourth period I'm a groaning mess. I haven't seen Kayla properly since

Friday and I kinda miss her. Which is sissy of me, right? It's not like we're a couple or anything. She just drives me crazy and the worst part? She doesn't even realise she does it. It kills me. She's all I can think about. It took me over two years to get over her.

I can still remember the first time I met her, well, saw her. She was walking down the hallway, her hair wild and falling in loose waves down her back. She was wearing her large black glasses that sat huge on her small delicate face. She walked with her head down, clutching a pile of books in her arms. I had stopped to stare. My eyes taking in every inch of her and I couldn't believe someone so beautiful was walking down the halls of our shitty school. She looked so out of place. In a good way, of course.

She had pouty, full, red lips that looked beyond kissable. It took everything in me to move my gaze away I was that overcome by her beauty. She didn't even wear makeup, or even dress up for me to notice. She was beautiful in every way that counts. She still is the most beautiful girl I've ever laid eyes on and no one else can even compare. She's beautiful inside and out.

"Dude, what the fuck is wrong with you today?" Toby, my friend, taunts next to me. We're in geography, another lesson I couldn't get with Kayla and I'm sure he's been talking to me for the past twenty minutes, but my thoughts have been consumed with Kayla, her beauty and those bruises I saw on her wrist this morning. I still don't buy that she got them from a fall. Does she really think I'm that stupid, or did she really believe her lie was good enough to believe?

"Seriously, dude, you've spaced all lesson. What the fuck is up with you?"

"Sorry, I guess I'm just tired," I lie, shaking Kayla from my thoughts.

"Are you sure? You've been grunting all lesson and every time I've asked you a question you've completely ignored me."

I shrug not knowing what else to say apart from 'I'm sorry'.

"Anyway, as I was saying, Dean is having a party later at his house. Do you want to come?"

I think about it for a minute and decide not to. It's not my thing anymore. The girls who throw themselves at you in hopes they can cop a feel. It's all the same. Once you've been to one party, you've been to them all.

"I've got plans already, but ask Max, I'm sure he'll be up for it."

"Max is always up for it," Toby laughs.

I smile back at him and my thoughts drift back to Kayla, wondering how I could get a girl as special as her to notice me. It's like she only sees me as a friend, and if that's all I ever get than I'll live with it. I'll take anything she will give me. After everything she's been through I know I can't push for anything more than friends until she's ready. If I try something now she might push me away for good. And that is something I don't want to risk.

SEVEN

KAYLA

CHARLIE ARRIVES RIGHT on time. Her mom's horn honks outside, notifying me of her arrival. I rush off down the stairs and make my way to the front door peephole. After a quick check that it is in fact Charlie, I rush to open the door. I'm so excited. I feel like I haven't seen her at all since I got back, when in reality it's only been three weeks.

"Hey," I greet her excitedly, but then my smile fades when I see how pale and tired she looks. "You okay?" I ask worriedly, inviting her in.

"Just a rough couple of days, it's okay. Can we just go crash upstairs for a bit, catch up?"

"Yeah! Yeah, sure. Do you want something to drink?"

"Yeah, can I have a glass of water?"

"Sure. Go on up and I'll meet you up there."

She walks away slowly, heading upstairs. She's usually bubbly, full of life, and chattering non-stop when she's around. This person reminds me of the girl she used to be, the one that was as quiet, and as shy as I am now.

Walking into my bedroom she's lying down on my bed with her eyes closed and for a few seconds I actually believe she's fallen asleep, but then her head turns and her eyes open.

"Come on, I want to know how everything at school is going," she smiles, sitting up and taking her glass of water from me.

"It's going good. I've caught up on all the work I missed with the trial going on, and only have a few assignments. How's college?"

"Boring," she groans. "And I didn't mean your school work, I meant being there, after, you know..."

"Oh! O-okay I guess. It's been good. Myles is with me most of the time," I shrug, ignoring the tingles I get from mentioning his name.

"Myles Carter?" she asks, her voice suspicious and my back straightens.

"Yeah, why?"

"Oh, no reason. So who else have you made friends with?"

I think about it for a few minutes and realise I haven't actually made any other friends apart from Max. "Max?" I ask, more of a question. I want to bury my head in the pillow knowing what's about to come.

"Are you kidding me? You've made no other friends what-so-ever?" she asks heatedly. "Kayla, we had a deal, when you came back you would make friends, go out, enjoy yourself. I've kept up my end of the bargain."

"Yeah, but you're so good at being bubbly, outgoing, and a people person. It's always been inside of you, Charlie. I'm lucky if I don't have a panic attack asking for no gherkins on my double cheeseburger. And technically I still made friends with Myles and Max. Plus, if you include Harlow then that's three people I've made friends with since I got back. I'd say that's progress."

She looks at me like I've lost my mind and then sighs, thankfully giving in. "Okay, I'll let it go, but you need to at least make a few more outside of the Carter family," she tells me and I smile, then remember the dinner I had with Lake on Saturday.

"Oh, and I made a friend at the church food bank. A girl called Lake who volunteers there. Some of the girls were being mean to her for no reason. We went out for lunch together," I smile big, feeling like a nursery kid needing praise for the painting they've just done.

"See, *that's* progress," she laughs, most likely at my enthusiasm. I ignore her and sit so that my back is against the bars of my bed and cross my ankles. "Oh, and talking of the trial, how are you after all that?"

"I'm still in shock, I guess. I know he would have been sent to prison with or without my testimony, but I'm still glad I did it. I just thought getting closure, him being locked away, would change things. Change me. But it hasn't," I tell her honestly, my voice quietening.

"What do you mean? Has someone said something to you at school? If they have I'll come kick their asses," she says vehemently.

I laugh. I can't help it. "No, Rocky. No one has said anything. I had people stare at me the first week or so, but it died down after that. I think the fact that whenever Max would catch someone staring, he'd walk right up to them and stare right in their face for a good five minutes."

"He didn't?" she laughs loudly, rolling to her side.

"He freaking did. One girl turned bright red, trying to getting away from him, but he just followed her, getting in her face," I laugh back, remembering all the times the crazy boy did that for me.

"It seems like those Carter boys care about you, she smiles, her laughing dying down to a contented chuckle.

I shrug. I try to come off not affected, but I can feel the blush rise in my cheeks when I think about Myles and him caring about me. I know he must in some way, but I fantasise about him caring about me in other ways. I know it will never be more than just friends, boys like him don't like girls like me, especially not broken ones.

"Oh come on! We both know Max doesn't associate with girls unless it's to do the nasty, and even then he never sees the same girl twice. For him to be friends with a girl is a miracle."

"He's friends with Harlow and Denny," I tell her dryly.

"That's different... Oh no, it's not. See, they're all dating his brothers, and Myles has a crush on you," she smiles looking giddy.

"Myles does not have a crush on me," I shout at her, my eyes wide, but I can't deny the rapid pulse that happens thinking that it's true.

"Pft, please. He so does."

"How would you know?" I say defensively.

"Oh come on, he was always making googly eyes at you. He could never keep his tongue from hanging out whenever you were around. I even heard he got into an altercation with Davis once, too, when, you know..." she doesn't finish. She doesn't need to. She means when he raped me, when he bullied me. The news that Myles would stick up for me against *him* surprises me. I didn't think anyone really believed me at the time. I remember the conversation I had once with Myles. I was sitting outside one of the school building and he came and sat down next to me. He was the first person I really opened up to. Yeah, I told Charlie what happened, but not the same way I told Myles. It was like everything came pouring out when he was there.

"He doesn't make googly eyes, you're mistaken," I roll my eyes, not wanting to talk about Davis.

"Keep telling yourself that, Kayla."

"Whatever."

"So, where is your dad?" she asks. I notice her fiddling with her fingers in her lap, she's nervous. Why she's nervous I have no clue. She has nothing to be nervous about. It's just me here.

"At work," I say gritting my teeth. He said he wouldn't be working so many hours, but he lied. Again!

"Take it things haven't changed? How about your mom?" she asks softly.

"I don't want to talk about them. What about you? How are you? You said you had some news to tell me." I'm hoping she doesn't call me out on changing the subject, but I really don't want to talk about my parents as much as I want to talk about Davis with her, or anyone.

"About that..." her tone doesn't sit well with me, and I sit up straighter feeling concerned.

"Go on."

"I had my check up a month ago. Things still haven't been going too well, and I didn't want to say anything until I knew for sure, but-" she chokes on a sob, not able to continue and I immediately crawl across the bed to her side and place my arm around her.

"Hey, it's okay. Take your time," I soothe.

"My body is rejecting my new heart," she sobs shoving her head into my chest. Charlie has dilated cardiomyopathy which weakens the heart muscle. Her father suffered the same diagnosis when he was younger. She had a transplant last year, so I know whatever else she is about to tell me is going to be bad.

"Shhhh, it's okay. Everything will be okay. They'll put you on the waiting list and you'll get a new heart and everything will be fine," I tell her, trying to sound convincing, but I don't know who I'm trying to convince...her or me.

"That's it though, Kayla. I don't think it will," she says, looking at me sadly. "I'm getting weaker and weaker by the day. I've already had a heart transplant. The chances of me getting another are slim."

"We can Google it. Find out what your options are," I tell her softly, feeling my own tears fall from my eyes.

"I have. It's rare, Kayla. I read this one story, though; it was about a woman who suffered with the same condition as me. Five years after her first transplant she got chronic organ failure that attacked her heart. She got put on the waiting list and received her second heart transplant. She died waiting for her third heart transplant."

"But it might not be the same results, Charlie. You can't worry like this, it won't do your heart any good," I tell her.

"I know. I know it's different, but reading her story, the way she was, how inspiring she *is*, it made me see things a little differently. I may not pull through this; the chances are really slim at this stage. I guess she inspired me. She helped me understand certain things. I even found myself looking up all the articles Google had on her."

I quickly jump off my bed and grab my laptop before bringing it back over to the bed and sitting down next to her. I don't know all that much about Charlie's condition. Yeah, I know it's serious, but I still don't feel like I understand it. When I load up Google, I ask her to show me. It's then we read through all the articles on this woman. I can see why Charlie got fixated on her. She really is an inspiring woman. She went through so much treatment, surgeries and hospital stays. She married a few months before she died from what we could make out. She was beautiful. She didn't look like a person who had a heart problem; she looked radiant, glowing, and full of life. We talk about it for an hour, both of us soaking in what we can.

"Everything will be okay, you can fight this," I tell her when I shut the laptop down.

"I'm scared. I'm eighteen, nearly nineteen, and I've not even been kissed. I haven't had a boyfriend, had sex, or hell, I've never left the UK. Reading about this woman, Donna, made me realise just how much of my life I've wasted away. Look at everything she achieved in life. She left this world knowing there was a man who loved her, had a child she could influence even after she was gone. She was looked up to. She'd be remembered for all the greatness and help she did.

This website isn't just about her, it's about everything and the support on there is out of this world. I've read so many other people's heart transplant stories on there, and for me, she started that, and I want to do something so people will remember me."

"Even if you were going to die, but you're not..." I choke out. "...You'd always be remembered, Charlie. You're more special than you give yourself credit for. I'm lucky to have you in my life. If it had not been for you I wouldn't have made it through the past few years," I tell her honestly.

"I'm just so scared," she sobs and together we lie down and cry. I hold her in my arms and try to soothe her the best I can, but the whole time my heart is breaking for her. Charlie doesn't deserve this; she deserves a long, full, happy life.

I don't know how long we lay there holding each other for, but it's not until Charlie's phone rings that I move for the first time. When I look over to Charlie, wondering why she isn't moving to answer her phone, I find her asleep. I shake her tired body and she wakes up slowly, looking disorientated and pale.

"Your phone. It was ringing," I whisper to her, just as her phone starts ringing again.

"Shit, I must have fallen asleep. Mom is going to kill me," she mutters before answering her phone. "Hey Mom... Oh! Okay, yeah. I'm sorry. I fell asleep. I'll be down in a second," she tells her mom before ending the call. "She's downstairs waiting for me. When I didn't come home by curfew she started to get worried, hence the reason she's downstairs waiting for me."

"Come on. Let's go downstairs before she starts banging the door down," I laugh, but the sound is sad and distant.

We both get up off the bed, stretch our taut muscles before heading off downstairs. Her mom is waiting outside in the car, and before heading down the path, Charlie turns around and embraces me in a tight hug.

"Thank you for being my friend. I love you," she whispers, before slowly turning around and heading to the car. Once she opens the door she gives me one last teary goodbye with a wave, and then gets in the car.

I watch as the taillights disappear in the distance, my heart aching that much more the further away they get.

Shutting the door, I sink down to the floor, my head resting on my knees and I let out the most blood curling sob I've ever heard. I choke on another sob, my chest heaving as I struggle to catch my breath.

Charlie could die.

Heart transplant.

I can't lose her. She's been here for me through everything, but it's more than that. Charlie has so much more to give in life. She doesn't deserve any of this.

With shaky hands I grab my phone from my back pocket. I don't even think about what I'm doing, I just dial the number I've somehow memorised off by heart and put the phone to my ear.

"Hello?"

"I need you…" I sob.

EIGHT

MYLES

The phone call from Kayla has me breaking in a sweat as I run through the streets to get to her house. Her sobs still echo in my ears. I hate knowing she's alone and hurt when there's nothing I can do. As soon as her words broke through the phone I was out of bed and rushing for my shoes and jacket. I never even explained to Mav where I was going when I rushed out either, but I know I'm going to have to give him a text when I find out what's wrong.

I rush up the pathway to her house and bang on the front door loud enough to wake up the neighbours. I hear a whimper on the other side and my heart clenches.

"Kayla? Kayla, are you okay? Open up," I shout through the door, and I sag with relief when I hear her start to unlock the door. As soon as it's opened I rush through the door, gently pushing her back and slamming the door shut behind me with my foot.

Kayla's eyes are red and swollen from crying and I take in every inch of her body for any signs of injury, but when I see none I take a quick glance around the room, noticing nothing out of place.

"Hush, baby," I comfort her, taking her in my arms. "Can you tell me what happened?"

"I-it's Charlie...her heart, her body's rejecting it and she may not survive," she sobs and my breath hitches. Shit! I know now why she's so upset, why she is so worked up. Kayla may not know this, but when she left before, I got updates from Charlie to see how she was. It ended though some time a year and a half ago when Charlie stopped coming to school. I understand why now. She's obviously been hiding her own secrets.

"I'm sorry," I tell her honestly, knowing how much Charlie means to her.

"She's scared, so scared she's going to die and all I can say is 'everything will be okay.' How lame is that?"

"It's not lame. No one can predict what's going to happen, baby. Come on, let's go lie down, you look knackered."

She nods her head and doesn't fight me when I lift her into my arms. She wraps her arm around my neck and cradles her head into my shoulder seeking comfort. I'm not going to lie and say I don't feel anything with her in my arms because I feel everything. How her body fits perfectly against mine and I love how her breath feels against my neck and how warm her hand feels palming my heart. It's heaven and no guy on this earth could resist feeling something for her.

"Did I disturb you?" she whispers once I lie us down on her bed.

"No you didn't," I tell her, pulling her back flush with my front. She stiffens at first, but soon relaxes when I run my fingers soothingly down her arm. I'm not going to lie; it feels good that she's comfortable around me to *even* relax after what she's been through. "What did Charlie tell you about her condition?"

"I already know some about it. When they first found it they thought it was due to stress from losing her granddad, but then when they did some further tests they found out she had Dilated Cardiomyopathy. They did a heart transplant around five months later. She called me to tell me and I wasn't here for her. My mother wouldn't let me come visit her and to be honest I wasn't in any fit state to leave on my own."

"If she's already had a transplant then, what will they do now?"

"Honestly? I don't know. She said they will be doing some more tests, and she'll be put back onto the transplant list. She's been getting short of breath easily and has been getting severer chest pains. It's not looking good."

"There has to be something we can do," I mumble feeling useless to her. She's called me because she needs me, and all I can do is hold her, I can't make this situation right.

"Nope, nothing but sit and wait to hear what the doctors have to say," she says wiping her eyes. "All I keep thinking is how scared she must be, how scared she was when she told me. She's so young."

"Has she always had heart problems?"

"Yeah. She was born with it, I think, but with the right medication she's been able to control it. When she came tonight I knew something was wrong the second I saw her. She looked drawn, pale, and even though she had put on weight due to the tablets, she looks so freaking fragile."

"God, this sucks!"

"Yeah, it does. I just wish I knew how I could make it better for her."

"How about a girl's night out?" I mention.

"We can't. She can't do anything that will exhaust her," she sighs, rolling over so she's facing me. I move down the bed a little so that my face is level with hers, our bodies not far away from each other, but close enough so I can still reach out and touch her.

"Okay, so what about a girl's night in? I know Denny could use one; she's been bored with Harlow at college all the time. Harlow would love one, too. She's been moaning about college," I shrug.

"Really? You think they'd be up for it? We could meet up here or something," she smiles, and it's genuine and I feel an accomplishment in that when she's just got bad news about her best friend.

"Denny will most likely have it at hers because of Hope. There is no way she will leave Hope." I smile, remembering the argument about leaving Hope with Grams while we all go away for the weekend. I'm hoping Kayla can come. I've asked, well, mentioned it to Denny. She said she would ask her, that it's a good idea, so I'm hoping she does it soon so that Kayla doesn't use 'it's too short notice' as an excuse.

"Yeah, okay, that sounds like a good idea. Let me text the girls," she smiles and my chest nearly bursts by the beauty of it. God, she's like sunshine on a cloudy day.

She leans over me and I suck in a sharp breath, her scent surrounding me, making me feel intoxicated.

"O-oh, I'm s-sorry," she breathes out as she lies back down, her phone in her hand, but her eyes fixated on me. She's so goddamn fucking beautiful.

"It's fine," I tell her, my voice low and husky.

She looks at me for a few seconds longer, her breathing heavy with the rise and fall of her chest. It's take everything in me not to look down, knowing her plump, full breasts will be spilling out of her strapped top with every heavy breath she takes.

Her eyes pull away, down to the light on her phone and starts clicking away on her buttons, a smile ghosting her lips.

"All...done," she smiles looking at me.

"Good," I smile, and then smile wider when her phone beeps with an incoming message.

"Denny is up for it," she laughs.

"What she say?"

"She said: Hell yes, baby. I need to socialise with someone other than Hope and Max."

I laugh along with her, knowing how Max is getting on Denny's nerves, but I know no matter how much she moans about him, I know she loves him all the more for it, especially with the way he adores Hope.

"That sounds like her," I chuckle as another message comes through on her phone.

"Harlow is up for it too, and I think Charlie will be asleep, but I'm sure she'll be up for it. That's if she can convince her mom to let her out of her sights. She was pretty obsessive with her the last time. Charlie said she would fuss over her, baby her, and follow her everywhere she went."

"Understandable," I chuckle. "Isn't Charlie an only child, too?"

"Yeah she is. I think that's why we're so close. Both of us haven't grown up with siblings. Must be nice for you to have all your brothers around you."

"It is, but sometimes it can become too much. Max can be a handful if you haven't already noticed."

"Oh, I've noticed," she laughs. It's decided, her laugh has just become my favourite sound ever. She seriously doesn't realise how breathtaking she is.

Looking at the clock next to her bed it reads midnight. Shit! Maverick. Quickly grabbing my phone out of my back pocket, I unlock it, and notice I've already received a few messages from Maverick.

Mav: Let me know you're okay. You ran pretty quickly out of the house. That can only mean two things. Either Max has done something stupid and

needs bailing out, or Kayla called you.

Mav: Max is back with a black eye and you're not with him so I'm taking it you're at Kayla's. Give us a text and let me know what you're doing tonight.

"Everything okay?" Kayla asks sweetly, looking at me with her big green doe eyes.

"Yeah, it's just Mav. I left the house in a hurry and didn't get to tell him where I was going or what I was doing, just going to text him back."

"Oh no, are you in trouble?"

"No, baby," I smile softly, loving it when a blush rushes to her cheeks.

"Do you want me to stay? I can go if you need me to," I tell her, hoping she doesn't send me away. Her dad's car isn't out the front again and from what Joan said the other day he's been seen with another woman. Something tells me Kayla doesn't know this snippet of information and I for one don't want to be the one to tell her. She has enough going on in her life without worrying about who her dad's banging.

Kayla looks over to the bedside clock before turning her attention back to me. "You can stay if you'd like," she says hesitantly.

I smile at her and nod, not wanting to look too eager, then fire off a quick text to Mav explaining Kayla was upset because she had some bad news, and that I'll be back in the morning to get showered and changed for school.

"We should get some sleep. We have to be up in the morning for school."

"I'm just going to get changed," she says, then moves off the bed, her body jumping over mine and I groan wishing I could grab a hold of her hips and pull her down on me so she's straddling my lap. I don't, though, instead I watch silently as she walks to her chest of drawers, grabbing her pyjamas then walking out to the bathroom.

While she's gone I quickly take off my trainers, then grab my shirt at the back of my neck before pulling it off and chucking it over the desk chair. I leave my jogging bottoms on, knowing it will most likely scare her if I only wear my boxers. Plus, it's an extra barrier for when I get a hard on. It's hard not to when I'm around the girl, She's a walking, talking, supermodel, and because she doesn't even see how beautiful she really is, it makes her that much more appealing.

She walks into the room after switching off the hallway lights. Just as she's about to turn off the main light to her room she comes to a sudden halt, her body locking tight, and her eyes fixated on my stomach. I'm not like Max who is a gym junky. I don't work out. However, it doesn't mean I don't have muscles where a lad should. But seeing her eyeing me, the way she is like she could eat me and lick every inch of me is making my dick uncomfortably hard.

She visibly swallows, the movement making my dick jerk and throb, especially when her eyes slowly lift, running up my body until they meet my eyes, and I swear I can still feel everywhere her eyes have just looked over on me. Her eyes are blazing when her gaze locks with mine and I can't look away from her. This is a side to Kayla that I've only seen twice. Once now, and the other is the last time I stayed and she woke up wrapped around me.

I cough, gaining her attention and she jumps. "You okay?" I croak out, not able to hide the huskiness in my voice.

"Yes, I-I was just thinking." She blushes and I want to chuckle. Yep, whatever she is thinking about I wish I had front row seats too. I'd do anything to be able to hear what she is thinking right now. I'd give up my left ball. Why not my right? I have no fucking clue. It could be because I'm right handed and now I'm talking bollocks so I'm going to shut up.

"Come on," I grin, lifting the bed-sheets up before sliding in, moving as close to the wall as I can get, giving her room to fit. Her bed is only a single, and I'm not a small lad, and the last time I stayed I slept over the blankets at the edge of the bed, nearly falling out every time I tried to move.

Slowly but surely, she walks over to the bed, stopping for a second to switch off the lamp before getting in. Her body is locked up tight and before I can give her a chance to freak out, I grab her hips and pull her against me.

"Relax," I demand softly, and I'm surprised she submits the second the word leaves my mouth. "Goodnight, Kayla."

"Thank you for being here for me tonight," she whispers into the dark. "I don't know what I would have done if you hadn't answered your phone."

"You're never going to have to find out because I'll always be here for you," I tell her honestly.

Her heart rate picks up, I can feel it against my chest and I smile inwardly. She seriously has no clue how I feel about her.

"Thank you," she whispers and for a second I swear she sounds choked up.

"Goodnight, baby." I whisper the words against her ear, kissing her head once before lying back down on the pillow.

She snuggles up against me; her body completely flush against mine when she whispers her next words, the sound of her voice going straight to my dick. I'm just glad she hasn't said anything about my current wood sticking against her ass.

"Goodnight, Myles."

NINE

KAYLA

THE WEEK PASSES PRETTY quickly and soon enough the weekend arrives. I was glad when my dad talked to my mom about letting me stay home this weekend. Any other time she would have refused, but then my dad told her about Charlie's condition and I know she couldn't say no without giving away her true colours to Dad. He still has no clue who she really is or what she's really capable of.

I know for a fact when I next go to her house there will be major consequences to face, but with everything going on with Charlie, I can't seem to care. For the first time in a long time I don't care what she does to me. I know that will soon change once I'm back in her house, in her presence, and under her lock and key. There is no way this weekend is going to go ahead without any further punishment from her.

I've honestly not really thought about it much, my mind has been too consumed over Myles and the way he's been with me over the past week. We've seemed to have gotten closer since the night he came over to comfort me over Charlie, and I'm actually loving it to the point I'm wondering when it's going to end. I loved waking up with his arms around me, the way they make me feel safe wrapped up in them. I know my feelings for him have always been more than friendship, but since moving back to Coldenshire they've grown into something more, something I can't describe. I just know it's a feeling I never want to end, but also a feeling I'm too scared to explore.

As I'm walking down the path towards Denny's house I get a message alert. Grabbing my phone I'm surprised when I find the message is from Charlie.

Charlie: I'm so sorry, but I'm not gonna make it 2nyt. I'm not feelin 2 gud nd mom wnts me 2 stay in and get sum rest.

Me: Is everything okay? Are you okay?

I look away from my phone and walk up to knock on Denny's door. Her house is at the back of the Carter house. The older Carter and Mason, Denny's fiancé, built it for themselves to begin with, but then Denny found out she was pregnant and the oldest Carter gave them his share of the house so they could move in. It's pretty sweet to be fair. The place isn't huge, but it is for them. It's a three bedroom, I think, and it's pretty spacious.

Raising my fist to knock on the door, I end up jumping back a step when the door flies open to reveal Denny looking bubbly and excited. She's always been beautiful, but since giving birth to baby Hope she's even more radiant.

"Hey," she smiles then looks behind me. I look too, wondering who she's looking at, but when I do, I don't see anyone.

"Where's Charlie?" she asks confused.

"Oh, yeah! She's just messaged me, she's not feeling too good so she's going to stay at home tonight."

"Why what's wrong?"

"She's got the flu," I lie, knowing Charlie won't want anyone to know yet. She hasn't had time to process it all herself, so I know she won't be able to handle questions from everyone else.

"Oh no, well, maybe next time," she smiles, inviting me in at the same time my phone alerts me of another message.

Charlie: I'm gud, jst tired and short of breath. I'll tlk 2 u tomoz, promise. Love u an hav fun :)

Me: I'll try. Wish you were here. LOVE YOU more biatch xoxo

"Who's that?" Harlow asks nosily as I walk into the front room. I burst into a fit of laughter. Denny or Harlow, or maybe both of them, have put a ton of blankets on the floor along with fluffy pillows. Ones I'm pretty sure aren't apart of the downstairs decor. I swear, I could probably jump on it and bounce back up softly it looks that fluffy and cosy. They have a bunch of snacks in bowls and plates, drinks, and sweets on the table next to all the blankets.

"Oh my God. This looks amazing," I grin, looking around.

"I know, when you text me on Monday about it, I got all excited," Denny laughs. "I've even got wedding magazines to look at after we watch the first movie."

"It looks amazing," I tell her, and start taking my coat off. Now I can see why she asked me to bring a spare set of pyjamas. It's like every teenage girl's sleepover fantasy. It looks so cool. I've never had this, and looking around the room and at my friends it makes me choke up with emotion.

"So... who texted you?" Harlow smiles.

"Oh, Charlie. She can't come, she's not feeling too good and she's going to be so bummed when she finds out what she missed out on."

"Is that why she hasn't been at college all week?" Harlow asks, watching me as I take my shoes off next.

"Probably yeah," I smile, wishing I could change the subject.

"Well the next time we have a girl's night in we will have to do this all over again," she smiles and I smile back. I love Harlow. She's sassy, beautiful, but so shy at times. She's kind, generous and I'm glad I got the chance to meet her, to get to know her.

"You need to get changed," Denny demands, rushing back in the room with a clear box full of God knows what.

"Yes, Mom!" I laugh.

"Ha-ha, now go get changed. Hope is over at the brothers' house with Mason so you don't need to be quiet going up. They'll be back in a bit, but Mason said he wouldn't disturb us."

I nod my head, smiling at her. I quickly rush up the stairs with my change of clothes before Denny chases after me and starts undressing me herself. I decided to bring my long pyjama trousers with a matching t-shirt. I usually wear shorts and a baggy t-shirt, but with the scars on the back of my legs I don't want to scare the girls by flashing them around.

Once I'm changed, and I've packed my bag with the clothes I already had on, I make my way out of the bathroom. A startled scream escapes my lips when I bump into a large, hard body.

"Hey, Kayla. It's me, Mason. I just came by to get some more nappies. It's okay," he soothes, holding onto my shoulders. Footsteps come rushing up the stairs and Denny comes into view.

"I told you to make yourself known, that Kayla was up here," she snaps at him.

"Babe," is all he says, rolling his eyes. I shake my head and smile at the both of them, trying to will my heart rate to slow down.

"It's fine. I just wasn't expecting anyone to be outside the door. I'm sorry. Bit of a good job you weren't putting a sleeping Hope to bed though, huh?"

"Yep, that scream would have definitely woken her up," Mason laughs bending down to give Denny a quick kiss.

When they pull away I'm blushing furiously. "Come on, Kayla, let's go downstairs."

We're all sitting on the blankets, all of us leaning back with our heads on the sofa wearing face masks. As soon as I walked into the front room after getting changed earlier, Denny dragged me to the floor where she plastered both me and Harlow with facemasks before doing her own.

"How has school been going?" Denny asks me after a minute.

"Okay," I shrug, and then silently curse myself when I remember they can't see with the cucumber they have over their eyes.

"What about you with college, Harlow?" Denny asks her.

She groans. "I swear, I thought school was bad at times, but college is so much worse. None of the other kids sit and take in anything the teachers are saying. It's a nightmare because half the lesson is wasted with the teacher telling everyone to be quiet. It pisses me off because if they didn't want to be there they could have taken a year out."

"Wow, I'm taking it you're not enjoying college then," I tease, and both girls start laughing.

"I am; it's just the others who don't take it seriously. I really want to go to university and I can't do that unless I pass college."

"Have you spoken with your tutor about it?" Denny asks.

"And look like a brownnose? Nope. I'm hoping in time they will either drop out or grow up."

"What about you, Denny, how is it being a mommy and a fiancé?" I giggle.

"Brilliant. I love it, but sometimes I miss you guys. I want to do something, but with Hope being so young still I don't want to leave her. Just the thought makes me sick. I'm hoping to open my own business, but I never got to finish my evening business course, so I'm going to wait for Hope to sleep through the night before I start it up again."

"That sounds like a brilliant idea," I tell her. I know she wanted to go to college, but when she found out about Hope she decided not to. The birth would have interfered with her timetable. There was no point in her starting college only to have time out not long after to look after Hope.

"How are things with Myles?" Harlow asks out of nowhere, and my heart stops. Choosing to ignore her question seems like my best option, so it's what I do. It's not like she directed her question directly at me.

"Kayla?" Denny speaks up, her arm nudging mine.

"Oh, you're talking to me?" and both girls laugh like my question is that funny. "What?" I say defensively.

"Oh come on, Kayla, I heard Mav talking to Myles the other day about staying over at yours. What gives? What's going on?" Harlow laughs, and if it had been anyone else teasing me I would think they were being mean, but I know with Harlow and Denny it comes from a good place.

"Nothing. We're friends. He came over and we ended up falling asleep. That's it," I tell them, only half lying. I think bringing up Charlie will only cause more questions and I know Charlie won't want anyone to know just yet.

"Yeah, yeah. Well, whenever you're ready to tell us, then we're here for you," Harlow tells me softly.

"I know you guys are; there's just nothing to tell."

"If you say so," Denny says with a smile in her voice. She shifts next to me before getting up. Come on, it's time to wash these off. Once we've done that I'm ordering pizza, that is if you don't mind pizza. I'm starving."

"I could eat pizza," I tell her, and Harlow agrees.

The pizza comes just as we put on a movie to watch. Harlow and Denny decided on a horror film saying they never get to watch one when the boys are around because they're big babies. How the Carter brothers can get scared watching a horror film is shocking. They're all big muscled, and Maverick, the eldest brother, is scary as hell. He's the only one with tattoos... that I've seen anyway. I asked Denny about it the once and she said they're new, he got the full sleeve a few months back, but apparently the tattoos on his back and chest have always been there. It surprises me that the other Carter brothers don't have them. But to think they're scared of horror films is just something else.

It took us ages to choose a film because Denny originally picked up *The Hills Have Eyes*, but when I looked it up online I found out it has a really bad rape scene in it. I told them there was no way I was watching it, especially when I read one of the most descriptive reviews that was very detailed about what happened. It's making me feel sick just thinking about it.

So instead, they've decided on an oldie called *Smiley*. The cover looks really freaking scary and I swear, if I woke up with that looking down on me I'd die of a heart attack. No questions. I even told Denny and Harlow that and they both agreed laughing.

"Yes, food is here," Denny groans, walking back into the room. The front door opens and Mason walks in with Myles, Malik, Max and Maverick trailing behind him. "Seriously, Mason?"

"Sorry, we smelled pizza," he shrugs and my face heats when I feel Myles' gaze on me.

"Hey," he smiles and I give him a small smile in return, feeling flushed that his brothers are all dominating the room. They're all big men, and in Denny's small front room they look like giants.

"I've got you a couple of pizzas too, they're in the kitchen. Now go away. And where the hell is Hope?" she screeches once she realises no one has a hold of her.

"Granddad has her. Joan went to bingo with a group of friends," he smiles, reassuring her.

"Good," she says relaxing. "Now go get your pizza and fuck off."

"Jesus, who pissed on your cornflakes this morning," Max grumbles, walking away to get the pizza from kitchen with Mason.

"Hey, Kayla," Maverick, the older brother waves smiling and I'm completely startled at first. We've never really spoken to each other so for him to call me out, by name, is just surprising.

"Hi," I shyly wave, earning a grin from him and Myles. I shake my head not meeting their eyes and pull the blanket further over my legs. It's gotten hot in the room and with all the blankets it's getting worse, but there is no way I'm removing it with these all the room.

"Boys, she got us meat feast, hot and spicy, and even got Max his pussy margarita pizza," Mason shouts, walking back into the room with three pizza boxes, four boxes of chips and another box of chicken wings.

"It's not a pussy pizza," Max groans carrying two bottles of pop.

"Yeah, bro, it is," Maverick laughs, along with Myles and the rest of us.

"Fuck-sake, it's not, okay? I just don't like spicy food, goddamn it."

"Max, you could have ham and pineapple, but you don't, you even moan over that," Myles laughs.

"I like cheese pizza, so sue me," he shouts, stomping out.

"See you later, babe," Mason grins, bending over to give her another kiss on the lips.

Denny kisses him back, then steps away to put our pizzas on the floor when Myles speaks up. "What pizza did you three get?"

"Pepperoni and a meat feast."

"Are you going to eat all of that?" Maverick asks wide eyed.

"Probably not, we have garlic bread, chips and barbecue wings, but I promise to call once we've consumed what we want," she smiles sitting down in the middle of me and Harlow.

Malik shakes his head. "I wouldn't promise anything just yet, Harlow could eat you out of house," he chuckles, earning a glare from Harlow.

"Are you calling me fat?" she asks deadly calm.

"No, babe, I like that you like your food. I'll see you later," he tells her, bending down to give her a kiss, and my heart constricts seeing Denny and Harlow both happy with their boyfriends. I wish I could have that. My eyes flicker to Myles to find him watching me with a strange expression. It's like he can read my thoughts. Before I can think any more about it, I hear Malik whisper to Harlow. "Make sure you call me first, these boys will demolish it otherwise."

Denny and I laugh as we're the only ones that heard what he said and his brothers look at him suspiciously. He just shrugs, gives Harlow another kiss before pushing his brothers out the door. Once they've gone, Denny turns to me with a sly grin on her face.

"Are you sure there is nothing going on between you and Myles?"

"What do you mean?" I ask her, confused. My cheeks flush, but I don't let my gaze falter.

"It means he couldn't keep his eyes off you."

I'm about to deny it when Harlow speaks up. "She's right. He couldn't keep his eyes off you. I think he likes you," she teases and my face heats up further.

"Shut up and eat your food," I snap lightly making them both laugh.

"Whatever you say," Denny laughs then clicks play on the remote.

The pizza is gone long before the film ends. Now, Denny, Harlow and I are looking through bridal magazines. Harlow has a clip board taking notes and ticking off her check list. As maid of honour she has the privilege of helping Denny organise the wedding. It's actually been pretty easy thanks to Denny's dad paying for it, no expense spared. My dad would most likely give me a budget, and with the way Denny loves her clothes and shoes, you'd think her dad would have had some sense in doing that too. In all fairness though, Denny hasn't booked anything extravagant as of yet. She's kept everything elegant and simple.

"What colour are the bridesmaids going to be?" I ask, flicking through one of the wedding gown books.

"I liked navy blue, but then I saw these coral dresses in one of the boutiques in town and have chosen them. You'll have to make sure you're free over the next few months for a dress fitting," Denny tells me before typing away on the internet. "Dammit, I'm going to have ta' book the pick-and-mix stand and the photo booth separate. *Party Fusion* isn't open anymore, it's closed down."

"Um, firstly, why would I need to book time in for a dress fitting? And secondly, why the hell are you having a photo booth?" I laugh.

"One," she says in a snotty tone, throwing my words back at me. "Is that you're a bridesmaid, you really should have known that already," she tells me, giving me a 'duh' look before typing something onto the laptop again. "And secondly, everyone needs a photo booth in their lives at least once. We had one once at one of the school functions, but the queues always took forever because of the lads jumping the line to go again. They were amazing though and you'll be surprised how many bridal parties book them. Plus, I love sweets. Why wouldn't anyone want a pick-and-mix stand at their wedding?"

"It might as well be a party for Hope," Harlow laughs, while my face is frozen on Denny.

Bridesmaid.

She wants me, yes, freaking me, to be bridesmaid.

That is so cool!

"You really want me to be bridesmaid? I ask, my voice not hiding the shock.

"Well, yeah, duh," Denny laughs looking at me like I've grown two heads.

I squeal before throwing myself over to her, my arms reaching around her and bringing her into a tight hug. No one has ever asked me to do something so special. This is just... it's freaking amazing and I'm so honoured she's asked me.

Denny laughs and I giggle too, knowing this is so out of character for me. Before I know it Harlow is laughing along with us and throwing her arms around us both too. We all end up rolling to the side, Harlow and I rolling on top of Denny.

"Now THIS is what I like to see," a voice booms with laughter, making me screech.

Harlow and I jump off Denny. Harlow is laughing on the floor at Max, while my eyes are wide, and my hands are shaking. I never heard him come in. My breathing picks up until my vision begins to blur. I should have heard him come in. I should have sensed him, but I didn't.

"Hey you okay?" I hear Myles' relaxing voice by the side of me. I hold my hand up not able to talk as I try to control my breathing, but it's not working. My lungs feel tight and I have to close my eyes tightly to try and push the dizziness away.

Strong arms wrap around me, pulling me onto their lap, and the minute I smell his strong, spicy scent, my body begins to relax. I shove my face into the crook of his neck, my lips lightly brushing against his warm skin. His hands start moving, brushing lightly up and down my back. The gesture is sweet and soothing, and I begin to feel lax in his arms. It doesn't last long, as soon as I remember where I am, and that I just freaked out for no reason other than Max scaring the hell out of us, I start to feel ashamed. Why can't I act normal around these guys?

"So you don't like people watching either, Kayla? It's okay. I get stage fright too," Max tells me from close by. I close my eyes tighter, fighting the urge to giggle, especially when I hear a hard slap against skin and then Max howl in pain. "Seriously, brother, you have a child in your arms," Max hisses on a whisper, to who I presume is Mason.

"I'm so sorry," I whisper against Myles. He holds onto me tighter and I'd be lying if I said this didn't feel good because it does.

"It's okay, babe."

I sit up not moving from off his lap and look to the others. Max and Mason are having a heated discussion over using violence in front of a minor, while Denny and Harlow are sending me worried glances.

"I'm fine. I just didn't hear them come in, and I got scared. I'm sorry," I tell them, feeling embarrassed.

"It's fine, chick, you just scared us is all," Harlow says softly, then jumps when the front door opens.

"Babe? Babe?" Malik shouts walking into the house.

"Seriously, MALIK! There is a *child* trying to sleep in here, keep it the fuc-fudge down," Max hisses.

Mason rolls his eyes and Malik just stares at him dryly before turning his attention to Harlow.

"Come on, we're going home," he says, and from the look in his eyes, something tells me she's not going home to sleep.

"But we haven't finished the next film. We got *A Little Bit Of Heaven* left to watch," she moans, folding her arms over her chest in a huff.

"Babe," he warns with a smirk on his lips before stepping over the magazines, the leftover pizza box we forgot to call them about, and all of the other bits and bobs lying around. Once he reaches Harlow he picks her up. She squeals loudly as he throws her over his shoulder and she shouts giggling at him to stop. I can't stop the smile spreading across my face at seeing the both of them so happy. I've known Malik a long time, he was in the same year as me at school when I first went there, and he was always so angry, getting into fights, and moody, but seeing him with Harlow it's like seeing a whole new person.

He slaps her ass telling her to be quiet. "Quiet, before Max has a hissy fit and calls the police for waking Hope up," Malik growls amused, then walks out the door. Once her squeals have disappeared we all burst out laughing, and I end up shoving my face into Myles' neck when I let out a snort.

"Angel, you ready for bed?" Mason asks Denny sweetly, a twinkle in his eye and she grins nodding her head.

She gets up and walks over to him grabbing his hand, the one not currently supporting Hope who is sleeping soundly in his arms, her head tucked snugly in his shoulder.

"Hey, don't you need your blanket?" I ask her, looking around the room at the three dozen blankets.

She waves me off with a smile. "I bought them especially for tonight, so it's no worries. Don't worry about cleaning up, I'll do it in the morning," she smiles. "Goodnight."

"Goodnight," I wave back smiling shaking my head.

"She bought all this *just* for tonight?" Max asks, eating some of the jelly tots we started to munch on earlier.

"It's Denny, do you really need to ask?" Myles laughs, snatching the jelly tots off Max who scowls back at him.

It's silent for a few minutes; the only noise in the room is coming from the television. My hands start to become sweaty and when I realise I'm still sat on Myles, I gently slide myself off, my face blushing red.

"God, this is more awkward than that time I looked for Narnia in my wardrobe," Max mutters standing up. "I'm out." With that, he turns and struts out whistling a tune. I try hard to cover up my giggles, but it's hard, so when I find Myles staring down at me, it only causes me to laugh harder. After a few seconds of watching me, he laughs too, his head falling back against the sofa just as a full belly laugh erupts from his mouth.

"I swear, sometimes I wonder if we're really twins," he chuckles, once he's calmed down.

I shake my head still smiling at him. Then he reaches over to the pile of magazines and grunts. When I realise he's packing it all away, I reach out and stop him.

"It's okay, I can clean this up," I tell him softly.

"I know, baby, but I want to help," he smiles and my belly does a summersault at hearing him call me 'baby'. I love it when he calls me that, it makes my heart flutter.

I nod my head and help him clear away all the rubbish, bowls, and pile the laptop and the magazines in a pile, dumping them on the sofa. There's no point in me sleeping on there, with all the blankets piled on the floor it's soft enough for me to sleep on.

"Do you want me to go, or would you like to watch another film?" Myles asks when he walks back in with fresh glass of pop.

"As long as it's not another scary movie then I don't mind," I smile, loving the fact I'm going to get to spend some more time with him. I love being around him.

"God, no! I don't mind horror movies, but I prefer an action, thriller, comedy, or hell, even a romance," he laughs.

"Well, if it's okay with you I brought *Ninja Turtles* if you want to watch that with me. Denny and Harlow don't seem like girls who would enjoy it," I giggle and he chuckles.

"You'll be surprised what they like, baby. Denny surprised us all when we found out she's a huge fan of horror movies, and Harlow when we found out she listens and watches anything that interests her. She doesn't have specific taste. So, if you'd have asked them, you would have been surprised that they would have most likely liked to watch it with you."

I run over his words in my head, and now listening to him say it like that I feel like shit. I judged them. Seeing how beautiful they are, how girly and well dressed they always are, I never stopped to even ask them what movies they liked.

I look to Myles and give him a small smile. "I'll remember that for the next time we have a girl's night."

"Maybe you shouldn't," he mutters under his breath, but I hear him clear as day as he starts the DVD up.

"Why?" I blurt out, wanting, no, needing to know why he said that.

"Because if you had watched this with the girls then I wouldn't be sitting here watching it with you," he says softly, his eyes boring into mine and I feel myself start to burn up, a blush rising in my cheeks. How can he look as good as he does, be a manly lad, a popular kid, and still be the kindest, sweetest, and most sensitive lad I know. Most lads his age would say shit like that just to get into their girl's knickers, but I know when I hear things like that coming from Myles, he truly means them. It makes me like him that much more and I'm starting to feel like I could quite easily fall for him and his charming ways.

Not knowing what to say, I keep quiet. My eyes flicker over to Myles every so often to find his eyes are fixated on the television, but every so often he'll catch me staring, his lips twitching when I look away quickly, and it makes my heart race.

I don't know how long into the movie we get before I start to feel my eyes droop. My head falls to the side and in doing so falling onto Myles' shoulder. He pulls me into him, his arm around my shoulders with his fingers rubbing slow circles on my bare shoulder. A few seconds of that and I can feel myself close down, my eyes closing, my heart rate slowing, and my mind clearing.

TEN

KAYLA

THE REST OF THE WEEKEND goes off without a hitch, and on Monday morning, waking up, alone, I wish I could rewind back to Sunday morning when I woke up wrapped up in a warm embrace against a hard body.

Of course, I'd skip the part where Denny was standing in the doorway with a huge smirk on her lips. That I didn't need to see first thing in the morning, especially when seconds later, Mason, Max and Maverick walk in wearing only tracksuit bottoms, or in Max's case, boxers. They all took one look at me and Myles and pounced on us. And I'm talking in the literal sense too. Their hard bodies took seconds to squash my small delicate one, and Myles' hard one. I'm sure he took most of the brunt too considering he had Maverick's weight and Mason's. I'm also pretty sure the hand that belonged to Max that "accidentally" copped a feel wasn't an accident; the jury is still out on that one.

We all ate breakfast together, and that's when I got roped into going to a theme park that is a seven hour drive away. With all of the brothers looking at me with puppy dog eyes, Myles' pleading glance, there was just no way I could say no to them.

The rest of the day at school passes quickly, Myles and Max keeping me company in most lessons and lunch.

Leaving early for my therapist appointment, other students give me curious glances. The only person, apart from the teacher, who knows where I'm going is Myles. Not even Max has had the luxury of knowing where I'm going today, and he's tried relentlessly to find out.

The bus stop is empty when I get there for which I'm thankful for. I need time to gather my thoughts, not concentrate on movements of others around me.

I'm glad my mother can't make it to today's session; she called my dad last night and told him she had an interview she needed to go to. More likely she had some rich schmuck taking her out for a date and she doesn't want to blow him off. The schmuck will never know just how thankful I am. I hate it when she comes with me to my appointments. She fills the therapists head with shit and I end up set back in my recovery because of it.

My dad is waiting in the reception area when I arrive at the therapist's office five minutes early.

"Darling, how was school?"

"Good. I did some mock exams today and pretty sure I nailed them," I grin, knowing there is no way I got remotely one answer wrong on those tests. I'd revised like a mad woman, and knew the answers confidently. There was not one I was unsure of.

"That's lovely," he tells me, smiling back. "Would you like to grab something for dinner once we're finished here?"

"Sure," I shrug, dropping my school bag to the floor by my feet. I won't hold my breath. Nearly every session he tells me the same thing, but as soon as I step out of the room, he has a phone call that has him stepping away for another meeting.

"Kayla Martin?" my therapist's receptionist calls.

I stand up just as my dad wishes me luck, and I make my way into the doomed room. It's not like the therapist rooms that you see on the television. You know the ones that have the fainting couches, the lightly dimmed room that's filled with candles, and the soft music playing in the background? Yeah, that is so not like my therapist's office. It's a basic room. Walking inside, the desk is straight in front of you, filing cabinets behind that run along the wall, and a large window with blinds half open on the next wall. Then to the left of the door are two sets of chairs that make the school chairs look comfy, with a little round coffee table centred in the middle.

Mr. Stanley gets up from his chair to greet me, holding his pudgy hand out to me. The man is overweight, balding, and the little hair he does have left is turning grey. His suit looks new, expensive, but he obviously hasn't looked after it considering he's still got crumbs on his tie, a coffee stain on his shirt, and I don't even want to imagine what the other stain on the sleeve of his suit jacket is.

Vomit!

"Kayla, take a seat. Would you like something to drink?" he asks, ever so politely. I'd love to say yes because after travelling on the bus, and being at school all day, I'm parched, but there is no way I'll accept a drink from him. The little made-up kitchenette he's made above one of the filing cabinets looks to have seen better days. I'm pretty sure I once saw a spider climbing all over his cup before he took a sip. I'd like to confirm this, but that poor spider had crawled off so quickly I didn't have a chance.

"No, thank you. I'm good."

"As you know from our last session your mother was quite concerned about your behaviour. You seem to be distancing yourself from people, becoming confrontational towards her. Has that changed since we last spoke?"

For the first time I can say what I really want to say. My mother isn't here to dig her fake manicured nails into my arm.

"Since we finally have privacy, Mr. Stanley, I'd like to point out that not once did you ever ask me any of this when my mother was in the room. So, I'd also like to point out I'm not confrontational. I also can't distance myself from people I hardly see, Mr. Stanley. I've made huge progress since the first time you saw me, and I'll also add I've made friends, and we're really close."

"I'm sorry. Your mother just seems to be very worried about you."

I want to laugh in his face, and although I've had this boost of confidence to finally speak my mind, I'm *not* that brave.

"Not to be rude, Sir, but you don't know my mother. She isn't worried about me at all. If she was..." I stop myself short before I can say anything more, knowing he can report her.

"Go on," he says, writing something down on his paper. I hate it when he does that because his eyes hardly move away from mine, and his gaze always has me feeling unsettled.

"It doesn't matter. What I'm trying to say is that, I'm the one who was raped, I'm the one my mother made keep it quiet, making me feel ashamed about it, and I'm the one recovering from it. I'd like to say I'm completely healed, that I've finally come to terms with what happened to me, but I'd be lying. Who can really get over something like that? I'm never going to be able to, but what I can do is move on from it, but having these restrictions on me, especially at eighteen, is not helping, Mr. Stanley, so I'm begging, no pleading, for you to reconsider your last diagnosis."

"It's my job to look after your best interests, Kayla. You tried to kill yourself twice, we just need to make sure you're better." I go to speak, but he puts his hands up stopping me. "That said, the last time I saw you I did feel like you were doing much better. I spoke with your father about it and he agrees wholeheartedly that you have overcome so much since moving back to Coldenshire. They were worried at first on how the move would affect you emotionally, but it seems you've been doing brilliantly. From now on, our sessions will be every six months. As for your restrictions, they've already been removed. I contacted your mother right after going over our last session, did she not mention it?"

"No she didn't," I grit out. His comment about me taking my own life also grates on my nerves. He knows nothing; no one does unless they've felt what I felt, suffered what I have. Every day was torture for me, all I wanted was for the voices inside my head to stop, the images of what happened to stop playing over and over in my head. It didn't, though, and each day was a constant reminder of what happened to me.

For the first few months I took the hottest showers possible, burning my skin, and scrubbing it to the point it would be red raw by the time I walked out of the shower. My skin would be sore for months and months afterwards.

You can call me weak. Tell me I don't deserve to live, that there are people out there fighting for their lives that would appreciate the chance I've been given.

But imagine having to live a life where your nightmare is playing constantly in your mind, whether you're awake or asleep. Hearing *his* voice around every corner you turn and being too afraid to leave your room. Then there's the not feeling clean. Having to shower every chance you get, but still not feeling any cleaner and still feeling his hands all over you. But the worst part of it all was being powerless to stop it. In a way, I guess ending my life was my way of gaining power, and not just ending my living nightmare.

I never made the decision lightly either, but no matter how much I played it in my head on how to try make it better, to make all the pain, hurt, and memories to stop, I always came back to ending it all.

It worked too. Until the very second I woke up in the hospital bed and everything came flooding back. As soon as I had the chance, I did it again. I'm a stronger person now though; I'm learning to deal with more than just my nightmares, but with everyday living.

"Right," he mutters, writing down in that damn pad again, interrupting me from my thoughts.

"We've got half an hour left of today's session, is there anything you would like to discuss?"

I shrug, hating this part. I never know what to say. And when I do finally talk, he listens, but he always stares, gauging every reaction, every movement I make, and it's so unnerving. I hate it. I'd rather have a crowd of a million people watching me than have just that one person stare at me.

"Okay, I'll go. You mentioned you made some friends. You want to tell me about them?"

And that's how I spend the last half an hour of my session. I tell him all about Myles, Max, Denny, and Harlow. I mention the other Carter brothers too, but mostly Myles and Max. I mention who Harlow is, what happened to her, and how it made me feel. I tell him about Denny, what happened to her and why, and he listens, gives me feedback, asks me questions. I'm glad he doesn't think it's not a good idea for me mentally to speak with Harlow. He even said it was great that I had the courage to do what I did meeting her, although he does believe I have nothing to be sorry for. He's wrong, though, if I had said something sooner, had the courage Harlow had, then he wouldn't have been able to have hurt her, and his brother wouldn't have hurt Denny.

"Carol, can you please send in Mr. Martin, please," Mr. Stanley calls through the phone.

A few seconds later the door knocks once before my dad walks in looking puzzled, carrying my school bag.

"Hello, is something wrong?" he asks Mr. Stanley concerned, before looking me over to check I'm okay.

"Yes, I just wanted to let you know that Kayla's restrictions were revoked at our last session. It seems Ms. Martin forgot to pass on this information to you and Kayla. I'll also be stretching our appointments out. Our session will be every six months, but with the progress I've seen, the confidence in Kayla in today's session; I can see us spreading them farther apart in the near future. Do you have questions?"

"So she won't need twenty-four hour monitoring?" I turn to my dad when he speaks. I'm surprised by the tone in his voice. He almost sounds relieved and it confuses me. When his eyes start to water my eyes widen in shock. What. On. Earth...? "Thank you, Lord. I've been so worried she'd have another relapse. Honey, I'm so proud of you," he tells me, his voice choked up with tears.

"Dad," I whisper, feeling my own eyes start to water.

He just shakes his head then turns to Mr. Stanley and shakes his hand. Then he takes mine and walks us out of the door. As soon as we get back into the reception area he turns to me with a frown and I automatically know what's coming.

"I know, I know, you've got another meeting," I grumble, waving him off, but he just looks at me confused.

"Huh?"

"You were about to tell me you needed to cancel our dinner date because you had a meeting, weren't you?" I ask stepping out into the fresh air.

"Um no, I was going to say you can invite those friends of yours to dinner. We can wait until they get to the restaurant to order," he tells me and I'm completely taken aback, even more so when he turns to me looking sheepish. "Do I really bail that much on you, sweetie?"

Not one to lie, I tell him the truth. "Every darn session."

"God, I'm such a shit father. I promise honey, no more. Actually, cancel on your friends, we can do that another time, tonight we need to celebrate. Plus, I have something I'd like to share with you, it's important."

When I look over to him I can't gauge his reaction, he looks worried about something, but his facial expression isn't giving anything away. It concerns me a little, but as I've not sensed anything major going on, or any tension coming from him, I nod my head and follow him down the street to where he parked his car.

He takes us to one of the nicer restaurants in town, which shouldn't have surprised me, but I'm still wearing my school uniform and feel so out of place. The restaurant is somewhere you'd take a date, not your daughter.

After ordering our food, the waitress walks off and I turn to my dad noticing him shifting in his seat nervously.

"What did you want to tell me?" I ask him, hoping like mad it's nothing to do with staying at mom's.

"Well, you know me and your mother have been separated for some time now?" he asks slowly.

Please don't tell me you're getting back together with that witch. "Yeah."

"Well, I've been lonely. Your mother and I haven't exactly had a great relationship; I think we were over before we were officially over..."

"Dad, just spit it out," I smile, keeping my tone light.

"I'm seeing someone. She works for me. At first it was just some fling, but I've come to really care about her."

He stops his nervous ramble and stares at me, trying to gauge my reaction. I should have seen it coming. He's a good looking man for his age, and extremely wealthy. I'm just unsure how I feel about it.

"Is that all?" I ask, not knowing how I truly feel. I think I'm more worried she's going to be like my mother. I know I won't be able to handle another gold-digging witch, especially if it's as serious as Dad is making it out to be.

"Well, I'm also hoping, if it's okay with you, if she comes over for dinner at the weekend?"

"Ah, Dad, that's what I needed to talk to you about. Now my restriction has been provoked, I was hoping you would give me your permission to go away for the weekend with my friends. They've planned a trip to a theme park, and they asked me to go with them. I said yes, but I wanted to check in with you first."

"That's okay, Honey. We can reschedule for another time. I'm more worried about how upset your mother will be. She's expecting you this weekend, right?"

"Actually, that's another thing I want to talk to you about. I'm not going to be staying over at Mom's again."

"What? Why? Don't you like it there?"

Shit. I said too much. "With all my homework and stuff, it's easier to work from home. The shelter I work at on a Saturday is closer to your house than it is Mom's. We still don't have the best relationship, and I'd really love it if you could support me on this, Dad. I'm a grown adult who has been through some bad stuff, but I know what I need. I just need you to support me," I ask him, my voice quiet and pleading.

He looks at my eyes and I start to panic he can see more than I told him. If he finds out what mom does to me, he'll end up in jail or worse, she'll kill me. I've never been brave enough to tell anyone anyway, just in case they never believed me. It's easier to keep it to myself.

"I understand. I just don't understand *why*. Your mother will be really disappointed and upset."

Like hell she will. Just wish I could say that out loud.

"Please, she'll be fine."

"Okay, let me just give her a call..."

"No! Just... let's enjoy our meal first. Tell me all about this new woman?" I ask, and like that his face lights up and he tells me all about his new girlfriend, who now has a name, Katie.

"I'll see you later," I wave off to my dad, hoping like hell that he listened when I asked him to talk to Mom over the weekend instead of tonight. He tried to talk me out of it, telling me it's unfair to cancel on such short notice in case she has plans to take me somewhere. Only I know different. So I lied and told him she has an important date tonight, and if she finds out I'm not going at the weekend it will ruin her date if she's being miserable over me. He seemed to perk up when he found out she wouldn't be on her own.

"Call me if you change your mind about me picking you up," he shouts, and then pulls out of Charlie's driveway.

I walk in, not bothering to knock on the door. I've never needed to. Charlie's mom greets me with a wide smile.

"Kayla, it's so good to see you. Charlie's upstairs in her room. She's feeling a little tired and sluggish today, so if you don't mind sitting up in her room with her?"

"I don't mind," I smile, moving towards the stairs.

"Would you take these up for me please, Honey?"

I turn back around to see her mom walk out of the kitchen with a tray of drinks, snacks, and other stuff along with a prescription bottle of medication.

"I don't mind," I tell her, taking the tray from her, thankful it's not too heavy.

"I'm so glad you're here for her, Kayla. You're a good girl," she tells me, her eyes glistening with tears before she turns and walks into the kitchen.

Charlie's house is smaller than mine, far smaller, but it's still the perfect size for Charlie and her family. It's a four bedroom, and with only her parents and Charlie occupying those rooms. They use one of the spare rooms as a cinema. It's great in there. I'm hoping I can get her to move into the room next to her, so we can chill and watch a movie.

"Hey you," I grin, walking into her room and heading straight for her desk to drop the tray down.

"Hey," she answers softly, her face yellow, yet pale, and her body looks drained. She has dark circles under her eyes and I know that the cinema next door is out of the question. She can barely lift her head let alone get up to walk next door.

"You don't look so good," I mumble, grabbing her prescription and her drink. "Your mom said to bring these up, I'm taking it that you have to take it now?"

"Yeah, sorry. I'm just so tired."

"It's fine. I pop the pill into her mouth after reading the label on the bottle, and then hold the straw in the glass to her lips.

"I'd ask how you are, but I can see it's not so good," I tell her, smiling gently.

She chuckles, but it ends up turning into a cough, her face wincing in pain. Once it stops she turns to me with her eyes filled with tears.

"Please tell me about your weekend," she stumbles, her voice soft, quiet and tired.

"It's been really good. I wish you were there on Saturday. Denny pulled out all the stops at the sleepover, buying a ton of fluffy blankets and pillows for us to lie on. She said she's keeping them so we can do it again next time, so hopefully you'll be better by then," I smile.

"Sounds like a plan, Stan," she teases, smiling at me. "How are things with Myles?"

"Good."

"Seriously, Kayla. Be honest. This is me."

"Gah, I swear he drives me crazy," I tell her, standing up to pace back and forth. "Every time he touches me he sets my skin alight. Every time he looks at me my face flushes red, and don't even get me started on the tingles, or the way my belly does a summersault when he's near. Then there's his voice, God, his voice, it's so deep, so mesmerising, gentle and loving. I could listen to him all day. In fact, he'd be perfect to do one of those audio books."

"You love him," she states, not a question, and I look at her horrified.

"I do not."

"Do too," she grins. "Admit it, you love him. You deserve this, Kayla."

"I'm dirty, though," I choke out once I realise I do in fact have strong feelings for Myles. It may or may not be love, I don't know. What I do know is there isn't anyone other than him I'd rather be with.

"Huh?"

"I'm unclean, dirty, tainted, ruined, and used. I'm all of those and more. He deserves someone pure. Someone clean, and perfect, not someone like me," I tell her, looking down at my lap now that I'm sitting down next to her again. She reaches out with her cold hand and places it down on mine. She squeezes it gently, and I'm sure just that movement has taken up all of her strength.

"Kayla, you're far from those things. Myles would be lucky to have you. The way he looks at you, is the same way you look at him, if not more star-struck. He's had a crush on you for years. Give yourself this, please. Promise me. I need you to promise me," she coughs out again and I turn my worried eyes to her.

"You're not getting better are you?"

"It'll be fine," she grumbles, not meeting my eyes. "I've just caught a chest infection or something." I can tell by her tone and her not meeting my eyes that there is more to the story than she's letting on. I let it go, not wanting to upset her more.

"I love you, Charlie, and I promise. I can't promise anything will happen, but I promise to start seeing myself differently when I'm with him. Just... promise me you'll fight. You'll fight whatever it is happening with everything you have because I can't lose you," I choke out, tears falling from my eyes.

"I promise to fight, Kayla, with everything I have in me, I'll fight, but you need to also be prepared for the worst."

She says it so confidently, so surely, it breaks my heart. I lie down next to her, wrap my arm around her stomach and cuddle up next to her.

"Nothing could ever prepare me, Charlie. You're one of a kind," I whisper, then hear her choke out a sob and we both lay there crying, both of us clinging to each other.

Her mother walks in not long after telling me it's time to go home. Her expression is full of pain, sadness, and I can see her eyes watering as she looks down at her sleeping daughter. Charlie exhausted herself from crying, talking to me about all her fears.

"Will you let her know I said goodbye and I'll be back soon?" I whisper, climbing over a sleeping Charlie.

"Of course, dear."

She waits until I grab my blazer before following me out of the room and down the stairs.

"Kayla," she calls as I reach the front door.

"Yes?"

"Thank you."

"For what?" I ask her, confused.

"For being a friend to Charlie, even when you moved away. She hasn't had a friend like you, one who will bring out the best in her."

"I didn't do anything, Mrs. Young. Your daughter did it all by herself. She saved me. She's extraordinary and I promise I'll be praying each and every night for her," I tell her quietly before opening the door. I hear her sniffles turn into sobs and it takes everything in me not to go back inside and break down with her.

ELEVEN

KAYLA

By the time I get home I've worked myself up over Charlie. I'm scared for her, but I know I need to be strong for her. Its horrible knowing there is nothing I can do to make her better, to reassure her that everything is going to be okay. I feel like I'm promising the impossible, but I suppose when it comes to the heart, it is.

I'm about to put my key in the door when my dad answers, both of us startled to find the other.

"Hey," I say, taking note of his work suit, his briefcase, and his flushed face holding his phone.

Interesting.

"Hey, Honey. I was just about to call you. I've got to head into work for a bit, but after I'm going round Katie's when she gets back from her other job."

Oh, so she's not a gold-digger like my mother. She actually works hard for her money. Another interesting fact I need to add to the list of things I know about her.

"Okay, I'll see you in the morning before school."

He smiles, bending down to kiss my forehead, shocking the shit into me. He's never been this affectionate towards me, but since he left my mother he's been different. Not just towards me, but towards everyone and everything. Even the way he walks is relaxed. At times it makes me want to ask if Mom beat him too, but I don't think that would go over so well.

"Bye, Honey..." he tells me, walking down the path to his car. Before he opens the door he calls back, stopping me. "Oh, Myles is in your room waiting for you. He said it's about homework. I told him you wouldn't be long."

"What?" I screech, but it's too late, he's in the car and driving off. What the hell? He let Myles into my room? He couldn't have started the conversation off with that. Oh my God, I look a mess. I've been crying, my eyes are swollen, my clothes are crinkled, and I don't even want to imagine what I look like as a whole.

Rushing in I lock the door behind me before jogging off to the downstairs toilet. I groan when I see my puffy face staring back at me in the mirror.

God, I look a mess.

After splashing some cold water on my face I dry off before quickly brushing my fingers through my red locks. Most people say I'm ginger, but my hair is too dark, so I always say red. It's not like I can get away with saying it's strawberry blonde and as a kid, going to school with a bunch of girls, you can imagine the names I got called.

Shaking my head of my thoughts, I sigh in disappointment. There's no taming my hair. It's sticking out in smooth waves down my back. It looks wild like it's not been brushed for weeks.

Leaving my hair is my only option. I don't even have a bobble to put it up into a ponytail. Making my way up the stairs I cringe when I hear my music playing from my room. I know exactly what he's watching before I even open the door. It's my year seven talent show where I sang *My Heart Will Go On* by Celine Dion.

"What are you doing?" I squeak out, rushing over to the DVD player to turn it off.

"Oh come on," Myles laughs and I stiffen. "I was really getting into that. Before that I watched you playing piano, and then another of you singing *Wannabe* by the Spice Girls. I was having fun."

"*That* is not having fun," I snap, making sure to make a mental note to find a better hiding spot for them. It's not something I want anyone to see. Don't get me wrong, it's not the singing part that bothers me, it's how I look. I had already started going through puberty, my small breasts at the time showing. I had just turned eleven on this video, I think, and had already had my period for a year. Most of the other girls in my year didn't even know what a period was, while I had to suffer through monthly cramps and mood swings.

"Lighten up, Kayla; you were brilliant," he says, and I can hear the smile and pride in his voice.

"What are you doing here?" I ask once the disc is safely in its original case.

"I came by to see you, but also to show you the introduction to the project. Hey, what's wrong?" he asks worriedly when I turn around.

Dang it!

I obviously didn't do a well enough job to hide my swollen, red eyes. Now he's going to think I'm a Debbie Downer.

"I've been to see Charlie," I tell him. It's my way of explaining everything. He's the only one who knows what's going on with her. I've still not told anyone else. Charlie's mom filled in my dad when she called him that time we never answered the door. The first time Charlie spoke to me about her heart.

"Is she okay?" he asks, bringing me into his arms. It's weird how easily I melt into him. If this had been anyone else there is no way I would have let them get close to me, let alone hold me tightly in their arms.

"She's not doing so well at the minute. She's been really tired and short of breath a lot. Her mom is really worried about her getting an infection."

"Shit! What have the doctors said? Do you know?"

"Nope," I sigh, sadly moving my head back to look up at him. "Now, how the hell have you finished that introduction so fast? I've not even finished my research."

"Aw, poor Kayla," he laughs, and I give him a playful glare. "I got bored the other day when I finished all my other homework, so I started up on this. I'll need you to proofread it because there is no way I'm asking my brothers. They'd make me pay them or some shit, and not even notice the mistakes. The whole process would just be useless."

I laugh at that. The thought of Max helping Myles to do homework is funny as hell. I could see Max pulling some prank, changing words to make a fool out of Myles.

"Point taken. Did you want to do this now, though? I just want to chill and relax." I hope I don't offend him. I'm just too tired to look over the introduction right now. Just the thought of it is giving me a headache.

"Nah, whenever you're free. Did you want me to go or do want to watch a film?"

"You want to watch a film?" I swallow nervously. No matter how many times we've watched movies together, the thought of being alone with him, snuggled up on my bed, has my skin breaking out in goosebumps. The other part of why I'm nervous is because I'm so shocked he always wants to spend time with me, away from our project.

"Yeah, I was hoping we could finish watching the one I just started," he teases with a mischievous grin.

It takes me a few seconds to catch on and when I do I send him another glare, wanting to wrap my fingers around his neck. "No way jose."

"Oh come on," he pleads, picking me up and my body shivers with delight.

"No," I glare, my lips twitching, especially when he starts to swing me around. My smile breaks out into a full on laugh. "No, Myles. I'll let you pick any other film, but not that one. I've even got Netflix so you can watch *Castle*."

He laughs and eventually puts me down on my feet by my dresser. "You play dirty, Kayla Martin; you know how much I love that show. Now go get dressed so we can get in two episodes before you start snoring."

"I do not snore," I growl. Yes, growled.

He laughs, throwing his head back. "No, you don't. You make these little cute noises that aren't quite a snore, yet. It's like listening to a baby cub trying to roar," he laughs, and I give him another glare. I seem to be doing that a lot tonight.

"I. Do. Not," I frown.

Myles steps closer to me. Bringing his hand up, he lightly runs his fingers across my frown lines, and down my nose, before giving the tip a tap once with his index finger.

"Cute," is all he says before turning and walking over to the bed to grab the TV remote.

I'm standing there, all heavy breathing, my whole body covered in goosebumps while he looks calm and collected. It's not fair.

"Kayla. Dressed, now," he reminds me, and I jump from my position to quickly find some pyjamas to wear.

Walking back into my room, Myles is already glued to the television. His mouth curled up into an amused smirk.

"What's so funny?"

"Huh?" he asks, only now seeming to notice I've walked back into the room.

"You. You're wearing a smirk, what gives?" I ask whilst climbing over him to get to my side of the bed.

"Oh, I was just remembering your dance moves to *Wannabe*," he laughs.

"You're such an ass," I scold trying to fight my own smile.

"We're watching the frozen episode again, you know the one where she's dumped and melting all over a construction site?"

"We've watched this one already. Why do you constantly watch all the old ones? You do realise there are, like, seven seasons or something?"

"Yeah, but they're all new in my head, I know them like I know my brothers," he grins giving me a quick glance before flickering his eyes to the television. "Plus, you fell asleep the last time when we watched this, and I want you to get the full *Castle* experience."

"That sounds so wrong. I'll make a deal with you. If I watch this with you, then you have to watch an episode of *Veronica Mars*."

"You drive a hard bargain." He grins at me and I smile wide. I love his smile. He really is the best looking boy I've ever met and there's no question that he'll be a handsome man.

"So is that a deal?" I smirk, trying my hardest not to squeal. I've been trying to get him to watch *Veronica Mars* for a few weeks now, but each time he'll make me watch some other movie. Then we started Castle and it's been all about that, but I always manage to fall asleep not long into it.

"Deal."

"Ha, you're going to be converted, I promise. Once you see how badass cool she is you're going to want to be her," I giggle and turn my attention to him when he doesn't reply. He's laying down on my pillows staring at me with so much depth it scares me a little. "What?" my voice coming out as a whisper.

"I love your laugh, and your smile, but when you giggle like that, it's just… beautiful."

His face is so serious. He really does believe that. My stomach gets those damn butterflies again and I find my eyes drawn to his full, plump lips. He makes a sound at the back of his throat that has my eyes snapping to meet his. The look has me moving my head back a little. They're so full of lust and desire it surprises me. Surely he can't be attracted to me? Am I seriously that dumb that I don't know the difference? I want to growl at my own experience, but what I do instead is flick my eyes back down to his lips.

I don't know who moves first, or if we move together, but I find myself moving closer towards him, his lips only a breath away. My attention moves to his eyes and what I find staring back at me has my stomach doing summersaults. They've darkened; his pupils nearly black as we stare into each other's eyes. That's when I feel his breath against my lips, then seconds after, the feel of his soft, smooth lips across mine. It's so soft and gentle it surprises me. I've never been kissed, and I know there is no one on this earth I'd rather give my first and last kiss to than Myles.

He moves in closer, his lips pressing more firmly against mine and when I feel his tongue against my bottom lip, I gasp, giving his tongue entry. At first I'm startled, unsure what to do, but when I feel his tongue massage against mine, I mimic his movements. It's still slow, sensual, and so soft, and I know it's more to the fact he doesn't want to scare me. I never expected it to be this good, to feel the way I do, like I could float on thin air.

We're both laying on our sides facing each other, our lips still locked together when I start to move my hand up his strong muscled arm, up to his neck, cheek, and then finally into his thick, unruly hair. It's soft under my touch, the strands feeling like silk and he growls into my mouth when I run my fingers through it, which spurs me on.

His hand moves down to my waist and my body stiffens slightly, but when he doesn't move to go any further I finally relax myself back into the kiss, hoping I've got the hang of it.

When we finally break apart we're both staring at each other in awe and wonder. His lips look redder, fuller, when I flick my eyes back down to them, missing the feel of them on mine already.

"God you're beautiful," he groans, and I feel giddy with excitement that he's not repulsed or running away from me yet. He seemed to have enjoyed the kiss more than I did, if that's possible. I just hope it was as good for him.

"Did I, was that...Oh God," I groan.

"It was perfect, Kayla," he smiles, moving in to kiss my lips one more time, before kissing the tip of my nose.

"Now, I think we should finish this episode so we can watch this Ronnie chick who's meant to be badass."

I grin at him widely, knowing he's not going to get enough of her, and hopefully he'll kiss me again. I liked kissing him. No. I *loved* kissing him.

Waking up in Myles' arms will never feel old. No matter how much I'm wrapped up into him, how tight he holds me; the only thing I ever feel is safe.

He left an hour ago to get showered and changed for school. He texted me not too long ago saying he was on his way, so after quickly rushing to finish off my hair and put on the light bit of makeup I decided to wear, I make my way downstairs. We have a non-uniform day today to help raise money for the new school library, which is why it's taken me longer than normal to get ready for school.

Apart from Myles and his brothers, Denny, Harlow and Charlie, no other kids see me outside of school, so I want to make sure I make a good impression. With the weather so chilly I decided to just put on my black leggings with my brown knit jumper that hangs off the one shoulder. I've finished it off with my matching brown boots that reach below my knees.

I'm wearing my hair down and straight for once, another reason I'm running behind. My hair is thick so it takes ages to straighten. Then there was the whole makeup debatical so I'm rushing down the stairs while zipping up my jacket.

The door knocks and a big toothy grin escapes me. It's only been an hour, but I've missed him and I'm excited to see him again.

"What took you so... Mom! What are you doing here?" I ask startled, my hands shaking. I look around outside not seeing Myles or my dad's car. He hasn't been back since last night which isn't surprising, but I just wish right now he was here.

"You little conniving bitch," she snarls, shoving past me and kicking the door shut behind her. "Did you think I wouldn't find out about your little plan? What have you been telling that psycho doctor of yours?"

"What? I don't... I... I need to go to school," I stammer, trying to sound brave.

"Like hell you are, Missy. We need to talk and then we're going back to that office and you're going to tell them whatever you said was a lie," she snarls and her eyes are bloodshot. I can smell the alcohol on her breath.

"I haven't said anything," I cry when her hand lashes out, thumping me in the top of my arm.

"Liar. He called me asking me a lot of questions, calling your father and asking him questions too. What have you been-"

"Kayla, come on. We're going to be late if you don't get your sweet ass into gear," Myles calls from the other side of the door. I begin to panic, hoping he didn't hear my mom shouting at me. God. If he finds out I've got more baggage he'll most likely want me gone. I could barely let his touch go farther than my waist last night, and he didn't seem to mind, but there's only so much I can expect him to deal with.

"Mom, I need to go to school," I tell her walking towards the door, but her hand lashes out grabbing me by the wrist and twisting. I bite my lip sharply to stop myself from crying out in pain and when I taste blood I start to panic more.

"Get rid of him. You ent going," she snaps, her eyes warning me not to push her.

I nod my head, but the hold on my wrist only gets tighter. "Okay, please, stop," I cry, my wrist throbbing. It's the first time I've begged her to stop in a long time. I just hope whatever she has planned is not going to be bad, but then I turn to the door and a risky plan falls into my mind. She'll never hurt me in front of someone. She wouldn't want anyone finding out about what she does. So with that in my mind I open the door to a smiling Myles.

"Hey, I've been the one waiting for you, come on," I grin, hoping it looks genuine and he can't see the pain behind my words. He looks at me and smiles until he frowns looking behind me to the door. I grab his arm quickly, not wanting her to think of something that has me staying. "See ya, Mom," I shout, my body shaking as I carry on dragging Myles down the path and onto the road.

"You okay?" he asks when we're a good distance away from my house.

"What? Yeah, why wouldn't I be?" I ask defensively, but deep down I'm shitting myself about the consequences of running out on her like that. I should have just stayed there and toughed it out, but I'm tired. I'm tired of being her punching bag, of the person she torments, yells at and hits. I just wish she could be like all the other moms, gentle, kind and loving. She's never been those things towards me.

"You just seem a little shaken and pale. Are you sure everything is okay? Was it something your mom said?"

"What do you mean what she said?" I ask quickly, worried he heard us through the door.

"Nothing, your mom was there, it didn't seem like your dad had come home at all since last night, so she can be the only person who has you tied up in knots like this."

"Oh, no. Sorry. I guess I'm just tired and I didn't want to explain where Dad was," I grumble, hating that I have to lie to him.

"Why, where is he?" he asks intrigued.

"He probably stayed the night with his new girlfriend, Katie. He's been seeing her for a while now, but he didn't want to tell me until it was serious. I'm meeting her next weekend."

"Oh, I know who she is. She's a really nice lady. She volunteers for a lot of things around town. I can see why you wouldn't want your mom to know about her, she'd get jealous, if I know your mom as well as I think I do."

His words have me pausing and I want to snap at him that no one knows who she really is apart from me. I'm the one she torments, hurts, beats, and hates. It's only when I look into his deep brown eyes that I stop myself and instead I smile and nod my head agreeing.

"So, um, I was wondering if you wanted to have another movie night Thursday. I can get Maverick to pick us up from yours. They've decided to borrow one of the people carriers from one of the volunteers at the local church, so we'll all be riding together. Joan told us about it and said the owner wouldn't mind lending it us as long as we left a car for her to borrow."

"Yeah, that sounds great," I sigh smiling, liking the fact I get to spend another night with him.

"So, I didn't scare you away last night?" he asks hesitantly and when I turn to look at his side profile, his head is down somewhat and his eyes focused on the floor, his hands tucked into his zip up jacket.

"No, you didn't scare me off," I tell him honestly.

"You sure? You seem a little off this morning since I got back."

"Myles," I call, stopping. Once he realises I've stopped he turns around and walks back to me. "Last night was the first kiss I've ever had. It was the most extraordinary, breathtaking, and you can take that literally," I chuckle. "It was also something that wasn't taken from me, but something I happily gave to you and I wouldn't change it for the world."

His face is a mixture of expressions. He looks shocked, smug and damn straight happy. I give him a wide grin, wanting him to know that every word I just said is the truth, no holding back. What I feel for Myles is something I've never felt before, even before the attack. It's something I never thought my body would allow me to feel, but then again, when I'm around him, that's when I feel like I'm at my safest. I'm not dumb to think Davis was my only enemy as such. He's not. There is a world of evil out there and I know what happened to me could have been a lot worse. But the times I'm with Myles I don't feel any of that. It's like he breaks down all the wall mechanisms that I built up to protect myself and my heart. I've never had that before. Never had a person or a place that I can feel like myself, feel safe, and he gives me that, but more importantly he gives me himself and I'll be forever thankful for that.

"I'm glad," he grins, moving forward. His one hand reaches up cupping my cheek and I let out a tiny breath, my eyes close and my cheek snuggles into his hand. God, his hands are soft. Tingles run down my cheek from his touch and I make a sound in the back of my throat. I hear him say something, but it falls on deaf ears when I feel his lips connect with mine. The softness envelopes mine and I clutch onto his strong biceps for support when my legs threaten to give out.

My stomach flutters dangerously and I feel like I'm about to combust, but then his tongue massages against mine and that's all I can feel, all I can think about as I mirror his movements as we explore each other's mouths.

Explore each other's mouths? Seriously? Could I sound any cheesier? I make it sound like I'm sticking my tongue right in there and wiggling it around, getting to know each and every part of his gums and teeth. Now I'm just ruining the kiss thinking about gums and teeth and inside I'm a giggling moron.

My hands somehow have made it up to his neck while my head ran away with my thoughts, and finding the courage I run my fingers through his hair, pulling him to me tighter and he growls low in his throat before breaking the kiss. I let out a tiny whimper of disappointment.

"God, I'll never get bored of kissing you," he whispers against my lips.

Catching my breath for a few more seconds I open my eyes to find his looking into mine and I let out a little smile. "Let's hope not."

My words have double meaning. I don't want him to get bored with me, but I also know I'm not going to be ready for anything more than kissing, and I'm hoping that will be enough for him. That's if we last that long. If we're even a 'we'.

"Are we a 'we'?" I blurt out, startling him and he chuckles.

"Yeah, Babe, we're a 'we'."

"What does that entail?"

He chuckles, shaking his head at me, looking down at me with amusement. "It means, sweet Kayla, that you are mine and I am yours."

I grin up at him giddily. I could quite easily get used to belonging to him and him belonging to me.

He reaches down, kissing me on the lips quickly before giving me another sexy smirk. "Now, let's get to school."

TWELVE

KAYLA

THE REST OF THE WEEK passed pretty quickly, and before I knew it, it was Thursday morning.

I've been looking forward to today for a while. Myles is staying for dinner and overnight because we have to leave early tomorrow morning for *Exhilaration*. I've never been to a theme park before and I'm beyond excited. I've been looking forward to going since I got invited.

I've been awake since four from another nightmare. They aren't as bad as they used to be lately and that shocks me. It's another reason I have so much to thank Myles for.

Anyway, when dad got up at half five for work he walked into my room when he heard me shuffling about. I started to pack my case to pass the time away and he gave me some extra cash to take with me. I didn't think he was happy about me going because there are no adults going. Well, who he would call an adult anyway. To me, Maverick and Mason are. But when he handed over the money to me, he told me to make sure I had a good time, and if I needed any more money to just call him and he'd transfer it into my bank. He left me with my mouth hanging open in shock.

When the doorbell rings half an hour before I'm due to leave for school, I'm surprised. Myles said he would meet me at school this morning because of having to talk to one of the teachers. Happy he will be walking me to school I basically skip to the front door with a huge grin, not bothering to do my usual checks in the peephole. I feel like I haven't seen him in days, when it's only been a night. He came over to do some homework yesterday after school, but then left when Dad got home around ten. Just thinking about having his lips against mine again is making me want to scream out with joy.

"Miss me alre-"

"Never, and I mean NEVER, dismiss me the way you did on Tuesday, young child. Who the hell do you think you are?" my mom yells and before I can brace myself for it, a hard slap connects to my face and I feel blood fill the inside of my mouth. My hand doesn't even reach up in time to cover my stinging cheek before I'm pushed to the floor with a kick causing me to scream out in pain.

"NO!" I scream, trying to block her blows, but it's no use.

Black dots blur my vision and I know I'm going to pass out at any second. Her words sound like white noise, but a few words I do make sense of.

Bitch. Ruined my life. I'll make you pay and so on, it's always the same. It's never ending and the kicks keep on coming until my vision finally turns black and everything turns numb.

BY THE TIME I WAKE up my mom is gone and my body is stiff and bloody on the front room floor. Bile rises in my throat and I throw up all over the laminate flooring, my body screaming out in pain when I turn over too quickly.

Rising up on all fours I wince in pain feeling like a truck has run over me. With my shaky legs I stand up, using the wall as leverage as I make my way over to the hallway, up the stairs and down to the bathroom, managing to close the door behind me without passing out again. Removing my uniform I don't turn around or inspect my injuries until I'm fully undressed and when I do I choke in horror. All of the right side of my stomach is covered in ugly, purple and blue bruises, the swelling severest near the hip area. A few bruises cover my legs and I know the pair of shorts I packed in my case for *Exhilaration* will be no good to me. There is no way I can use an 'I fell down the stairs' excuse with these bruises. They're ugly, swollen, and angry looking, and in no way or hell will they be better by tomorrow morning.

Tears fall from my eyes and I open my mouth, pulling my bottom lip down to inspect the damage and, as I predicted before I passed out, she has cut open the inside of my bottom lip.

I hate her.

I seriously fucking hate her.

Angry tears fall from my eyes and I wipe them away feeling furious with myself. I don't even know why I carry on hiding her secret anymore. I'm not the naive little girl I once was. I'm stronger. I have people who love me, who care for me and will stand by me, goddamn it.

So why the hell do I feel so fucking alone? Why do I constantly feel like I can't tell anyone what she's really like, show them what she's capable of? It scares me to think of the extent of damage she'll do to me before I finally find the courage to open my mouth and tell someone. It's not just about her, though, it's about protecting me. I've always been that poor, weak, little girl that got raped, who got bullied; I don't want to be the girl who was abused by her mother too. It's stupid and idiotic, I know, but I just don't want people to know how weak I really am.

Opening the cupboard, I grab a couple of painkillers and swallow them down dry before swilling my mouth out with some water out of the tap.

The bruising isn't as worse as it usually is and I should be thankful for that. It still doesn't excuse the fact I'll be going to a theme park tomorrow and going on rides that will jolt me about. With my bruises taking the brunt of it I'll be doing nothing but suffering in pain the whole day. It's going to ruin the whole entire experience, I can feel it already. With tears blurring my vision I manage to grab my dressing gown off the back of the bathroom door and cover myself.

With a defeated sigh I take another painkiller, wanting to sleep the day away, before heading back to my room. I grab my phone where I've got missed calls and a few messages from Myles and Max. A small smile plays on my lips when I read Max's message.

The fit twin: You playing hooky without me? It's not fair. I know all the best places to hide out at and Myles didn't have to know ☹

After registration one day I found out Max had programmed his number into my phone without me knowing. That is until it started ringing '*Let's talk about sex, baby'* in the middle of classroom with 'The fit twin' as the caller. I could have killed him. I died with embarrassment. I was just glad the teachers couldn't confiscate my phone from me.

I scroll down and find the message from Myles and feel my eyes water again. My mom is *nothing* to me anymore. I'd give everything to have him here with me, but she's ruined that. He'll see me for who I really am.

Weak.

The only twin: I'm outside school, where are you?

The only twin: I have got you a hot chocolate.

The only twin: Now you're driving a hard bargain.

The only twin: Is everything okay? I'm worried. I have to go in, but if I haven't heard from you by lunchtime I'll come around.

Looking at the time on my phone quickly, I'm thankful to find out I wasn't out very long. So I quickly type back my lie and hate every second of it.

Me: I'm spending the day with my dad. He feels bad he has been spending too much time at work, and because I'm gone the weekend he said I may as well call in sick. I'm going to have to cancel tonight too, but don't worry about collecting me, I'll meet you at yours. X

Putting my phone back down on the bedside table I quickly go downstairs in case my dad comes back to see puke and blood on his front room floor. I'll never be able to explain the blood and sick.

It doesn't take me long to clean up the mess and when I look up I find my mom's handbag on the floor by the front door. Panicking that she's going to come back for it, I rush over to it, wanting to chuck it as far as I can outside without hurting myself further. When I get to the bag though my hands shake and I end up dropping the entire contents all over the floor. In a mad rush I throw it all back in, wondering why the hell my mom needs all this crap in her handbag. She has a fucking bottle opener in here for Christ's sakes. A letter grabs my attention, from the corner of my eye, and I pick it up with shaky hands and open it.

I scan it quickly, not wanting to get caught reading it, but it's all a bunch of words on paper that I don't understand. The basics is that she owes money, but that isn't what concerns me, it's the *why* she owes money. When she and my dad got divorced the costs were covered in the settlement, so I don't understand.

Not wanting the bag in here a second longer, I put the letter back in the envelope and remind myself to mention it to my dad when he's back. I look outside the window checking the drive before opening the door and putting the bag right outside the door, not wanting her to miss it or for it to get stolen which will have her banging it down and punishing me even more. It's more than likely I'll get the blame for her forgetting it anyway.

I seriously hate her. Just thinking about her is making me angry and I end up slamming the door shut, another stream of angry tears falling from my eyes.

The whole of my body is throbbing and all I want to do is go curl up in ball, lie down on my bed and cry myself to sleep. I just want to forget about today, and concentrate on tomorrow, knowing I've got to somehow manage to fake being fine in front of seven other people. I've done it for years now, fake my own happiness. I've perfected it to a T, but Myles and his family, they see right through it.

My eyes are sore when I wake up, and everything around me is a blur my head is killing me that much. It also doesn't help the pain killers I took earlier make me dizzy and nauseous, but it's got to better than the pain in my side, which seems to have dulled a little thanks to them.

When some of my senses start to come alive, I feel a presence in the room with me and my whole body goes ramrod straight. After cleaning up the sick earlier downstairs, I put on a pair of pyjamas and in my rush to just go to sleep, I just threw whatever was at the top of the pile, which happened to be a tank top with a pair of skimpy shorts, and I know for a fact whoever is in the room has seen my bruises.

My face is to the wall and ever so slowly I roll onto my back and immediately look over to my desk to where I find Myles sitting down on my desk chair, looking sad. His head is bent down, and his eyes look red, but from this angle I can see his jaw is clenched.

"Myles?" I call out making him jump. His eyes reach mine and I tear up when I see the depth of his sadness seeping out through his expression.

"Who?" is all he manages to say, his voice hoarse and firm.

"Pardon?" I ask, pretending not to know what he's talking about.

"Don't play me, Kayla. Who did that to you? I've seen the bruises. Your shirt rode up when you were asleep, so when I came in to check on you I saw them. So did Max. We were worried when we saw your dad in town with Katie and said he hadn't seen you since this morning. So tell me, Kayla, who did it?" he bites out and my eyes widen in shock.

"I really don't want to talk about it, Myles. Please don't make me," I whisper.

"I'd never make you do anything," he says hurt, standing up to walk over to me.

I watch him closely, so many emotions running through me, one of them embarrassment. I can't believe they have seen me like this, that Max saw me like this.

"Where is Max?" I whisper, looking away and down at my blanket.

"He's gone to get some food. We didn't want to leave you like this."

"You can go," I whisper, not wanting to torture him anymore than he already is. It's obvious this is bothering him and I hate that I'm hurting him like this. I just want him to hold me, to tell me everything is okay, but I know it's not going to be now. The way he's looking at me, it's something I never wanted.

"I'm not going anywhere, Kayla. I need you to tell me who it is. Is it your dad?"

I laugh, and I laugh hard, not caring about the ache in my side or that Myles is looking at me like I'm crazy. If only he fucking knew which of them was the crazy one.

"My dad has never laid a finger on me. No one did. I'm just clumsy. I fell in the shower," I lie and I know he knows I'm lying because I can't look him in the eye when I tell him. My inner thoughts are screaming at me to tell him, to finally let go of all this pain my mom has made me carry around for years. She blamed me for having to move house after I was attacked, she blamed me for everything.

"You're lying, goddamn it. Who did this, Kayla? Why won't you tell me?" he shouts, his voice piercing my ears.

"Yo, bro, chill," Max calls, as he walks into the room. His eyes flick to me quickly before they move back to his brother and I envy their twin bond. I envy their whole family. They are always there for each other no matter and if one is hurt, they all hurt, but they all fight back.

"Not now, Max," Myles grits out, his eyes watering as he runs his fingers through his hair, pulling at the ends in frustration. He looks lost on what to do and I did that to him. I feel myself becoming angry. Angry at myself, at my mom and at the whole world.

"I fell in the shower. Please, don't make me talk about it," I yell. "Why won't you just believe me, why? If you don't want to be here then just go, I never asked you to come." Tears run down my face and I wipe them away not looking away from Myles. Max moves so he's closer to us before kneeling down by the side of my bed. His huge frame in my room makes the bedroom look like a tiny box room.

"Why don't you want to talk about it?" He asks softly and Myles' eyes meet mine, intrigued in hearing my answer.

"I just don't. Please. I just don't," I plead, looking away from Myles to Max. He nods his head looking like he understands then puts his hand on the bed next to mine.

"Then don't. But I do think you should. If someone is hurting you then we can stop it. We're here and we can protect you. I know we didn't do a good job with the other two, but with Harlow and Denny, we were like training GI Joe's," he jokes, making me chuckle. Harlow and Denny have had their own troubles, their own demons and they've come through it. Hearing him put it like that has me wondering if I'll be safe to tell them. My biggest problem is no one believing me.

"We need to know who it is, though, Kayla. Maybe we can help," Myles speaks up, his voice full of emotion.

"I'm fine, I promise. It's just a few bruises."

"It's more than a few bruises," he grits out, his eyes hard, lingering on the bruises that are showing on left arm.

"Myles," Max warns. "Look, we're not going to push you tonight, but until you decide to tell us who it is that's hurting you, then you're going to have to put up with the both of us, possibly Maverick too, as Mason and Malik are all loved the fuck up. Not that they wouldn't help if we asked," he shrugs and my mind screams out in alert.

"No! No! You can't talk about this. It was an accident. It's not like it's happened before," I rush out, lying my ass off again.

"If you say so," Max says eyeing me curiously and Myles just looks pissed.

"Please don't be mad at me. I didn't want you to see me like this. I didn't want you to know," I tell him softly and hear him take in a deep breath.

"Kayla, someone is hurting you. I came back to check on you because I've been worried all goddamn day thinking the worst, and when I get here it's so much worse. This isn't the first time it's happened, I can see it in your eyes, but I've also seen bruises on you before. I always believed your excuses. I'll let it go until we're back from the weekend, but after that all bets are off, and if I have to find out myself then I won't be happy," he growls and this is a side to Myles I've never seen before. I've never had anyone want to protect me the way he wants to right now and it's warming my heart to know I have that when I've never had it before.

"That sounds better than my idea," Max mumbles and Myles and I look to him confused.

"You said you'd let it go," I snap.

"Yeah, to you. Didn't mean I wouldn't beat your fucking dad up to get some answers."

I look at him with wide horrified eyes and he just chuckles looking at me with a smirk. "Don't worry, Daddy is safe.... For now."

"He hasn't done anything," I snap back furiously. He holds his hands up in surrender and I wish I could wipe that smirk off his face.

"Well, until Sunday," he winks and I frown, hoping like hell I can think of something before we're back on Sunday. There is no way I can tell them who it is, if that's what they'll do. Not that I think they'll hit a woman, but I've seen Max, he loves playing pranks on people, and my mom will most likely wake up glued to her bed or some shit.

I just shake my head then my empty stomach growls, echoing around the quiet room and both boys look to me with big grins.

"Luckily I got us a Chinese," Max grins, then stands up walking over to the door. "I'll go get it plated up."

"We'll be down in a sec," Myles says, and I can feel his eyes on me still as I watch Max leave the room, leaving me alone with Myles, the tension is still thick in the room.

"Are you okay? Do you need painkillers? I wasn't sure if you'd took any," he asks softly, his face full of worry and concern.

"I'll wait until after I've eaten. It looks worse than what it actually is."

"Yeah, and Max is a virgin," he mutters standing up. "Where's your robe?"

"Oh, here," I mutter, grabbing it from the end of the bed where I dumped it before going to sleep. I step out of bed once it's secured around me, hiding the bruises from his prying eyes. I can feel them burning into my skin where I know marks cover my body.

After eating, Max puts all our dishes in the dishwasher before walking back in and deciding we were all watching a film. When I go to stand up my body is sore and stiff and I wheeze out a breath. Max hears me and moves to my side, and for a second my body freezes until I remember it's Max, Myles' brother.

"What's going on?" Myles asks walking into the room with three cans of pop.

"She's just stiff," Max says, his eyes on mine as he carefully lifts me from the sofa. He guides me to the hall and by the time we reach the stairs my body is stretched and the pain lessens somewhat.

"I'll grab you some painkillers once we get upstairs," Myles tells me, and I'm not all that surprised he knows where they are with the amount of time he spends here.

Settling in on the bed, Max sits next to the wall, I sit down next to him and when Myles walks in, looking at us, he takes the space next to me and I become a Carter twin sandwich.

Myles hands me a glass of water along with two painkillers and I take them greedily, wanting the dull ache in my side to ease off a little. Max has been quiet since we got into my room and Myles has just been as bad and it's driving me nuts, and calming me at the same time. I can feel the tension suffocating the air in the room and sandwiched between the two boys, it's starting to suffocate me. Deciding to just go with it and let them deal with it on their own, I snuggle down in the bed, thankful Max thought to grab the extra pillows I keep on my beanie.

"Getting comfy?" Max grunts and that's when I notice he's trying not to touch me. I'm not sure whether that's because Myles is in the room, or because he doesn't want to hurt me, so I decide to give him some space and snuggle closer to Myles, who seems to be okay with that. He looks down at me with a small smile, his arm going around me and pulling me closer so I have no choice but to use his head as a pillow.

"Ahem," I grunt, my lips twitching a little when I feel him shift again, my eyes feeling droopy once the sound of the movie starts to play.

THIRTEEN

MYLES

I'VE TOSSED AND TURNED all night long, so when my eyes open in the morning from the sound of my phone alarm blaring, I groan. A warm body is cocooned tightly around me and I look down to find Kayla's wild red hair falling all over my chest, her face snuggled into my chest. I smile slowly, loving the feel of her wrapped around me and I want to show her just how much by kissing the ever-loving-shit out of her.

Then *he* happens.

"Please don't have a boner while I'm in the bed with you. This just feels so fucking wrong," Max groans rubbing his eyes. My head turns fully to him and I give him a glare, forgetting he was even in the bed with us.

"What the fuck are you still doing in here?" I snap.

"Jesus, calm the fuck down. One, your girl's legs was lying across mine, she's freaking flexible," he grins and a low growl comes from my throat. He just rolls his eyes at me, ignoring the line he's crossing. "And two, I didn't want to risk sneaking out and her dad catching me. He'd walk in here wanting answers and if he saw you here too he'd wonder what the fuck we were doing here," he whispers quickly to me.

"So you stayed, because?" I deadpan, not caring for his excuses.

"Fuck's sake, I was comfy as fuck. We only freaking slept. I didn't even cop a feel," he smirks and I lean across with my one arm and smack him across the head, nearly squashing Kayla in the process.

"Please tell me you're really good at voice impersonating Max, and that he's not lying next to me?" Kayla groans sleepily, making both Max and I burst into a fit of laughter.

"Sorry, babe, I'm here," he teases, and tickles her under her armpits making her squeal and jump closer to me giggling.

"Please stop! Stop!" She laughs and I watch with amusement as my brother makes her laugh, careful not to harm her bruises. "Please, stop. Mercy! I'm going to pee myself," she yells through laughter.

"That's my queue to get to the loo before you," Max shouts jumping over the both of us and off the bed. "Fuck, that rhymed," he laughs, walking out of the room still fully dressed.

I roll us over so we're on our sides and I give her a soft smile. And in return she gifts me with a lazy, soft smile. Fuck, she's beautiful all of the time, but when she smiles it's something else and it causes my chest to tighten. Every. Single. Time.

"Morning," I rasp, giving her a peck on the nose. She relaxes into me, her hands finding my shoulders as she looks up at me with those big doe eyes.

Leaning in I give her another kiss, not able to stop myself, only this time opening my mouth to taste her. She goes to pull away from me, mumbling something about morning breath, but I couldn't give a fuck. She tastes even better than she normally does. She doesn't try to fight me for long, her mouth opens and her sweet tongue touches mine and I lose all senses. Shit, she can fucking kiss. She has my balls drawn up so tight she's given 'blue balls' a whole new meaning.

"Good morning to you too," she rasps out when I pull away and I grin down at her. Then I remember last night and I lose my smile. She looks at me worriedly, losing her own smile.

"How are you feeling?"

"Okay, I guess. Those tablets worked, but my skin still feels tender when I move."

My face hardens and I know I'm going to kill her dad. I'll never be able to look at him again and not want to beat the ever-loving-shit out of him. He has to be the one hurting her. He was the last person to see her yesterday and he lives with her. I just don't get why. He seems so protective of her, adores her, yet he hurts her. I just don't get it. If she lived with her mom on the other hand, I'd totally get her hurting her. Her mom is a raving lunatic. I swear I wish she was a bloke for the shit she has put Kayla through. It makes me furious to think of all the stuff she pulled after Kayla was attacked. The bitch has karma coming for her.

"Relax, otherwise your face will stick like it with all those frown lines," Kayla whispers.

I relax and decide to change the subject and to make sure she has a banging time this weekend. "How'd ya sleep? Did you have a nightmare?" This is a question I've wanted to ask her for a while now. Every night I've stayed I've not woken up to her screaming out in her sleep, or found her already awake.

"No, I didn't have a nightmare," she smiles, but it doesn't reach her eyes. She seems to be mulling that over in her head, so I ask another question.

"Have you not been having them? The last few times I've stayed you've not had one."

"I've had them..." she stops for a second before her eyes go wide.

"What?" I ask worried.

"Nothing. It's just...well, I had a nightmare the night before, but now you've mentioned it, I don't remember having one when you've been in bed with me," she says, biting her bottom lip.

"Maverick is on his way in fifteen minutes so I'd get a move on if I was you. I'm going to make something to eat, is that okay, Kayla?" Max calls interrupting.

"That's fine," she calls back and looks back at me with excitement shining in her eyes. She kneels up off the bed before climbing over me and making her way to her drawers. "Let me just have a quick shower. I've packed everything already, but I need to put last minute things in."

"Take your time," I grin, happy to see her excited.

"MAX, WILL YOU JUST PICK one fucking song and let it play?" Maverick snaps and Kayla giggles beside me. We're sat in the far back of the people carrier with Harlow. Malik, who is currently sulking after being separated by Harlow, is sat in front of us with Denny and Mason. Poor Maverick got the short straw and had Max up front. Unlucky is all I can say.

"How long we got left till we get there?" Max whines again for the fiftieth time since we left Kayla's two hours ago. "I'm hungry and I'm bored."

"You ate twenty minutes ago, Max, plus you had breakfast at Kayla's, made us take you to McDonalds and when we stopped off at the garage you bought a shit ton of crap to eat. And we'd get there sooner if you'd stop making us fucking stop every ten minutes."

"You just said I ate twenty minutes ago, not ten. Don't be so dramatic. I'm a growing lad."

Kayla giggles again beside me and I look down at her, amused. She hasn't moved away from me since we got in the carrier. I didn't even have to put my arm around her and pull her closer, she just got in and snuggled up next to me. When everyone started staring at us with wide eyes and their mouths hanging open, she just smiled and waved like it was no big deal. It made my fucking heart swell, I swear, and something else but I don't want to go there. I feel fucking good with her in my arms, but what has the permanent grin upon my face is the fact I've chased her nightmares away. I just wish when I wasn't with her that they'd leave her alone too, but knowing that I chase them away for her is incredible and makes me feel really fucking good.

"Pass me that," Maverick snaps, and I look up in time to see him snatch the phone from Max's hand.

"No, don't," he protests, and Maverick glares chucking the phone behind him to Mason.

"Pick some music," he tells Mason. The car radio doesn't work and none of us thought to bring CDs with us. Thankfully Maverick had thought of the cable that connects a phone to the car's stereo system, but so far, Max hasn't let a damn song play all the way through.

"What the fuck?" Mason roars with laughter, and Max stops fighting to get it back and turns back in his seat, slumping down in a huff. "He has lists of music."

"So fucking play one already," Maverick snaps, clearly getting annoyed with his younger siblings.

"You sure?" Mason laughs again and it has me looking over his shoulder at the screen. As soon as I read the first few, I burst out laughing along with him.

"What's so funny?" Kayla asks me the same time Denny starts giggling. Next thing you know *Cotton Eye Joe* starts playing over the radio and everyone bursts out laughing, including Maverick. He looks over to Max with a huge grin on his face.

"Seriously, Max?" he laughs then shouts over his shoulder to Mason. "What else does he have?"

A Disney song starts to play and everyone laughs harder. "*Frozen*, Max? Fucking, *Frozen*?" I laugh.

"It's catching, so fuck off," he grunts.

"Sing it then?" Mason taunts and the girls start singing along with it, not able to stop through their laughter. When Max finally joins in, his voice overpowers theirs. That's when I notice Malik has finally snapped out of his sulk and is recording Max singing wildly to *Love Is An Open Door* with an evil smirk on his face.

A car horn honks from the side of us and I've never laughed so hard in all my life when a group of girls in a mini convertible with the hood down drive next to us.

I didn't even notice we had hit slow moving traffic and were gaining an audience.

When the girls start laughing, Max turns around in his seat and glares at all of us. "I'll get you back, you bunch of pricks."

One of the girls shouts something to him and he rolls down his window, sticking his head out.

"What'd ya say, babe?" She says something back, but from the back I can't hear. "My brother has kids," he shrugs and we all snicker, but then Mason changes the song and we all burst into laughter again. God, my face hurts from laughing so hard. Kayla joins me, shoving her head into my chest when she lets out a snort which only makes her laugh harder.

"Seriously, Mason," Max glares. Mason put on the *Vengaboys We Like To Party*, skipping straight to the chorus.

"Will the wire stretch so I can have a look?" I laugh leaning over. Mason passes it back and surely enough it does reach.

I scroll through the phone at his lists. When I see a 'do not play' list I click on it. On it is every love song and break up song that you can think of.

"Max? Why do you have a 'do not play' list with a bunch of love songs and shit in it?"

"Oh, I'd drive you in the fast lane…" he finishes as our lane starts moving faster and then turns back around to look at me. "Because I do, okay. Look on someone else's phone."

"If you don't like them why have them on your phone?"

"Because chicks love that crap, that's why," he growls and we all snicker.

"Here, give me the wire," Kayla says pulling her phone out of her bag and I smile passing her the wire to plug into her phone. When she hits an album on her phone I grin at her. It's one with various artists on.

Looking down at Max's phone, it vibrates with a text message.

Poppy: I thought we had something special. Why are you ignoring my calls and texts? We shared a night together

I snicker reading it and thankfully Max is in a mood and not paying attention, or even noticing the fact it's not his phone that is now playing the music. So I decide to text back, wanting to pass the time. Kayla looks over and notices what I'm doing and grins.

"He shouldn't mess with girls' emotions like that," she whispers.

I nod my head in agreement and start typing out a reply.

Max: We did have something special, Poppy bear. I'm not ignoring you; I'm just trying to let you down easy, I'm not good enough for you.

Poppy: Oh Max, you are. What we shared was the best night of my life. Do you want to be my boyfriend?

Ash: Want to meet up later?

"Here, I'll text Poppy back, you can text Ash. I can't believe he has this many girls on the go," she scolds, glaring at the phone.

Max: Poppy, I need you to know something… I'm not good enough because I like boys. What we shared was me getting my frustration out on a boy that I'm in love with. I'm sorry if I've hurt you, I'm a complete asshole who doesn't deserve friendship from you. Please forgive me.

I laugh hard as I watch her type, loving this fiery side to her. She passes me the phone looking unsure, so I chuckle bumping under her chin with my knuckles. "It's fine. He deserves it." She smiles and nods her head, her eyes soft and I bend down to kiss her softly before paying attention to the phone. I re-read Ash's message and can't think of an Ash at our school. Not that all the girls he meets are from our school.

Max: I'd love to meet up, but I'm hanging with my boyfriend tonight.

Poppy: Oh Max, why didn't you tell me? I would have totally understood? If you ever need to get that frustration out again, just give me a call.

"What a hussy," Kayla whispers at me, making me chuckle just as another message comes through.

Ash: What the fuck?

Max: I know you wanted something special with me, and I dig that you're into me, but I'm spoken for.

Ash: Max, dude, are you gay?

I re-read the message then chuckle. "Do you think Ash is a girl or a boy?" I ask Kayla and she shrugs, grinning, her eyes darting to Max, before taking the phone out of my hands.

Max: Want to find out?

Ash: Excuse me?

Max: There's only one way to find out if I'm gay, care to have a night with the Maxter?

I chuckle reading the message she sent and 'Maxter', seriously? She's been watching too much *American Pie*. I take the phone from her wanting to send the next text.

Ash: Fuck off. I ent gay u prick.

Max: Don't knock it till you try it. Every hole's a goal right?

A couple of minutes pass with no reply and we end up laughing quietly to ourselves in the back.

"Hey, where's my phone?" Max calls from the front.

"Here," I shout back, smiling, making sure to delete the messages before passing it over to Mason to pass to Max.

We all fall into comfortable silence, listening to the music playing as we pick up speed on the motorway, now that the traffic has disappeared.

Then Max happens, and Kayla and I start laughing.

"What the fuck, Dude?" he shouts, his phone pressed to his ear. "Why would I want your cousin Adam's number for? A date? Please tell me this is some prank right now. What has Ash got to do with anything?" he growls, and Kayla starts giggling, hiding her face in my shoulder. Max's head whips around in his seat and he sends me an evil glare. "No, I'm not fucking gay. I love pussy. Love the taste, love sticking my dick in it and love tits, so you can put that in ya pipe and smoke it. Now tell Ash my brother's sense of humour isn't what it used to be," he growls before throwing his phone on the dashboard.

"Not gay?" Maverick asks, his voice filled with amusement.

"This Adam, he not your type, Max?" Kayla teases, and it shocks me that she spoke up and made a joke. I can't help but staring at her before laughing at what she said. She giggles, hiding her face again, when Max turns around and sends me a glare. Then his phone beeps again and he growls, the noise filling the car.

"Now fucking Poppy Little is texting me asking me when I want to release my frustration out. That she'll let me practice in her ass," he snaps. "That bitch is crazy. I spoke to her one night and now she thinks we're a couple. Apparently I was drunk enough to kiss her. What the fuck did you do, Myles?" he snaps while furiously snapping away on his phone.

"Let her down gently?" I laugh and everyone joins me.

"I'll get you back for this, asshole."

"Yeah, yeah," I laugh, not worried at all.

"I need something to eat," he snaps, still typing away on the phone.

"We're not stopping again," we all shout simultaneously.

FOURTEEN

KAYLA

It's taken longer than the seven hours it should have taken to get to Glensaugh because of Max and his ever empty stomach. To be honest, out of all of us I think I was the only one who never really complained about all the stops. My legs and back started to ache a bit, but I was too busy enjoying the talk and laughter we all shared along the way. It was by far the best road trip ever.

Now we've just booked into a Travelodge closest to the theme park. It's still a fifteen minute drive to the park, but it's the closest we could get, and staying on the actual park would have cost us all a fortune.

"Did you hear me?" Myles asks, and I shake my head. I'd zoned out, staring at the beautiful landscape outside.

"I'm sorry, what?"

He chuckles, his smile bringing out one of my own. I love his smile. "We're going to have to share a room, is that okay? I don't fancy sharing one with Max or Maverick and they don't have any rooms left."

"That's fine. We sleep together most nights anyway," I grin, and then blush when I hear gasps from beside me.

"Well, get you two love birds," Denny teases.

"Myles and Kayla sitting in the tree, K.I.S.S.I.N.G..." Harlow sings.

The boys just grin, waggling their eyebrows and it's then I realise they think sleep as in, *sleeping together*, and not sleeping, as in snoring together. Jesus, I sound like a two-year-old.

"I didn't mean it like that," I blush, my face heating.

"Now, now, Kayla. No need to get all shy on us," Maverick laughs and I send him my best scowl. I like Maverick. He's the quietest of the bunch of brothers and that's saying something if you've ever met Malik, that lad is just straight to the point. The most I ever hear him talk is with Harlow and it's so goddamn sweet. Maverick, though, is a mystery, always has been to me and everyone who is close to all the brothers. Denny even mentioned one night she'd like to get to know him more, and Harlow said the same. I think he likes it this way. He's close, but he still keeps people at arm's length.

"Shut up," I grumble pouting, making everyone laugh.

"Come on, you," Myles grins, giving me a wink.

Damn him! He looks good doing that too.

We get to the room and put our stuff down on the bed before taking a quick look around the room. It's pretty basic. There's a double bed, a dresser with a mirror above it with plug sockets along the wall and a kettle with cups in the corner. On the wall at the end of the bed is a plasma TV and the bathroom is the door to the left as we walked in. There's also a little place by the door where you can hang clothes, but only enough for about six or seven items.

"This is great," I smile looking over at Myles who is staring at me with a huge grin. "What?"

"You look like I've walked you into fairyland and not a basic Travelodge," he chuckles.

"I'm just happy to be here," I smile, telling him the truth. I can't wait to explore the town and the park tomorrow. It says on their website they have an Enchanted Forest, and I love Disney, so I'm so going to be checking that out. I also checked with everyone if we were hanging around for the firework display and boat parade they have going on later on the night, and they said yeah.

"Good, now which side do you want?" he asks looking at the bed.

"I'll take the right," I smirk.

"The right?"

"Yeah," I blush and he looks at me curiously.

"Now, tell me why the right side?" he grins back, stepping towards me.

"I'm not telling you, you'd think I was evil or something," I chuckle, my face turning red.

"I'd never think that of you," he says seriously and I shake my head rolling my eyes at him.

"Okay, but remember you asked for this," I tell him, giving him a pointed look. "I don't like being the closest to the door."

"Why's that?" he asks curiously.

"Because if a murderer with a chainsaw or something comes barging in then they'll see you and get you first, and I'll have time to escape," I shrug like it's no big deal.

He bursts out laughing and I have to look at him. His head is thrown back and he's roaring with laughter and I can't help but smile at him.

"You'd seriously run out of this room and leave me to get murdered?" he chuckles, his face red from laughing.

"Yeah, but I'd set the fire alarm off and call the police. I certainly wouldn't run and hide until they came to find me," I shrug and he starts laughing again.

"You, sweet Kayla, are something else. Come on, the rest will be waiting downstairs for us. Max is hungry."

I giggle at that. When is Max *not* hungry? I'm surprised he looks the way he does with what he eats. If I ate even half of what he does I'd be the size of a house and needing a crane to lift me to and from my bed.

I grab my handbag and take Myles' hand when he offers it, smiling big when he doesn't let go, even when we get to the gang.

Dinner goes over a treat. I slouch back in my chair and groan. Stick a fork in me, I'm done. The table falls into silence before everyone roars in laughter. That's when I look up to find everyone staring at me, laughing.

"I said that out loud didn't I?" I groan, feeling my face heat up.

"Aw, she's going red," Mason teases and I cover my face in my hands.

"She's going redder now," Maverick laughs and I know he's telling the truth. I can feel the heat radiating off my face.

"Well, if you stopped pointing it out I wouldn't be so red," I scold, pouting.

"So cute," Myles says from my left and I turn giving him a smile.

"You finished then?" is all Max contributes before polishing off the leftovers on my plate.

"Myles says you've never been to *Exhilaration* before, that right?" Maverick asks me.

"No. I've never been to one at all," I smile, happy for the subject change to something other than my reddened face.

"What you excited to try out?" he asks and everyone starts talking about some new rides that have opened.

"I want to see the Enchanted Forest, the fireworks and boat parade sounds awesome too. I'm not keen on that ghost ride, it looks scary as hell, but Myles said there's a boat one that takes you around the park or something. That sounds good too."

"Such a girl," Max laughs. "Don't think I'm walking through a prissy Enchanted Forest," he scoffs, with a mouthful of food.

"Shut up, Max. We're all going together. If she wants to go, she'll go," Myles snaps, giving his brother a warning look. It makes me feel uncomfortable, but then Max rolls his eyes shaking his head.

"Myles is right. If she wants to go to the Enchanted Forest she can," Maverick speaks up before Max can protest.

"I want to see that too. It says on the leaflet we had come through the post that the best time to go is at seven on the night. It's not as magical in the day otherwise," Harlow speaks up.

"I read that somewhere too. From the pictures I've seen, the whole forest lights up," I smile feeling giddy with excitement already.

"We should go there before the parade starts at eight thirty then," Denny interrupts, typing away on her phone.

"Babe, she's fine," Mason groans looking adoringly at his fiancé.

"I can't get freaking signal and I want to Facetime Hope."

"I've tried too and I can't get hold of her," Max speaks up, finishing his food.

"Seriously, you two are as bad as each other. Hope is a baby, she doesn't have a phone and I'm sure Gram's is fine with her. She has Mark and your Nan there, Denny," Harlow giggles.

"She's my niece, I should be able to talk to her when I like," Max growls, putting his phone in his pocket. "I swear Joan has turned her phone off or some shit, because ever since I called an hour ago, she seems to be avoiding my calls,"

"That's because between you, Denny, and Mason her phone hasn't stopped ringing all day," Malik speaks up.

"What do you know about it?" Denny speaks up, her eyes full of concern and worry. "Is she okay?"

"Jesus, she's fine, Denny. Joan is fine, but you're driving her and Granddad mad. Between you three, her phone has been ringing every ten minutes. Now, stop worrying. Joan said to tell you she will ring you at half ten when her last bottle is due."

"Jesus, Malik. You make us sound like stalkers," Mason grumbles.

"How about we go to the bar down the road? Max and Myles never get asked for I.D and the girls are all old enough," Maverick speaks up. Everyone agrees, but I feel apprehensive and wish I had the courage to speak up so I could politely decline. I've never drunk before and I don't really want to. I never want to lose any sense of control over my body and I know alcohol does that to you. I've seen it enough with my mom over the years. I also don't like crowded places. They terrify me, and with drunken lads around, I'll most likely black out from a panic attack.

"Kayla and I brought a film with us to watch. Why don't you guys head on out and we'll see you in the morning? The park doesn't open till half ten so we can grab breakfast first. There's a Little Chef next door," Myles speaks up and my body relaxes. I don't bother turning to look at him to know he must have read my body language. I feel shitty for ruining his night. He's a teenager who is still at school, he'd jump at the chance to go out and get blazing drunk, but I'm holding him back. It's the first time today that I've felt the sadness that usually hangs over me like a stormy cloud, hit me.

I feel eyes on me, but don't bother looking up from the table napkin. When everyone tells us they'll see us tomorrow, we start to gather our things to go and pay the bill. When I reach into my bag to grab some money a hand touches my arm stopping me. I look up into Myles' dark brown eyes confused.

"It's on me, babe," he smiles. His eyes lighting up.

"No, I'll pay; I have money," I tell him, going to reach into my bag for my purse again.

"No, I'm paying, end of," he scolds and hands Maverick our share of the bill.

Once everyone leaves we make our way back to the Travelodge, both of us walking in silence. I open my mouth a few times then close it, never knowing how to start. Then Myles speaks, breaking the silence.

"Are you okay? You've seemed really quiet since we finished eating. Is it cause I paid for our food?" he asks softly, and I turn my head to look at him. He seems sad, withdrawn a little, and I wonder if it's because he's not out having fun with his brothers and their girlfriends.

"You don't need to come back with me, ya know. You should go catch them up, I can stay by myself in the room," I blurt out.

"Huh? Why? Are you mad at me?" he asks, and stops walking when we reach the entrance of the Travelodge. A man is sitting at the reception desk with his feet up reading a magazine. I guess there isn't a lot for the night staff to do once they have all their guests booked in.

"No, I'm not mad," I whisper quietly.

"Then what's wrong? Why do you want me to go out with my brothers?" he asks in a stronger voice this time.

"Because the only reason you're not with them is because you're babysitting me."

He laughs, startling me, and I look up at him with wide eyes. Why is he laughing? When he looks back down at me with soft, crinkled eyes I look at him confused.

"You think I came back with you because I'm babysitting? I'm not babysitting," he states. "I have brought us a couple of films to watch. I had it planned before they even mentioned going out tonight. Going out wasn't even on the agenda until Maverick brought it up. I promise you."

"So, you don't want to go out, you want to stay in and watch a movie with me?"

"Why, did you want to go out?" he asks not answering my question.

"No! I thought you only said no because you noticed how uncomfortable I was when he brought it up."

"No, Kayla, I didn't just say it. Yes I noticed the tension in your body, but I promise you I already had this planned. We've got a long day tomorrow and after the car journey today I just wanted to lay back and relax. Plus, going out isn't my thing."

"Mine either," I blush, feeling embarrassed about my response to him coming back with me.

"So, film? You in?" he asks smiling.

"Yeah. You just better have brought that *Adam Sandler* movie with you," I warn and he bursts out laughing.

"The one with *Jennifer Aniston* in it?"

"The one and only," I grin as we make our way into our room.

"I may or may not have," he smirks and I push on his arm softly, giggling. I like him teasing me. He doesn't do it to be mean like other kids used to; he does it because it's him.

"That was so good. How funny was the part where he kicks the wrong woman under the table? I'm still crying over it," I laugh, and I laugh hard. This has to be one of the funniest films I've ever seen. It had everything in it and the romance, awwe, the romance. They were falling for each other like they were seeing each other for the first time. I'm not even going to mention those kids of hers, they had me in stitches. The little girl tries to impersonate a British accent. I swear, we don't sound like that, posh, sophisticated and well...snobby.

"Want to watch another? It's only half nine."

"What did you bring... a video store?" I giggle, wondering how many he brought with him.

"Are you teasing me?" he asks seriously, and I bite my lip to try and stop myself from giggling. He smirks, a look of amusement washing over him. Then his hands reach out of the blanket and come towards me and before he can reach me, I jump out of the bed squealing, laughter bubbling out of me. "Oh no you don't," he shouts, amusement in his voice. That's when I feel his large hands wrap around my waist, careful of my bruises and pulling my back to his front. My laughter echoes around the room and his laughter follows as he throws me across the room, I gasp, a rush of air leaving me before I land with a bounce on the bed, wincing a little when it catches my side. Myles follows, jumping over me, but his body doesn't touch mine, he just hovers over me.

I'm surprised I haven't freaked out over the intimate position, but Charlie's words about giving him a chance settle in, and I look up at him and smile. My eyes gaze down to his luscious mouth. God, his lips look so full, so ripe, and so mine. I reach up, my mouth slowly caressing his and I'm surprised when he lets out a growl, the only other sound in the room apart from my heavy breathing. The bottom half of his body is pressed against mine. My mouth opens around his and I gasp. The sensations overwhelming my body are becoming too much. When he reaches down, his hand to my neck, his lips to my mouth, I can do nothing but kiss him back.

Shit, he can kiss.

Not that I've got anything to compare it to.

His tongue reaches mine and I moan shamefully, and loudly. Myles reacts by tightening his hold on my neck and where his hand lays on my hip.

The tingles shoot down my spine and butterflies flutter in my stomach as the kiss deepens and I know I'll never feel anything as good as this. When my body moves on its own accord and rubs against his hardness I gasp in horror, but Myles doesn't give me time to freeze, to panic, he just moves his leg over so he's now straddling one of mine and in that moment I know I'm definitely in love with Myles Carter.

The hand on my hip moves slowly up my body until he reaches my breast, then with his thumb, he strokes underneath, earning a startled moan from me. I feel him smirk against my lips before pulling away. When he doesn't move in to kiss me again, I open my eyes, confused.

"You're so fucking beautiful it hurts," he whispers, his eyes boring into mine.

"So are you," I whisper back, my face flushing.

A deep chuckle vibrates against my chest and I tilt my head to the side wondering what I said that was funny.

"Babe, I'm not beautiful, never call me beautiful, not in front of anyone, especially Max," he grins.

"But you are. Would you prefer I use the words sexy, handsome, rugged, flawless-" I start, but he cuts me off, slamming his lips down to mine and I find myself lost in the kiss. So lost I don't realise I've started grinding my core down on his thigh, all I can feel is his lips on mine, and the sensations overwhelming my body from everything that he's driving my body towards. My movements become jerky and Myles' kiss becomes hungrier, his hands exploring every inch of my stomach, his fingers light as to not hurt press into my bruises and when he pulls back, looks at me in the eyes, and says, "Can I?" I don't hesitate to nod my head, wanting, no, needing Myles to be the one to touch me intimately for the first time. When his hands reach under my t-shirt my body stiffens at first, the touch foreign, but at the same time welcome. I'm nervous, and honestly, a little scared. But then Myles reaches back down, his mouth pressing against mine and I lose all coherent thoughts as makes my mind dizzy with lust.

Slowly, knowing my reaction, my past, Myles slides his fingers against my stomach, his skin feeling smooth against mine and I moan into his mouth. They work their way up, stopping short of my bra covered breast before hesitating.

"Please, touch me there," I plead, not having time to feel embarrassed about how blunt I'm being. He growls into my mouth again, the noise becoming one of my favourite sounds. He doesn't waste another second before slowly peeling down my bra cup, my breast falls free and I arch into his touch. I'm more than a handful, even to Myles who has large hands and he groans, his hips coming down to my leg, rubbing his erection against me and I decide I don't mind that much, I'm just not ready for it to go any further than it is now.

His fingers circle my nipple before lightly pulling and my body craves something unknown, something I've never had before and that scares me in a way, but in another it's something that excites me. My hips start to rub faster against his leg, the friction stirring sensations in my lower belly and I can feel it tightening in a good way.

I moan again, more loudly, not caring if anyone can hear me now, all that matters is Myles and the feelings he's inflicting on me.

"Fuck, you are incredible," he moans into my mouth and then I explode. It's the only way to describe it. One minute I felt like my whole body was coiled up real tight, and then the next second I just exploded. My eyes close tightly and a silent puff of air escapes my mouth just as my back arches off the bed, my head now thrown into the crook of Myles' neck.

"What was that?" I whisper shocked, and overthrown from the sensations still tingling all over my body. What the hell did he just do to me? Not that I'm complaining, it felt good, *real* good.

He leans up before looking down at me, his eyes glassy and dark. He gives me a soft look before leaning down to give me a peck on the lips.

"That, Kayla, was an orgasm."

"But...but we...we didn't... you know," I blush, feeling my cheeks redden.

He chuckles, a small smile playing on his lips and I decide I love that look on him. His erection is still hard and pressed against my leg and I wonder if it's hurting him. I'm not naive, I know what boys do to get off, I'm not that much of a hermit, but it has to be painful for him.

"You can have an orgasm without having sex. Are you feeling okay? I didn't hurt your bruises did I?" he asks softly, his voice worried and eyes drawn together.

"No. No you didn't hurt me," I tell him truthfully. I haven't really thought about them. They've ached all day, especially sitting in the car for so long, but other than that they've surprisingly been okay. I think it's helped I've had Myles and the others to keep my mind off it.

"Good," he smiles, leaning down to peck my lips once more. That's when I feel his hand still up my top and I giggle. He looks at me and when I look to his hand he chuckles. He pulls my bra cup back up before sliding his hand out of my T-shirt. "I'll put on a film."

I watch his ass jump out of the bed, over to his rucksack and pull out another DVD. This one is one I've already seen, *Red Riding Hood.* After putting the disc in, he's just about to jump back into bed, but then a commotion from outside stops him in his tracks. He looks to me and grins and because I'm feeling mellow, my whole body relaxed and sated, I don't find the energy to feel the same enthusiasm as him, so I just give him a weak smile. I know it's the others coming back, I can hear Max bellowing down the hallway from here.

Myles shakes his head and jumps back into bed, and chuckles when he hears Max's shouts.

"She wanted me, I'm telling you," Max shouts, sounding so sure.

"Bro, she threw a drink in your face," someone else says, I think it's Malik, but I can't be too sure, it could be Maverick.

"She wanted me," he declares again, their voices coming closer.

"Bro, get over it. She made it clear how she really felt about you once she found out your real age."

"I weren't going to lie to her, man. If a woman can't handle me, fuck um, but I'm telling you, she was all over my junk. Have you never seen it in the movies when chicks will 'accidentally' on purpose, just to get their hands on the man's junk?"

"Bro, like Malik said, she threw it in your face," Maverick laughs, answering my earlier question.

"Girls?" Max whines, obviously needing back up and I giggle loudly into Myles when neither Denny nor Harlow answer. "Great, now Kayla is going to think I got a drink thrown in my face," he says and I giggle harder.

"Night, Max," Denny laughs, sounding like she's right outside our door. Denny and Mason are in the room next to us, Max on the other, and down from Max is Maverick. Malik and Harlow are a room down from Denny and Mason, both out of the way.

"Kayla, she wanted me," Max shouts through the door and Myles and I burst out laughing.

"Is he drunk?" I ask on a whisper, but wasn't quiet enough, because Maverick shouts through the door to answer me before Myles can.

"Yeah, Kay, he is. Idiot thought he was cool doing shots of sambuca with a bunch of college chicks," he laughs. "Night, guys," he shouts through, still laughing.

"Night," I shout back, giggling, Myles shouting the same.

"Night, twinny, may you have a shit night's sleep," Max shouts. "Love you, brothers, and ladies, but you, Myles, you, my twinny are my bestest. You gave me food so you could starve," he shouts again, but gets silenced by Maverick. We hear him push Max into the room telling him to get some sleep before we hear Max groan. "Okay, okay, damn it, I'm going."

"Twinny?" I giggle, more quietly than before.

"Don't ask. He gets affectionate when he's had a drink. He's all hands on," Myles chuckles.

"What was he on about when he was talking about starving?" I ask curiously.

"Oh, I was the smallest when I came out. Max had taken everything," he laughs. "He was 7lbs newborn, while I was only 4lbs. He thinks he owes me some sort of gratitude."

"Bless him. That's kind of sweet when you think about it," I chuckle, and then shiver when the night's cold air hits me.

"You cold?"

"A little."

"Come on. Let's get you into bed," he tells me. We both jump up off the bed, pulling the blanket back, but end up struggling. We look at each other and laugh, and then both pull at the same time. It's like someone has glued the bloody bed sheet to the bed it's that hard to pull down.

"Shit, did they super glue the thing down to the mattress or something?" Myles groans then steps back a foot when his side of the blanket comes loose. I look at him and shake my head, wondering how the hell he made it look so easy. I try again, pulling with all my strength. I pull that hard I don't feel the blanket coming loose, and I end up on my ass, Myles still on the other side of the bed, laughing.

"Jesus, this bed should come with its own warning label," I laugh, Myles laughing harder at my gracefulness.

"Some of us are trying to get to sleep," Max shouts through the wall and Myles and I start laughing. "Fuck, someone stuck my blanket to the bed," we hear next and I laugh harder, falling down on my back.

We hear him muttering about the blanket before we hear a thud on the floor and I know he's done the same thing I just did which makes me laugh harder.

Myles helps me up from the floor and as soon as I look at him I fall into another fit of laughter. I can't help it, it's funny. We get into bed, shutting the lights out and playing the DVD.

It's not ten minutes before my eyes start drooping. With the long drive and the intense orgasm I just had and the emotions from having one have drained me and a yawn escapes my mouth before I can cover it.

"Tired?" Myles asks, followed by a yawn of his own.

"Yeah," I mumble tiredly.

He gets up turning on the side light before getting out of bed and shutting the DVD down and turning the tele off. He gets back into bed wasting no time in pulling me to him. I don't bother fighting, I love being in his arms, I love the feeling of safety he provokes in me.

I'm just falling in a deep slumber when banging on the wall above our head starts.

Myles groans and I giggle wondering what the hell Max is doing that has the bed banging against the wall. When it doesn't stop Myles sits up and bangs on the wall.

"What the hell are you doing, Max?" Myles shouts.

"Breaking the bed in," Max shouts back and I stifle a giggle.

"You went to bed alone, Max," Myles laughs through the wall.

"Not that," Max shouts before we hear another thud. "The fucking bed is rock solid, man. You could get more softness out of a cardboard box."

I start laughing, burying my face into the pillow.

"Max, just go to sleep for fuck's sake," Myles laughs.

"Kayla, laugh all you want because if I don't get my eight hours I'm an unhappy Max, and nobody likes an unhappy Max. Everyone loves a happy Max."

"How much has he had to drink?" I giggle.

"Kayla baby, you should have come with us, I'd have rocked your world," he shouts then we hear another shout from another room and it has to be one of the others. I also want to shout, I doubt he could rock my anything, his brother does that by just being him, but then they'd know how close I am to Myles and I'm not ready to share that.

"Maverick, I'm going to sleep now. Did you break your bed in?" he pauses. "Fuck, yeah, goodnight. Night, Twinny. Night, Kayla," he says before one last thud on the wall happens. That's when Myles turns over, onto his side, grabs me around the hips and pulls me to him, keeping his hand away from my bruised ribs. I snuggle back into him, my ass to his groin and before I know it, I'm fast asleep.

FIFTEEN

KAYLA

After an eventful night of listening to Max fight with his bed, I woke up this morning to Myles peppering light kisses all over my face. I was so darn sure after what happened between us last night that I would wake up drenched in sweat from a nightmare, but for the first time in over two years, I had a dream. I dreamt about Myles. Him kissing me, him touching me, and him making me laugh. So, for once, I woke up not plagued by a nightmare, but in a dream, one that felt like I still hadn't woken up from.

We arrived at the park a few hours ago. The place is jam-packed with people from all over the place. It's had me a little on edge with the place so crowded, but then I'd feel Myles' touch or presence and my heart would calm down. In fact, I think everyone noticed I felt a little on edge. I've found Maverick hovering close by me too, and when we've gone on a ride that has three seats he's always made sure I'm sitting between him and Myles. I know this is on purpose. I heard Maverick talking to Myles about it when they thought I wasn't paying attention.

Now we're stopping for some lunch. Max is slouched over the picnic bench looking a little green.

"How are you holding up, Max?" I ask softly. He's sitting opposite me, Maverick and Myles on either side of me, and the rest scattered in the empty seats.

"Starting to wish I didn't do that last shot of sambuca last night," he groans.

"Well, *Twinny*," I tease. "You've only got yourself to blame," I giggle.

"Oh God, I called him Twinny again, didn't I?" he asks, mortified, and I giggle. Myles and Maverick chuckling beside me.

"Yep," I giggle, and look up when I see Mason, and Malik walking over with our trays of food.

They set the trays down and hand Max a full breakfast and a glass of orange juice.

"Get this inside ya, kid. It will do you some good," Mason tells him with a grin. Max groans, but grabs a knife and fork anyway from the tray and tucks in.

Once we've eaten we sit talking, letting our food go down and going over where to go next when I mention *Swamp*. It's not a ride I particularly wanted to go on, but with Max looking so green it seems like our best option. I really don't want to be on one of the big rides and have him throw up, especially if I'm sitting behind him.

"Isn't that the boat ride, the haunted one? It's meant to be good," Maverick grins mischievously. Max has gone to the toilet so he doesn't have any input, but I'm sure he'll be thankful his stomach is getting a rest.

"Yeah, sounds ace. Plus, don't we need to do that ride in order to get the graveyard trip tonight?" Myles pipes in. His arm goes around my waist, sliding me along the bench closer to him.

"We're doing *Dead End*, the graveyard maze?" I squeak. That is definitely something I didn't want to do. Walking around in a maze, with no way out, with dead people chasing you, is my worst nightmare come to life. I can see it now. I'll be running around in circles screaming for my life and one of the characters will jump out at me and I'll end up going berserk, or worse, have a panic attack.

God, I'm ruining this weekend.

Stop being a party pooper, Kayla, and have some fun, I hear Charlie telling me in my head. She's always telling me to let go, to have fun and to hell with the consequences. I turn, looking up to Myles and see him giving Maverick a look, his face full of amusement and excitement and I know then if I don't want to do it, he'll stay back with me and miss out on all the fun.

He looks down at me, sees my expression, and his face turns serious, but soft, relaxed even.

"We don't have to do the maze if you don't want. We can sit in a concession stand and get something to drink."

"No... I... Just don't leave me in there, please," I plead, not realising just how much being trapped with no way out bothers me. With Myles, though, I know he won't leave me, he makes me feel safe, safe enough to go into a graveyard maze in the dark with dead people chasing you.

"I won't, babe. I promise," he smiles softly.

"I'll be there too. If it gets too much we can run around to the exit, ask whoever is monitoring the exit to let us in so we can play tricks on everyone else," Maverick whispers and I giggle.

Max walks back to the table with more colour to his face and it makes me wonder if he just spent the last ten minutes in the loos throwing up. I'm about to ask when Denny grabs my attention, and I turn away from Max.

"Are you free in a few weeks to look at some bridesmaid's dresses?"

"I should be; depends on what time. I'm at school, remember," I smile, still excited about being a bridesmaid. I've always wanted to wear a bridesmaid dress, or even a wedding gown. When I walk past a wedding store in town I have to stop and stare, admiring all the beautiful dresses.

"Oh, I've booked it for a Saturday. I got us an appointment at that *Flora's Boutique*, near London. I know it's a long drive an' all, but..."

She doesn't need to finish. Even I, who knows nothing about fashion, knows how big Flora's dresses are. She's one of the top wedding gown designers in the UK. It takes celebrities months to even get a consultation with her, let alone a fitting. So for Denny to get a consultation at one of her new stores says something, big.

"Will she be there?" I breathe out, my body giddy with excitement. I've never met anyone famous. The closest I got was when I went to the big shopping centre where they had some meet and greet with a cast of some TV programme called *TOWNIE*, or *TWOOIE*, shit, no, it was *TOWIE*...I think. It doesn't matter, what does matter is that I might get to meet the famous *Flora*.

Denny gives me a big toothy grin and starts squealing 'yes'. "My nan, if you can believe it, knew her. I mean *knew* her. When we informed her about us getting engaged she called her and told her about me, about my mom and what happened. I know it's wrong to use what happened to me to get an appointment, but Flora understood why my nan wanted the best for me. Flora has even offered to pay for all the bridesmaid dresses. I couldn't believe it."

"Wow! How? I mean, I know your nan is one tough cookie to say 'no' to, but this, this is huge. I heard Flora turned down an actress who just wanted an appointment. She even offered to pay millions to get her to change her mind and make time to see her. I forgot her name now, I was too busy staring at the dresses they had on the page," I gush happily, and notice everyone around the table apart from us girls have gone quiet. "What?" I ask looking to Myles who is grinning widely at me.

"Cute," is all he says before Denny grabs my attention again.

"See, that's where it gets weirder. When I told Nan I couldn't afford that kind of money for a wedding gown, she told me Flora has opened up a discounted store that is open to the public. You still need to be put on a waiting list. I couldn't believe it. Nan showed me a few of the gowns before telling me about it, asking my opinion, because the dresses are different from Flora's other designs. But when I looked at this one, my God, it stole my breath away," she breathes, her eyes shining. I flick my eyes to her left to see Mason watching her with an amused, loving expression on his face. He really does love her, I can see it in the way he looks at her; it's the same way she looks at him. I swear the two couldn't be better made for each other. I just wish the beginning of their relationship wasn't as rocky as it was. Denny and Harlow filled me in on everything that happened, but I'm glad everything turned out okay in the end.

"I'm so happy for you. I can't wait to see the dress," I smile, starting to feel uncomfortable with the silence around the table.

"We also need to talk about bachelorette-" Harlow starts.

"Can we please go? As much as I love you as a sister, I don't want to hear about Flora dresses and shit. Can we go on *Turn* now?" Max whines.

"We're going on-" I start, but I'm cut off by Myles, his hand gripping my leg and interrupting me.

"Let's go."

I look at him confused, wondering what that was about, but shrug it off when he just grins at me. The way he grins at me has me forgetting my own name, and I end up forgetting what I was about to say anyway.

We walk over to the *Swamp* and Myles takes my hand, not for the first time today either. I like it. It's soft, and warm. My eyes are cast to the floor, looking down at my scuffed vans with a small smile on my face.

"What the fuck!" is boomed in front of us and I snap my head up to see Max turning and glaring at all of us. "Is this some sort of sick joke?"

"What is he going on about?" I whisper to Myles.

"No idea, Babe," he chuckles. Max hears his brother's chuckle and snaps his head in our direction.

"You!" he points to Myles walking over to us. The expression on his face has me stepping back. He notices and he stops advancing on us, and instead, gives his brother a glare.

"Why would you bring us here?"

"It was my idea," I blurt out, not wanting him to shout at Myles. I find courage inside me and step in front of Myles, blocking what I can of him with my tiny body, from Max. Max's eyes widen for a second, his eyes flicking between me and Myles before he grins at me.

"You sticking up for Myles, Kayla?" he teases, amusement in his eyes.

"Why are you mad?" I ask confused, and when I look around, Denny, Harlow, and the boys are all grinning at Max, or me, I don't know, all I know is it's making me feel uncomfortable.

"Mad? I just don't want to go on this ride," he snaps.

"Are you scared?" I ask and sigh when I feel Myles step up behind me, his arm going around my waist. Other people walk by, their curious glances making me blush. I hate being given any sort of attention and with the way we're all standing it looks like we're in a standoff, especially with the angry expression now on Max's face.

"No. I'm not scared. Why would I be scared? It's a ride. It's not real, Kayla."

"So why are you getting so worked up?" I snap back, feeling frustrated. I never get like this ever. I never snap. At all. At anyone.

"I'm not, I would have just liked to be informed is all."

"Well now you know, so pull on your big girl pants and move it. The line says it's half an hour wait."

With that I walk off leaving everyone's laughter behind me as I start queuing up in the line. They all follow, and when Myles walks up behind me, bending down to give my neck a light kiss, I begin to relax. I thought he might be funny with me telling his brother off like that, but he seems to be fine. I know my face is bright red, but I don't care.

When the ride is over I know why Maverick gave Myles that mischievous look and why Max got so worked up over going on.

We all walk off the ride, everyone in a fit of laughter, but me. Why? Because I had no choice but to sit next to Max on the ride, even after we tried to tell the ride operator that I wanted to be next to Myles. He said he needed to keep the line moving and to not argue, and because I heard people moaning about us holding them up, I stopped complaining and got on next to Max. Why I didn't complain further is a mistake I won't be making twice.

I have nail marks imprinted into my hands and arms, my left ear is ringing and it's all from the death grip Max had on me, and the screams that escaped his mouth.

"You sounded like you were being murdered," I glare when we finally reach a secluded area. I stop, making sure I get my point across, feeling brave. It could be to do with the fact he seriously fucking hurt my hand.

I kick him in the shin and he howls in pain while everyone else bursts out laughing.

"Don't you laugh, you... You mean boy," I stutter, snapping at Myles.

He holds his hands up in surrender. "What did I do?"

"You knew. You all knew. I'm going to be hearing his screams for months. Months! Why would you do that to me?" I whisper-yell defensively.

"We did try to get him next to Maverick or Malik if you remember, but that jerk operator wouldn't keep his eyes off your, um, chest long enough to listen to anyone," Myles says sheepishly.

He was staring at my chest? Ew. Really could have done with not knowing that, at all. Myles gives me a sheepish grin and shrugs his shoulders.

"He screamed in my ear," I whine quietly, my eyes looking around for the person in question. He still hasn't come out of the bathroom that he ran off to when we walked out. Well, *we* walked, he ran like a big baby.

"I'm sorry, Baby. I promise not to let him near you for the rest of the trip."

"He dug his nails in my hands and arm, and did you know he tried getting in my lap at one point? In *my lap*. In the middle of a ride, Myles, it was horrible. I swear to God, I didn't even get to see anything going on because he was all over me like a rash," I growl, kind of thankful in a way that I didn't see anything. If Max's screams were anything to go by then it must have been scary. I even heard Denny and Harlow squealing at one time, but I couldn't be too sure over the screaming in my ear. I rub my ear again trying to get rid of the buzzing noise, but it doesn't work.

"*Now* can we go on Ride?" Max says from behind me, making me jump. I squeal loudly jumping into Myles' arms and Max laughs.

"Jesus, Kayla, don't be such a baby, it's not like I snuck up on you," he laughs and I turn from Myles to look at Max and growl. He gives me a wide expression but I know what that fucker can do with those nails and God, God, his screams. I shudder just remembering it.

"Okay, wild cat, let's go on Ride," Myles laughs, pulling me with him as we walk across the park.

The last of the sun has gone down and the moon and stars are finally out. I've wanted to go to the Enchanted Forest all day, but from what Malik said, we have to do the graveyard stint first. Which is probably best, it will give me time to calm my beating heart.

We've been queuing for an hour and a half. In that time we've watched the sun go down, the stars and moon come out, and Max and Malik eat their own body weight in junk food. I swear the Carter brothers can eat.

We're getting closer to the start. We're the next group to go through and I begin to fidget when Myles nudges me.

"You going to be okay doing this?" He whispers so the others can't hear him. I look up at him with soft eyes, loving how attentive he's been to my nervousness all day. Whenever I've become uncomfortable he's picked up on it and has put me at ease. After we went on Ride my side became really sore, so I took a few painkillers. Then I saw what the next ride was and Myles picked up on the same predicament. There was no way I could go on that ride. The name said it all.

Twist.

And that's what the ride did; it twisted, and turned, twisted and turned and spun so fast I noticed people still spinning walking off the ride. I would have done more damage to my already bruised side going on that ride, so Myles told the others he wanted to sit this one out and actually *asked* me if I would keep him company, like I was doing him a favour.

The only person other than Myles who knows about the bruises is Max, so the others had no idea that Myles was only doing it for me. He got teased the rest of the day before going on rides.

"Kayla," he calls in a teasing voice, and I shake away my thoughts.

"Sorry, yeah, I'll be good," I smile, trying to relax my nerves. "Just don't run off and leave me."

"My name is Myles, not Max."

"We're moving."

I look to Malik who spoke to find him looking at Mason with a devilish smirk on his face. The girls are none the wiser, they're too busy squealing with excitement and I smile at their antics.

"Come on, Kayla, we're next," Harlow giggles, and I shake my head no.

"I'll take my chances with Myles, thank you," I tell her softly, not wanting to tell her I have a feeling Malik and Mason are planning on playing their own tricks on the girls.

"Come on, us girls have to stick together, don't we, Max?" Denny teases.

"Fuck off," Max mutters, his feet shifting from one foot to the other.

That's when the line starts moving quickly and we make our way through the first set of gates. We follow the rest of the group in front of us. There in front of us is a man dressed in white overalls, blood splattered all over them standing in front of five sets of doors.

"I need you to get into groups of six and stand in front of a door. If you've come today in a large group, split up," he shouts to us as a female worker walks out and starts directing people where to stand. I cling to Myles when I notice Denny and Mason being separated. She looks to Mason with wide eyes, but he just grins sending her a wink.

"Door number three, please," the woman says, and I jump not having seen her approach us. Myles laughs and walks us over to door three, and I groan when I see we've been paired with Max, thankfully Denny is with us, but it still doesn't make me feel any better. Another two girls are added to our door and then haunted music starts playing, a creepy deep voice booming from the speakers.

"Enter at your own risk."

Like I have a choice, I think to myself.

We huddle through, the place pitched in darkness and I hear Max squeal which makes me squeal. The doors slam, one by one, and the sound of locking is overheard on the speakers around us.

The lights start to flicker on and I look around, looking for that person who is bound to jump out at you, but I'm even more startled when all we find is mirrors. We hear Max and Denny scream and I giggle. I love having Myles near me instead of Max.

"Find your way out and you shall live," the ghostly voice says.

Max and Denny start touching the glass, making sure they're not walking into any mirrors.

"Oh my God, is that Maverick?" I laugh, when I look to my right. Maverick and a group of people are struggling the same as us, trying to find our way out.

"Yeah," Max laughs. He walks closer, noticing the glass, is just that, glass. This one isn't a mirror, it's just a divider separating each group. The lights dim more, so Max chooses that moment to shove his face closer to the glass, shouting Maverick's name over the creepy music that's still playing. The two other girls have taken the lead, both of them giggling and feeling their way to the exit. Just as they reach a moving door, the booming voice startles us, and the place goes pitch black, all of us freezing in place.

"Do not move. Keep very, very still," the ghostly voice says.

"Is it bad I'm going to pee my pants I'm that freaking scared?" Denny whisper-yells and I silently agree with her, my body frozen and rooted to the spot.

All of a sudden a crack of thunder fills the room and the room is bathed in light and we all scream loudly, Max the loudest. Up against the clear glass where Max was standing is now a scary looking dead woman. Her face is deformed, the makeup artist making her look like something from *The Walking Dead* T.V. programme. We all turn to run, Max smacking into a mirror, before we head towards the sounds of the girls screaming.

"Time is running out," the voice booms above the speakers and my heart rate speeds up when I hear the distinct sound of a chainsaw behind us.

"Oh my God, we need to go," I squeak, pulling on Myles' arm to move forward. We catch up to the girls, and notice why they've stopped.

"Are those real people?" Myles whispers to me, his hand clutching mine tightly. On the floor lying down are a bunch of dead bodies. Obviously not real, but you get my drift.

"Maybe this is the wrong way?" one of the girls in our group says.

"Nah, look, it says exit over there, babe," Max speaks up. "Why don't you go first?" he tells her, pushing her in front of him. She laughs pushing back, refusing.

"What if they're real people? I'm not stepping on them," she laughs.

Myles steps forward when we hear the chainsaw coming closer. He nudges the body with his foot and laughs.

"It's a dummy. Just don't step on them," he laughs as he steps over the first one. I follow having no choice in the matter. Denny follows clutching my spare hand. When we're half way to the exit, the floor boards beneath us move and we all scream, then louder when sprays of water hit us from above. We all move faster and I can't believe how fast my heart is going. The adrenaline is pumping through my veins and I can't help but laugh as I hear everyone effin' and blinding behind me.

Reaching the exit door a body jumps out from the side of us and we all scream in fear, pushing each other forward to get away. Once we're all out we stand catching our breath, laughing our heads off. The two girls start eyeing up Max and Myles and I feel myself stepping closer to him, not wanting them to get his attention.

One of the girls notices and gives me a small, shy smile making me relax. When I turn to look around we're in a graveyard. Not a real one. It looks like a graveyard, except the grave stones are bigger, the grass is more like wheat and the place is full of fake cobwebs. We hear a squeal to the left and I swear that it's Harlow's scream, which makes us all giggle.

"Reminder," an announcement calls from a speaker at the entrance of the graveyard. "The rules from the beginning apply. No actor will touch or harm you in any way. They may come close, but will not make contact. Please keep the journey safe for both you and actors and enjoy the ride."

We all look at Max and give him a warning look. He just looks offended and huffs out an annoyed breath.

"The chainsaw man has escaped," a woman wearing a ripped dress says, scaring the shit out of me. Where the hell did she come from? Everyone else must be thinking the same thing when I see them looking in the direction her voice had first come from. "You need to go..." she tells us frantically, looking around, her eyes wide with fear. "He's coming, he's coming," she screams, then runs.

Then little twinkle lights shine on the ground, and we enter the maze. The grave stones look real, and my hand reaches out to touch one, but it's just decorated poly blocks. They look so real. I'm just about to take my phone out to take a picture when we hear the chainsaw again. We all turn around to the sound and scream. A man dressed as the Chainsaw Massacre is standing at the entrance. We all turn and run when he takes a step towards us.

Denny is in front of us, Max and the girls behind, all of us screaming our heads off. We end up in a bigger field, and it's obviously joined with the others because I can hear other people screaming around us.

I'm between laughing and peeing my pants when Max comes shoving past us, nearly sending Myles and I to the floor. He just gets ahead of Denny when a zombie walks out of the open grave. He screams, pushing Denny in front of him and running off in another direction, leaving us all behind.

"Are you okay?" I laugh, rushing over to Denny, who is quick to get back on her feet.

"I'm going to kill that fucker. Did you see his face, though?" she laughs and we all laugh with her. We turn around to find the girls have gone too, and when we turn in the direction we came from I can see why. Standing there is the man with the chainsaw, the noise of the engine making me quake with fear. That's when we hear 'argh' from behind us and remember the zombie. We all scream, laughter following, and run in the direction where the smoke is still lingering from how fast Max hightailed it out of here.

"This way," Myles shouts, grabbing my hand. I grab Denny's and together we rush through the pathways between what I think is supposed to be a corn field. Rounding another corner we all scream to a sudden stop, then burst out laughing when we come face to face with Maverick and Harlow.

"Where's Mason and Malik?" Denny asks.

"Mason legged it before this bloke came out to warn us," Maverick says dryly.

"And we lost Malik when I pushed him out the way and legged it," Harlow laughs.

"Max did that to me, but literally pushed me over....then legged it," Denny laughs and the others laugh with her.

"Come on. Let's go. That has to be the way out because we've been back there and all the other paths are blocked by either zombies, or a bloke with a hatchet."

We follow behind Maverick and Myles, us girls linking arms and squealing every time we pass a grave that has a zombie trying to escape. It's not long before we come to another building. One says exit, the other says Enchanted Forest. We take the Enchanted Forest, and walk in to find Max, Malik, and Mason all sat around laughing.

"Seriously, Max, you'd leave the mother of your niece to be murdered?" Denny snaps, walking over to Mason.

"She'd be in good hands with me," he tells her rolling his eyes. I giggle.

"Yeah, until another zombie walks into your life and you leave her to defend herself."

"I wouldn't do that to her, she's my princess."

"Liar," Denny snaps, and Mason cuddles her to his chest, kissing her neck.

"Cheers, Babe, nice of you to leave me to get here by myself. I nearly got took out by a group of girls and this one," Malik growls, looking pissed at Max.

"I needed to scope out the place before I let any of you walk in," Max snaps, defending himself.

"Whatever, bro."

"Sorry, I thought you were behind me," Harlow says blushing.

"Babe, you ran out of there that fast I'm surprised your feet didn't set on fire."

We all laugh, and then join the queue, still talking about the ride and what a chicken Max had been. We're all in our own little world that we don't feel the outside air until we're standing in an archway.

Just like on the water ride we went on earlier they have a platform moving clockwise with mini boats waiting to be loaded.

"It's four to a boat," the man tells us when we are closer to the front of the line.

"Max is not with me," I shout quickly, and then blush when Max turns to me glaring.

"We'll come with you," Malik and Harlow offer, and I smile.

Myles takes my hand when it's our turn to load the boat, and quickly we rush over to get in, the rest of the group in the boat behind us.

"Are we on the right ride? I thought we walked through the forest?" I ask Myles, not seeing anything about boats in the leaflet.

"Yeah, I heard one of the groups in front of us mention it takes us through the back way. When it's the end of the ride, we can walk through to the main park area. That way we don't have to walk all the way through and miss the boat carnival."

"Okay," I nod, and then snuggle into his side starting to feel chilly from the night air. It doesn't help I'm wet from being sprayed in the graveyard.

"Do you reckon there are crocodiles in this water?" we hear Max from the other boat, and we all snicker, the other boat full of groans. Not wanting to miss a minute, I lean my head on Myles' shoulder, his arm wrapping around me and take in the lanterns, fairy lights and sparkly decorations surrounding the beautiful wildlife. I can see why this attraction isn't open all the time. It must take a lot of work to keep the decorations in good condition, not to mention lighting all the lantern candles.

They change the theme every once in a while, but the fairy lights have always been there.

The atmosphere on the boat is smooth and relaxing. With all the dull lighting, and the glow from the moon it gives off a romantic feel.

Malik and Harlow are making out in the front of the boat and I blush before looking away. That's when Myles turns my head, his lips moving towards mine before giving me a tender loving kiss. It's soft, and gentle, and I feel it with every fibre in my body. Every time he kisses me it just gets better and better.

When we pull away we're both out of breath, my heart beating at a rapid pace. He gives me a small smile then pulls me into his arms. I sigh, feeling content and rest my head on his shoulder. The ride continues for another five minutes before we come to the end.

Myles steps out first before helping me out, then we stand off to the side to wait for the others, this part of the day becoming one of the best parts, hell, it's become one of my best memories.

SIXTEEN

MYLES

"THIS WAS THE BEST DAY ever. I'm gutted Charlie missed it; she would have gone gaga over those floats. She loves taking photos," Kayla gushes from the other room. I bite back a grin.

The rest have headed to bed too, wanting to get an early start back tomorrow, but Kayla and I went to get some drinks from the corner shop along with some snacks.

"It's not the same, but we took some pretty good photos between the two of us, maybe we can get them printed out to show her," I offer, around a mouth full of toothpaste.

"Oh my God," she beams. "She'd love that. Why didn't I think of that? Maybe we can get one of the firework display printed on a canvas for her. She loves fireworks. Always has. When we moved she came to visit me in the six weeks holiday and dragged me to this firework display that was happening where we lived. She gushed over it for months and I remember her telling me that if she could, she would paint her room to look just like that firework display."

"I love seeing you like this," I grin, walking out of the bathroom. She's all pent up with excitement and energy and has gone over every detail of today like I wasn't there right along with her.

It's freaking cute.

She's cute.

"Like what?" she asks, her face red and flushed. I watch her grab her pyjamas in a rush, not making eye contact with me. She's all flustered and that's when I realise it's because I'm only wearing my Calvin Klein boxers.

"Happy, carefree, excited," I chuckle and she looks back at me to glare, but then takes one look at my body and gets all flustered again.

I sit on the edge of the bed shoving today's clothes into my rucksack, listening to Kayla ramble about the walk through the Enchanted Forest. I'm not usually into all that girly shit, but I have to admit, the place looked fucking amazing.

I look up when I hear clothes rustling. Kayla rushed in so quick she forgot to close the door, so when I look up, my whole body locks up, completely freezing. My jaw locks and my hands clench tightly into fists.

Kayla's bruises are worse than I first anticipated. They're fiery red, blue and purple, looking nasty across her side, ribs and stomach. I knew it was bad, but not this, not fucking spread so far across her stomach and side, damaging her flawless skin. The fact that someone could hurt someone so kind, so innocent, and already fragile makes me want to repay them the favour. I'm trying to rein in my anger, not wanting to scare Kayla, that I don't hear her walk in. She must have taken one look at me and known something was up.

"Is everything okay? I know I've talked a lot... and I'm rambling again."

"I'm fine, sorry. Just tired," I tell her, lifting my head and giving her a warm smile. She smiles back, but her eyes look unsure as she gets into bed. I shove the last of my shit into my bag, making sure to take out the clothes for tomorrow before joining Kayla on the bed.

"Did *you* have a good day?" she asks softly.

"I had the best day," I grin, my body relaxing.

"You did?" she asks, beaming, and being all cute.

"Bet your ass I did," I chuckle before leaning over and giving her a kiss. And as always, my lips reach hers and my whole body lights the fuck up. No one has set my body on fire the way she does. God, it's like it burns only for her. She only has to make contact with me and I'm fighting back a hard on, but now, her lips drive me to the point I could quite easily cum in my pants.

"Goodnight, Myles," she whispers sleepily.

"Night, Babe," I smile, leaning down to give her one more peck on her lips.

"Thank you for today," she whispers again before I hear her breathing even out.

My mind has been on Kayla since we dropped her off three hours ago. She's going out for dinner with her dad and there was nothing I could do to get her to change her mind. I'd wanted her to stay with me, to come to mine for dinner, just something to get her away from that house. I'm still not sure who's hurting her, but with my past experience, my guess is it's her dad. He was the only one there that morning that could have done that to her. She's not been having any problems at school, so it's not something she could have gotten from there, and there is no one else in her life. I know her mother is an only child so she doesn't have any aunts or uncles on that witches side, and her dad has a brother and sister, but both live miles away for her to have any contact with them. So the only person it could be *is* her dad.

I've finally snapped, needing to get out of the house I stand up towards the door, but I'm stopped short when my granddad walks in holding a plate of food.

"Joan wanted me to bring you over a plate. Is everything okay, son?"

"Yeah, why wouldn't it be?" I lie.

"Don't lie to me, boy. Talk to me," he demands, sitting the plate down on the table and taking a seat opposite on the recliner.

I groan, scrubbing my hands down my face before addressing him. "Granddad, if you knew someone was being hurt, but you couldn't prove who was hurting them, what would you do?" I ask him, looking at him with pleading eyes. It's been killing me not knowing how to help Kayla, to keep her safe. She's been avoiding my calls and texts since we dropped her off and she promised we would talk about it when we got back. I know what she's doing, but she can't avoid me forever.

"Someone's hurting Kayla?" he asks shocked.

"What? I didn't..."

"Your face says it all, plus, she's the only one I can see you looking ready to commit murder for."

"Max and I went to hers on Thursday when she didn't show up for school. She texted me saying some bullshit about being with her dad, but then we saw him in town with his new missus. So Max and I went there and found her asleep in bed, but the blanket had moved down and showed she had some bruises on her side. Granddad, it was fucked up. She's had bruises before, finger marks and shit, but I've just pushed my worries aside hoping she'd come to me, but she never did. Then last night I saw the bruises full on, and Granddad, it looks like someone took a fucking hammer to her stomach and ribs. I don't know what to do. I've left her alone with her dad tonight, and he could be the one hurting her," I groan, feeling angrier by the second.

"What the fuck?" a voice behind us booms, and I jump, turning around to find Maverick watching us with a thunderous expression.

"Don't let her know that you know, bro," I beg him, panicked.

"Who the fuck would hurt her? She's like a freaking fairy," he snaps.

"Sit down, both of you," Granddad snaps, looking at us both with a determined expression.

"Maverick, calm down before you set him off even more, and Myles, how do you know it's her dad?"

"Who else would it be? She's with me every day at school, plus I would have heard if someone was hurting her there. And the only other place she could be hurt is at home. And the only other person there that early to hurt her was her dad. I left her before she went to bed, so unless he did it then or waited until the morning, I don't know, but it all makes sense."

"I dunno, Kid. I've known her father awhile and although he let a lot of shit slide before, he loves that girl."

"What has Kayla said?" Maverick grits out.

"She won't tell me anything, she said she would talk about it today, but now she's ignoring me."

"Maybe she's out or she's asleep," he offers, which could be true, it is nearly ten at night.

"What do I do?" I plead.

"Son, I've only had the privilege of meeting the girl a few times now, but she's strong. Yes she's beyond fragile on the inside, but I believe with you by her side she will talk to you. Don't go pushing her for answers, or suffocating her, it won't work. Her will has been taken from her, her whole life; she doesn't need that from you too."

"But what-"

"But nothing, Son. I know what you boys are like. You're loyal to the bone and when you love, you do it strong and you do it fighting. Kayla doesn't need that, she needs you, just you," he smiles softly.

My eyes water and I don't care if I look like a baby in front of them. She's everything to me. I couldn't protect her the first time, and I don't want to make the same mistake twice. Knowing I could be doing something is killing me. She could be at home now wishing someone would save her from her dad.

"He's right, Myles. I saw the way you looked at each other over the weekend, and that girl worships the ground you walk on. I'm not saying I agree with Granddad, that we should wait until she agrees to tell us who is hurting her, but I do agree she needs to be the one to make the decision. All you can do until then is stand by her and be there for her," Maverick offers, coming to sit down next to me, patting my back in what we call our brotherly hug.

"When did you become so sentimental?" I chuckle, my eyes still glassed over.

"The day I had to raise you guys and watch you grow into men," he shrugs, before getting up and walking over to Granddad. He pats him on the back before leaving us with one more thing. "And the men you've become is thanks to this man, so take his advice." And with that he walks away, up the stairs and when I hear his bedroom door shut I turn to Granddad who is watching me with curious eyes.

"So what are you going to do?"

"I'm not going to run over there knife blazing and threaten the fucker if that's what you're worried about. I'm going to wait until she replies, if she hasn't called me by tomorrow morning, before I leave to meet her for school, then I'll make sure I go see her."

"Good lad. I'm really proud of who you boys have become. You never had a great upbringing, and a part of that was due to my negligence."

"No, Granddad, it wasn't. It was because we had two fucked up parents who didn't deserve to produce kids. You were the best thing that ever happened to any of us, without you we would probably get into trouble, robbing stores for our next meal. Don't ever blame yourself," I tell him heatedly.

He chokes up, his eyes watering and I know that must be hard for him to show his emotions like that. He's not one to sit and have a heart to heart, he usually tells us to 'shake it off and carry on' or 'build a bridge and get over it'.

He nods his head twice before standing up and walking over to the sofa. "I'll be next door if you need me son, day or night, for whatever you need."

I wait for him to close the front door before getting up and locking up after him. Max is out at some party. Some chick texted him when we were twenty minutes away from home inviting him to go and he said yes. Knowing he has taken the back door key, I push the chain across the front door before heading upstairs to bed.

Lying in bed I stare up at the ceiling, watching the reflections that the moon and street lamps are causing. I've been in bed for a good half an hour to an hour, mindlessly thinking about everything Kayla. She's consuming my mind more and more, especially since we first kissed. I crave the taste of her cherry lips, and the smell of the vanilla scented body lotion she must wear.

I'm just about to give up on her texting me back when the light from my phone lights up the bedroom, the screen flashing.

In a rush to hear from her I fall from the bed, my knees banging on the carpeted floor with a thud.

"Fuck!" I yelp, getting back up, and slowly this time, grabbing my phone.

Kayla: Soz, went 2 Charlie's after my dinner with Dad. I was 2 excited 2 tell her about our trip to wait until tomorrow. My phone died and only just got back. Is everything ok?

Me: Yeah, baby. Did you show her the pictures? And are you okay? Your dad home?

I wait for what feels like hours after sending her a message back. I hate the thought of her being alone with him in that house, especially when her neighbours would never hear her screaming for help. Just the thought has tremors raking through my body and I have to bite my lips to calm myself down.

Kayla: She begged me 2 show um 2 her, but I sed I wnted it 2 be a surprise ;) Wen do u wnt 2 go get them done? And he's in bed asleep already. He was snoring away when I walked past. I'm gud, why wouldn't I be?

Me: We can go Tuesday after school if you like? That way we can get some more of our presentation finished. Just asking, I miss you xx

Kayla: Awwe, ain't u sweet. Tuesdays cool. I miss you 2 <3 x

Me: Really?

Kayla: Really, really. I thought you'd be asleep by now.

Me: Nah, I'm missing you sleeping next to me.

Kayla: U can sleep Tuesday. Dad will be away for the night again. I think I heard him telling someone on the phone that he was going away 4 a weekend in a few weeks 2. Maybe we can get everyone 2geva around mine 2 watch a movie?

Me: It's a date. You looking forward to him been gone for the weekend?

When she doesn't answer right away, and when the three flashing dots don't appear to show me she's writing back, I start to panic. It's just confirmation that it is her dad hurting her. Otherwise she'd answer simply instead of taking so long. I'm about to dial her number after a few more minutes of silence, until my message alerts goes off.

Kayla: Not really. I hate it when he's away. I don't like being on my own in the house.

Me: Well, now you never have to be.

Kayla: Promise?

Me: Pinky promise.

Kayla: LOL Pinky promise LOL I'm off to bed. Are you still meeting me at the corner shop in the morning to walk to school?

Me: Yes, I'll meet you there at 8.15. Night, Baby, and make sure you dream of me ;)

Kayla: Always ;) Night xx

I set my alarm with a grin on my face. Knowing she's going to be dreaming about me makes me hard as fuck. God, the girl is beyond fucking sexy. I'm not even going to mention her rubbing herself off at the hotel on my leg. Fuck, that shit was hot.

Re-reading the messages again, I'm surprised she's not happy about her dad going away. It just makes it that more and more confusing. She confuses me. Why wouldn't she tell me who was hurting her, why is she protecting them? I just don't get it, it's not like she has siblings she could get separated from and she's old enough to move in by herself. There has to be more to it. The feeling I had the first day I saw those bruises on her wrists comes back and I know, deep down, something is brewing and it's only going to get worse before it gets better.

Although I'll see her tomorrow, I plan on waiting until Tuesday to get her to talk to me. I need her to know she can trust me no matter what and trust that I'll do everything in my power to help her. She shouldn't have to live with this. She shouldn't have to suffer anymore than she already has.

I just hope my girl is strong enough to withhold the interrogation she's going to get on Tuesday, because there is no way I'm going to take 'no' for an answer.

SEVENTEEN

KAYLA

Yesterday with Myles didn't feel right, he seemed off, out of sorts and it's had me worried ever since if he regrets what we did at the weekend.

Well, what I did.

I don't want him to regret me, or for him to leave me. Our friendship means more to me than my own freedom from my mother. I'm not going to be able to cope with losing him.

He was so quiet, so withdrawn and distant yesterday I had a hard time not bursting into tears. I just wanted to beg and plead with him to tell me what I had done.

I love him.

I love him so much that yesterday has scared me more than anything I've ever experienced. I've been going over and over the possibilities of what I could have possibly done, but keep coming up short.

The door knocks startling me and I look at the clock. He's early. We cancelled getting the pictures done today because he got them done yesterday on his free period. I had science so I let him take my phone with him. He's picking them up today and said he'd be by at five after he got showered and changed. It's only four.

Opening the door, I'm surprised to find Maverick on the other side.

"Um, hey," I whisper, surprised to find him here, and if I'm honest, I'm nervous. Has something happened to Myles? Has he sent Maverick to come and dump me?

"Hey, can I come in? I need to talk to you," he says softly and I shake the horrid thoughts from my mind. I don't even hesitate opening the door, knowing Maverick would never hurt me.

"Is everything okay?" I ask, gesturing him to take a seat. I take the chair, curling my feet under me.

"I was hoping you could tell me," he says evasively, looking at me with sad eyes. Maverick is bigger built than the rest of the Carter boys; he's also the rugged one and the only one that has tattoos.

"I'm sorry. I'm confused," I tell him quietly, feeling my nerves pick up.

"Has Myles ever spoken to you about our past?"

"Yeah, some if it," I answer, still feeling confused. My hands begin to shake, so I place them under my legs to try and keep them still.

"Well, whatever he said is true, but there's more. Our dad, he was sick, I mean really sick. He didn't care what happened to us, whether we were fed or clothed. He didn't care when he hurt us or if people hurt us, hell, he'd watch with his sick fascination.

"Our mom was just as bad. The boys were too young to remember and I think Mason just blocked it out. I'm not sure. But I remember everything. I'd remember the feel of the fag's she'd stumped out on me, the bite of her nails digging into my skin, and the feel of high heels kicking into my ribs," he finishes calmly, his eyes distant like they're stuck in the memory.

What he said has hit so close to home. The way my mom would burn me on purpose with an iron when I wouldn't get the creases out of her clothes, or when she'd kick me after coming home drunk from a night out with her friends. It was never ending and I don't think I'll ever forget the pain in those memories.

"I...I don't know what to say," I tell him honestly, confused as to why he's telling me all this. A few tears fall free my eyes and I free my hands to swipe them away.

"You don't need to say anything. I just need you to know that I know what it's like. I know what it feels like to have the one person that should protect you, love you unconditionally, and supposed to be your hero, hurt you."

"He told you," I whisper, feeling hurt.

"Don't be mad at him. I overheard him talking to our granddad, worried sick. I didn't hear everything, but I heard the worry, the heartbreak in that kid's voice over you. I know it's killing him not being able to protect you, and even worse not knowing who is actually hurting."

"No one's..."

"Don't lie," he demands taking me off guard. I'm surprised by his bluntness, at how rough his voice is.

"I'm sorry."

"Don't be. When Myles comes round in a bit you need to talk to him. Don't protect the person who is hurting you because if the roles were reversed they'd kick you in front of a bus. You don't owe your dad anything, so talk to Myles. You're old enough to move out, you can come stay with us, whatever you need, but you need to know you've got choices," he tells me softly and I snap my head to his, looking him in the eye.

"What? My dad isn't the one hurting me," I yelp, panic in my voice. Oh, God, they think my dad is the one hurting me. What if they go to the police and accuse him of it? He'd never forgive me, and then he'd find out that someone was hurting me.

This is such a mess.

"I know. I just needed to confirm that it's your crazy bitch of a mom. Tell him. And don't go near her. If she bothers you, or shows up, call me, or Myles. We won't let her hurt you, but Myles needs to know."

"But you said... How did you? I don't understand," I say shocked, my mind jumbled with everything that was just said.

"I knew your dad wouldn't hurt you. He has come into the bar a few times with business associates and he has praised you non-stop. But Myles thinks he has it figured out because of you living with your dad. You need to put him right, and out of his misery. You also need to help us help you so that she can't hurt you anymore and if you ever decide that you want to go to the police then we'll be here to support you."

"Why are you doing this for me?" I whisper, tears falling from my eyes.

"Because we're your family," he states, and I look at him just as a sob escapes. He gets up and kneels down in front of the chair, his hands resting on my bent knees. "Don't cry. You're not alone and no one will understand more than us about what you're going through."

"Telling someone will make it real, will make the years I suffered all the more painful," I whisper.

"It could also set you free, make you stronger," he tells me softly.

"When I was raped, I walked through the house and sobbed to her, begging her to make the pain stop, but you know all she did? She shoved me away like I was filth, telling me to go get a shower and to stop being dramatic," I sob. "All I wanted was for her to love me, to hold me, and it was in that moment I knew I was everything she thought of me, but then I came back and Myles changed that. He makes me feel clean, worthy and I don't want that taken away by telling him."

Maverick's jaw is clenched, his hands tightening on my legs and I know he's reining in his anger.

"He'll never see you any different. Do you see him differently because of his upbringing?"

"What? No! I'd never..."

"Exactly. Have more faith in him, Kayla. You'll be surprised at the lengths he'll go to to protect you."

"I can't lose him," I sob and Maverick pulls me into his arms, and into his lap as he moves to position himself against the sofa.

"You're not going to lose him, but if you keep crying you might lose your brother-in-law. He's due any minute now isn't he? If he finds us like this he's going to string up my balls for making you cry. Or worse, he'll get Max and gang up on me, and the two together I can't handle."

I chuckle wondering what they've done to him in the past for him to be worried about them teaming up, but I keep my mouth shut and pull away.

"Thank you," I tell him, wishing he knew how much it means to me that he came to talk to me. I know it's because he doesn't want to see his brother hurt, or worse, involved, but for him to come to me and understand is refreshing.

"I didn't do anything, Kayla. You just needed someone who understood everything you're going through and to tell you everything will be okay."

"You did more than you'll ever know," I tell him, giving him a small smile. He gives me a smile back and lifts me up, literally, until he's standing so that I'm placed in front of him.

Shit, he's strong.

"I best be going before he comes and punches me for thinking I'm hitting on his girl."

His girl!

"He wouldn't... I'm not..." I stutter, blushing.

"You're his *beginning, middle,* and *end,* Kayla. Don't ever doubt that," he winks before walking over to the door.

I don't know what to say so I don't say anything; I just nod my head, feeling flabbergasted.

"See you soon," he tells me before quietly leaving the house, my mind still reeling over what he said.

"See you soon," I whisper, knowing he's long gone to even hear me.

I don't know how long I'm standing there staring at the locked door for, but when a loud knock comes, I nearly fall over it startles me that much. I smile shaking my head at how ridiculous I am. I get so lost in my own thoughts sometimes that time escapes me. It's always been the same. I guess it's my mind's way of protecting itself.

I walk over and open the door and give Myles a small smile when I see it's him. He returns my smile with his own and butterflies erupt in my belly.

He looks good today. He's wearing a pair of ratted jeans, with his white t-shirt, and his Vans. I hate that he can wear the simplest of things and still look so freaking good.

"Hey, you okay?" Myles speaks, and then I notice he's waving his hand in front of my face. I blink, gaining back focus and chuckle.

"Sorry, I spaced out."

"Checking me out?" he chuckles and I blush knowing he's caught me.

"Shut up. Have you eaten? I have some leftover meatballs in the fridge."

"I'm good, babe. Is your dad here?" he asks, his teeth gritted together. Now I know what is going through his head, I'm picking up his distaste for my dad. It also explains the million and one questions he asked about him over the weekend.

"No, he's out for the night, remember? You said you were staying over," I remind him, feeling panicked that this has nothing to do with what Maverick brought up earlier. Maybe he really does want me alone so he can break up with me nicely. Is there even a nice way to break someone's heart?

"Oh shit, yeah. Sorry. Yeah, I'm still sleeping over," he smiles, but it doesn't reach his eyes. When he reaches for my hands, I pull them away at the last second.

His face lifts to mine, hurt and confusion written across his face.

"What is going on? Are you okay with me? Have I done something? You've been really off with me."

"WOW! Slow down. Nothing is going on, I promise. I just need to talk to you about something. It's about Thursday and the marks on your body," he says quietly, not meeting my eyes.

"It is?" I ask, half relieved, but half panicked that I'm going to have to talk to him about it.

"Um...why do you seem so pleased about that?" he asks.

"I thought you were breaking up with me," I admit sheepishly, feeling my face heat.

"Never," he says, a frown lining his face.

"Good," I smile. "Do you want to go upstairs and talk? I'd feel more comfortable there." My bedroom is my safe haven. I swear, whenever I'm ill, or feeling lonely or whatever, I like to be in my room, with my own personal surroundings, and my bed. My dad tried for months to get me to go out more, or to sit downstairs, but then we moved and he stopped trying when he had to work so much. Not that I'd have listened to him. I love my room.

We walk up the stairs after I grab us a can of Coke, and take a seat on my bed, pulling the pillows behind us.

"Sooo..." I begin when he doesn't speak.

"I know it's your dad. I don't want to push you, I don't want to force you and I certainly don't want you to feel suffocated, but I want you to think about going to the police, or social services."

"I'm eighteen, Myles. What can social services really do for me?" I ask, because I've thought about it myself. If only in fantasies, or in my dreams, but the thought has lingered nonetheless.

"He's been hurting you for a while, Kayla. Did it start when he got custody of you?" he asks softly, his fingers running down my hair.

"It's not my dad, Myles." I pause before continuing. "It's my mom."

"What? You're fucking mother? She... She's the one that's been hurting you? Why the fuck did I not see this before?" He growls before getting up off the bed and pacing the floor in front of me. I shovel down so I'm sitting on the edge and watch him with wide eyes. Maverick was right. He's worried and he's been scared over it all, and it's my entire fault.

My eyes water, and as much as I want to hide them from him, I can't seem to take my eyes away from him, watching his muscles tense, his strong, lean legs pace and his handsome face flicker before me with different emotions.

"Please stop," I whisper, my throat choked up.

"I should have known that bitch had something to do with this. When you were attacked, Joan and my granddad could never understand why your mother went to such lengths to stop you from testifying, why your so called mother would let you take what happened like a punishment. They bullied you," he rants and I feel like my heart has stopped beating.

"Please stop talking," I whisper, my hands and body now shaking. I can't think about that, I can't go back to that place, to that time. It was horrendous, and no matter how much time I spent in therapy, I'll never be able to move on from the taunts, the bullies, name calling, or the pranks they so cruelly played on me.

"Did you know I beat up a couple of kids from your year? Yeah," he nods, his temper rising. "My granddad thought they mixed Max and I up, that it was Max getting into the fights. It was me. I hated watching you walk down those halls enduring everything they did. And all along your fucking mother was the cause of it all. She'd been hurting you long before then hadn't she?" he asks, finally looking at me, and that's when the blood drains from his face when he takes me in. I'm shaking like a leaf sitting on the edge of my bed, tears streaming down my face. "I'm so fucking sorry. Shit, Kayla, I... I didn't mean to. Fuck!"

He grabs me from under my arms and lifts me in the air, sitting me down on his lap. I cuddle into him, my body cold from the shaking. When I feel the fleece throw-over, thrown over me, I cuddle up to him tighter.

His breathing is hard and ragged, and I know he's trying to rein his temper in for me, and I love him for it. Maverick warned me he was going crazy over this; it was only a matter of time before he exploded over it too.

"She started hurting me when my dad took me out of the all girls' boarding school. Katherine, who looked after me the majority of my life, died when I was thirteen. She was everything to me and showed me love that my parents never. When my father told me I'd be moving home, back with them, and attending a public school, I'd been so thrilled. I loved my parents. Well, I guess I loved the idea of them.

"My dad and I had a good relationship. He'd come see me every weekend and a few times in the week when he was passing through, but most of the time our visits were scheduled in the holidays. My mother was always distant. I've never really had a relationship with her, but at thirteen years old, I guess I wanted one. Then I came home and she was just so formal," I tell him, remembering sitting down at the large oak table, the smell of the food the cooks were busy making in the kitchen and then stilled conversation at the table. It was nothing like I had experienced with Katherine. She'd always make me laugh, talk about our days and make fun of stupid commercials. I even tried to make one up at the table with my parents to break the ice, but my mom looked at me with a horrified expression, telling my father they didn't pay thousands of pounds a month for me to be raised like that.

"You okay?" Myles asks when I get too lost in thought.

"Yeah," I croak, then cough. "Anyway, the weekend after I was back, my dad had to leave again for work. I guess that's when it all started," I tell him, not wanting to dive into it anymore. He knows all he needs to know and that's as far as I'm willing to go, for tonight anyway.

"Does your dad know? He has to have seen the bruises," he tells me, his fingers still running through my hair, making me sleepy.

"If he does he acts well at hiding it. It's laughable how you and Maverick guessed so quickly about what I'm going through, but my own father, who I live with, doesn't know a thing," I laugh, but sob at the same time, my throat hoarse, and dry.

"Maverick?" he asks confused, a hint of hurt laced in his voice.

"Oh, um...Well, he came over before you turned up. He wanted to talk to me. He told me some things, and the way he said it made me realise a few things. Please don't be mad at him. He loves you; he was just worried about you. I guess with my situation hitting so close to home with you all, he was worried how it would affect you. I dunno," I shrug; feeling embarrassed all of a sudden.

"He didn't tell me. Did he upset you?" he whispers.

"No, God, no. He honestly just wanted to talk to me before you did. He wanted to know my reaction and explain that me not talking to you was hurting you. I'm not ready to tell you everything, I don't know if I'll ever be, but I don't want you to worry over me because of it."

"I'll always worry about you," he tells me, leaning in to kiss my head. "Haven't you realised yet? No matter what is ever going on I'll always worry about you. Because you, Kayla Martin, are everything to me."

EIGHTEEN

KAYLA

Another week at school has flown by. I can't believe how quickly it's gone. I'll be finished soon, and will be able to start looking for colleges, work, just something to get me out of that house, away from *her*.

This is the first Saturday I've arrived at the Salvation food bank feeling happy. After Tuesday I thought Myles would treat me differently, look at me differently, but he hasn't. It's been refreshing.

"Morning, Joan," I sing happily when I walk in carrying one of the food boxes from outside.

"Well, aren't you a sight, child. If I wasn't mistaken I'd say you were in love," she teases, winking at me.

I laugh. I love how easy going Joan is. Even the volunteers half her age aren't as laid back as she is. It's one of the reasons I love helping her out.

When I don't say anything she stops what she's doing with her chart. She gives me a once over before grinning mischievously at me.

"If only we could get our Max all loved up," she grins evilly. "I knew my Myles would, and I know for a fact I couldn't have picked anyone better for that boy, but

Max, now Max I'm going to have fun with," she chuckles.

"I don't think Max is the settling down type," I tell her, not wanting to crush her hopes, but I also don't want her to get her hopes up.

"Oh, Kayla, you have a lot to learn. That boy is going to get what's coming to him sooner or later. We had to drive down to the station last night because he got caught trespassing and vandalising someone's barn."

I gasp, not believing Max would do such a thing. "Oh my goodness, why would he do that?"

"That boy will never learn. Even with a firm talking to from his Gramps and I, did he still sit there and have that cocky, lazy smirk on his face. Anyway, it got me thinking what punishment would be good enough and then I realised falling in love," she sings sweetly, but her grin looks anything but.

"I don't think that's going to work, Joan. He loves a lot of girls," I choke out, feeling awkward.

"Sit back and watch, dear, all will be revealed, real soon," she laughs, and then walks out. I stare at the open door where she left not sure whether to feel sorry for Max or Joan.

"Hi, lady," a sweet voice says from behind me.

I turn around not seeing anyone, but then I feel someone tugging on my top, so I look down. A cute girl, around four or five years old is standing in front of me. She looks so freaking adorable. Her clothes aren't the cleanest, and they look like they're two sizes too small, but her chubby cheeks, blonde wavy her, and her big blue eyes are what stand out.

"Hello, pretty girl," I greet, kneeling down.

"My mommy is gwetting t'us some food. Do woo need food too?" she asks sweetly.

"Everyone needs food, Sweetie. Want to go see what toys and girly clothes we can find if your mommy says it's okay?" I ask, not wanting to overstep anything.

She nods her head excitedly, grabbing my hand and dragging me out of the side door, into the main hall. This is where we ask the people who come in to wait, have a cup of tea and biscuits while we get their bags ready.

"Mommy, dis wady sways I can gwet some new twoys and cwose. Can I?" she asks sweetly, looking up at a middle aged woman. She's dressed in trousers that are tearing at the bottom from being too long for her, and has a t-shirt that has faded from the amount of times it's been through the washer, but even with that she is still beautiful, just like her daughter.

"Oh, Pippa, I don't think…"

"If it's okay with you I can get her some bags done up of clothes while she picks out a few toys she likes. We had someone bring in a big order of donations, so it's fine."

She smiles at me warmly and I can tell this means something to her. She's obviously a single mom, having trouble paying the bills, keeping a roof over their heads and keeping a growing child fed and clothed. I've seen so many families like this since starting and it breaks my heart.

"If you're sure? Dean, do you want to go with your sister?" she asks a boy around eight or nine years old. He's sitting on one of the chairs chewing a cookie, looking like he'd rather be anywhere than here. He shakes his head no and his mother turns back to her little girl and smiles.

"Be good, and listen to this nice lady when she tells you what to do, okay?"

"T'way, Mommy," she smiles widely, before grabbing my hand again. I show her the way through to the back, where we don't usually let anyone other than staff come in and show her the toys. She squeals loudly talking about Santa Clause coming early while looking at everything like she only has seconds before moving onto the next item she sees.

I giggle watching her for a few seconds before moving over to the clothes. I grab the box of girls dresses and from what I guessed of her age I start rummaging through, picking a few dresses and folding them up on the table. I do the same with the trousers, tops, and being lucky, I find a nice warm coat the right size for her. I smile when I find enough things to tide her over, and then notice the boys box labelled eight to nine. Not knowing the boys size I still walk over and make another pile just for him.

When I'm done I fold them all into the big shopper bags that we have especially for the clothes and walk over to Pippa to find her playing with a soft rag doll. It's a pretty little thing, and even I had to admire it when I saw it a few weeks ago. Apparently one of the ladies who volunteers for the church makes them. They are beautiful.

"Do you like her?" I ask, sitting down next to her, quietly putting the toys she's thrown out back.

"I wove it. I want it, pwease?"

"You may. Would you like some books and jigsaw puzzles too?"

She nods her head yes, but her attention is focused on her doll. I smile and move over to the end of the isle where I noticed a few boys stuff that was given in second-hand. When I notice an old Nintendo Game boy, I snatch it up along with the games brought in with it, and bag them up for the boy. I'm just praying he doesn't already have one.

When we're done I'm carrying out two shopping bags filled with clothes and a pair of shoes for each kid, a plastic bag with a book and jigsaw for Pippa, who hasn't let go of her doll and another shopping bag with a few bits of women's clothing that I guessed was their mom's size. They've all got tags still on them, so I'm hoping it won't offend her.

When we walk out her mother's eyes bug out and she rushes over to us.

"Oh my God, we can't possibly take all this," she rushes out.

"It's fine. We need to get it cleared before our new donation boxes come through. I hope you don't mind, but I picked up some outfits for both the kids. I guessed their sizes, so if they don't fit, just bring it back and I'll find something new. We also had some women's clothes donated a few weeks back. They've all still got their tags on. I was hoping that they might be some use to you, if that's okay?" I blush, hating this part of the job. I feel like we're sticking our noses up at them when we're not. We just want to make them feel welcome, and know that we only want to help make their home life easier.

The woman's eyes well up and she nods her head as the first tear falls free. "Thank you. Thank you so much," she chokes out, taking the bags from my hand. I quickly grab the Game Boy, I left on the top in a separate carrier bag to give to the boy.

"Hi, I'm Kayla. I got you this. I weren't sure if you already had one," I tell him quietly, as I hand him the bag. He looks bored when I first hand it over, until he looks inside and his eyes bug out like his mom's did earlier, then his face lights up like Christmas lights. It's times like this that I love volunteering here. Nothing can get much better than this.

"No way! Mom, look at this?" he shouts grinning, before rushing over to his mom to show her his new game. My chest aches watching them, and feel my eyes fill with tears watching the look of pure happiness on their faces. It's nice how little things like a second-hand Game Boy can please a boy.

Most of the kids I grew up with weren't happy unless they had top of the art gadgets, or handbags. Yes, handbags at ten years old. It's like the newer the generation, the earlier they think they're adults. It's alarming.

Needing to finish unpacking the food orders, I turn to walk around, when a hard body jolts me forward, tiny arms going around my legs. I smile big when I turn around to find Pippa smiling.

"Tank you," she smiles real big.

"My pleasure, Sweetie." Giving her a hug, she wraps her tiny arms around my neck and squeezes making me laugh. She's so freaking cute.

She gives me a peck on the cheek before running back off to her mom, who is waiting by the door holding her hand out for her. I watch them leave with a smile on my face before turning around to find Lake watching me.

"Oh hey, didn't know you were in today. You been hiding?" I smile.

"I was in the back stacking some shelves. That was real sweet what you did for that family," she says quietly.

"It's what we do." I shrug her words away, knowing any one of us today would have done the same. Well, maybe not everyone. There are a bunch of girls who volunteer who do nothing but take the piss out of people coming in needing help. It's people like them that stop us helping more people. It's the same with charity shops. People turn their noses up at the idea of going in and selecting items, but then they have no problem buying second hand items off Facebook. It's the same and if anything charity shops clean the clothes beforehand, well, at least we do.

"Not everyone here would do what you just did, Kayla. Take a compliment," she winks and walks with me to storage room.

"Joan wants me in here with you. One of the girls is getting on my nerves and I think Joan knows I'm seconds away from snapping."

I'm surprised she has said so much to me. Even when we went out for lunch the once she hardly spoke to me about anything. I'm a shy, quiet person, so keeping conversation was really hard. I also find myself feeling confident around her.

"What have they done this time?" I ask, not needing to ask what bunch of girls has said stuff. It's the same group of girls I mentioned who make people feel uncomfortable earlier. I don't know why they let them still volunteer.

"The same. Not knowing when to keep their mouths shut," she shrugs, as she starts emptying a box.

"I don't know why no one has said anything to them by now. They've been like this for as long as I've known them."

"It's because some of their parents donate big to the church. I already made a complaint about them. I can't afford to get into trouble by saying something back to them."

"Is that why you haven't said anything back to them when they've been talking shit to you?" I ask bluntly.

"Yeah," she sighs. "If it was a few years ago, I'd be all up in their faces, yelling to demand what their problem was, but I suppose it's my punishment," she says, the end part at a near whisper that I barely hear her.

Opening my mouth to question her further, I'm stopped short when Myles walks in looking handsome as ever.

"Hello," I grin, surprised to see him here. "What are you doing here?"

I rush over to him and give him a kiss, then before I realise it I'm blushing, forgetting we have an audience. I look shyly at Lake, who just grins and shakes her head.

"Go, I got this covered," she says before I can speak.

"Well, that saves me asking," Myles chuckles. "I was wondering if you'd come out with me."

"Like a date?" I ask scrunching my nose up.

"Cute," he mutters, confusing me. "Yes, a date. Mason needs me to clean out the storage unit at work, so I thought I'd come take you out now."

"Okay then. Let me just check with Joan."

"Already asked her. She didn't even let me get my words out before she said make sure you spoil her," he grins.

I grin back. That sounds like Joan. Then I remember our conversation earlier and open my mouth to tell Myles to warn Max, but then close it. I think seeing what she has in store for Max will be much more exciting if he doesn't see it coming.

*** *** *** *** *** ***

"Where we going?" I ask once we get out the taxi.

"We are going to a roller disco. They have an over eighteen one here at the leisure centre," he tells me as he points behind me.

Oh my God. He has to be joking. Please tell me he's joking.

"Please tell me you're joking?" I ask wide eyed, fearing for the people's lives who I'm about to take.

"Nope," he grins, and I can't help but melt at the sight. He's so freaking hot when he grins like that. I think I've said this a few times before. Or maybe every time he grins.

"Do we have it rented out for ourselves? Do people know you're going to let me loose on there?"

"You can't be that bad," he laughs, looking at my deer caught in headlights expression.

"No! No because I'm worse than bad, I'm freaking terrible. I'm like Bambie learning to walk when I put on skates. I tried it once when I was thirteen. I took out the two front teeth off a girl my age, and nearly broke a little boys arm skating over it. Then they kicked me out after I skated into the DJ box and smashed his system to the ground. This is a disaster," I yell, not caring I'm getting people's attention.

Instead of taking me seriously, he laughs. He laughs so hard that his face turns bright red, to the point he looks like he got his face painted.

"Don't laugh," I hiss, stomping my foot, but it just causes him to laugh harder.

"This is just… I wish I brought Max now," he says through laughter, moving to take out his phone.

"Don't you dare! I'm not going in there if you call him," I tell him, then groan when I realise I just told him I'd be going in there.

Shit!

I really wasn't joking about the destruction I caused when I came to one of these the last time. I swear, I was only thirteen, but everyone around me looked like professional freaking dancers, like they had been doing it for years and years. They definitely didn't look how I looked at only thirteen years. It drove me nuts.

"I won't. Come on; let's go pay for our ticket. I've booked us some skate hire too," he laughs.

"You should have got Life Insurance while you were at it," I mutter, and he laughs in return, guiding me to the small line waiting to enter.

By the time we've paid and got our skates on I'm shaking like a leaf, and ready to bolt. *I can't do this!* I tell myself everything will be okay, but then we enter and I freak out.

"Oh my God, they are professionals. Look at him skating backwards, and I'm not going to go there with that bloke over there. I can't do this. This must be an advanced session or something. We're in the wrong place," I ramble. I get so lost trying to talk him out of taking me that I don't feel him sliding me across the wide open hall. The place is where they must play ball games and stuff. It's like a huge school gym.

Music is blaring through the speakers around the hall and I can barely hear what Myles is saying.

"What?" I shout.

"Just hold on to me and you'll be fine," he grins, and I look at him confused. Does he seriously believe I'll be vertical at any point during our time here? I should have made it clear I'll be on the floor, horizontal, the whole time.

I wobble when he moves me forward, his arm no longer around my waist to keep me up and I end up failing to keep upright. I try to grab onto Myles so we don't fall at the same time. He tries to grab a hold of me tighter, but I end up smacking him in the mouth and taking him to the floor with me. We land with a loud grunt, Myles lying on top of me. We haven't even made it to the group of skaters, skating around in a circle, clockwise.

"Shit, girl. As much as I love this position we are in right now, now isn't the time," he smirks. I just roll my eyes and push him away. My face flames beet red when I notice a bunch of lads and girls staring our way. Some are laughing outright, and some are trying to hide their amusement.

They haven't seen anything yet.

"Why don't I just walk while you skate?" I ask hopeful.

"Not allowed, babe, unless you're a member of staff," he grins. He's totally freaking lying. I just saw a group of girls wearing ten inch high heels. I playfully go to punch him when he has us standing upright, but end up wobbling and falling on my ass again. At least he didn't fall with me this time.

Jesus, my ass is going to be bruised.

He holds his hand out to help me up and I gratefully take it. When I'm up, I shove my hair out of my face and puff out a breath.

Right, we can do this. Just one time around the circle, and we can go, I chant to myself, hoping one circle will be enough to make Myles happy. Let's face it, we've been here ten minutes already and haven't even made it *to* the circle.

"Don't move a second," he shouts near my ear over the music. I listen to what he says, I really do, but I'm on freaking skates for Christ's sakes. They have round wheels. I end up rolling a little, but thankfully he's ready for it and places his hands around my waist. I silently thank him, not caring that he can't hear me.

When he's behind me he presses his body against my back, his hands firmly on my waist. He kicks my feet together gently, not enough to make me topple, then leans in again.

"Keep your feet still, don't lift them or try to move. I'm going to skate and you're going to...roll with it," He chuckles, the sound deep and husky in my ear.

He starts to move and I squeal, and with a mind of their own my feet start to separate, sliding away from each other.

Like I said. Bambie!

"I can't do this," I whine, and curse myself for becoming that girl. You know, the type that whines over the most stupidest things.

"Come on, you can do it. Let's try it this way," he tells me before skating effortlessly in front of me. He skids to a halt and takes my hands and starts skating backwards. "Keep your feet together," he shouts and I concentrate hard on keeping my feet together with my hands gripped firmly in his.

We finally make it to the circle and I squeal with happiness and that's when the first incident happens. I end up flying forward, but to catch my balance I use Myles' hands to pull myself up, the same time he does the same thing, which causes me to fly backwards. I roll backwards, my arms flailing everywhere before landing into a hard body. Before I know it, I've caused a pile up in the circle.

Myles skates over to me grinning ear to ear before helping me up from the floor. I look behind me to apologise, but gasp when I see the lad I bumped into hold his dangly arm grunting in pain. I look to Myles, horrified, but he just shakes his head, and turns away looking amused.

Then I look to the chaos around the lad I hit and feel like crying. A girl not far behind has a nose bleed, another one is clutching her red fingers for dear life and another lad is rubbing frantically at his leg, while his head has an egg shaped lump on it.

"We need to go," I tell him before trying to skate off, but end up falling on my knees. Staff members come rushing over to the injured and my face flames in embarrassment. When one asks what happened the one with what I think is a broken arm turns to me with a thunderous expression.

Oh, shite.

I rip my skates off, not bothering to pick them up before running out of the hall. I'm so freaking embarrassed.

Myles rushes out behind me on his skates, his face full of amusement. He's carrying my skates and I'm glad he picked them up when I remember that I can't get my shoes back without them.

He hands the guys our skates and we wait for him to bring back our shoes.

"So, do you want to talk about..." Myles starts, but I hold my hand up to stop him.

"Not now. Not now," I warn.

It's quiet for a couple of seconds until I hear him laughing all over again, his hands on his knees bent over and gasping for air.

"Oh my God, that was... that was. How could you be that bad at skating?" he asks amused.

"I just am, okay? Can we not talk about it? I want to forget the whole ordeal," I moan, feeling my face heat up when a couple come out of the hall and glare at me. "Oh God, they're cancelling the rest of the session aren't they?"

When more people come walking out with grumpy faces I can tell I must have caused some serious injuries in there. I look to Myles with wide eyes, but he just laughs handing me my shoes. Before anyone can jump me or start spouting nasty words off at me, I slide them on and rush out of the building, sighing when the cool air hits my hot face.

"Come on. It was funny. You should have seen your face. I have a fat lip, a guy has a broken arm and I'm not even sure what the other injuries were. I had tears blocking my vision," he laughs, wiping those imaginary tears away.

"Funny," I snap, then notice a cinema over the road and an idea forms in my head. My favourite author has just released another film this week and I'm just betting it's not something Myles usually watches. "Come on, we're going there."

He looks over to the cinema and smiles. "Babe, there isn't anything good on. There's only some crappy chick flick and some cartoon crap."

"But, babe, we're seeing that chick flick," I tell him sweetly. He just looks at me shocked before grinning. He then takes the few steps to stand directly in front of me and bends down and lifts me over his shoulder. I half squeal and half laugh when he rushes over the road with me still over his shoulder.

"It's like a hideout while the skater crews calm their skates down," he shouts over the traffic and my laughter.

Even with nearly killing a room full of people on skates, he still makes me laugh. Only Myles could do that to me and I'm thankful every day I have him in my life.

NINETEEN

MYLES

Kayla and I walk out of the cinema hand in hand, both comfortable with our own thoughts. When she said she couldn't skate I didn't believe her. Charlie had called me telling me to get her out of her comfort zone and that skating is one thing she's always wanted to do. I have a feeling Charlie is playing tricks on me and knew exactly what she was doing when she called me.

We walk over to the deserted taxi rank to wait for a taxi and I'm surprised she hasn't mentioned the movie. Usually when we've watched something new she starts telling me everything like I wasn't right there next to her. Lately she's come out of herself more. I've also noticed her attitude is more confident since we found the bruises on her last week. She's sassier, braver; it's a real change in her and one I think she needed.

"So, shall I address the elephant in the room, or street," Kayla mentions and I look down to her confused.

"Huh?" I say wondering if I was spaced out enough to miss some of the conversation. I do that a lot when I'm thinking of her. Spacing out that is.

"Oh, come on," she laughs pushing at my shoulder. "I saw, Myles. I'm not blind."

"I didn't say you were blind and I have no idea what the hell you're going on about."

"The tears; you totally cried."

Fuck! Fuck! Fuck!

I thought I hid that well. How can she tease me? That would make someone suffering with emotional disorder cry.

"I had dust in my eye," I lie, not looking at her. She laughs. The little minx laughs. I look down at her and laugh with her. I'm totally busted. "Okay, okay, but so did you, so you can't tease me."

"I totally can," she giggles. "You said before it started that films like this are so unreal it would make Essex girls look real."

"Let's not get into that right now, okay. Let's just take you home, enjoy the rest of our Saturday with pizza and a movie," I tell her just as my phone starts ringing.

I answer it with a 'hello' when Kayla's starts ringing too.

"Hi, Denny…" she answers, but her conversation is drowned out by the annoying twit in my ear.

"Dude, you have to come right now. Hope said 'ma ma'," Max squeals like a girl.

I grin big; though I feel sad I missed it. That girl is just something else, and cute doesn't even begin to describe her. She's looking more like her dad every day, the poor sod, but thankfully at the moment she still has her mother's looks.

I look to Kayla who is staring at me, smiling. I know what she's going to ask before she even speaks. "We'll be there in ten," I tell him before cutting him off. A taxi pulls up the same time Kayla says her goodbyes. We give him Denny's address and sit back.

"I can't believe she said ma ma," Kayla coos.

"She probably just had wind," I laugh.

"No, she's seven months now, she'll be talking more and more," she smiles.

"True, when she first walks they'll be throwing a party. When she first smiled it was to Max and we never heard the end of that shit. Took her another day before she did it again."

"He really loves her doesn't he?"

"Yeah, we've always wanted a sister, but having a niece is so much better. She's going to be spoiled rotten."

We pull up to the house and we barely pay the taxi driver and get out when Max is running down the driveway with Hope in his arms.

"Say ma ma," he coos, talking like an idiot.

Hope giggles, smacking his mouth with her tiny chubby fist before repeating his words.

"Ma maaaa."

"Oh my God, aren't you a clever girl. Yes you are, aren't you," Kayla says and I have to chuckle. I don't know why I'm laughing; I talk to her the same way. I can't help it. Plus, Hope loves it when we do. I think she knows we're all off our rockers.

Hope repeats it again, making it into a game and loving the attention she's getting.

"You're going to be the cleverest girl in the world. Aren't you, Hope? 'Cause, you're a Carter aren't you? Yes you are, yes you are," Max starts and leads us back to Denny's.

"We're ordering pizza for dinner, you want in? We thought we'd wait for you before we ordered anything," Mason says as we walk in.

"Yeah, I'm in. We were having pizza anyway," I tell him as I take a seat.

Kayla is now holding Hope in her arms, so when she comes to stand next to my chair I pull her down to my lap, bringing Hope with her.

"Who's your favourite uncle, Kid?" I ask, lightly running my finger down her soft cheek. She's so freaking cute.

She rambles some 'goo, goo, ga ga' back and I smile. "I know, Kid. I love you too."

Kayla chuckles and brings her lips to Hope's neck and blows raspberries. Hope laughs loudly, her fist clinging to Kayla's hair. I try to untangle them, but it causes Hope to hold on tighter.

"Hey, princess, can you let go of my girl's hair?" I ask, still trying to pry her hands away. I hear Kayla's breath deepen for a second before she lets it out. Every time I've called her my girl she's had the same reaction. It's like she doesn't believe it, and whenever she hears it, it's like a shock. I'm just going to have to work harder for her to realise that she is, and she always will be my girl.

Hope finally lets go of Kayla's hair, but only so she can reach her arms out to me, her body flying towards me. I laugh and grab her from Kayla who doesn't move from my lap. I tickle Hope under her arms and watch as she throws herself backwards, nearly flying off the chair altogether.

"So, what have you two done today?" Denny asks and before I can think of the consequences I open my big mouth.

"Kayla took out a whole hall full of skaters by just being there," I laugh and they all look at me smiling.

"What happened?" Mason laughs.

"She literally caused a huge pile up that you'd see on the news, but with skaters. Oh my God, this one dude had a broken arm, and the rest were all bloodied and injured. She was so freaking cute. She said she couldn't skate, that she'd caused accidents before, but I didn't believe it. Look at this video I got before she stormed out," I tell them, then lift up reaching for my phone. Hope tries to make a grab for it the same time Kayla does.

"No, no, no! You didn't. You can't show them that," she squeals horrified. She tries to grab the phone off me, but I lift it up out of her reach, laughing.

"Oh, come on, Babe, they have to see this. This shit belongs on YouTube," I laugh as I move the phone to the other side before she can grab it. She tries to tickle me into dropping the phone but it doesn't work. Hope thinks it's a game and starts smacking her fists against me whilst laughing.

The phone is ripped from my hand and I turn to see Maverick looking at the screen before laughing his head off.

"Shit. How the hell did you manage all that?" he laughs.

Mason and Max walk over and ask him to replay it. They all crack up laughing and Kayla sighs, sulking in my lap. I pull her to me, still laughing.

"Babe, it was funny," I chuckle. She doesn't say anything and it makes me laugh harder.

"Come on, how did this happen and why didn't you record it from the beginning? I'm sending it Malik," Maverick grins while tapping away on my phone.

"I can't skate. It took us ten minutes to even get me into the actual room I was that off balance. Then when Myles finally got me to move without falling over I got excited and you know the rest," she pouts not looking happy. "Just please don't post it on anything else," she pleads to me, and the look in her eyes tells me she's being serious.

"I promise, Babe," I tell her, and hope she can see the truth in my eyes. I know she's been on the receiving end of a bully's pranks, which they've recorded for their own amusement.

Her phone rings, vibrating against my lap. She scrunches her eyebrows up in that cute way that she does before grabbing it out of her bag.

"It's my dad," she mutters before answering. "Hello. I'm with Myles at Denny's, why? Oh no! I'm so sorry, Dad. No, I've not eaten. Okay. See you in a sec," she says before hanging up. "It's my dad. I forgot I have that meal tonight to meet Katie."

"Oh crap," I say forgetting all about. I know she's been worrying over it, not knowing what to expect. She's got nothing to worry about, though, Katie is a lovely woman.

"Yeah," she sighs. "He's going to pick me up in a sec, but I feel bad for forgetting. Well, I knew, but with everything that's happened this afternoon I forgot."

"That's what happens when you take a whole hall of people out," I laugh and she smacks my arm. I rub where she hit me, pretending to be hurt, but she sees right through me and rolls her eyes.

A horn beeps, and Kayla sighs, standing up. "I'll see you all another day. I've got to go. I forgot I had a meal with my dad," she says to the room before bending down and kissing Hope on the head. "Bye clever pants."

She stands back up, looking unsure, before I stand up ready to hand Hope over to Maverick, but Max is there prying her from my arms. I give him the 'what the fuck' look, but he just shrugs and starts talking to Hope.

I walk her out, but before we get to the road I grab her arm and pull her backwards against me.

"Want me to come after your meal?" I ask softly, my hands wrapping around her waist.

"Can I text you and let you know?" she asks shyly, and I smile nodding my head. I'd do anything she told me to do, so if she wants me to wait around for her to text then I will. Some might call me pussy whipped, but I call it knowing what is worth waiting for. And anything Kayla will give me will definitely be worth all the time in the world.

"Sure, Baby. Now kiss me," I whisper, but don't bother waiting for her to lean up and kiss me, instead I kiss her softly, my lips against hers.

The car horn beeps again and I grin. Kayla looks hesitant to go, but I give her an encouraging smile."You'll be fine. Call me. Anytime," I wink.

"Okay. I'll text you later," she smiles but it doesn't reach her eyes. I wish I had more time with her, more time to persuade her that everything will be okay, but then her phone rings and she growls making me chuckle.

"Go on," I laugh and she moves forward so quickly I don't have time to prepare myself before her lips are against mine in a quick, soft kiss. Before I catch my bearings, she's gone.

Turning around I head back to the house with a smile on my face. The others stop talking when I walk in, looking at me like I've grown two heads.

"What?" I ask throwing my hands up.

"You are so freaking whipped, my twin," Max groans, still holding Hope in his arms.

"Says the person who can't go ten minutes without seeing his niece? It's unhealthy, and I don't just mean for you," I tell him playfully.

"One day you're going to meet a girl, fall head over heels and wonder why you didn't do it sooner. It's going to knock you over so goddamn hard, you're going to take a while to recover," Denny sings in a teasing voice.

"Yeah, until I get my sanity back and realise what a freaking pussy whipped mistake it was. Don't you guys get bored? Not asking you Myles before you go kung fu on me, I'm asking the others. You know, having one pussy each night, every night."

"Best kind," Mason says.

"Not done the whole girlfriend thing, but must be better than random hook-ups," Maverick mutters looking at Max distastefully. "Can we not talk about it please, they're like my sisters."

I grunt in agreement and Denny leans over smacking Max up the side of his head, making Hope giggle.

"Whatever, I'm just saying, falling in love and having one girl just isn't for me. Whatever floats your boat, but I'm into the whole sharing is caring motto," Max says.

"That's how STDs are spread," Mason interrupts. "Maybe sharing is caring shouldn't be the motto you follow?"

"When is the pizza coming?" Max snaps, wanting out of the conversation, making me grin. "Wipe that grin off your face, Myles, it doesn't suit you."

"Grouchy," I tease laughing. He chucks one of Hope's building blocks at me, but I manage to catch it before it reaches my head.

TWENTY

KAYLA

ON THE DRIVE BACK HOME, my dad does nothing but moan at me for being so inconsiderate. I try to explain that I forgot, that Myles took me out and I completely lost track of everything. He just gave me a look that said he wished he could say more, but didn't want to embarrass himself, or me. I could only imagine how *that* talk would go. I'd literally cry.

We arrive outside our home before he turns to me, his expression serious and concerned.

"Are you sure you're okay with me seeing Katie. I know you love your mother, but we're separated," he sighs.

I want to snort.

Love my mother? Is he freaking serious right now? Not wanting to touch on the subject of my *mother*, I reach out, placing my hand gently on his arm.

"Dad, I'm fine. I'm really happy for you. You deserve to be happy," I smile genuinely, because hell, I never understood why he stayed with my mother for so long, or why he continues to provide for her. I don't even go to her place that much, and I plan on never stepping foot inside her house ever again.

"Good, now let's go in, she's due any second," he says, jinxing us. A red car pulls up behind my dad's as we step out, a tiny brunette with wild, curly hair getting out of the driver's side.

"Hey, darling," my dad greets, a huge smile on his face. His eyes are soft and he's looking at her in a way I've never seen him look at anyone before. A smile breaks across my face, but then I notice them both hesitantly looking my way and I start to shake.

Why are they looking at me like that?

Dad sends me a glare and nods his head gesturing to Katie beside him. She looks as shy as I am, but I'm not going to let that fool me. My mother can act better than most Hollywood actresses, so I know all too well how conniving people can be.

"I'm sorry. Hello, I'm Kayla," I introduce myself, and she smiles shyly before reaching her hand out to me. I shakily move my hands from behind my back and reach out to take hers. They're warm, soft, and it has me quickly dropping my hand and dropping my arm to my side.

She smiles, not seeming offended by my sudden move.

"Well let's go in, it's getting colder," my dad says, his hand at the bottom of her back. "Kayla is making her special seasoning steak."

I stand behind them with my mouth hanging open. Since when was I meant to be cooking? Really starting to wish I had never answered my phone and just stayed at Denny's snuggled up to Myles and eating pizza. Pizza I wouldn't have to stand around for an hour or so cooking.

I walk in after them and head straight to the kitchen. I'm grabbing all the ingredients out of the fridge and cupboards so I don't hear Katie walk in behind me, scaring the hell out of me.

"I'm sorry; I didn't mean to scare you. I just wanted to come in and help, if that's okay?"

"Oh no! That's fine, I can totally manage. I don't mind," I lie, but my words are rushed, not wanting her to think I'm being rude or anything, or that I can't handle cooking dinner. Hell, I've probably cooked more dinners than I've actually eaten.

"I don't mind, Sweetie. Your dad has just gone to answer a call, so he'll be back in a second. I like to keep busy," she says, and before I can blink she's grabbing the peeler out of the drawer and peeling the potatoes.

I nod my head and give her a small smile, then carry on with preparing the steak, before putting it to the side so that I can prepare the rest of the dinner.

"Do you like peas?" I ask quietly, and notice from the corner of my eye that she is curiously watching my every move.

"Yes. So, your father says you want to become a social worker, is that right?"

"Yes, but I'm more interested in the therapist side of it. I want to be able to help kids get through certain areas of their life," I tell her.

"That's great. My mother was a foster parent. Mostly she looked after troubled teens and she helped them through so much, so I can envy you wanting to do that for a living."

"How many teens did she foster?" I ask, curious to know all about it.

"I think she is currently on her twenty-ninth. She has a teenage boy called Daniel, who was abandoned by his parents when he was eight. He moved in with some relatives shortly after, but they died, and because of his age, it's hard to find someone to adopt him. Then there is a girl called Sally-Ann, she arrived not long ago after suffering years of abuse from her parents. It's the same case as Daniel's, with her being too old for people to adopt."

"What your mother is doing is incredible," I whisper, thinking of the girl who suffered years of abuse. I wonder if that would have been me had I spoken to someone sooner. No. I don't think my dad would have let anyone take me.

"She's an incredible mother. You should talk to her about doing a placement, you'll need the hours to get your degree," she says. I look to her after putting the potatoes on to boil. Is this her way of buying my approval, to lure me into a false predicament? I'm still unsure if I can trust her.

"I'll think about it," I tell her quietly, not looking at her.

I stand staring at the potatoes for awhile, watching them boil, and I lose track of the time. It's not until a hand touches my arm that I jump out of my trance, screaming in fright. Katie stands looking at me with a horrified expression, her hands both up in a defence position.

"I'm sorry. I'm so sorry. I didn't mean to scare you. The potatoes are boiling over," she whispers, and if I'm not mistaken she actually sounds genuinely concerned.

"You just startled me is all," I tell her, turning around to turn the heat down. I turn the other hob on, needing to put the steaks on. My hands visibly shake and Katie walks up to me slowly, placing her hand on mine.

"I'll finish off the dinner, why don't you go sit down or lay the table."

I nod my head, wanting some space to myself for five minutes. She gives me a soft smile before turning her attention back to the stove.

My dad walks out of his office at the same time I walk out of the kitchen, and gives me a look of concern.

"Is Katie okay?" he asks. I sigh, knowing I shouldn't have even thought he would be concerned about me. It just makes my chest hurt and my eyes begin to water.

"Yeah, she's just finishing the dinner. I need to just go send an email to my teacher. I forgot to hand in an assignment yesterday," I tell him, then hurry off up the stairs, but not before I hear him and Katie laughing and giggling in the kitchen.

By the time I make it back downstairs, I still can't shake away my nerves. I know how much my dad likes Katie and I don't want to ruin it for him, and I will if she thinks I'm this scared little freak.

I'm sitting at the table when Katie walks in struggling with some sauces. I stand up quickly nearly knocking my chair backwards to help her. I take the sauces and place them in the centre of the table before heading to the kitchen to grab the plates.

I pick up the two closest to me while Katie picks up the other along with a plate of garlic bread.

"Whose is who?" I ask her when we reach the table.

"That one is yours, and that one is mine," she smiles and my hands begin to shake. Just remembering how my mother would be angry if I sat and ate food with her, or heaven forbid, ate any food at all. So with shaky hands I move to the other end of the table as she takes a seat next to my dad. I'm about to set the plate down when my hand shakes that badly I drop it. I watch in horror as it lands on Katie's lap, her squeals of pain ringing in my ears.

"Oh my God, oh my God, oh my God," I chant, tears filling my eyes. I grab a tea-towel from the side and wipe the hot food from off her tight fitted, knee-length skirt. "I'm so sorry," I tell her, then see her hand lift in my side vision. Taken off guard, I launch backwards, knocking my head into the table with my hands covering my face. When I don't feel anything for a couple of seconds, I peek through my fingers, and through my tears I see my dad and Katie both looking at me with an expression that I can only describe as baffled. My dad looks like he wants to cuss a storm but is too stunned by my reaction and Katie looks like she wants to say something to me or my dad, or maybe throttle one or both of us. I'm so clueless it makes a sob break out of my mouth.

"I didn't mean to, I just…I'm sorry, I was nervous," I cry, feeling embarrassed, and the longer no one speaks the worse it feels.

My words must have snapped something into Katie, because she takes one look at my father before rushing down to me where I'm laying on my ass on the floor.

"It's okay, it was only an accident. Why don't you go upstairs and clean up then come and eat your dinner, yeah?"

"No!" I nearly shout in her face. "I'm fine. You can have mine. I ate a big dinner before I came," I lie, wiping my tears. "I'm sorry, Dad. Why don't you eat with Katie and I'll clean everything up in the morning. I'm sorry," I rush out before running off upstairs, taking two at a time. Once I make it to my room, I slam the door behind me and fling myself onto my bed, burying my head in the pillow.

How could I have been so freaking clumsy? Will I ever be normal? I wouldn't be surprised if my dad has an appointment with my therapist already lined up for Monday morning.

I hear my door creak open and I turn my head in time to see Katie shutting the door slowly behind her. I knew my instincts to protect myself were right. She's come for payback, just like my mother.

"I really am sorry," I whisper when she doesn't do or say anything.

"I know, honey," she sighs, then sits down on the bed next to me. My body freezes, and I completely tense not sure how to act around her. With my mother I know what's going to happen, how to react, not that it matters how I act, but still, I've learnt how to not make it worse. "Remember I told you about my mother?" she questions out of the blue, her hand slowly reaching out to touch my knee. I try to hold back a flinch, but my efforts are tireless.

"Yes," I whisper, not moving my eyes away from the hand on my knee. She hasn't made any move to hurt me, or to grip tighter so her nails can dig into my skin, but even still, I keep my body tense and on alert.

"Well, I remember that we once lived down the road from an old friend of my mom's. Her daughter would always come round our house and play, even though she was a few years older than me. She was the happiest when she was at ours, just me, my mother and my dad, but if we went to her house, she was always on edge. Always distant. I noticed after awhile that she never invited me to play in her room, no matter how much I begged," she says before taking a deep breath. I still don't look at her, in fear of where this story is heading, and why she is telling me this. "We'd go round for dinner at least once every other week at her house. Her parents were really good friends with mine. So one day when we went for dinner I asked to be excused to go to the toilet. They agreed and because their downstairs toilet was blocked I was finally allowed to use the upstairs. Instead of going into the bathroom, I went into her room and I was so taken aback, so confused I went to the next room. The room was her parents, all decorated fancy, double bed and all their knick-knacks. There weren't any other bedrooms."

"What was so confusing about her bedroom?" I ask before I can stop myself, my eyes moving away from her hand to her eyes. They look distant and sad and I feel bad for asking in case it hurts her to talk about.

"The only thing in her room was a sponge mattress and a bucket. Later that evening I told my parents and they didn't believe me, not at first. They even joked about it to her parents who laughed about it with them. I never understood it, until the next day when ambulances and police cars were lining the street on our road, all of them parked heartlessly in the road. They killed her," she says quietly.

I gasp, feeling my tears begin again. How? Why? I just...I'm about to ask, but Katie's voice breaks into the silence of the air.

"I blamed myself for years afterwards, for not saying anything and for saying something. If I had never had told my parents what I saw she might have been alive today. It took me a while to realise I was wrong. The way her parents had been beating her, we were later told that she was lucky to have lived as long as she did. She was nine when she died."

"Why are you telling me this?" I voice aloud.

"Because I know how it feels not to know who to trust. For a long time after I was scared to tell my parents anything, and not just them either, but other adults. It might not be the same, but I feel like you need an adult that can just be here for you, to guide you on what to do and to be on your side."

"What do you mean?" I ask quickly, my eyes wide with fear. Does she know? Does she know my mother hurts me? How? I know I dropped the plate in her lap, flinched a couple of times, but no one could know just from seeing that. Hell, if she's lived around here long enough then she would know I have other reasons to flinch as well.

"I have to ask, and please don't think I'll be running to the authorities, or downstairs to your father. I promise to keep it between us until I can figure out a way to help you," she says softly, bringing her arm around my shoulders. I stiffen again and pull away to look at her. To really look at her. She has soft features, her eyes soft, a light shade of blue, and is so tiny you could fit her on a shelf, but it's the kindness that shines in her eyes as she looks at me that has me taking in a deep breath. Could she really be that person I can turn to? She knows what it's like not knowing who to turn to, who will laugh in your face, or just plain ignore you. I guess it was one of my worst fears, especially after I was raped and people didn't believe me.

"I don't understand what you're getting at," I evade, not wanting to talk to a stranger about this.

"Does your father hit you, Kayla?" she asks, and swallows.

I laugh. I laugh so hard I fall back onto my bed, the tears running freely down my face. What is with everyone thinking my dad hits me? Does he really look that evil? I know looks can be deceiving, don't get me wrong, but come on, my dad? He's like a giant stuffed teddy bear that can be a little ignorant at times. Okay, most of the time, but let's not get into that.

"No, my dad doesn't hurt me. He'd never lay a finger on me. For one he'd have to be around a lot more to want to hurt me, and as he's not, so you've got nothing to worry about," I bite out, sitting back up.

"I'm sorry. I just needed to make sure," she replies softly.

I laugh again but it sounds wrong, disturbed and I know I need to keep a lid on what I say before I do end up screaming out the truth.

"You couldn't be more wrong if you tried, Katie. Did you ask because you really do care, or because you wanted to know if you'd be dating a child abuser?"

My harsh words sound so foreign to my ears that I wince, biting my bottom lip till I taste blood in my mouth.

"I'm sorry, I didn't mean that," I whisper.

"No, you're right, but you're deadly wrong. No child, no matter the age, should suffer through abuse, Kayla. No I'd never date your father if he did, but I also wouldn't leave you to fend for yourself either. I may not know you, but I want to. I'm not going to lie to you, your father has come to mean so much to me, more than you'll ever know."

"I'm sorry for the way I reacted to everything," I tell her truthfully, hoping I hadn't put her off dating him.

"So, can we call it a clean slate? And maybe when you begin to trust me you can confide in me about what's really going on." When I go to interrupt she holds up her hand stopping me. "I may believe that it isn't your father, I've heard the way he talks about you so it didn't need much convincing, but someone out there is hurting you, and I want to help you," she says before leaning over and kissing my head. I'm so in shock with her words I don't even say goodbye when she gets up and leaves.

Instead of going downstairs to tell her she's wrong, that no one is hurting me, I fall back onto the bed and fall into sobs. I'm sobbing so hard my chest aches, my throat is sore and my eyes sting from the constant tears.

I've known Katie all of five minutes and already she has shown me kindness and love. Her softness and the way she handled me with care means more to me than she'll ever know, it's also foreign for me to receive kindness like that and it's completely knocked me back. So, I'm mourning my stupidity and my constant fucked-up reactions to situations, but also for the mother I never got to have.

Apart from Katie, I've only received kindness and love from a few other older adults. Joan, Harlow's nan is one, and another lady I met called Hannah at the Salvation food bank is another.

I don't know how long I'm crying for, but when the hallway light shines through the room blinding me, I'm pulled back from my thoughts. A large stiletto is barricading the doorway and I gasp in fright until I smell him.

"Myles," I choke out, and he wastes no time in rushing over and climbing into bed with me. He pulls me into his arms and I sob harder, and with broken words I explain everything that happened, from the beginning to the end when Katie left my room. All through it Myles stays quiet running his fingers through my hair.

TWENTY-ONE

KAYLA

A FEW MORE WEEKS HAVE passed since the disastrous dinner with Katie and my dad. Thankfully I was able to make it up to both of them on Sunday when I cooked a roast. I think that time around it went better due to Myles being there.

After Katie returned from my room, she informed my dad how upset I was and if there was anyone he could call. When he saw my phone on the side he dialled Myles' number, knowing I've been spending all my time with him. I've not told him we're a couple, but from the rules he laid out in the morning on the Sunday, I'm guessing he has an idea. He basically told Myles that under no circumstances was he allowed to sleep in my bedroom when he wasn't in the house. Yeah, like *that's* going to happen. Katie winked at me. After that I began to feel at ease more around her, liking how she put my dad in his place when he was wrong. It's funny to watch because she doesn't do it nastily, or spitefully.

Today we're heading to London to try on the bride and bridesmaid dresses. The boys have decided to tag along since we're staying overnight at a hotel.

It's good they have an excuse about getting their suits, otherwise I think

Denny's Nan would have thrown a hissy fit, though she did mention she liked looking at those Carter boys.

Whatever that means.

My phone rings when I walk out of the restroom at the restaurant we're all eating at.

Dad calling.

Ugh.

He told me he wouldn't call me to check in every hour when I left this morning. Since the disastrous meal happened he's become closer to me, involved in every aspect of my life. Even asking questions about school, my future and about Myles and my friends. When I told him I'd been asked to be a bridesmaid his eyes had watered, although if you asked him he would have said a fly flew into his eye.

Whatever!

"Dad," I groan into the phone, although I secretly love that he calls to check in on me now. Before he left me to my own devices.

"Hey, Kayla. I'm sorry to interrupt what you're doing but I've had a call from Bob in Leeds. He needs me to go down and sort out these accounts for him before they shut him down. I'll be back by Monday but your mother has offered to stay the weekend with you."

It takes me a second not to panic. The thought of my mom tainting more of that house is unquestionable. "Dad, I'm not going to be there anyway. Plus, you've let me sleep at home by myself before."

"Well, that was before you fell on your ass, fear filling your eyes, with tears down your face," he bites out. "Sorry. I'm just stressed. I've been a shit dad to you for years, Kayla, and I know no matter what I do it will never bring back those precious moments in your life that I missed. I'll ever be regretful of that, but I want to be in your life now, I want to be the dad you always deserved."

I get choked up, and move to a large pillar so that the table with all my friends on can't see me.

"It's fine, Dad, but no need to call Mom to stay over. I'm here until Monday then I'm sleeping at Denny's remember?" I lie. I'm totally not sleeping at Denny's. I'm sleeping at Myles' for the first time. I'm actually pretty excited about it.

"I'll give her a call now. Be safe and I'll call you when I get to Leeds. I'll be back by Tuesday evening at the latest," he tells me before we both say our goodbyes and hang up.

"Everything okay?" Myles asks making me jump. I smack his arm smiling.

"Don't scare me like that. It was my dad. He called to say he was getting mom to come stay over, but I explained I wouldn't be there," I tell him, and I watch as his jaw gets hard at hearing her name. We haven't spoken much about her since I told him who was hurting me. I know he's trying to give me space and I'm thankful for that. I'm also grateful he doesn't pressure me into telling him anything more. I need him to just be here for me, without piling on all my baggage.

"Are you okay to sleep at mine still?" he asks, and his eyes soften and his mouth turns up into a smile.

"Yes. He thinks I'll be at Denny's. It's only a half lie. I will be there, but I'll be sleeping at your house, in your bed," I grin and reach up and kiss him. My arms wrap around his neck, and I moan when he wraps his around my waist, pulling me flush against him.

God, I'll never get tired of kissing him. Ever!

"Hmmm," I groan and chuckle when we pull away to see he has pink lipstick smudged across his lips. Before I have chance to tell him or to wipe it away, Joan grabs our attention when we hear her shout across the restaurant.

"That's it, you tell him, dump that sad loser," she chants and everyone turns to look at her in shock. We look to where she's shouting to, and believe it or not, it's only a few tables across from us. The way she was shouting, you'd think they were outside on the pavement.

"Grams," Harlow hisses, and smiles an apology at the couple, but the girl at the table stands up nodding her head.

"You're right, old lady. I'm dumping this loser's ass. He slept with my mother and my sister, you know," she shouts, picking up her glass of wine and throwing it over her boyfriend's head. I gasp and try to cover my giggles when he stands up to defend himself only to get some green looking sauce thrown at him.

"Grams, don't throw food," Harlow hisses louder. "You're going to get us kicked out."

"Oh girl, you know nothing. Us sisters have to stick together, you hear me? Oi, girl who got fucked by her mother and sister, I ain't no old lady. I got more stamina than most you young folk," Joan says and the table erupts in groans and protests. Other tables are looking by, watching the show with amusement. Myles walks us back to our seats, making sure to keep us out of everyone's attention.

"Eww, I did, didn't I? You had that penis in my mother and sister and in me, it means we shared more than DNA, eww," the blonde squeals, then lands a hard slap to the man's cheek.

"It didn't mean anything. I thought she was you," he defends himself just as an older lady and younger girl walk in.

"Oi, Mom, Sandra, come 'ere," the blonde shouts and everyone's heads turn quickly to see the newcomers. They walk slowly over to the table, looking around the room at everyone's curious glances.

The two waiters come to intervene, but then the manager we met earlier walks over to stop them, shaking his head grinning.

"Old lady, can she be mistaken for me?" the blonde asks Joan, and Joan being Joan stands up and looks the other girl up and down in distaste.

"I hope you get diseases," Joan hisses before turning to the man at the blonde's table. He looks pale and looking around for a way to bolt, but then Blondie grabs a hold of his arm.

"Don't even think about it. So?"

"You're blonde, thin, tall, got fake ass tits, and blue eyes. Your sister has brown hair, small, chubby, no tits, but a huge ass, there is no way he could have mistaken the two of you, and what's your excuse for the mother?" Joan asks taking a seat again.

"Please keep out it, Grams; you're not *Jeremy Kyle*," Harlow hisses quietly, but her nan just waves her off. Everyone else is just transfixed on the commotion going on at the table. I don't know what the hell we missed but all of a sudden a plate of food is thrown in the sister's face, and her mom's hair is dripping with soup. When I look to the table in front of them I can see where it came from. Blondie obviously used the couple's starters to get her revenge.

"Cheers, old lady. You really should get your own show," Blondie says before walking out of the restaurant with her head held high. When she gets to the entrance a man walks over to greet her, whispers something in her ear making her laugh before they both walk out holding hands.

We then look back to the table where the three stand sopping wet with food, looking at each other with expressions I can't explain.

"So, I guess now isn't the time to tell you I'm pregnant?" the mother says before taking her daughter's hand and rushing out. We all look stunned, watching the man rushing out after her before we all look to one another. Then the whole restaurant erupts in laughter and endless chatter.

"What the hell was that?" I whisper, feeling like we just entered an episode of Jerry Springer.

"That, my dear, is London. Full of drama," Joan cackles before taking a sip of her martini.

I shake my head before looking at Myles. He's still laughing and when he feels me watching him he looks down with a soft expression.

"I've got a surprise for you after. You up for it, or are you tired?" he whispers so no one else can hear.

I nod my head. "Yes."

"Bro, why the fuck you wearing lipstick?" Max shouts across the table and I giggle uncontrollably, just remembering I hadn't wiped it off. He gives me a look that only makes me laugh harder. The table then continues to tease him while finishing off their food and I look around at the people I've come to love and call my own family.

"Oh my God, you brought me to the London Eye," I squeal, jumping up and down. I wrap my arms around Myles, squeezing him to me. I've wanted to go on the London Eye since forever.

Myles laughs at my behaviour, but I don't care. I'm so freaking excited I could scream from the rooftops. I laugh out loud, not caring if people think I've lost my trolley.

"You're excited then?" he asks, and I give him a look before giving him another hug.

"Thank you, thank you," I chant, and grab his hand excitedly as he pulls us over to the small queue. The view from down here is beautiful. The place is lit up with so many lights, changing from blue, to green and then to pink. It's breathtaking.

We move into a room for our photos, and I look at the green screen behind me in confusion. Why would we want a photo with a green background? I ignore it and smile up at Myles just as the photo is taken. I blush when the photographer chuckles and tells us to move on. It's not long before we're seated in a 4D cinema and laughing our heads off.

Myles gets a few calls and text messages when we're in there, but he presses ignore before clicking it on silent.

"That was amazing," I laugh, my hair a little wet as we leave the cinema room. Myles laughs, his hand still clutched in mine.

Then we notice people queuing at a booth and when we make our way over to it, it's the photos we had taken before entering the cinema. I gasp when I see ours. I'm standing so my front is to Myles' side, my face looking up at him and smiling. I didn't know when the photo was taken, but Myles is also facing me and smiling. We look... we look like a young couple in love. I know I love him, but I don't think he's there just yet. Not wanting to put a downer on the evening, I grab my bag to get my purse, but Myles' voice stops me.

"I'll take two of number 109 please," he says handing over a twenty.

"I could have gotten them, you got the tickets," I pout, while we wait for our photos to be printed.

"It's my treat, and seeing your face light up like a Christmas tree is worth every penny," he tells me softly. I melt into him, feeling all mushy inside.

"You really know how to sweet talk me," I tell him softly, kissing his cheek.

"Anything for you," he tells me before taking the photos the lady hands over. He keeps the bag as we walk up to the gates, the queue's getting smaller and smaller as we arrive.

We walk onto a passenger capsule and I feel giddy with excitement and nerves. I rush quickly over to the far end of the capsule, looking out at the water. The doors close and we're left in a capsule with six or seven other people, all of them taking photos of each other or selfies. I smile at them before watching the river lit up outside.

It's not long before we're at the top, the ride stopping to give us all time to appreciate the view. The houses of Parliament lights up golden, and I take in all the street lights and sigh. It's more beautiful than I ever imagined. It's perfect.

"This is beautiful," I sigh, leaning my head against Myles' shoulder.

"Yes it is," he whispers, his one hand rubbing slow circles on my hip. I turn my head, pulling away a little and look at him, expecting him to be watching the view but he's staring down at me, his eyes glazed over.

"I love you," I blurt out, then gasp, covering my mouth with my hand. Shit! Why did I just go and ruin it and say that. Tears spring from my eyes and for the first time since walking onto this capsule I wish I could run off it, escape from my verbal vomit.

"I love you too," I hear, but I can't be hearing things right. Did he? Did he just say what I think he said?

I look up at him with wide eyes, not bothering to wipe away my tears or check to see if people are looking. The capsule starts moving again, but I don't tear my eyes away from his.

"What?" I ask, shaking my head, feeling like I'm in a dream.

"I said, I love you. I love you, Kayla," he whispers, his lips now against my mouth. How did he move that close? Jesus, I need to get it together.

"I...I lov-" but I'm cut off when his lips reach mine, the soft texture against mine and I moan into his mouth, wrapping my arms around his neck.

His hands on my hips tighten a fraction before sliding around to the bottom of my back, his fingers pressing into my back and pulling me against him. I can feel his arousal against my stomach, long and hard between us and instead of feeling freaked out like I normally would, it just makes me groan into his mouth. Knowing I do that to him, and knowing he's feeling it, not just from desire, but from love too, means everything to me. I never thought anyone would ever feel like this towards me, especially after Davis.

A cough interrupts us and I quickly take a step away, my breathing erratic.

"It's time to come off," a staff member says, amusement in his voice.

I nod my head, and grab a hold of Myles' hand. I'm not even disappointed I missed the rest of the ride, him telling me he loves me is by far the best experience I'll ever encounter.

"You want to get some snacks before heading back?" Myles asks.

I nod, feeling my cheeks heat. "Yeah, I need to get some skittles," I tell him, remembering I forgot to bring some with me. I love them.

"Okay," he laughs and walks us away from the London Eye, back towards the hotel we're staying at.

BACK AT THE HOTEL, WE'RE lying down on the double bed, watching a movie from the laptop in front of us. The TV in the room doesn't have an HDMI lead, or even a DVD player built in, so it's a good thing Myles thought to bring his laptop.

We're half way through watching Bridesmaids – and yes, I know, the irony – when I move for the millionth time. I haven't been able to keep still since we got back from the London Eye and Myles took his clothes off getting ready for bed. I don't know what's wrong with me. One minute I was fine, the next I was hot and bothered. I even got up and opened the bedroom window, but it's doing nothing to cool me down.

"Are you sure you're okay?" Myles rumbles and his voice hits straight to my core.

"Ahem," I mutter, squeezing my legs together to see if that gets rid of the ache.

"Kayla?" he calls softly and I turn to look over at him. He's watching me with half mast eyes and a soft expression.

"Yeah?"

"Are you turned on?" he asks, moving down to move the laptop to the side of his bed.

"Hey, it was getting to a good bit," I half protest. Curious as to what he's going on about.

"Don't ignore me. Is that why you've been restless, crossing and uncrossing your legs?" he asks, his tongue flicking out to lick his bottom lip.

"I don't know," I tell him truthfully.

"Can I touch you?" he asks, moving forward. His mouth moving closer to mine.

"I don't know," I whisper, feeling my chest rise and fall heavier.

His finger lightly runs down my cheek and I have to close my eyes, enjoying the sensation. His breath tickles my lips for a second before he presses them against mine. My hand automatically reaches for him, landing on his strong, hard chest.

His hand runs lightly down my side, the warmth from his hands seeps through my night shirt. When he reaches my ribs, I giggle. "That tickles," I whisper.

"It does?" he whispers back his lips at my jaw, kissing their way up to my ear where he takes my earlobe into his mouth.

I gasp, completely taken off guard by the sensations running through my body. I can't get enough oxygen to my lungs, the feelings are that overwhelming. When his fingers run on bare skin where my shirt has pulled away from my pyjama shorts, I moan against his cheek. My fingers move to his cheek just as he rolls us so he's positioned above me. The position doesn't scare me, especially when I look into his eyes and see nothing but love. My hand travels up his chest, drifting into the scruff of his hair and the back of his neck. He moves his face into my neck, the rough texture of his jaw rubbing against the sensitive skin below my ear.

My body aches, and the urge to move my hips into his like I did last time is building to the point of pain. I feel like my whole body is strung up so tight it will only take one touch for it to diffuse.

I feel him pull away and when he makes no move to touch me, I open my eyes to find him looking down at me with worry in his eyes.

"I don't know what to do," he groans looking pained. "You're not ready."

He goes to move, but I put my hands around his neck, stopping me. "Don't stop. I'm not ready to have sex, but please touch me. I don't just mean my boobs either," I blush, feeling my face heat and redden.

"You're killing me."

"If you're not ready, then we can wait," I panic, not thinking he might not be ready.

"I've only ever slept with one person, I just want this to be good for you," he says biting his bottom lip.

My eyes widen. Even back when I was fourteen and he was thirteen I heard rumours about him with girls. They'd gush and talk about him like he was a piece of meat in the bathrooms. It always made me blush, especially when it was one of the older girls doing the talking.

"Everything you do feels good," I promise him, not wanting to think about him with other girls anymore.

He smiles down at me before his hand runs across the gap between my shirt and shorts. When he sits up and peels the top up, I lift up on my elbows, helping him remove it.

I lay back staring up at him with nerves and excitement, the only sound in the room is my heavy breathing and the laptop still playing *Bridesmaids*. His gaze burns into mine and I watch fascinated as he gazes down at me, his irises black.

His finger lightly crosses over my cleavage and I moan loudly, my back arching towards him.

"Sit up," he asks hoarsely.

I do as he asks and sit up, and bite my lip when he runs his fingers around to my back to unclip my bra. His touch is torture, especially when he lowers the straps from my shoulders, slowly, his eyes never once leaving mine.

Everything after feels like a dream, one I don't want to ever wake up from.

He's sucking, licking and biting, his fingers tugging at my taut nipples.

When I'm ready to beg him, to shout at him, he finally removes my shorts and knickers. His gaze again never leaving mine, giving me the strength and encouragement I need. He makes me feel sexy, beautiful and it's something I've never felt before, but he also lets me experience gentle, which is something I never thought I'd have after everything I went through. Just the thought of someone's hands touching me intimately would make me throw up, but with Myles, I feel like I'm dying without his touch.

His fingers explore my wet heat and I bow my back off the bed, loving the sensations he's driving through my body.

Needing to touch him I move my hands to his chest, slowly tracing the little hair he has between his pecks down to his six pack. The lines define each one, and with my finger I trace down the middle until I get to a trail of hair leading into his boxers.

I look up at Myles unsure, and that's when I notice he's stopped moving. His eyes are tightly clutched together, and his jaw his hard, making me pull my hand away quickly.

"Touch me," he groans, grabbing my hand to move it back to where it was. I trace the edge of his boxer shorts with my finger, dipping in slightly before pulling back out. I'm so nervous. I don't know what to do. When his fingers find my clit I moan loudly, not feeling the embarrassment I first had when he touched me down there.

He gets up on his knees and shocking the hell out me when he pulls his boxer briefs down, moving so he's no longer positioned between my legs. He's large, thick, and the tip is bulging red and I swallow thickly, scared at the thought of that being inside me. I reach out gently as he moves towards me still on his knees, and reaches out to grab my hand obviously reading my nerves.

"Remember, any time you want to stop just say the word and we'll stop," he says softly, his voice deep.

I nod my head 'okay' then wrap my hand around his hard length. I'm surprised at the softness, and how big it feels in my hand, and when he jerks it startles me, and he lets out a chuckle.

"Now move up and down like this," he whisper hoarsely, his voice strained. I can feel myself becoming wetter, and I feel my cheeks turn pink and I hope he doesn't notice.

After a few seconds of getting into a rhythm, and Myles showing how he likes it, he moves his hands from over mine and his fingers carry on exploring my sex. My hand stops enjoying the feeling, but then Myles stops with me.

"You stop, I stop," he tells me, and when I look up at him, his eyes are sparkling with mischief.

I shake my head smiling at him and continue moving my hand up and down, every once in a while wetness from the tip will drip down onto my hand and I'll swipe the tip with my thumb which Myles likes, if the noises he makes when I do it are any indication.

I swear it feels like hours, but only minutes before I feel my body tighten, and I know it's about to happen again, I'm about to orgasm. My hand holding his dick moves faster, and faster, matching the pace of my breathing and I feel him swell in my hand. Then I tighten around his fingers completely, my eyes closing and a hiss leaving my mouth at the same time I feel him pulse in my hand and hot spurts of his cum land on my stomach and chest.

When it's over, I look up at Myles and my eyes start to water.

"Hey, what's wrong?" he says worriedly and I shake my head and wave him off.

"I didn't freak out. I touched you, you touched me and I didn't freak out. I never thought I'd have that," I tell him and burst into tears.

"I don't know whether to take your tears as a compliment or as a bad sign," he grumbles holding me.

I laugh, the same time I wipe my eyes and look at him. "It was beautiful, Myles, amazing."

His eyes soften, his finger running softly down my cheek. "You're beautiful," he whispers.

TWENTY-TWO

KAYLA

Last night was amazing and I haven't been able to keep the grin off my face all morning. Everyone had been giving me curious glances, or, with Max, conspicuous winks he would send my way, which I ignored.

After we all said our goodbyes to the lads we made our way to *Flora's Boutique*. The shop is huge. After Denny had said it was only going to be a small set up I presumed it was going to be a small shop, but it's anything but.

"I'm so excited but so freaking nervous," Denny breathes, fiddling with her fingers.

Mary walks in behind us just as another lady her age walks out of the back. She's wearing a white floral suit, the skirt falling loosely to her knees with a measure tape wrapped around her neck like a piece of jewellery. She's got white hair styled in a bun low at the back of her head. She looks like money.

"Mary, darling," Flora coos, wrapping Mary up in her arms.

"It's so good to see you, Flora. You're looking fab-oh-lous," she winks and Flora laughs, lightly smacking her arm.

"So do you," she smiles. "Now which one is Denny?" she asks smiling.

We shove Denny forward and Flora's smile widens. "My God, aren't you a walking beauty. I have just the dress," she says going into business mode. She ushers Denny upstairs.

"Charlotte, can you take Miss Denny here to cubical five, and get refreshments for her guests?" she orders and I turn to see a young girl looking flabbergasted and stressed, nodding her head. She's wearing a similar suit to Flora's, but in a dark blue colour with a white blouse. She looks like a stewardess, but I don't voice that.

"Yes, Flora." We follow Denny up the stairs that are decorated with bridal flowers. The place is beautiful. The gowns look expensive and completely out of this world.

When we get to the top we all take a seat on the half-circle love seat. The place is even bigger up here. In front of us is a line of curtains and Charlotte ushers Denny to the one directly in front of us.

"What's that for?" Harlow asks quietly next to me and I turn to find her looking at the stand in the centre of the room.

"That's where the brides stand when they're showing their dresses off," I whisper, feeling like I'm in a library. The place is so quiet; the only noise is the light music playing in the background. If we're here for long then I'll definitely be asleep by the time we leave.

A clanging noise to my right makes me jump and I follow the direction it came in. Flora walks out of a lift with a rack full of bridal dresses.

"That damn lift is going to be the death of me," she mutters before looking over to Mary. "I had workers come in to take a look at it and they said it was fine, it was just rusty. Did that sound fine to you?" she asks Mary and I look to Mary.

"It's fine," she chuckles.

"Right then, introduce us. I'm guessing you're Joan? I've heard a lot about you," Flora winks at Joan and we all laugh.

"Whatever she said is most likely all true," she cackles back, waving at her.

"Me and you are going to be best friends then," Flora laughs, before looking back to Mary.

"This is Harlow, her maid of honour. And this tiny one here is Kayla, her other bridesmaid."

"Hello." Harlow and I wave and she smiles.

"Oh God, your dresses are going to be pains," she mutters and I notice her staring at my chest. I cover myself self-consciously, which just makes her grin.

"Why?" Mary asks looking worried.

"Have you seen their chests? They'll either have cleavage that will have everyone's attention on them and not the bride, or a dress that they'll never breathe in to cover them up."

"I don't want people staring at me or my cleavage," I panic, and everyone's eyes come to mine. I duck my head feeling pathetic, and embarrassed. But then Joan's hand comes from the other side of me and pats it soothingly making me relax somewhat.

"Baby girl, you'll be fine, don't worry," she assures me and when I look back up I catch the end of Mary giving Flora a silent look that she'll fill her in later. I know both Joan and Mary know about my past and how it's affected me, so I'm kind of glad they're here for support.

"I'm not rich for no reason. I'll make you look beautiful," Flora smiles before heading over to a nervous Denny. "You, my girl, need a glass of champagne."

As if it was magically conjured, Charlotte walks out with a tray of glasses, a bucket with champagne in and a bowl of strawberries.

"There's also a little kitchenette in the back where Charlotte just came from if you need a hot drink," Flora advises. "Just let Charlotte or me know, or just go help yourselves."

Harlow and I are both old enough to drink, so when we're handed our glasses, Mary makes a toast.

"To Denny, may she find the wedding dress of her dreams, and lingerie that will have Mason bursting in his pants," she winks and we all laugh.

Without thinking I take a sip of the champagne, the sweet, grape, bubbly taste filling my taste buds. I cough at the taste and put the glass down. I don't drink. Even though it's just us girls I still don't feel safe enough to drink. I don't want to be feel out of control ever again.

"Nowm, you, let's try this dress on. We'll save the best for last," Flora grins and moves over to the rack grabbing one of the dresses that are hidden inside a protective bag.

"God, is it normal to be this nervous and excited," Denny mutters again and we all laugh.

"Go get out of your clothes and put this on for me, but keep your own knickers on," Flora instructs. "Shout when you've finished."

By the seventh dress we've only all agreed on one. Denny is trying the last one on now, which Flora said is the best one she has in the shop and one that Denny is guaranteed to fall in love with.

"I'm ready," we hear Denny whisper and we all stand up waiting. None of the dresses have made Denny's list, and I know she's starting to feel nervous, but this is the first time we've heard her sound in awe.

The second she steps out from behind the curtain the whole room gasps, our hands covering our mouths. I hear a sob from the left of me and want to chuckle. Every dress she's tried on, no matter if it didn't look right, Mary has cried, but to hear her sob, I know this is the dress. Denny has tears of her own in her eyes and is looking at us for our opinion as she stands on the little round stage.

"You look so beautiful," Mary says.

"Completely breathtaking," Joan adds.

"Seriously hot," Harlow winks and I chuckle.

"Like a princess," I add with my own wink.

"This is the one," she whispers and turns to look in the floor length mirror. Mason is going to be knocked off his feet over the dress, never mind the lingerie.

The princess-cut, sweetheart, strapless, long length gown is tight on her bust, enchasing her cleavage. The natural fitting waist has rhinestones, crystal beading, finished with a grey/silver ribbon that fits snug at the waist. The dress then flares down in layers and layers, looking elegant and fairytale like with a cathedral train.

Mary asks her to do a twirl and from the back it's just as beautiful. The ribbon has been tied up in a bow and the back is laced up like a corset.

"I love it," Denny gushes, tears streaming down her face.

"We have to make a few alterations, but nothing that will take much time. You will need to come back for one more fitting, but that's it," Flora smiles. "I knew when you were introduced this dress would be perfect for you. You've got the tiny waist that is perfect for this dress. Now, what colour bridesmaid dresses are you going for? I'd recommend the dark grey. We have two designs and as you're only having one bridesmaid and one maid of honour... I'll go get them," she finishes before rushing off down the stairs.

"Denny, you look beautiful," Mary gushes, wiping her eyes as she goes to stand next to Denny.

"You really do look like a princess," I smile, taking a sip of the water I grabbed earlier. Harlow agrees, before continuing to type on her phone.

"I hope you're not texting that boy of yours?" Mary scolds Harlow.

Harlow's face turns red and she guiltily looks up from her phone frowning. "Why?"

"Because it's bad luck."

"To text my boyfriend to see how the suit shopping is going?" she frowns looking adorable. Joan cackles and I slyly take the nearly empty bottle of champagne away from her. Harlow had a sip of her drink then left it the same as me, but it didn't stop Mary and Joan finishing our glasses, stating 'waste not, want not' to us.

"Oh, I thought you were spying for Mason. I know he's desperate to see this one in a dress," she giggles, most likely three sheets to the wind with the amount of alcohol in her system. "Just don't take pictures."

"Here we are," Flora shouts, coming out of the lift, that screeching noise ringing in my ears.

"Before we get you changed so the girls can get changed, you need to decide if this is the style. We have this one which is a sleek, lighter grey for Kayla. It has flower ruffles to hide her ta tas. It's just a straight length, but the dark grey flowers on the breast give it character. It's sleeveless too. Then for Harlow we have this one. It will make you stand out as maid of honour. It's a bit like a greek dress, one that wraps over the one shoulder. With your hair you could wear it like this," she says. Then shows us a picture of another girl wearing a similar dress. Her hair is plaited like a band around her head, coming in a bundle at the bottom of her neck. She looks freaking beautiful.

"Of course you don't need to take my advice, have whatever you feel is right. I'd also wear your hair down, Kayla. I know you don't want attention there," she says, pointing to my breasts with her eyes. "So have it down, in loose curls, maybe have some of it backcombed to give it character with a flower brooch in the back to clip it there."

When she's finished Denny is standing wide eyed with her mouth hanging open. "You just described exactly what I wanted," she breathes and Flora naturally waves her off.

"It's my job, Dear. Now go with Charlotte, get unchanged while we get these girls into their dresses. Charlotte, when you've finished help Harlow here into her dress," she orders before taking the dress for me off the rack. "Come on."

I get up and look at Joan nervously. I didn't think when I was asked I would be dressing in front of people. Now that I've got to get changed in front of a stranger no less I feel like I might pass out. Not wanting to cause drama, I follow Flora into the changing room next to Denny's and start to undress slowly. I know the second she sees my scars. Her gasp fills the changing room and I can feel my eyes water.

"Right. Ok. Let's get you in this beauty. I'll turn around while you change into this," she says, handing me a strapless bra. I give her a small smile, but I don't look in her eyes, not wanting to see the horrified expression on her face.

Once I'm changed I turn back around. "I'm ready," I tell her, still not looking at her.

"Look at me, Dear," she says, quietly. I look up startled she called me out on it and I find her eyes watering, and instead of looking horrified, she looks completely upset. "I don't know your story, and I won't ask, but don't ever be ashamed. You carry them scars with strength, not weakness, my Dear. Whatever you went through that caused them, you survived. You should be proud of that. Most people can never move on from that kind of pain. You, my sweet girl, hold the world on your shoulders, I can read it in your eyes, but for today let all that go and let's get you dressed up," she smiles gently, her hand rubbing gently up and down my arm.

A few tears fall from my eyes and I nod my head. I've never looked at my scars that way. Every time I see them I just remember everything that happened, everything they represent, but with Flora putting it the way she did, I might be able to start looking at them to remind me what I've overcome, what I've pulled through.

I step into the dress, the material smooth against my skin. She messes with something at the back before I feel her zip the dress up.

"Turn," she orders, back to bridal dress mode. I turn and turn bright red when she starts fiddling with the seam by my breasts, not asking permission to touch me. When she positions my breasts so that they're not showing so much cleavage, I nearly run from the changing room. Myles would have a field day if he knew another woman was touching my breasts. I giggle just thinking about it and Flora, being the woman she is, just looks at me and smiles.

I step out and find Harlow isn't ready yet. Everyone is still standing, including Denny and when I walk out she starts crying.

"That bad?" I tease which makes her laugh.

"No. You look so freaking beautiful. This day is going be everything I dreamed of. I didn't think I was ready for a huge wedding, only wanting to keep it small, but I'm glad I let Mason talk me into doing it properly. Picking a dress, and seeing what you guys will look like next to me is just… Oh God, I'm going to cry again," she babbles before blowing her nose into a tissue.

I'm glad when Harlow steps out and Joan whistles. She looks like a greek goddess in her dress.

"So?" Harlow asks, twirling. "Are these the dresses because if they're not I'm buying it anyway." Everyone laughs including me, but I can totally see where she's coming from. She turns to me and grins and it makes me feel nervous.

"Myles is so going to have a heart attack when he sees you," she giggles, and I blush. "Aww, she's blushing, again."

"Stop," I laugh.

"I don't usually do this, but for you girl, I will. Where's your phone?" Flora asks and I point to the table where it's sitting. My dad texted to check in on me and I ended up leaving it there.

She grabs it from the table, presses a few buttons before taking a picture of me in the dress. She presses a few more buttons before looking at me and grinning.

"What did you just do?" I ask, but I have a feeling I already know.

"Well, I teased him. I only got so much of the dress in the picture to make him want to see the rest," she winks, then laughs when a text message immediately comes through. I just make it off the stand when Harlow's and Denny's phones go off too. They both grab their phones and burst out laughing, just as I'm taking mine from Flora.

"Mason said, 'As much as I want to see you in your dress, can I have a picture of what's underneath' with a wink face," Denny laughs.

Harlow laughs then reads her message. "Babe, why the 'fudge' is Myles getting pictures, but I'm getting left in the dark? Take a selfie for me; I want to see you in a dress again. Just make sure you ent showing your boobs again because there's only so much of hitting Max all night I can take."

"That boy is terrible. I can't wait for the day the roles are reversed," Joan scolds, smiling. Shit! I forgot about that. I was going to tell Myles so he could warn Max.

"What did Myles say?" Denny asks and I look down at my screen and smile.

"I can't wait for the day I get to walk you down the aisle in a white dress, especially with how beautiful you look in a bridesmaid dress."

I blush, my smile widening. *He wants to marry me.* I want to squeal, but instead

I do it inside my head. Everyone awwes at his sweetness, and Joan comments about saving up for another wedding, making me laugh. We are nowhere near ready for that sort of commitment, but I know Myles will be the man I marry, so I don't tell them any different.

"Let's get you changed, girls, so we can get the last dress on."

"Last dress?" Joan asks confused and Flora grins.

"Nan, you didn't really think I'd have a wedding without my mother would you."

"I certainly freaking hope you would," Mary snaps, looking angry, but Denny just laughs.

"Nan," she says taking her hands. "I'm talking about you. I know you're not my mother, but you've been more of one to me than my own ever has, and instead of mother of the bride, I'm having a Nan of the bride, so you'll be getting your own special dress," Denny smiles softly.

Mary, finally understanding starts to cry again. Luckily, Joan already has the box of tissues handy and hands one to Denny to give to Mary.

"But I just bought a dress," Mary whispers, and I think she feels completely taken off guard. I don't think she expected anything like this and my eyes water watching. You can see in her eyes how much the gesture means to her.

"You can save it for Harlow's or Kayla's wedding," she teases. "Or Hope's christening."

"Well then, how can I say no to that," she says to Denny before turning to Flora. "I need to get me a young man, so push these beasts up," she says grabbing her breasts through her blouse, making us all laugh.

"What?" Mary says. "I need me a man that can go all night, and I can't get me one of those unless my beauties are standing up right and not hanging around down south."

We all crack up and Flora just shakes her head before heading into the changing room with Mary.

"This has been the perfect weekend, thank you for coming," Denny says before bursting into tears, making us laugh.

TWENTY-THREE

KAYLA

THE WEEKEND HAD BEEN perfect, but my nights spent with Myles at the hotel and at his, were the best part. We didn't do anything after that night, which I'm kind of frustrated at him for, but also thankful at the same time. My feelings are confusing the hell out of me, but I know he knows me better than I know myself sometimes, so I'm glad we are taking it as slow as we are. Although, I wouldn't mind touching him again.

"I'll see you tomorrow," I tell him as he walks me to the door. The place is filled with darkness because my dad isn't back yet. My battery died last night at Myles' house so I haven't had chance to speak to him either.

"I can't. I have to go to that college interview," he groans. "Then my granddad wants to take us out for a lunch."

"Well, we have the whole week off, so we'll arrange it for Thursday. Okay?"

"Okay, but make sure you text me. I'm going to miss you," he says hugging me to him. I willingly go, knowing I'm going to miss him just as much.

"I'll miss you too," I whisper against his lips, hating having to say goodbye after such a perfect few days spent with him.

He kisses me and I cling to him, my arms wrapped around his neck, my fingers playing with his hair at the nape of his neck. I love doing this to him. And when I pull it, he makes this growling sound that hits me straight between my legs. I love it. So I do it often enough that I hear it, but enough so that he doesn't get used to it.

"I love you," he whispers when he pulls away and Mason beeps the horn for Myles to hurry up. Myles groans and I smile.

"I love you too. Now go. He misses his girls," I tell him, giving him another kiss. He kisses me back looking hesitant to go.

"I don't want to go. I don't know. I just feel like I should be with you," he tells me frowning and I just laugh him off, pushing him towards the car.

"Go before he comes and gets you himself. I'll be fine," I laugh.

He gives me one more look, worry filling his eyes but I ignore it. I know he's just going to miss me, because I'm going to feel the same, but we promised to see each other Thursday. It's only one day.

"Just text me," he says and heads over to the passenger side. "Love you," he shouts and I shout it back.

"Love you too, Babe," Mason calls and I burst into laughter. I shake my head before turning and heading inside. I turn around to watch the car's headlights drive away before turning and shutting the door behind me. I flick on the light and scream, an object flying right at me before everything turns into darkness.

I DON'T KNOW HOW much longer I can keep going. It's been hours, maybe days. My mother has had me locked up in my bedroom, beaten, tied up, sore and I'm pretty sure she's broken my arm. It hangs limp against my chest, swollen and throbbing. The pain has long been forgotten, fear and shock overriding it's place. My mouth is sore and dry from screaming and having no water or food for days. The last thing I remember before everything went fuzzy was saying goodbye to Myles. After that everything else is a blur. I woke up tied to the bed with my arm twisted at a weird angle, the swelling and throbbing too much for me to cope with and I ended up passing out. The few times I did wake up was to receive a beating from my mom. Any time I tried to talk to her it only fuelled her anger.

The front door slams, the only indication that I know it's not someone coming to my rescue. Her footsteps are heavy on the stairs before the door to my room slams open.

She stands in the doorway, her face thundering with anger. Her normal up-kept designer clothes are dishevelled. Her hair that was up in an up-do this morning before she left is now in messy waves down her shoulders, like she's been pulling at it in rage.

"Please can I have some water?" I beg again. Not that it works, but I need to keep strong, I just need to try.

She laughs manically and I wince at the sound. "Water? Water? No dear, no." She starts pacing in front of me muttering things I can't understand until she looks at me with an evil look in her eyes.

"Your father thinks he's clever. Took my wedding ring in the divorce because it's been in his family for generations, but it's mine," she laughs, looking up at the ceiling before looking back down at me. Her leg kicks out hitting me in the shin and I wince in pain, not bothering to cry out, it only pleases her. "Took all his jewellery and he won't be able to prove who it was because you, you little brat aren't going to tell him a thing are you? No, because if you do I'll make your life a living hell. He thinks the ban he has on selling his ring will stop me, but it won't. Some dealer bought it off me for a few grand, even though it's worth a lot, lot more."

"You're doing this for jewellery?" I breathe out, mystified.

"No. I'm doing this for fucking money. When you decided you were too good to visit your mother, your father decided it was time to end sending me money. Now he has his fancy slut of a girlfriend, a brat of a kid, he thinks his shit don't stink."

"You've got what you want, so why not leave?" I beg, just as banging on the door starts. My name is called through the letter box and my heart beats faster.

Someone's come for me.

Tears spring to my eyes but my mother just scoffs then her eyes widen in fear when a loud kick bangs against the door.

"I told you someone would come for me," I smile smugly, hating the words she threw at me. No doubt the same that is about to come from her mouth now.

"For you? No one loves you, Kayla. You're a weak little girl who no one will ever respect. You think that boy loves you?" she asks and my eyes widen. How does she know about Myles? "Yes, I know about you spreading those legs for him. I'm surprised you haven't already cried rape," she laughs. "I won't just make your life hell but I'll make his too." Then she grabs some things from outside my bedroom door before turning back to look at me. "Keep *that* shut," she says motioning to her mouth before disappearing.

Another loud bang startles me before my name is shouted through the house. Myles.

I smile for the first time in days and open my mouth and scream as loud as my throat will take me. "Here, Myles. Myles!"

He comes charging up the stairs like a bat out of hell and stumbles into my room. He takes one look at me and his eyes widen in horror.

"Holy fuck!" comes from behind him.

Myles, snapping out of his thoughts, rushes over to me, his eyes a mix of anger, guilt and relief.

"Are you okay?" he asks, trying to free my hands.

"I think my arm is broken. Other than that I'm fine," I pant out, my body shaking. I'm free. Finally free.

"Jesus, you're not fucking fine. Who the fuck did this?" he asks, his voice stronger and louder which makes me flinch.

"My…"

"You're fucking Mom," he bites out.

"What's going on, bro?" Mason asks looking concerned, and to be honest, a little horrified, which is what makes me start sobbing.

"Her mom beats her. Come on, we need to get you to the hospital," he tells me as he lifts me up into his arms, letting me stand on my feet. I sway from dizziness for a few seconds, not having any food or water has made me nauseous.

"What day is it?" I ask quietly as we walk down the stairs.

"Fuck!" Mason grits out.

"Friday, Babe. I've been trying to get a hold of you since Wednesday morning. Mason, go start the car," he orders and Mason runs off ahead.

The cool air hits me first from the air drifting through the broken door, but once we step out of the house, I'm blinded by light. The clouds are grey and miserable, the rain pouring down in thick drops, but I've never been so thankful to be outside.

Freedom.

"We need to file a report," Myles mutters as we step off the road to cross over to Mason's car.

"What?" I ask, stopping. "We can't," I tell him panicked. "It will make things worse, she said...she said she'd make my life hell if I told *anyone*," I tell him. "She'll make you pay too," I whisper quietly.

"She won't do shit, Kayla. You need to really think. You've been studying childcare, child abuse for a few years in school, would you tell a child in your care to not to tell anyone, to keep it to themselves and just suffer?"

Horrified, I blink up at him through the rain, ignoring Mason's calls to hurry up.

"Of course I wouldn't, Myles. It's why I want the job. I want to help kids who've gone through what I have."

"So why not help yourself," he yells, throwing his hands up.

I drop my head to the floor feeling ashamed of myself. I nod my head in agreement, knowing he's right. Damn, I've known it for a long time, but I've always let fear overrule what's right.

He takes my arm again and helps me step further into the road. My legs are shaky, but I'm managing. When I hear a car engine I try to quicken my pace, not wanting anyone slowing down enough to see the state I'm in.

A hard push to my back sends me flying to the ground near Mason's car and I yell out in pain. The next thing I hear is a loud thud, a sound of a window cracking, and Mason's yells. I roll over slowly in time to see Myles being thrown off a car that is speeding away, its tail lights disappearing off into the distance.

"NO!" I scream, crawling over to his lifeless body. "Myles, Myles, wake up," I shout at him.

Mason comes up behind me, his phone to his ear with his eyes watering with tears.

"Come on, bro. Wake up and shake it off," he chokes out, getting down on his knees. He doesn't make a move to touch Myles and I can see why. His leg is at a weird angle, his head is bleeding severely and his face is covered in bruises and blood.

"Please don't leave me, please," I beg.

"That was your fucking mother wasn't it?" Mason shouts and I stumble back on my ass. I look up at him with wide eyes. She left. She wouldn't. Oh my God. I roll over choking up bile at the same time a powerful sob tears through my chest.

"No, no, no, no," I chant over and over until I hear sirens not too far away. "I'm sorry, Mason. I'm so freaking sorry," I tell him and he looks at me with soft eyes.

"I don't blame you, Kayla. I blame your bitch of a mom. I know who she is and recognised her when she drove past."

"I'm sorry."

The ambulance pulls up and has Myles on a stretcher and in the back of an ambulance. When they ask who was coming Mason tells him to take me, that I've been hurt too. They also inform us the police will want to ask questions but we tell them to meet us at the hospital. Everything seems to happen so fast. One minute I'm tied in my bedroom being saved by the love of my life, and the next I'm sitting in the back of an ambulance praying he survives. They won't tell me what's going on, that they'll know more once the doctors at the E.R. check him over.

My arm was confirmed broken in two places an hour ago, and I've only just had someone come and plaster it up. I'm edging to go to see Myles, to see how he is, but no one will tell me anything and I can't go until I've been seen to.

The police called my father, informing him of the incident, my mother's involvement and the stolen items she took and sold. I couldn't tell them what she took, the only thing she specifically talked about was the wedding ring dad got in the divorce.

"You can go now, Miss," the kind nurse tells me when she walks back in.

"Do you know where they took the boy I came in with, Myles?" I ask, wiping tears away.

"If you go to the waiting area on level three, his family and friends are waiting to be spoken to by the nurse."

I nod my head and waste no time in rushing to the elevator, my legs still shaky from no food or water. It feels like the lift takes forever and by the time it reaches level three I'm a nervous wreck. I run down the corridor and push my way into the waiting room.

Everyone's heads jump to the door and I feel bad for rushing in. They're in here waiting to see if their brother is alive or not, and for a doctor to walk in and tell them.

Maverick is the first to reach me and when his arms wrap around me I fall into his embrace. I cry quietly into his chest, telling him how sorry I am.

"You're not to blame, Kayla," he tells me, his voice rough.

"If he never had come, if he didn't know me, this wouldn't have happened," I yell at him.

Harlow walks up to me slowly, her demeanour mournful, and I wonder if they've already had the news.

"Is he okay?" I ask her, knowing she knows something. It's the way she's looking at me, like my world is about to change and she wishes there was an easier way to break the news. I look around the room at everyone else and they all have a similar expressions. The atmosphere in the room spirals to the max. The intense, uneasy feeling overcoming me. The only person who hasn't looked up is Max. He's sitting down on the hard floor in the corner with his knees up to his chest, his face buried in his knees. It breaks my heart seeing him looking so helpless, so broken. His granddad notices where my attention is and looks with sad eyes to Max, shaking his head like he has no clue what to do.

"Kayla, we've been trying to get hold of you since yesterday morning. When I couldn't reach you, and Myles couldn't, we thought you were already told. So Myles said he'd give you until today. He's been worried about you. He said he felt uneasy, but he thought it was just because of the news."

"What do you mean? What aren't you telling me?" I ask her, feeling hysterical. I try to push Maverick's comfort away from me, not wanting it, but he grabs both of my arms behind me, hugging me to his front. "Tell me," I scream, struggling against Maverick. Tears run down both mine and Harlow's faces.

"It's Charlie. She was brought in on Monday. Her mom tried to call you, and when you didn't answer she called me to inform me. When we couldn't reach you we just assumed she had gotten in touch with you," she cries.

My knees give out but Maverick's ready and lifts me up, pulling me against him, supporting my weight.

"Is she... is she?" I sob out, but can't find the words.

"No. But it's not good. She's on the floor below us if you want to go see her."

"I can't leave Myles," I whisper, feeling torn.

"It's what Myles would want," Maverick tells me.

"I'll come down with you. I need to stretch my legs. Will you call me if you hear anything?" Denny asks Mason, speaking for the first time since I arrived. Malik is sitting in the chair next to where Max is sitting on the floor, his eyes now downcast.

"Yeah I will," he agrees.

Denny walks me out of the room and back down towards the lift, both of us silent until we're alone in the confined space.

"You could have told us, Kayla. I know what it's like to have an abusive mother. Yes, mine was emotionally, but I would have understood," she tells me sounding hurt.

"I didn't know this would happen, I would never want to see him hurt," I cry, and she shakes her head, disappointment shining in her eyes.

"That boy jumped in front of a car today to save your ass. That there proves how special you are, and how much he loves you and no doubt you feel just as strongly and would do the same if the roles were reversed.

"We all care about you. Each and every one of us would do the same for you, Kayla. You should have felt like you could have come to us. We would never have let her hurt you again," she says, tears running down her face.

"I've been alone for so long. I'm used to keeping everything to myself, keeping it all bottled up. I didn't know how to project my feelings," I admit. I've been so closed off, especially since the rape. After that I closed myself off from trusting anyone."

"Well, from here on out, don't keep shit to yourself," she warns me, before giving me a hug, both of us crying.

"I won't, I promise," I tell her just as the lift door opens.

I HARDLY RECOGNISE THE girl lying on the hospital bed. She's so pale, yet yellow looking. I want to run over and hug her, but she looks so freaking fragile.

"Kayla?" Charlie whispers, her eyes wide when she sees my cast. "Oh my Gosh, what happened?" she asks and just hearing her voice has me breaking down and rushing over to her. I sit on the bed and lay my head on her stomach.

"It's my entire fault. He could die and it's my entire fault. If only I had told someone about what she was doing sooner than none of this would have happened. I feel like I'm losing everyone," I cry out. I feel her lift her arm before her fingers start running through my hair, her fingers getting tangled in the still knotted strands.

"Kayla, what happened?" I hear her whisper, tears in her throat.

I look up at wipe my own tears and instantly feel selfish. "I'm so sorry. I'm being selfish. How are you feeling? What have they said?"

"What happened, Kayla?"

"My mom, she beat me and held me tied up in my room. I didn't even know how long for. Then Myles was taking me out to the car when my mom ran him over in her car," I ramble, still shaking.

"Oh, no! Where's your dad? Have they got her?"

I shake my head, 'no', feeling deflated. "I don't know what to do, Charlie."

"You'll figure it out. You have to remember we made a pact," she tells me and I roll my eyes.

"Whatever. Now, what did the doctors say?"

"Not a lot really. I've got a chest infection, and my liver and stuff are on the fritz. I guess if I don't get a transplant soon..." she shrugs trailing off, her eyes looking back down at her blanket. "I'm just so scared, Kayla. What will my mom do when I'm gone? Will she be okay? How will my dad cope? Everyone I've ever met, ever known will move on, but then, what will happen to me? Where will I go? Will I be there, will I still be able to think, to remember? It's all going around in my head, a million questions running through my head and I'll never know the answers until I die, and then it will be too late to know anything."

"Oh, Charlie. If there is one thing that I believe and that's that you'll reincarnate. Your soul will be reborn, and in time we'll meet again. The only other option is that you'll go to heaven, haunt our asses and watch over us for the rest of our lives until we're able to be with you.

"I can also tell you that days may turn into weeks, weeks into months, and months into years, but no matter how much time passes, no one who has ever known you will forget you for a second. I promise you.

"But you need to stay strong. I'm not ready to lose you. I can't. You're my bestfriend, and I can't live without my best friend. You have to be here to make sure I keep leaving the house, keep eating, and keep to our pact, because we both know I'll throw that crap into the bin," I laugh, tears still running down my face.

She laughs with me, but her laughs soon turn into sobs and it's heartbreaking. All her fears, all her questions are natural, and I won't lie and say I haven't asked myself the same questions.

When I attempted suicide after the rape, I asked all those questions and more.

Would I go to hell for taking my life? Would I be accepted? Would I reincarnate or would killing myself ruin my chances?

"I'm going to miss you," she sobs. "Just promise me, that no matter what, if I do die, you'll live enough for the both of us. Don't waste life on what ifs," she wheezes out just as the door to her room opens.

"Hey, how you feeling?" Denny asks softly.

"Better than this one," Charlie chuckles.

"I know, can't leave her alone for five minutes," Denny teases back.

"I'm right here," I snap, sitting up on Charlie's bed.

Charlie's mom walks into the room not long after, smiling when she's sees I'm finally here, but shocked when she sees the state of me. She doesn't ask any questions, just gives me a quick hug before telling us she'll be outside.

Half an hour passes and although I want to stay with Charlie, I'm anxious as hell to hear what is going on with Myles. Charlie yawns as the doctor walks in reading a chart.

"Oh my God, is Myles okay?" Denny gasps when she sees him and it has me on alert.

"Oh, Myles Carter?" he asks her, confused.

"Yes."

"I can't discuss patients with you, I'm sorry. I'm here to see Charlie here. We're short on doctors so I'm filling in," he explains.

"Oh," she sighs, looking disappointed. "Well we should go and see what's going on."

"I'll see you later, Charlie. I'll be back," I promise and reach over to hug her. "I love you."

"I love you too, and remember what I said."

I lean up and look into her eyes, reading the strong plea in them. I nod my head, 'yes', giving her another tight hug, feeling torn about leaving. I want to stay here with her, but I also want to see how Myles is doing.

The atmosphere back in the waiting area is tense. Everyone is still sitting in the same places as they were when we left just under an hour ago, their eyes rimmed red from the tears they've shed.

"Any news?" Denny asks walking over to Mason, wrapping her arms around him. I stand feeling awkward at the door, hating seeing the misery on all their faces and knowing it's my fault. I hate this. I hate that this has happened to such good people.

"No, we're still waiting. The nurse said they're short staffed and someone will get back to us as soon as possible," he says sarcastically. "He could be dead and those fuckers have us in here like sitting birds."

"Sitting ducks," Denny corrects, and he shakes his head before dropping it to her chest, where she wraps her arms around him.

"He's fine," Max says and from the hoarse sound in his throat I think this may be the first time he's spoken since he arrived.

"What?" Malik croaks, looking at his brother.

"He's not dead," Max replies sounding stronger. "I'd know right? I'd know if the other half of me had copped it. I'd know. I'd fucking know," he shouts, making everyone and me jump.

"He'll be fine. He's strong like the rest of you boys," Joan tells him softly.

"I know. He's the strongest," he whispers before dropping his head back into his knees, his shoulders shaking.

"Sit down," Maverick whispers, making me jump. I'm still standing by the door feeling like I don't belong. When the others hear his voice they all look up to stare at me making me fidget.

This is so awkward.

I nod, and with shaky legs I make my way over to the empty seat between Maverick and Mark. Time passes and the more I hear the clock ticking on the wall, the more I feel like I'm going to lose my mind.

Tick tock! Tick tock!

When the door to the waiting area opens, everyone shoots up from their seats, but I know, I know as soon as I see his face and his eyes meet mine.

"No! No, no , no, no," I scream, just as my feet collapse.

TWENTY-FOUR

KAYLA

THIS CANNOT BE HAPPENING.

No, no, no, no, no, no, I can't... I can't breathe.

"Kayla, breathe. Breathe," I hear Maverick shout, but it all sounds foggy to my ears. How can he be so calm?

"She's dead isn't she?" I ask. The pain in my chest feeling like a thousand knives slicing through me, it's excruciating. "It hurts. Oh my God, it hurts," I sob, rubbing my chest.

"Mrs Roberts asked me to come and inform you of her daughter's passing. She's still with her," I hear the doctor reply sadly before he starts talking to someone else in the room. I don't even know what about, I can't seem to hear past the loud ringing in my ears.

"Kayla, you need to snap out of it."

I've never felt anything like this. I've been beaten, raped, beaten and tied up by my mom, but I'd rather suffer through that kind of pain than this. At least I can recover from bruises, but this, this is something I'll never get over.

"How?" I whisper. "I was just with her, it can't be right. The doctor must have got it wrong," I suddenly blurt out, getting to my feet on shaky legs. I wobble, losing my balance, until someone's strong arms grab a hold of my waist. "It's not true. It's just not."

"I think you need to sit down," Maverick tells me softly, but I shove his hands away from my waist.

"No. No. I'm going to talk to her. She'll probably laugh at me for being silly. For getting worked up. I'd know right? I'd know if she died. She's not gone," I tell him before turning and running out of the room.

Loud footsteps thud on the floor behind me, but my mind is focused on getting to Charlie. I skip past the lift and move over to the exit, running up the stairwell to her floor. The footsteps behind me draw in closer, and if the person following speaks, I don't hear it.

Charlie's room comes into view and I relax. Her dad is sitting outside her door in a chair with his head down.

See? Surely if she was gone he wouldn't be sitting there? Right?

My heart is pumping in my chest so hard, my breath coming in short, deep, fast pants. Her dad doesn't even look up when I approach, his head stays bowed and my anxiety spikes.

I fling the door open startling Hannah, Charlie's mom, but I don't give her a second look, my attention solely on Charlie. She's sleeping. My body relaxes and a few more tears spill from my face. She looks so peaceful.

"They told me she was dead," I whisper to nobody. My hand reaching out for Charlie's. She's here, she's alive, she's breathing.

"Honey, she's gone, her heart couldn't take anymore," her mom croaks out and I look up at her, really looking for the first time and notice tears streaming down her face. Her eyes are red, her face worn and tired and she looks to have aged ten years.

"No, she's just sleeping. She always looks peaceful sleeping," I tell her, giving her a small smile.

She gives me a sad smile, her chin quivering and I look away.

"Sweetie, she's gone. Please, she's gone," she chokes out on a sob.

"No, she's not!" I yell, another sob breaking free. "She's not. Charlie, wake up, wake up," I plead, tears streaming down my face. She makes no move to open her eyes and I feel myself becoming angry.

No, no, no, no!

Please, God, no!

"Honey," is all Hannah says before covering her mouth with her hand. I notice a few other people have entered the room and I turn to find Denny, Maverick and Charlie's dad standing staring at me.

"SHE'S ALIVE, SHE'S NOT GONE," I roar. "She can't be. Wake up, wake up," I beg sobbing, shaking her shoulders gently. "Please wake up. You have to. We have loads to talk about."

"Maverick, do something," I hear Denny cry.

"Come on, Kayla. Let's give her mom and dad time to say goodbye," he whispers, coming up behind me. "Myles is awake, he wants to see you."

"No, not until she wakes up. Not until she tells everyone this is just a big lie," I choke out, looking down at her. Looking closer her skin is pale, and her lips are turning a bluish colour.

Maverick pulls my back to his front, wrapping his arms around me, and I lean back and choke on a sob. Mrs. Roberts walks around the bed with a white envelope in her hand and I shake my head over and over.

This can't be real.

I'd rather wake up back at home, tied up to a bed and having my mom kick me for the fun of it, than have this be real.

"She wrote this to you yesterday when no one could get a hold of you. She knew she was going, Sweetie. She made us promise things she'd never make us promise if she knew she'd survive," she chokes out. Her husband comes and wraps his arms around her and she falls in his arms crying.

I look down at the letter and pull away from Maverick, sitting down on the chair next to Charlie.

"Can we have five minutes?" I whisper, hoping they give us this time.

"Of course, we'll be outside," I hear her dad say.

A large hand lands on my shoulder, giving it a light squeeze before murmuring that they'll be outside.

"I'm sorry," Denny whispers, her voice hoarse from her tears. I nod my head not having anything to say. What can I say? There's nothing to say. I've just lost my best friend, my reason I got out of bed each morning after the rape, she helped me through so much and all I could do was sit back and watch her die. I made out that her dying never bothered me, because, in all honestly, I never thought she would die. She's strong, she's a fighter and she didn't deserve this.

I sit up from the chair and, wobbly, make my way over to her bed to sit down. She looks peaceful, like she's sleeping, it doesn't feel real. The blanket has been tucked under her armpits so that her arms rest by her sides, her hands resting on each other on her stomach.

The letter in my hand crinkles. When I look down I notice my tears soaking through and I quickly move it away, not wanting to ruin or smudge her words.

I feel like it takes all my strength when I tear the letter open, pulling out two pieces of paper.

Kayla,

What do you say to your best friend knowing you're not there to console her? Hard, huh? I want to go on and on about how fabulous I am, but we already knew all that, so I'll get to you.

When I first met you, I was in a bad place. I was lonely, bullied, and friendless. Then you came into my life and I felt like I was the most popular girl in school. You have this thing about you that draws people to you. You're kind to the point I think you'll be posted on YouTube one day for helping a snail across the road just to make sure it made it safely. I'm laughing (okay wheezing) writing this.

You're gentle, loving, superstitious, you love the same programmes I do, and you hate horror movies just as much as I do. You're also the most genuine person anyone can meet. I was lucky to have you in my life and it killed me when I watched you slowly killing yourself and I don't want to see that again, even from the heavens.

So all those promises I've hopefully already made you make me, keep them, and don't ever break them. Because my life was short it doesn't mean yours has to be as well.

I'm also going to ask you to do two more things, and I know you're crying and can hardly see these words, but I NEED you to do this for me.

1) *I need you to sing at my funeral, because let's face it, your voice always soothed me, and hearing it made me feel like I was floating, free, and alive all in one. So please, no matter how hard it will be for you, sing to me, just to me and ignore the people who have come to the church to say their goodbyes. Just focus on me. Even better, bring your phone and sing into it, just like you always did for me.*

2) *I need you to be there for my mom. I know it's a lot to ask with your own grief, but I need to know she's going to be okay. That no matter what, she will still have a part of me near. She always said you were more like my sister than a friend.*

While everything else is going to be hard, I need you to also do me a few other things, but they're on the other page. Look at it like a bucket list, not a chore list.

My hand is starting to cramp, so I really should finish this up, but know that I love you. I love you so goddamn much.

I don't like the thought that I won't be able to miss you where I'm going, but if there is one thing I do know, I'll love you forever.

Please don't grieve for me forever; it's not what I want. When you think of me, know I'm not suffering; know I do not have to go through another op, another procedure that will cause me to stay in hospital for weeks. Know I'm free, free from it all.

I love you, Charlie.

P.S. Tell my mom that her and dad's letters are in my pant drawer at home. Couldn't risk her reading it before. You know what she's like. She'd have informed the media.

Love you.

I stare at the words, but they're just a blur now through my tears. I cry, I cry for everything she's missing out on, everything she'll never experience. The paper falls from my fingers and I sob into my hands.

Wiping away my tears to clear my vision I notice the piece of paper that was underneath and I laugh. In bold letters at the top it reads CHARLIE AND KAYLA'S BUCKET LIST!

I don't expect you to tick them all off, but I'm hoping you know which ones I'm most serious about. I love you no matter what. Even if you don't tick any off, but know, I'll haunt your ass.

1) Fall in love, although, I know you're already there, just never give up on it.
2) Make love. Feel what s.e.x. is supposed to feel like. You never got to experience gentle, but I believe with Myles, he'll be that and more. (Make sure you come to my grave and tell me all about it)
3) Tell someone about your bitch of a mom. I know you think you hid it well, but you didn't. I may still be wrong, but in the case I'm right; push that witch off a cliff and forget all about her.
4) Make friends. You're worth being friends with. There will be someone out there feeling lonely, like I did, that would worship your friendship.
5) Get drunk. Yes, I so did this. I think you're in a safe place where you can have a drink, throw up and savour the raging hangover the next day. I've already told Denny to work on this one.
6) Do something reckless. Personally, I'd like to see you do this one because if there is something you aren't, it's reckless.
7) Get a tattoo.... you know you want to. I saw you eyeing those angel wings, don't deny it.
8) Pull a prank on someone who bullied you back in the day. I have the

perfect candidate. Bruce Lockwood. He was such an asshole, and as pranks go, I'd so show people what a little pecker he has. LOL

9) This one will be a hard one. Tell someone about what happened to you. People should know just how much you suffered. People should see the strength that you have inside you.

10) Never forget me and please don't be sad when you think of me. I want you to smile when I'm mentioned. You've got a few weeks to get all your tears out, but after that, all bets are off. You need to move on and not wallow. I don't want that for you, I want you to be happy.

The last number on the list drives me into another fit of sobs and I fall down onto Charlie, my head resting on her hands while I cry.

Not much time passes when the door creaks open and footsteps walk towards me. Thinking it's Maverick I turn to find my dad instead, his eyes red rimmed, and worry and concern filling his expression. I don't know what comes over me, but I jump off the bed and fall into his arms crying. He seems taken aback at first until I feel his arms wrap around me.

"I'm sorry, Kayla. I really am sorry," he tells me softly.

"It's not fair," I cry, still not understanding why God takes away the good people in life, but keeps the bad down here on earth. Sometimes I believe that we live in Hell, and when we die we go to Heaven, or we just reincarnate to stay down here in Hell. It'd make sense, wouldn't it? Whatever I believe doesn't matter because I know somewhere out there Charlie's soul is floating around looking down on us, making sure we're all okay. I can feel it.

"The police are here. They have your mother. I don't understand what's going on. I had a phone call that you had been in an accident, but the police officer said your mother was involved," he tells me, completely flustered.

"I need to give them my statement," I tell him, feeling like a zombie.

"Come on, they're outside, but I think they'll understand if you want to have a couple of days until you feel up to it. That way I can see to your mother."

Not understanding his meaning about my 'mother' I shove it off, but a niggling feeling has me wondering if he cares. Surely he knows what she's done if they've told him her involvement, but the way he says 'see to your mother' it doesn't seem venomous in any way.

We walk out the door and Denny and Maverick get up from the floor where they were perched. Maverick gives my dad a hard look before his eyes soften looking down at me.

"How you doing?" he asks, his eyes flicking to the pieces of paper in my hand.

I shrug, and jump when a gasp startles me from my left. I turn to find Katie rushing down the corridor, her face flustered and red.

"Oh my God, Honey," she gasps, breathing hard when she gets to our little huddle. I put my head down knowing she'll see the shame in my eyes from lying to her. I'm thankful when she starts firing questions at my dad and I manage to pull myself out from between them and walk over to Mrs. And Mr. Roberts.

"Hey, Hannah. I'm sorry for the way I acted," I tell her, feeling ashamed by my reaction.

"Oh, Sweetie. Are you okay?" she asks, wiping her eyes.

I nod my head, but deep down I'm falling apart and I need some space to get myself together.

"She wanted me to tell you that she has letters written for each of you back in her room. They are in her knickers drawer."

Hannah looks at her husband with wide eyes, tears filling them, and I can see she's torn between staying with Charlie, and leaving to go read the words she wrote for her.

"I'm going to give my statement to the police, but I'll come round very soon to see you. Charlie wanted me to sing at her funeral," I tell her, not looking her in the eye.

"She always said she felt at real peace when you sang to her, but she would never let me hear you," she tells me, which makes me look up at her shocked.

"She didn't?"

"No. She said you weren't ready for the world to hear the voice of an angel," she says and I can hear Charlie saying that.

"I tried recording some songs onto her phone the once because of our phone bills getting too high from me calling her, but she said it wasn't the same. I had to beg my dad for a contract phone just so I could sing to her," I laugh, but it's low, and sad.

"Well, you go and sort out what you need to, and we will see you soon, Darling," she tells me before falling softly into her husband's arms and silently crying.

"Kayla. Kayla Martin?" A deep voice speaks and I turn around to find two police officers standing behind me.

"Yes?"

"We would like you to come down into a room that the nurses have let us use to ask you some questions. We understand this is a tough time for you, but we need to get your mom booked."

"Booked?" my dad asks shocked, looking at me with questioning eyes. I look away to see Maverick take a step towards my dad, but Denny reaches out to stop him.

I nod my head to them. "I'll meet you back in the waiting room?" I ask Denny and Maverick sadly.

"Okay. I don't know if you heard me, but Myles is awake and he's okay," Maverick replies and tears of relief fill my eyes.

TWENTY-FIVE

KAYLA

We're in what I think is a staff room. It's got a table centred in the middle with four chairs surrounding it. A little kitchenette sits along the one wall and boxes fill the other.

The police officers asked Katie to stay outside. They tried the same with my dad telling him they wanted to talk to me alone, but he was having none of it. Because I didn't want to repeat myself over and over again to everyone, I asked them if it was okay to have him there. They didn't look too pleased, but I think that's more to do with the fact they think I won't speak up about what my mom did, but boy are they wrong. I'm about to tell them everything.

"I'm PC Howard, and this is my partner PC Smith..."

"I'm sorry, but I can't see why you have arrested Jessica?" Dad interrupts, but the police officer asks him to keep quiet until after the interview. Both officers take notes and it makes me nervous. It reminds me a lot of my therapist when we're in a session.

"Earlier today a call was made from a nurse here, requested by you. From the little information we have, it seems you want to press charges against your mom for assault, is that correct?" the police officer starts, but my dad holds up his hand interrupting. His face is red with anger and his fists are clenched, which is not the response I was hoping for. This is going to get worse before it gets better. Why did I ever think he'd take my side, stand by me?

"Mr. Martin, I'll ask you again, please abstain yourself from interrupting or we will have to ask you to leave. We need to talk to your daughter and ask some questions."

"I asked the nurse to call you," I blurt out, confirming, just wanting to ease the tension in the room. Only it makes it all worse, and it's only coming from one person.

My dad.

"Why would you do that?" my dad asks me, but I ignore him and talk directly to the officers, wanting, no needing, to get all this out of my system.

"On Tuesday my boyfriend dropped me off at home. I watched his car leave before shutting the door. I didn't even get to turn around," I tell them, swallowing the lump in my throat. "I don't remember much, just waking up tied to my bed, bleeding and hurt. She beat me for I don't know how long," I tell them, my voice rising. I'm angry at her, angry she hurt me, but more angry at her for hurting Myles. He had nothing to do with any of this.

"Have you been seen by a doctor?" PC Howard asks looking at me directly. It makes me feel safe, like it's a safe place to open up. I nod my head yes, before he carries on. "Has your mother hurt you before Tuesday?"

"Of course she hasn't," my dad shouts, outraged .

"Yes, every time I was in her care," I answer honestly.

"Kayla," my dad asks. "How? When? Why?"

"Sir, I understand this is a difficult situation, but we really need to talk to Kayla here," he tells my dad, before turning his attention back to me. "What made this time worse? Different?"

"I don't know what made her do what she did this time. She usually makes sure no one will see the bruises.

"She's taken jewellery of my dad's, and kept going on about selling it, needing the money. She's always acted like I owed her, but more so when they got divorced."

"And what about the hit and run?"

"My boyfriend, Myles, got worried when I never texted him, or called him back. And we planned to meet on Thursday, so when I didn't turn up, he knew something was wrong, especially when my friend," I swallow, feeling the pain hit my chest thinking of Charlie. It doesn't seem real.

"Take your time. You're in a safe place," he encourages.

"My friend, she was ill and we're like sisters, so when I never turned up or answered back he knew, so he turned up at the house. He kicked the door in and found me tied to the bed. My mom was there when it happened, I don't know how she got out without him seeing her, but she did. He knew about it, some of it, and told me I needed to tell someone. That's when the car came out of nowhere and he pushed me out of the way. He saved my life," I tell them, my eyes watering. "Is there anything else, I need to go see him," I tell them, knowing what I need to do.

"Yes…for now. We will be in contact to get an official statement. Your mother got picked up just over an hour ago. Another witness on the scene identified your mother as the one from the hit and run."

"What will happen to her?" I ask, not really caring.

"She will be charged with a hit and run, and will also be charged with the assault towards you."

I nod my head understanding, hoping she gets jail time and has to share a cell with some butch woman who farts a lot and eats with her mouth open.

"Can I go?" I ask attentively. "I haven't seen my boyfriend yet."

"Just a second," PC Howard tells me before addressing my father. "Could you wait outside for two minutes? There is one question that we would like to ask Kayla in private."

My dad looks too stunned, shaken up by the news he's just heard. I can't blame him. He's always hid his head in the clouds. Even Katie clicked on to what was going on with me and she met me for five minutes.

My dad stands up, looking down at me with watery eyes. "I'll wait outside," he says quietly, touching my shoulder lightly before walking out, leaving me with the two officers. My attention turns to them and notice them give each other a look.

"Kayla, I know this has been a difficult day for you, but your safety is important to us."

"Okay," I murmur, wondering where they are going with this. They have my mother in custody; it's the safest I've been since forever.

"Would you like us to arrange for somewhere to stay tonight, or are you safe to leave with your dad?"

"My dad's never touched me if that's what you're wondering. I promise."

"Okay. We will leave you to visit with your boyfriend and will contact you soon to get a full statement."

"Thank you. Thank you for everything."

"It's our job, Miss."

I nod my head, not agreeing. No one goes into the police force thinking *it's just a job*. They go into knowing they are making a difference, helping people.

My dad is outside when we leave, the police officers nodding their goodbyes before making their way down the hall.

"I'm going to go see Myles; there's something I need to do," I tell him feeling numb. I just want to process everything, but my mind won't stop with its whirlwind of thoughts to just stop on one. I feel like I'm a tornado heading towards a volcano.

The room is silent when I walk into Myles' room. He's in a private room until they find him a bed. When I spoke to Mark, his granddad, outside, he told me he'd be released by the end of next week, which made me breathe a sigh of relief.

"Hey," I whisper when he meets my eyes. He has bruises covering his face, and scratches from the curb. He leg is elevated in the air, covered in a cast. He has a bandage wrapped around his head and looks like he got hit by a truck instead of a car. "How are you feeling?"

I can't look at him any longer, the guilt of everything is weighing me down.

He coughs, making a wincing sound and I look up, worried he's hurt.

"It's not your fault," he croaks out as if reading my thoughts.

"Don't say that, we both know it is," I whisper ashamed. "What have the doctors said?"

"I'm fine. Just a broken leg, a few bruised ribs, and a concussion from my head injury. Have they talked to you about your mom?" he asks, not looking at me in the eye.

"Yes, she's been arrested. I want you to know I've told the police everything. She's been arrested," I tell him in a panicked voice, not wanting him to think I've continued to cover for her. After seeing what she's really capable of, there is no way to cover for her, especially now that she's hurt Myles.

"I wasn't sure... They came to talk to me before. I heard about Charlie, I'm so sorry," he says, his voice still sounding off.

I feel like there's a barrier between us now, and it's shifting us further and further apart. The silence between us is killing me; it's drawing out longer and longer between each word.

"Are we okay?" I ask in a whisper, scared to repeat myself if he didn't hear me.

"Yes, Babe. I'm just tired. The drugs they have me on are making me drowsy."

I nod my head, glad we're okay, but scared about his reaction to what I'm about to say.

"I need to do something, and to do it, I need time to myself, if only for a little while."

"You don't need to do this," he says, trying to sit up, but I put my hand on his chest stopping him.

"I'm not breaking up with you, but after everything that's happened I've realised I rely on you too much. I need to learn how to be strong by myself without having to lean on you, to pile everything on you. I nearly got you killed today and it's killing me inside."

"I don't blame you," he chokes out, looking at me wide eyed and panicked.

"I know you don't, but I do. If I was stronger none of this would have happened, Myles. Being with you has made me stronger. Well, now I need to prove it, not just to you, but to myself. I know what I need to do to achieve that, but I need to do it on my own. I need to be the one to take those steps."

"So, we're not breaking up?" he asks, looking hopeful.

"No. Never. I could never break up with you. I love you," I smile.

"I love you too. How are you doing?" he asks, his hand lightly rubbing my fingers where the cast on my broken arm meets.

"I'm good. My dad is waiting for me outside so I need to go," I tell him regretfully.

"When will I see you again?" he asks, his eyes watering.

"That's the other thing. I know you need to rest, but I need you to be at school next Thursday."

"I'll be there," he tells me, and I lean down to give him a light kiss, but as every time our lips touch, it turns heated, our tongues massaging against each other's. Tears fall down into our kiss and I realise it's me crying and I pull away. "It won't be forever."

"I know. I love you. Get better soon," I choke out and before he can reply, I turn and rush out the room, knowing the next two weeks are going to be hell, but I need to do this. It's also another box I can tick off on Charlie's list, and I'm sad she won't be there, but hopefully, wherever she is, she will hear me.

Everyone greets me outside, giving me their condolences, which makes me break down, and in Katie's arms of all people.

Maverick is the only one who knows my plan and promises to keep me informed on Myles' progress, and to make sure he's at school on that Thursday. All I need to do now is clear it with the school.

Thursday is going to be the day I tell everyone my darkest secrets.

TWENTY-SIX

KAYLA

"Hey, I just wanted to let you know I've dropped Myles off in the hall," Maverick says making me jump.

Jesus.

"Where the hell did you come from?" I ask, looking around backstage. I'm in the school drama hall where our school presents our assemblies. Today it will be me giving out the assembly speech and I'm scared shitless.

"Sorry," he laughs. "I didn't mean to scare you. I saw an old teacher of mine, I asked if he knew where you were, and well, here I am," he chuckles. "How are you feeling?"

"Nervous," I tell him honestly, wringing my fingers together.

"You can do this," he compliments, taking me by the shoulders. "He misses you ya know."

I hear the sadness in his voice. It's been so hard staying away, not answering Myles' messages or phone calls. The only person I've spoken to, bar the police and my dad, is Maverick.

"I miss him, too."

"Then make sure you go to him after your speech. He wants to be there for you tomorrow."

I breathe in, my heart rate escalating when I think about tomorrow. I've tried not to think about it, it hurts too much, but I know either way tomorrow I will give Charlie the best send off. She deserves it after everything she has been through.

"How has your dad taken everything that has happened? Has everything at home been okay?" he asks thoughtfully.

"He's taken it hard, but I think he's getting there. At first he didn't want to believe what happened with my mom, at how long she was hurting me, but I showed him a few things," I mutter, looking away.

"I feel like there's a 'but'," he asks curiously.

"*But*, he's driving me crazy. I know he will never be the dad that shows up to a school play, to spend time with me or take me away on holiday, but he loves me. I know he does. I just wish he'd give me some space, ya know?"

"He's just feeling guilty. It happened to you while he should have been protecting you," he shrugs.

"Kayla, we're ready for you," Principal Collins interrupts. "Hello, Maverick. Iit's good to see you," she smiles warmly at him, not the same frustrated look I've seen her give Max.

"You too, Miss. Collins," he smiles at her before turning back to me. "Good luck, Kid. You're gonna smash it."

"God, I'm so nervous," I admit, wiping my sweating palms down my school trousers.

"Go! You'll be fine," he tells me with confidence that I wish I had right now. I nod my head, too afraid I'm going to choke up and burst into uncontrollable tears on him. I watch him leave backstage before turning to the curtains and taking a step, listening to Miss. Collins as she introduces me. The school applaud making me more nervous and I end up walking onto the stage with shaky legs.

I hate being centre of attention, especially like this. Everyone is staring at me, all their attention purely directed at me. I stand directly in front of the podium, moving the mic into a better position before looking around the room nervously. Everyone, like I had feared, is staring up at me, looking confused as to why I'm standing up here today giving our assembly.

My focus lands on the back of the room, my heart stopping. Myles is sitting down in his wheelchair, dead centre of the aisles, giving me a clear view of his injuries. Even from up here I can see he's healing nicely, and when I shift my gaze up to his eyes I nearly stumble backwards when I find him looking right back at me. I give him a shaky smile when I notice the rest of his brothers, Harlow and Denny are standing there, too. They're all wearing prideful expressions. Knowing I have the support here in the audience, my nerves begin to calm somewhat.

"Hey. For those who don't me, I'm Kayla Martin. I'm here today on behalf of Principal Collins to support anti-bullying, and for the presentation Miss. Watson has given me in childcare on the affects of child abuse.

As both subjects are something I feel strongly about, I volunteered to stand up here today and give you my story, and how it all affected me.

"Over 50,000 children are identified as needing child protection in the UK, but what about the other large number who suffer in silence? The ones not added into statistics? What happens when they have no one to talk to, no one to turn to? In my personal experience, it only ends badly with people you love around you getting hurt.

"Statics show that most bullies are suffering at home with abuse and they take out their frustrations out on people weaker than them, others just do it to feel big, to feel better about themselves. But ask yourself this, that person you're bullying, the person's life you're making a living hell, what happens to them after they leave here, leave the halls of torture? Do they leave to a happy, safe environment, or do they have nothing more than to endure more bullying and torturing when they get home.

"All my life I've lived feeling unloved, not wanted, and always feeling like an outcast in this world. Then I turned thirteen and enrolled here, and for the first time in my life I was excited, excited for all the possibilities. I wanted to make friends that would last a life time, meet boys for the first time, and act like a teenager, to just be accepted. Instead, I started here and I was bullied. My clothes *weren't fashionable*, I was *too skinny*, my boobs *were too big*, *I was weird*," I blush, hating that I notice the attention of a few lads in the front row has been drawn to my boobs.

"They made me feel unworthy, inadequate, lonely and I hated that I let people have that power over me. But, what hurt the most was the people that looked on and watched, standing by and doing nothing. It was those people who could have helped me, but more importantly, I wished I'd helped myself. It took me a long time to believe their name calling was just that, names. I ignored them, moved past it, and started believing in myself. Unless they said something *I* believed to be true, I paid no attention.

"Then when the bullies knew they couldn't hurt me anymore, one took it to the next level, he raped me. He didn't just steal my innocence; he stole my soul, my dignity. I'm not telling you this for you all to feel sorry for me, I'm telling you this because it's my story, it's what I know, what I've lived. The first person I turned to was my mother, and you know how she reacted? She pushed me away with a disgusted look on her face. It was then I never felt so ashamed of being myself, I felt dirty, and it took me until recently to stop taking showers every chance I had.

"From that day forward my life got worse. I found everyday chores hard, even leaving the house, being in a public place so much harder, causing me to have panic attacks. School got that bad with other kids taunting me, their constant name calling, reminding me every day of what he did to me that I couldn't stand it anymore. It made me want to end my pain, which I tried to do, unsuccessfully, twice," I tell them, feeling choked up admitting that part. I wipe away my tears before looking up again.

"Thankfully, we moved not long after and I prayed so hard I'd be able to relax in my own body. But it was all a fantasy. I dropped out of school and got homeschooled and my home life got much worse. Long story short, since I was thirteen my mother abused me. She not only physically beat me, but she beat me down with her cruel words. A lot of people who are in my situation will tell you they'd rather take a beating than have cruel words thrown at them and I can totally sympathise. Those cruel words will live with you for the rest of your life; eat away at you from the inside until you start believing them.

"My life has been filled with so many doubts, so many what ifs. But one thing I learnt was suffering in silence just made me lonelier.

"So, I'm standing up here today to ask you, no, to beg you, to fight back. Whether it's a bully, or a parent, speak up. Don't hold on to your silence. They may scare you into silence because it's them that are afraid. Afraid of the consequences bound to happen to them. If they threaten you to keep quiet it's only because of the control they have over you. Take back that control, speak up. Get proof of what they're doing by recording it on your phone; get a friend to record it. I'm not standing here preaching that it will be easy; I know firsthand how scary it is, but from this day forward make a stand.

"I also want to tell the people, if they're listening, to think about their actions when you're bringing down another person. What are you achieving? If power is what you want join a school club, don't bring another person down with you. My education got put at risk, my dream job, my way out of the abuse at home because of a fair few bullies.

"So I will leave today with this. Parents are supposed to be the ones that you run to, confide in, and support you, so when it's one of them that is destroying you, it ruins you.

"That stops today. After a lot of begging on my part, I have got funding for the school to have a councillor on their payroll. It won't be like your career councillors, this one will be for you to talk to and confide in.

"I hope my story made people look at life differently, will change the way they behave towards another human being."

My heart is beating rapidly, and my mind is in a daze, but I come through when a deafening applause rings throughout the hall. I blink rapidly, tears blurring my eyes when I find everyone on their feet applauding me. I give a shaky smile before looking down to my family, and freeze when my eyes find my dad's and Katie's. I didn't even see them come in.

Needing *his* comfort, I rush down the stage steps, smiling at a few people before rushing down the aisle towards the one person I need right now.

I fall into his lap, burying my head into his neck and sob. I sob for everything I just released, all the pain and hurt I had bottled up inside me.

"How did it feel?" Myles whispers, his arm rubbing softly up and down my back.

I look up at him and smile. "Freeing."

"And how do *you* feel?" he grins.

"Lighter," I admit, glad to have everything off my chest. Whatever people decide to do with what I told them today is up to them, for me it was a way to let go of everything that has been weighing me down.

"I'm glad, Baby." His smile is bright, and I realise just then how much I really do love him, and I don't mean crush love, but a forever kind of love.

He leans in, his lips reaching mine, and for once, I don't care about the audience watching us, I press my lips to him and give him everything through a kiss, my love, my gratitude, and my soul. Wolf whistles reach my ears, and I laugh against Myles' mouth. I look around blushing but still grinning like an idiot.

"So, now that you're free, what is the first thing you're going to do?" Myles questions.

"I'm going to live," I answer immediately.

"Kayla," Mrs. Roberts greets sadly. "I just spoke with your father, he told me about yesterday. I'm sorry we missed it."

Mrs. Roberts always knew something wasn't right with me at home, but always aimed her dislike towards my parents towards my dad, not my mom. Charlie knew, and even told me a time or two, that her mom had questioned her over me.

"It was no big deal," I brush her off, looking around at the people entering the church. There are so many people here. Many of them I recognise from when I was at school with Charlie and I want to scream at them and ask what the hell they are doing here. Not one of them talked to her when she was alive, not one, but then I realise this is something Charlie would look down on and feel loved. She'd see it as people noticing her, which was hard not to, she was an incredible person with a bright personality. I just wish the people walking into the church knew her the way I did.

"It looks like a lot of friends have turned up, I didn't realise she had this many," Mrs. Roberts chokes out, grabbing a tissue from out of her purse.

"She was loved, Mrs. Roberts," is all I can manage to get out, before I move around her and into the church. I spoke with her last week when she organised the funeral about what would happen. I'm going to sing a song as the coffin is brought down the aisle, and again when they carry her out. Myles called Mrs. Roberts a week ago apparently, and told her his brothers offered to carry Charlie's coffin. Mr. Roberts agreed immediately, so he and his brother, along with the Carter boys will be carrying Charlie and placing her at the front of the church.

Walking into the church people I know, and some I don't give me their condolences. I give them a small smile, before moving on, and ten minutes, maybe longer, I finally reach the front where the vicar is talking to Myles who is waiting for me.

"Just the girl. The Carter boys, Mr. Roberts and his brother are ready. Everyone is taking their seats now, so if you'd just go get yourself ready," he tells me softly, patting me once on the shoulder before standing centre on the steps near where the casket will be placed.

I nod my head before shakily turning to Myles, my eyes watering already.

"You can do this," he tells me softly.

"My heart hurts," I tell him honestly, grateful for his support. We spent last night together. My dad didn't get a choice in the matter, but he did say we couldn't shut the door, which I didn't really mind.

"The pain will soothe in time, baby. Let's just get you through today, now go sing your little heart out," he whispers against my lips. My lips meet his as the first tear falls from my eyes, and we stay like that, kissing softly, until Myles pulls away to hug me, his strong arms giving me the strength I need.

Standing at the podium, I cough before taking a sip of the bottled water Myles brought me. I'm actually thankful because my mouth is dry and swallowing past the lump inside my throat has become difficult.

When everyone is seated, I begin; my voice soft and sweet carrying across the room.

Spend all your time waiting
for that second chance
for a break that would make it okay
there's always some reason
to feel not good enough
and it's hard at the end of the day
I need some distraction
oh, beautiful release
memories seep from my veins
let me be empty
and weightless and maybe
I'll find some peace tonight

in the arms of the angel
fly away from here
from this dark cold hotel room
and the endlessness that you fear
you are pulled from the wreckage
of your silent reverie

> *you're in the arms of the angel*
> *may you find some comfort here*

My eyes look up for the first time and I choke out the next words, the lump in my throat expanding when I see Mr. Roberts and his brother at the front carrying the casket that carries my best friend. She's in there, she's laying in there, in the dark, but then I remember, her soul isn't in that box, she's an Angel now.

> *so tired of the straight line*
> *and everywhere you turn*
> *there's vultures and thieves at your back*
> *and the storm keeps on twisting*
> *you keep on building the lies*
> *that you make up for all that you lack*
> *it don't make no difference*
> *escaping one last time*
> *it's easier to believe in this sweet madness oh*
> *this glorious sadness that brings me to my knees*
>
> *in the arms of the angel*
> *fly away from here*
> *from this dark cold hotel room*
> *and the endlessness that you fear*
> *you are pulled from the wreckage*
> *of your silent reverie*
> *you're in the arms of the angel*
> *may you find some comfort here*
> *you're in the arms of the angel*
> *may you find some comfort here*

I end the song on a choked sob. My voice had been a quivering mess since the second I lifted my eyes to see them carrying the casket down the aisle.

Without a second thought I rush down the few steps on the podium and over to the casket, where Charlie's body is sleeping.

"I love you so much," I whisper, tears falling from my eyes and onto the casket. My feet feel heavy, the same as my heart as I walk away and to the front row where I meet Myles and his brothers.

I miss half the service the vicar is giving, my eyes and head focused on the coffin, hating that she's there, sleeping and not moving. It's all that keeps going on in my head and I hate it. It's the first funeral I've ever been to; my mother never let me go to Miss. Niles', saying I wasn't family, even though the woman brought me up as her own child. I never expected it to be anything like this, how hard it would be to see the coffin, to know she's in there, it's breaking my heart.

I feel Myles nudge me and I look up at him and see him giving me a concerned look. He shifts his eyes over to the front and I shake my head.

"Your speech, Babe," he whispers, and I gasp, horrified I forgot. Mrs. Roberts wanted me to stand up and say something. When I asked who else was speaking she looked sad, telling me she couldn't, she couldn't stand up there, she'd break further. I can understand. Just singing the song Charlie chose for me to sing killed me.

Clearing my throat, I stand, giving Myles a small smile when he squeezes my hand in encouragement. I'd prepared a speech, something small and simple, and I had it memorised, but standing up here, looking over at everyone's tear stained faces, I go blank.

I clear my throat again, before addressing everyone, needing them to know, just know she was special.

"This is the second speech I've given in two days, and by far the hardest," I choke out, wiping away another tear, they just keep on coming. Bracing myself, getting myself together I take a deep breath. "I could stand up here for days and tell you how great Charlie was, how beautiful and kind she was, but for whoever knew her will know that already. They will know how lucky they were to have her in their life, to have her as a friend.

"So instead, I'm going to stand here today and tell you what she meant to me. Charlie wasn't just my best friend; she was my sister, my rock. She was the rainbow on a rainy day, stars on a dark night and the light on a dark day. She was everything and not a day will go by that I will forget that, or forget her.

"I love you, and will miss you," I say, now facing the casket, my hand resting on the top. I hear Mrs. Roberts cry out a sob, and I move quickly, not able to look at her, knowing it's going to set me off. I shouldn't have worried, as soon as I feel

Myles' strong arms around me, I break down, my sobs heavy and strong, and I cling to him with all the strength I have left.

I vaguely hear the vicar talking, about what I don't know, but when I hear him talking about donations going to the British Heart Foundation and Organ donation forms available at the back of the church; I know I need to get my act together. Charlie not only wanted me to sing one song, but also her favourite song she loved hearing me sing.

I get up from my seat wiping my soaked face with the tissue Denny handed me not long ago. It's already soaked, but it's all I have. I make my way back up to the podium, the strength I had for today beginning to weaken, my mood downing, and my energy falling too exhausted.

"Charlie requested a very special song, close to her heart, to be played by her best friend, Kayla. Please remain seated until Kayla is up and standing behind the casket," the vicar speaks, just before the tune to the song I'm singing starts to play.

Myles had to mess around with this one as I won't be able to sing all of the song, and walk Charlie back down the aisle, so we decided I'd sing the half of it before the boys get up to lift the casket, and then I'll slowly lower my voice until the actual singer starts singing.

When tomorrow comes
I'll be on my own
Feeling frightened of
The things that I don't know
When tomorrow comes
Tomorrow comes
Tomorrow comes

And though the road is long
I look up to the sky
And in the dark I found, lost hope that I won't fly
And I sing along, I sing along, and I sing along

I got all I need when I got you and I
I look around me, and see a sweet life
I'm stuck in the dark but you're my flashlight

You're getting me, getting me, through the night
Kick start my heart when you shine it in my eyes
Can't lie, it's a sweet life
Stuck in the dark but you're my flashlight
You're getting me, getting me, through the night
'Cause you're my flashlight (flashlight)
You're my flashlight (flashlight), you're my flashlight

I'm a sobbing mess by the end of my verse. My tears soaking my face and my throat raw from crying. *Flashlight* was the song Charlie always made me sing when she couldn't sleep. But now that she's gone, it has such a deeper meaning, she is my flashlight. She gave me hope on my dark days, she gave me light, and she definitely got me through the night and one thing is for sure with her around I had a sweet life, now all I pray is, her ever presence lives on around me, guiding me through all the good and bad times.

I make it down to Myles where his granddad has brought round the wheelchair for me to push him out with. Mrs. Roberts wanted Charlie's close friend right behind her when the boys carry the casket back down the aisle.

Looking up, I notice the boys and Mr. Roberts and his brother making their way to the casket. Her dad is a mess, sobbing and crying, and when he struggles to gain his composure, Mark walks over clapping him on the back and whispering something in his ear. When Mr. Roberts nods and looks at his wife with a lost expression, I almost collapse. Only Myles must sense I'm about to lose control and reaches around for my hand clutching the handles of his wheelchair and gives me a light kiss. I watch as the men lift Charlie, and I'm so proud of them, watching them carry her like the precious angel she is.

The song still plays in the background as we follow them down the aisle, Mrs. Roberts clutching her husband for support. My own tears keep falling, but I push on, needing to give her the send off she needs.

Even with saying goodbye to my best friend, I know this isn't the end for us, that one day we will meet again in the afterlife, and carry on being the friends we were.

EPILOGUE

KAYLA

It's been just over a month since Charlie's funeral, and everyday has been hard without her, but tonight has been one of those nights that I need her more than anything.

Myles invited me to our end of school prom, and I assumed it was just a party. You know, a school disco that you can just wear something fancy to, and Bob's your uncle. But, no! Instead, I was told yesterday by Denny and Harlow that it has to be a special gown. So now I'm screwed.

I've been throwing clothes out of my wardrobe for the past hour, trying to find something good enough, none of my dresses are that fancy. After the attack I made sure to buy clothes that bagged on me, or didn't show much skin. Now I'm actually regretting it. I want tonight to be perfect, but it's already a disaster.

The door to my room knocks and I let out a, "Come in," sigh.

When Katie sticks her head around the door I'm shocked. I didn't know she was going to be here tonight. Dad said they had a meal they were going to and that he would be spending the night at her place to give me and Myles some privacy. I think the privacy had more to do with Katie than my dad. I could tell he was biting his tongue when he told me.

"Hey," she smiles.

"Hey, what are you doing here?" I smile back. I've come close to Katie and love having her around and for some reason she loves my dad. I'm just glad he has someone like her in his life. She is nothing like my poisonous mother, who, by the way, got jail time and is having a psyche evaluation.

"I bought you something," she grins, then steps from behind the door with a white garment bag and a smaller black bag.

"What?" I gasp surprised. "What... I... What. I don't know what to say," I laugh when I fall over my words. She laughs back before hanging it up on the door. I'm still standing with a towel wrapped around my body, and one wrapped around my head.

"Myles called saying Denny called him, telling him you didn't have a dress. He asked if there was something you could borrow as both Denny and Harlow didn't go to their prom."

"He did?" I ask, melting on the spot.

God, I love him. I really do.

"You have it bad sweetie," she smiles and I just nod smiling back. "Anyway, I got you this..."

She reveals a stunning black and green puffy ball gown. The top half is tight fitted, a metallic green with black patterns. I can't make out from here if it's a rose at the bottom with little branches and thorns coming from it, or if it's just a pattern. I don't care. What I care about right now is that this woman went out of her way to get me the most stunning prom dress ever. The bottom half is my favourite. From the waist down it puffs out in layers and layers. It has these little white dots that sparkle, almost making it look glittery.

"It's beautiful," I whisper, my eyes watering. My mother would have made me go in trousers and a top, not caring what I wore. In fact, she'd probably go out of her way to get me the most horrendous dress she could find just to humiliate me.

"Don't. You'll set me off," she tells me, waving me off. "Myles said it was a 'Far Away' theme, and this is all the shop had left. It's a little on the fairytale side, but it will work. The woman said most of the dresses girls have been in for have looked the same," she shrugs.

"Thank you," I tell her, rushing over and hugging her, keeping one hand on my towel so I don't lose it. "Now all I have to do is do something with my hair," I groan, when I pull away. I need it cut. It's getting too long, frizzy, but it's the only time the curls stay loose and look like little ringlets.

"Don't worry, by the time I've finished with you, you'll be fit for a king," she winks and gestures me over to my desk where she parks my bum on the chair.

After that it's whirlwind. She does some magic with my hair, gets makeup to look right on my face, and by the time I'm finished and in my dress I have two minutes before Myles is here. I turn around when Katie finishes zipping the back of the dress up and make my way over to the mirror.

I stand still in shock, not believing what she's done. My hair is up in what can only be described as a work of art. She's used my curls and put them into a bun on the top of my head, but she's also got two plaits running around the side of my head to the back doing God knows what. My fringe has been blow dried to the side, looking full and bouncy. It's beautiful. I feel like Cinderella.

My makeup has been kept light apart from my eyes. She's made them look smoky, with a little green eye shadow on them making my green eyes stand out perfectly.

The dress, however, is just another story. It fits perfectly and although there is a dip between the breasts it still doesn't show off a lot of cleavage. Not that I really care.

When I hear rustling behind me, I turn to find Katie going through the other bag she brought with her.

When she finally grabs what she needs she throws them down on my bed before turning and walking over to me.

"Hold your hand out," she tells me grinning. She hasn't stopped praising how beautiful I look and if it wasn't for the fact I have seen the magnificent job she's done, I would tell her to shut up.

She places a black sparkly band of bracelets on my wrist that matches my dress perfectly, then she puts on a matching ring.

The doorbell rings and I'm thankful we're finished in time. That is until Katie looks up at me with wide panicked eyes.

"Oh God, turn around," she rushes and I do as I'm told, quickly turning around. When I feel something cold against my neck I look up to the mirror behind my door and gasp. On me she has put the most stunning necklace I've ever seen. It has black diamonds as the chain, with a green diamond in the middle, sitting snug on my chest.

"It's perfect," I whisper, feeling excited.

When she throws a clutch in my hand, grabbing my phone, keys and a bit of money, I giggle. She really is like a mom. She then rushes over to her bag grabbing something before coming over to me.

"Shit!" she says making me giggle then nearly choke when she sprays perfume on me.

"Okay, okay. Let's go before he thinks I've done a runner on him," I giggle.

"At least he can walk on the cast now," she winks and opens the bedroom door for me.

Myles doesn't get his cast off for another four weeks. The doctors gave him another X-ray a few weeks ago and it still needs a little more time to heal. He's just grateful he can get around on his own now.

"Thank you, Katie, for all of this," I tell her before we reach the door.

"It's my pleasure. You look beautiful. I've got to meet your father, but if you need me just give me a call," she smiles before kissing me on the cheek. She moves over to the door and opens it, the same time Myles is just about to knock. He stops mid-stride and opens his mouth, but nothing comes out. He's staring at me with a shocked, or an amazed expression, I'm not really sure, all I know is that it makes me nervous.

Katie laughs before moving past him, waving at me from behind his back.

"Hey," I whisper, when he doesn't say anything.

"Hey," is all he whispers back, before he shakes his head. "Goddamn, Kayla. You look fucking beautiful. Really fucking beautiful."

"Thank you," I tell him shyly.

"Come on, Dude, the party's waiting for me to arrive," Max shouts from the limo we all pitched in for. And before you ask, Max not only brought one date, but he brought three. Yes, three. How the monkeys he managed that is beyond me. I'm just glad only one is riding in the limo with us and she seems the quietest out of them all. But don't take the word quiet to heart, when you meet her you'll be begging her to shut up.

"Remind me again why we decided to limo share with him," Myles groans, his eyes still staring at me up and down. "God, I don't even want to leave or go now. Can't we stay in so I can stare and admire you all night?"

"No," I laugh. "Katie spent hours fixing me up to look beautiful for you, so we are going."

"You always look beautiful," he tells me, making me blush just as a dark figure comes up behind me making me jump.

"Hot fucking damn. I feel the need to go ditch my dates and just take you to prom," Max whistles, eyeing me up and down until Myles slaps him at the back of his head.

"Dude, girlfriend, and her eyes are up there," Myles points to where my eyes are and not to my chest where Max's eyes were lingering.

"Shit, sorry. I get horny when I've had a drink," he shrugs, his eyes straying until he hears Myles groan.

I giggle and grab Myles' hand before shutting the door behind me.

Tonight is going to be a good night. I made a promise to Charlie to enjoy every day like it's my last, and that is what I'm going to do.

MYLES

God she looks fucking stunning. I have to adjust my pants before we walk into the Rosemary Hotel where the school is holding our prom. I feel like a right creeper. I haven't been able to take my eyes off her and much to my dismay, neither has fucking Max. He's all but forgotten his date.

Kayla starts to fidget with her dress and I have to bite back a grin.

"You look beautiful. Stop fussing," I tease, my breath brushing across her ear.

"I can't help it. Are you sure – Oh my God, this is incredible, is that a, a castle?" she gasps and I watch her face in bewilderment. She's looks fucking breathtaking.

When I don't say anything she turns her head to the side to look at me, and gives me a small smile when she notices me staring at her.

"Why do you keep staring?" she asks, the dark blush rising on her cheeks making me chuckle.

"Because," I tell her, grabbing her around the hips and pulling her front to mine. "You look fucking beautiful and I can't keep my eyes off you. How could I when you look so fucking good?" I rasp, leaving her mouth hanging open in an 'O'. Leaning down I kiss her lightly on the corner of her mouth, the same time some flashes blind us. I turn to the side to see Liam, a kid in my science class, holding a camera up towards us. When he waves his hand, not moving his eye from the camera, indicating for us to pose, I grab Kayla around the waist and pull her to my side. She grins up at me, the same time I give her a soft smile, and again the flash clicks off, blinding us once again.

Kayla giggles then once again looks around the room. For the first time I take my eyes from Kayla to look around the room and I have to admit, it looks the shit. It's been a masquerade, to a fairy tale theme.

I grab her hand in mine and move us towards the twinkling dance floor. I take her in my arms, swaying in tune to the music, loving the feel of her in my arms. I don't think tonight could get much better than this.

I was wrong.

It gets much better.

We've been back for twenty minutes when Kayla excuses herself to go get out of her dress. We left the dance in the limo, leaving Max to get a lift back from someone else. He was too busy getting drunk to even care we were leaving anyway.

My jaw drops to the floor when she walks, wearing only a strapless bra and lace knickers.

Fuck me!

"What... Kayla... I... What are you doing?" I rasp out, my voice husky.

"I'm ready," she tells me, her arms wrapped around her belly.

"Kayla, we don't need to do this," I tell her, needing her to know I'd wait a life time for her.

"I know we don't, but I want to. I know tonight is a bit cliché, but I can't think of a better time than now. Tonight has been perfect and what better way to end it then to be with the person I love," she tells me softly, her cheeks flushed right before she loses her smile. "I want to be able to wake up tomorrow and know you were the last person to touch me, to be inside me. I want to be able to go to sleep tonight knowing I'll be thinking of your touch, not *his*, but mostly, I just want you, Myles. I want to show you what you mean to me, what we mean to each other, I'm ready for this step."

Holy fucking shit.

I wasn't expecting that. Her eyes fill with tears and it kills me. I know it's taken a lot to mention *him* tonight, so I give her a gentle smile and get up from the bed to walk over to her. Her body is fucking hot. I know she's self conscious about her scars, but to me, her imperfections just make her more perfect.

"Having you in my arms all night would suit me fine, Kayla, but if this is something you want, then we will try, okay?"

"Yes," she whispers, meeting my gaze.

Slowly, so I don't startle her, I lift my hand, meeting her warm, soft skin. My fingers trace her hips, to the band of her lace knickers and up her stomach. She shivers, goose bumps following my touch and she giggles.

"That tickles," she whispers softly, and I bring my gaze up to meet hers.

"You're so fucking beautiful, it hurts."

"So you've told me," she smiles, lifting her hand to my shirt. I threw my jacket and tie off the minute we got into the limo, hating that I had to wear it. One thing I'm not a fan of and that is wearing freaking penguin suits.

My hand shakes when I lift it to her breast, nervous about us doing this. I don't want to scare her off, or bring back bad memories, but I also want this to be good for her, and to popular belief, I haven't slept with as many people as people presume I have. I've slept with one girl, and that was years ago and only because I was drunk and in a bad place after what happened to Kayla. If I ever thought she would be back in my life, I would have waited for her.

I love her.

In a matter of minutes I'm standing before her wearing only my boxers and I have to blink back my surprise. My hands had been too busy roaming her soft skin that I didn't even feel her undress me.

She takes my hand in hers and pulls me over to the bed, and I'm in too much of a lust-filled haze that I let her. I'd follow her anywhere. It isn't until she lays down on the bed and starts to remove her bra with a unsure expression that I wake up, shaking my head. This is about her, not about me.

My fingers lightly brush her breasts, moving the thin laces covering her nipples away and dropping it to the floor.

Reaching down I bring my lips to hers, kissing her with all my love, showing her how much this moment means to me. Even if she tells me no, then this moment, this day, this night, will still be one of the best nights of my life.

Our kiss turns hungry and neither of us let up for air. She clings to my hair, pulling at it making me groan, God, that feels so good. When her sex brushes against my hard as fuck erection I almost cum in my pants and I have to pull away from her, my breathing erratic.

"Are you sure?" I croak out, not recognising my own voice. Fuck, she ties me up in knots.

She nods her head unable to speak and I sigh against her mouth, giving her another peck before lifting up on my elbows to look into her eyes.

"I need to hear your words, babe."

"Yes. Yes I'm sure. I want you," she tells me urgently, tugging at my head to bring me closer. Fuck, she's killing me.

I lift up to my knees and run my hands down her stomach, my tanned skin against her pale skin. My hands feel rough against her soft skin, but my touch seems to be lighting a fire inside her. Her breathing is heavy, and she watches me through heavy-lid eyes. Her knickers curl up to the size of a string as I roll them down her thighs, her legs and then off her feet. She giggles when I fling them behind her, before covering my body with hers. It's the first time we've both been naked like this, in this intimate position and just the feel of her wet core rubbing against the head of my dick has me ready to burst. I already feel like it's close to happening, and I don't know if I'll be able to control myself once I'm inside her.

"Please, Myles. Don't treat me like I'm made of glass," she pleads and I look down at her in awe.

"I'm nervous, baby. I just want this to be good for you," I admit. My brothers would take the piss out of me if they heard me talking like this, but I don't care, with Kayla I feel like I can tell her anything.

"I'm nervous too, but if it continues to feel anything like it does now, it's going to be mind blowing," she breathes out.

My fingers run down her stomach to her sex, where I rub her juices over her clit. Fucking hell, she's soaked. A fiery whimper escapes her lips before she begs me to stop teasing her.

I stand up off the bed removing my boxers and her eyes widen and a small smirk plays on my lips. I love it when she looks at me like that. It's fucking heaven.

Nearly over the bed, I'm about to position myself at her entrance when I remember something.

"Shit!"

"What?" she asks panicked.

"Baby, I don't have a condom," I groan, shoving my face into her neck. As much as it kills me having to stop, at least I can still make this good for her; that is until she breathes into my ear.

"I have one. I put it here earlier," she tells me, and shoves her hand under her pillow, grabbing a foiled packet. Her cheeks flame red with embarrassment, but I can only stare.

"Been planning on seducing me for a while then?" I tease, kissing her mouth lightly.

"Uh huh," she breathes, moaning when I pepper kisses over her jaw, and up to her ear, where I take her lobe into my mouth and softly nibble.

Taking the foiled condom out of her hand I open it up and roll it on my tip, groaning when her hand reaches out to help roll it down the rest of my length.

My heart pounds hard against my chest, blood pumping through my veins. Positioning myself I have to stop myself before looking into her eyes again, needing to see she is ready for this. When she gives me a blinding smile, and her hands hold onto my biceps, giving them a squeeze, I push in, all the while gauging her reaction.

Her face pinches in pain, so I stop, letting her get used to my size. When she moves, pushing up, I groan and enter her a little bit more.

"Are you okay?" I groan out. Feeling her tight walls clamping around my dick feels so fucking good and when a tingling starts to get heavy in my balls I know I'm not going to last, especially if she keeps clenching around me so tightly.

She nods her head and moves her hips again, the movement causing us to moan.

"God, you feel so fucking good," I tell her, pushing into a little bit more.

"Oh God, it stings," she cries out, and I look down at her with worry.

"Shall I stop?" I ask, bracing to pull out.

"No, God no," she moans, and moves again. Letting her set the pace I reach between us and rub tight circles across her clit, making her squirm and moan beneath me. I can feel her wetness dripping down my balls and it takes everything in me not to pull out and taste her.

"Move, please," she begs, then looks away embarrassed, and I don't think she planned to say that out loud.

"Keep your eyes on me," I demand, reaching up to cup her face. "I love you." Pushing in the rest of the way she lets out a startled gasp before shifting her hips. The biting pain of her nails digging into my skin causes a shiver to run down my back, as I thrust in and out of her, my movements slow and steady.

"Oh God," she cries out, her core tightening around me.

Oh God, don't do that. I'm hanging by a thread. My throat clogs with emotion when I look down at her, her eyes wild with desire, her cheeks flushed, and her movements and touch filled with love. I can feel it. Right down to my soul.

My movements speed up causing Kayla to cry out, and her movements to start matching mine.

It's not long before we're both crying out our release, our sweaty bodies lying together.

"That was... Fuck, Kayla. I love you," I breathe heavily.

Wetness drops onto my shoulder and I stiffen, moving so we're on our sides facing each other.

"Kayla, are you okay? Did I hurt you?" I panic, hoping to fucking Christ that I haven't. I'd been so wrapped up in what I hoped was her pleasure, I didn't even think about hurting her. With every cry of pleasure reaching my ears, just spurred me on more, making me float on ecstasy.

"Thank you," she croaks out, her voice hoarse from her tears, but also from her cries of pleasure.

"Baby, speak to me," I plead, my fingers holding her possessively. "You're worrying me, Babe."

"No! I'm not crying because I'm sad, but because I'm happy. I love you, Myles. You don't know how long I've waited for this moment. I didn't even realise until now how much. It was perfect. You're perfect. We're perfect. This moment is one I'll cherish forever," she tells me, her words a whisper at the end.

"Oh baby, you have no idea how long I've waited for you to be mine. I love you too; I always have and always will. You gave me something precious tonight, and if one us will be cherishing it, it will be me," I tell her, leaning in and kissing her.

It's not long before the kiss grows heated and we're taking each other's bodies to another high, both of us sticky with sweat and exhausted from the night's activities.

The last words I speak before I drift off, with the love of my life wrapped safely in my arms is, "I love you."

Ringing brings me out of a good fucking dream, one I didn't want to wake up from, but then I feel Kayla's naked body pressed against mine and realise none of it was a dream. I groan, rolling over and pressing my erection into her tight ass. She moans sleepily, but then the ringing that woke me up starts all over again making me growl.

A small giggle makes me jump and I playfully tickle Kayla on her hip bone causing her to squeal with laughter. I lean over her and grab my trousers, grabbing my phone out of my pocket. When I see Maverick's name on the screen I scrunch my face up.

Kayla sits up and switches on her bedside light, wrapping the sheets around herself, covering her chest. I shake my head in disappointment causing her to giggle and swat my arm. Giving her a wink and a playful smirk I answer the phone.

"This better be good. It's," I pause for a minute to look at the clock before continuing. "Four in the morning. Fuck! Okay, shit, I'll be there, okay, see you in five," I tell him before putting the phone down and looking at Kayla with a sorry expression.

"I've got to go, Babe," I tell her, hating that I have to leave, especially after sharing what we've shared. I wanted to wake up to her, make her breakfast in bed and laze around watching movies all day, but instead, I'll be getting picked up by Maverick in ten minutes.

"What? Why? What's happened?" she asks, wide-eyed and pale.

"It's Max.... He's been arrested."

THE END

ACKNOWLEDGEMENTS

I love and hate writing these. I feel like I'm missing someone out, or my words don't seem like enough of a thanks to the people that have supported me through this whole journey. It's been a tough road and I know it's only going to get tougher, but with all the support I've been getting, I know it will be worth it.

I was shocked from the amount of love for I had for Malik and Mason. That when I started writing Myles it took me a lot longer than both of them put together. I don't want to let anyone down. I was worried people would say, "Oh, the first one was good, but they got boring after that," or something along those lines. I want people to love the Carter brothers as much as I do. I've loved writing about them, and getting their stories out of my head. It's been a fun road and can't wait to get Max written down.

To my kids who are never patient with me when I'm writing, but still cheer me on to write. For the help they've given me making swag, packing up swag bags to winners, and even giving me character names. I love you, with all my heart.

To my best friend, my sister from another mister, and my book geek, Charlotte Perry. Thank you. Thank you for listening to me ramble when I've lost my writing mojo, or I'm plotting another story line. Thank you for volunteering to be my assistant at the author signing I'm going to, and for being my biggest supporter. Not that I give you a choice or anything. I love you lots, but you really do need to get off my back about finishing the Carter brothers LOL

To my Editor, Elisia. She's new to my team and has edited this book with only a short amount of time. So that's the reason there may be a few mistakes here and there.

I can't actually thank her enough. I've been saying it over and over, but she'll never know how much. You can't begin to realise just how hard she has worked on this for me. Or the time that has gone into it.

So from the bottom of my heart, Elisia, thank you. And welcome to the team.

To my Beta readers, you girls really do rock and without you I'd be stuck. Your faith and support in me means the world to me, and words will never describe just how thankful I am.

To Rachel for becoming my online assistant, helping me with release parties, blog posts, and everything else she can do across the internet. You really do rock, and have become a good friend of mine.

To Cassy Roop, my cover designer, thank you. From a simple picture you bring my book to life, designing the perfect cover for me. My book isn't complete without you, and I'll be forever in your debt. I love you girl!

To all my author friends, thank you for your unwavering support. You help make my releases successful and I appreciate all the help you kindly give me, and hopeful one day, I can return the favour.

To all the bloggers and readers out there who have read and supported me since I become an Indie author. Thank you.

This is one of them moments when thank you is not enough. What you ladies do for me is something I could never repay.

Thank you, from the bottom of my heart.

Printed in Great Britain
by Amazon